OF MORTAL VINTAGE

Immediately, one of the attendants next to Finn bent to the intravenous tap on his arm and opened it. His dark red blood began sliding down the tube and into a silver goblet.

He watched in fascinated horror as the servant closed off the tap and brought the goblet around to where the Lady Zillabar sat. The young Vampire held the cup to the Lady's lips and she drank from it eagerly. When she had finished, she licked her lips appreciatively. Another servant approached and delicately touched a silken cloth to the corners of her mouth.

The Lady Zillabar sighed. "Ahhh. I enjoyed that. Finn, thank you so much. Truly a delicious experience. I intend to have you share all of your meals with me." She turned to the rest of her guests. "Would anyone else like a taste?"

A COVENANT OF JUSTICE

■□□□□□□□□□□□□□□□□□□□□□□□□□□□□□□□■

David Gerrold

Based on "Trackers" created by
Daron J. Thomas and David Gerrold

BANTAM BOOKS
NEW YORK • TORONTO • LONDON
SYDNEY • AUCKLAND

A COVENANT OF JUSTICE

A Bantam Spectra Book / May 1994

SPECTRA and the portrayal of a boxed "s" are trademarks of Bantam Books, a division of Bantam Doubleday Dell Publishing Group, Inc.

ISBN 0-553-56188-X

Published simultaneously in the United States and Canada

Bantam Books are published by Bantam Books, a division of Bantam Doubleday Dell Publishing Group, Inc. Its trademark, consisting of the words "Bantam Books" and the portrayal of a rooster, is Registered in U.S. Patent and Trademark Office and in other countries. Marca Registrada. Bantam Books, 1540 Broadway, New York, New York 10036.

PRINTED IN THE UNITED STATES OF AMERICA

RAD 0 9 8 7 6 5 4 3 2 1

For Wilma and Wes Meier,
with love

A
COVENANT
OF
JUSTICE

Contract Negotiations

oooooooooooooooooooooooooooo

When they finally pulled Lee-1169 off Sawyer, both men had multiple minor cuts and abrasions, and Lee had blood streaming from his nose.

"I can't believe your audacity!" Lee shouted as he struggled in the grip of Drin and Tahl. The two larger men held him firmly back. "The rebellion will have a death sentence put on your head. To hell with both of you."

Sawyer spat back, "A death sentence from the Alliance of Life? The same Alliance that believes in the sacredness of life everywhere? You've revealed your true colors. Life only for those who believe *your* way. Now you know why we won't give our allegiance. We hate hypocrisy."

"Both of you, shut up," said William Three-Dollar, stepping between them.

Lee tried to shake free. "Don't you talk to them, goddammit! These two trackers don't even have the decency to stay bought."

William Three-Dollar reached out and grabbed Lee's throat. For the first time since they'd met him, his face clouded with emotion. He looked furious. He spoke in a voice as ferocious as any Dragon's. "Don't *ever again* tell me what I must or must not do. I walk my own path!" He released the smaller man. Shaken, Lee fell back, his face ashen.

Three-Dollar turned away from him. He lifted his

1

gaze to study Sawyer and Finn Markham. Finn let go of
his brother then; so did the other man holding Sawyer;
Tuan loomed larger than Drin and Tahl together. He
shoved Sawyer quickly away, leaving the two trackers
alone in the center of Three-Dollar's scrutiny. The
TimeBinder approached them slowly and looked mournfully down at them.

The TimeBinder looked from one to the other, with
very real disappointment in his eyes; but even though he
looked as if he had volumes to speak, he remained silent.
He just stared at them ruefully. He looked so disappointed that neither Sawyer nor Finn could meet his
penetrating gaze for long. Finally, Three-Dollar turned
his back on them and returned to the others. Sawyer and
Finn felt more than dismissed; they felt *discarded*.

"Let me instruct you in the way," Three-Dollar
spoke patiently to Lee-1169. He spread his hands wide
to bring in the other three rebels as well. Drin, Tahl, and
Tuan moved closer to the TimeBinder. "We might describe these two trackers who share our imprisonment as
ethically retarded, except that in their case, such an ap-
pellation would serve more as compliment than epithet."
He put his hand on Lee's smaller shoulder and spoke in
soft, gentle tones. "My son, you need to learn the compassion that extends beyond those who deserve compassion. Real compassion goes out to all, whether they
deserve it or not.

"These two men *seem* undeserving, and so we feel
justified in withholding our care. But if you could look at
them from a compassionate context, you would see that
these two poor assholes have simply never learned the
same loyalty that you have. They have no vision larger
than their stomachs. Because of that, they have no *real*
humanity. They can never truly understand the nature of
justice. So for you to expect or demand behavior consistent with such training only demonstrates more foolish-
ness on your part than theirs."

"Excuse me—" Sawyer started to interrupt, insulted.

Three-Dollar turned and looked at him calmly.
"Please don't interrupt. This conversation doesn't concern
you."

"Yes, it does!"

"Soy—" Finn grabbed his brother's arm and pulled him back. "Shut up."

"But he said—"

"I heard what he said. Shut up."

Three-Dollar turned back to the Alliance rebels. "We can only speak to them in their own language. We can only speak to them in terms they can understand."

Lee held up his clenched fists. "Then why did you stop me?"

"Because *you* didn't understand.

"Eh?" Lee shook his head, as if to clear it. But he closed his mouth and swallowed hard, and allowed the TimeBinder to educate him.

"Watch," he instructed. The TimeBinder turned back to Sawyer and Finn. He spread his huge bony hands out in a calming gesture—as if smoothing the troubled waters between them. "I will offer you a contract," he said. He turned his palms face up as if to demonstrate his good will. "Indeed, I'll offer you the only deal you appear capable of understanding."

"Good," said Sawyer, showing a pleased smile. "Let's talk terms. How much?"

"Your lives in exchange for your service."

Sawyer's smile collapsed. "I hate deals like that," he said.

"I have no other offer to make," the TimeBinder said. "Either take it or leave it."

Sawyer looked to his brother. Finn's expression demonstrated no more enthusiasm for the contract than Sawyer's. Finn shrugged. "It sounds like a fair deal to me," he said to Sawyer dryly. "Does it sound fair to you?"

Sawyer scratched his head. "I don't suppose we could discuss the hazardous-duty allotment . . . ? I didn't think so." He sighed and put on his bravest smile. "Okay, we accept." He held out his hand to the TimeBinder. So did Finn.

"Done," said the TimeBinder, clasping both Sawyer's and Finn's smaller hands in his great ones.

"All right," said Sawyer Markham. "*Now* we go to Plan B."

"Plan B?" Lee-1169 approached the two suspiciously. Despite his smoldering anger, he had not forgotten the peril of their circumstance; they still remained guests of the Lady Zillabar's dangerous hospitality.

"We *always* have a Plan B," Finn said. "You can't trust *anybody*."

Three-Dollar laughed aloud at that. Lee looked at the TimeBinder, puzzled—then he too got the joke and snorted in amusement. Finally he turned back to the brothers Markham and said, "All right, tell us your Plan B."

Sawyer held up a hand for silence. "Shh, I have to make it up."

Departures

□□□□□□□□□□□□□□□□□□□□□□□□□□□□□□

Abruptly, the floor shifted under their feet. It shuddered and began to tilt. The men looked at each other, alarmed. Only Three-Dollar remained placid. "We've lifted off," he said. "Whatever the Lady plans for us, she wants to keep us close."

To observers on the outside, the liftoff of the Lady's vessel presented an astonishing sight. First, the great sprawling structure of the palace lit up like a gaudy confection. The gleaming spires sparkled and shone, dazzling brighter than the Eye of God.

Then ... a great deep note began to resonate throughout the city. It swelled and ebbed as a grand tide of sound, vibrating up through the rock itself. Finally the entire top section of the palace lit up in frosty beams of light. It lifted off its golden cradle, and rose gently into the sky above the city.

The people poured out into the streets, gasping, shouting, and pointing. Even the normally stolid Dragons stopped to stare upward. Shouts of celebration and joy rose into the air, rising like the Lady's bright vessel. The ship slid gracefully out over the desert and began gathering speed. It swung around in a great arc and pointed itself eastward. Then it began rising straight up into the spangled night.

Kernel d'Vashti watched the Lady leave without visible expression. He stood on the highest balcony of his tower at the opposite end of the city and watched as the pebble of light streaked away toward the stars. At last a faint smile appeared on his face. His mouth tightened, his eyes narrowed. He understood the Lady's retreat better than she did. The males of his species knew this dance much better than the females—because the males had a lifetime of practice.

She danced away, thinking she danced in anger— even she believed it. But in truth her actions sent a much more tantalizing message. She dared him to follow and prove his worthiness. He would have to demonstrate his ferocity before she would surrender to his triumph.

d'Vashti allowed his outer face to wear the same expression as his inner one—a grin of happy expectation. He had the strength, he had the will, and he had a clear track toward his victory. He had eliminated everyone who might have challenged him for the Lady's bed. The inevitability of his victory gave him a surging feeling of pride. He would topple the arrogant Lady Zillabar into his nest, and he would shortly father the next generation of Zashti children.

He waited until the distant mote disappeared into the Eye of God; then he turned crisply about and reentered his tower, shouting as he hurried down the corridors, summoning his aides, and spitting a stream of ominous orders.

Far above, far away—the great vessel climbed majestically above the sea of air, climbed out of the well of gravity, and headed toward an enormous spired web that wheeled proudly in high orbit. It sparkled even brighter than its counterpart on the crown of MesaPort. From a distance it seemed as graceful as a dandelion drifting on the wind, but as Zillabar's vessel approached, its details became clearer and more deadly looking. It was a golden weapon, all daggers and spears. Among its many towers stood myriad projectors, accelerators, launchers, and disruptors. The Lady had decreed herself a chariot, *The Golden Fury*. Others, less respectful, called it simply, the Zillabarge—but not in the Lady's hearing, of course.

Now the part of Zillabar's palace that served as shuttlecraft slipped into its final docking maneuver. It fitted itself gracefully into the center of the great turning web of light and power. Once again complete, *The Golden Fury* glowed in readiness.

History

Inside the vessel, inside her hold, inside her prison, her human cargo felt the final soft thump of the docking. The men looked at each other's eyes, searching for a reason to hope.

Sawyer Markham quashed the impulse. "Burihatin," he said grimly. "We go to Burihatin-14." He saw the TimeBinder react sharply to this information.

"How do you know this?" asked Lee-1169.

"The Lady herself said so. She told d'Vashti. She did this in our presence, then she dismissed him. I don't think she likes him very much."

"Don't let her anger fool you," Three-Dollar said. "Vampire women like to torture their mates before they eat them. They don't have the same kind of emotions as humans. They don't have love; they have a form of intense hatred for that which attracts them. It produces terrible, frenzied matings. Sometimes the male survives, more often not."

"It sounds dreadful. Why would anyone want such a goal as desperately as d'Vashti seems to?"

Three-Dollar smiled gently. "In ancient days humans practiced much the same kind of mating. And desired it every bit as desperately."

"I find that difficult to believe."

The TimeBinder nodded gently. "I remember it well. Before the Phaestor began licensing wombs, humans numbered as many females as males."

"No—you joke with us. I can't imagine that," Sawyer said.

"Whether you can imagine it or not, it happened," Three-Dollar said calmly. The men in the room listened, fascinated. Even Drin, Tahl, and Tuan, who normally kept to themselves, came closer to hear this history. "Any man and any woman who chose to mate could do so, simply by publicly declaring their commitment to each other and signing a formal contract which guaranteed their responsibility for any resulting offspring. The female actually carried the children within her own body, within her own organic womb. She grew the children one at a time. Sometimes she gave birth to male children, sometimes female. Without selection the process remained totally random."

"It sounds . . . very haphazard," said Finn. "And dangerous."

The TimeBinder nodded. "Indeed it does sound haphazard and dangerous, but it worked. It worked for humans, at least. Most of the time. Apparently, it didn't work for the Phaestor. The Vampires don't like to have this fact known, but human scientists created them. Apparently, we created them too well—*too* aggressive. After destroying the Predators, the Vampires began uncreating their progenitors.

"Using their authority on the worlds they controlled, they began licensing all breeding to keep the resident populations from getting out of control. Over a period of many centuries, they have drastically reduced the populations of their subject worlds. Now if a human wants a child, a Vampire has to approve it, and the child—almost always male—will come from a synthetic womb. The

Vampires allow female births only where their control of the child remains assured. They fear unlicensed breeding, because their enemies could grow an army that way."

"Well, we would—" said Lee. "Wouldn't we?"

"You really don't know, do you?" said Three-Dollar. "They've even taken that away from you. Try to imagine," he continued, intensely, "what it means to hold your own child in your hands, the product of your loins, a laughing infant, so pink and delicate and so utterly helpless and dependent on you. Try to imagine the surge of emotion you would feel every time you look at your baby, the overpowering need to shelter and protect it from all harm. Try to imagine the *love*. Humans don't breed children like Vampires. We don't raise our offspring as weapons. We raise them as family—as pieces of ourselves. Your children become your way of achieving immortality.

"What you feel for your brothers, Lee—what Sawyer and Finn feel for each other, what Ibaka and Kask felt for their families—that same emotion grows even stronger for your mate and your children. The Vampires don't have that emotion. Because of the way they breed, they can never know it. But they know we have these feelings and they fear us because of it. In the calculations of their minds, they might know that we don't think like they do; but in their moment-to-moment hormone-maddened existence, they can see us only as reflections of themselves. Because humans never act as they expect us to, we trouble them immensely." He smiled wickedly. "The poor Vampires. They imagine themselves the warriors of the Cluster, but in truth they remain trapped in their inability to imagine."

The men fell silent for a while, each one examining in his own soul the meaning of the freedoms that William Three-Dollar had described. Such concepts had never before occurred to them, and the visions they produced had a disturbing quality. "When we defeat the Vampires," Tuan said, with an almost reverent awe for the possibilities that Three-Dollar had evoked, "we really *will* live differently."

"Your children will benefit from your victory," Three-Dollar said wisely. "If you follow in the path of every rebellion before you, you yourselves will probably have a great deal of trouble appreciating the fruits of your victory."

"Do you think we'll win, TimeBinder?" Drin asked.

"I predict the past," Three-Dollar said. "Not the future."

"Burihatin," Sawyer said. "What does that mean to you?" Sawyer pressed him. "I saw you react to it before. Why?"

The tall man allowed his concern to show. "We've known for some time that d'Vashti has sent many Marauder squadrons to Burihatin-14. We know that they've searched for the TimeBinder, but haven't had any success locating. Zillabar wants *that* headband in particular, because she knows that it has much more interesting knowledge than this one—" He tapped his forehead. "Much of the history of the creation of the Phaestor rests in the Burihatin memories. If she gains that knowledge, who knows what power it could give her?" He added grimly, "The fact that we go there now could indicate several things. Perhaps she's become too impatient to wait for d'Vashti's agents. Perhaps she doesn't trust d'Vashti. Perhaps her own people have located the headband. If the latter case, then they may have already killed the TimeBinder." He looked around at the others. "And if the latter has occurred, then she will have the power to destroy the Gathering and *all* the TimeBinders."

The Bridge to the Stars

∎∎∎∎∎∎∎∎∎∎∎∎∎∎∎∎∎∎∎∎∎∎∎∎∎∎

The command bridge of *The Golden Fury* looked like an elegant drawing room. One end of it fell away to become a railed terrace overlooking a giant window onto empty space, actually an enormous holographic display. Below this balcony the ship's flight crew, all specially neutered Vampires, worked busily at several ranks of workstations. The Lady glanced down at them only perfunctorily. Neuters held no interest for her. She turned back to her guests—in particular, the Dragon Lord.

"Have you had enough to eat, Your Grace?" she asked with elaborate courtesy. The Lady offered her greeting purely as a formality; her question did not refer to the Dragon Lord's immediate consumption aboard the starship.

The Dragon Lord belched contentedly and grinned a metallic smile. The stench of his eructation reached her delicate nostrils a moment later; but if it offended her, she betrayed no sign.

"Feed well? Yes, indeed I did," the Dragon Lord grunted happily. "For the first time in many years, I have not only filled myself to the point of satiation, but I have actually had to leave part of my meal uneaten because I could not hold anymore. I had not believed I would ever know such joy again. Indeed, had I not received your delicious invitation to join you on this expedition, I would have gone dormant for days while I digested. Perhaps I still might."

The Lady hid her reaction to the Dragon Lord's unexpected admission. Whatever surprise she might have felt, she carefully kept herself from showing it. She realized unhappily that the great Dragon's candor about his

10

own recent excess represented his way of chiding her, of letting her know that he remained very much aware of the hunting rites that Drydel—and by implication, herself—had practiced at the now-razed nest in the desert. She had asked the Lord to personally oversee the destruction of the remaining evidence. Of course, the bloody-damned lizard would use his knowledge to its maximum benefit for himself. He would remind her of this dishonor for years to come, subtly pushing her this way and that—a much more elegant way of throwing his considerable weight around than directly challenging her.

She gave the Dragon Lord her sweetest smile—an industrial-strength dose. "I hope that all of your future assignments shall prove as pleasant." And by that phrasing she reminded him that he still worked for her, not the other way around.

The Lady turned off her smile abruptly and said, "We have to clean up a mess on Burihatin. d'Vashti's mess. I shall require the complete cooperation of your best Dragons."

The Dragon Lord didn't answer immediately. He rumbled deep in his throat, a sound the Lady knew represented a ruminative contemplation. "I wonder what the people on Burihatin taste like."

"You'll find out soon enough," the Lady remarked, surprising even herself with her straightforward reply. "I would advise you to take extraordinary care, though. We do not enjoy the same control on Burihatin that we do on Thoska-Roole, and you already know too well how precarious the situation on Thoska-Roole can sometimes get."

"Madame Zillabar"—the Great Dragon bowed in elaborate obeisance—"you may count on the total support of myself and all the warrior-lizards under my command. We will place ourselves completely at your disposal."

"Thank you, great Dragon. You honor me with your service." The Lady turned to her Captain then, a near-featureless neuter, and nodded her command.

The Star-Captain bowed and proceeded to his station. Quietly, he began whispering orders. A moment later a solemn chime sounded throughout the vessel. It broke its orbit and headed out toward the darkness between the stars.

When it had finally put enough distance between itself and the worst effects of the gravity well created by Thoska-Roole and its bloated red sun, the starship activated its faster-than-light stardrive. It wrapped itself in a fold of *otherness* and leapt into *otherspace*.

Questions Without Answers

□□□□□□□□□□□□□□□□□□□□□□□□□□□□□□

Sawyer sat alone for a long time with his thoughts. He hadn't liked some of the things that the TimeBinder had said about his brother and himself. It bothered him. In particular he did not like the phrase "ethically retarded." It implied that he and Finn had never considered these so-called higher concerns at all.

In fact Sawyer and Finn had had many long discussions about morality, ethics, philosophy, and individual responsibility. After a number of direct exercises and experiments in the physical universe, their unique experiences had revealed to them the limits of trust in the realm, and based on that information, they had developed a system of personal behavior consistent with their discoveries. They trusted no one, sometimes not even each other.

For William Three-Dollar to call that "ethically retarded" seemed to Sawyer evidence of a terrible prejudice against self-contained individuals.

The only "alliance of life" that Sawyer had ever really noticed remained the unbreakable relationship between predator and prey. The universe offered you a choice between diner and dinner. 'Tis better to dine, Sawyer and Finn had decided. All life feeds on death.

Even plants, that depend only on sunlight for the energy to drive photosynthesis, feed on the heat death of a star. To characterize death as an enemy rather than accept it as part of the process seemed stupid, shortsighted, and narrow-minded. On the other hand, when death threatened you or someone close to you, it concentrated one's attention immensely. It put the matter into the subjective domain, which, Sawyer knew, always skewed one's perceptions.

In other words, the very real possibility of Finn's death scared the hell out of him.

Maybe they had made a very bad decision here. Maybe, as a result of their actions in tracking and capturing the TimeBinder, Lady Zillabar would now have the power to do a lot of harm to many unsuspecting people.[1] Did he and Finn bear the responsibility for that?

The question gnawed at his mind, coming back again and again to torment his peace. Should he have let Finn die to protect some people he didn't even know? He and Finn had always considered rebels just as bad as governments. They shared equal arrogance, both claiming moral authority and righteousness of purpose. Governments and rebels not only deserved each other; if either didn't exist, the other would have to invent them as an opponent. They needed each other. Why shouldn't the Markham brothers profit from the pigheadedness of those who believed they knew better than anyone else what other people should or shouldn't do? And besides, what else could they have done here? d'Vashti hadn't given them much choice—death or *boonga*.[2]

---

[1] The term *innocent* as applied to bystanders never occurred to Sawyer Markham. After a short while on Thoska-Roole, he no longer believed in anyone's innocence.

[2] Three explorers landed on a strange new planet and discovered a race of ferocious four-meter-tall, blue-skinned natives living there. The natives practiced many bizarre customs, worshiped strange gods, and circumscribed the structure of their lives with a complex set of rigid taboos and rituals. Very shortly, all three of the explorers had accidentally violated one or another of the native laws and the tribesmen seized them all. They brought the three unfortunate explorers before the High Chief for judging. "You have violated our most sacred laws," the Chief told the explorers. "I will give you a choice. Death or *boonga*."

The first explorer, a very young man who had not yet fully tasted life nor yet

Later, after Finn had lain down to rest again, Sawyer approached William Three-Dollar quietly. "Can I talk to you?"

The spindly man sat in a corner, his bony knees folded up in front of his chest, his arms carelessly wrapped around them. He nodded. He moved over on the bunk and made room for Sawyer. "You look like a man who has swallowed a live toad."

"Huh? I don't understand." Sawyer sat down next to Three-Dollar.

"You've never heard the old saying, have you? Swallow a live toad the first thing in the morning. Nothing worse will happen to you all day. Your face still shows the aftertaste of toad. You haven't yet figured out that things can only get better."

Sawyer scratched his head in puzzlement. "I guess I still don't get it. We had toads back home. Big things too"—he held up his hands, half a meter apart, to demonstrate the size—"I don't see how you could swallow one live. We used to eat them all the time when we

---

grown jaded with its variety, could not bear the thought of imminent death. He told himself that whatever horrors *boonga* might inflict, at least he would survive the punishment, so despite his ignorance of the nature of the ritual, he reluctantly chose *boonga*. "Good. Good," exclaimed the Chief, whereupon the biggest and surliest-looking of the ferocious four-meter-tall, blue-skinned warriors seized the unfortunate fellow, stripped him naked, nailed him to the ground, and proceeded to sodomize him and perform all manner of other grotesque obscenities upon his pale body for seven full days and nights. At the end of that time, the warriors released the lad; shaken, battered, bruised, aching, and sore—but alive.

The sight of this punishment, and the screams of the unfortunate victim, very much terrified the second explorer; but the thought of death terrified him even worse. So, he too reluctantly chose *boonga*. "Good. Good," exclaimed the delighted Chief. "A very good choice." This time the punishment lasted *two* weeks. And every single one of the ferocious four-meter-tall, blue-skinned warriors sodomized the poor chap *twice*. But he too survived his ordeal, albeit somewhat worse for wear, and the natives released him with the admonition to go and sin no more.

The third explorer, however, refused to consider this option. The whole thing appalled him more than he could say. He had never allowed another male of *any* species to touch his body, and even the promise of ultimate survival did not outweigh the horror that he felt at the thought of passive anal intercourse with a tribe of ferocious four-meter-tall, blue-skinned natives. So bravely, sternly, he stood up to the Chief and announced, "I choose death.'"

This pleased the Chief immensely. A broad grin spread over his huge ugly face. "I acknowledge your courage and I bow to you as the greatest warrior of all. You shall have the most glorious death imaginable. But first *boonga!*"

couldn't get anything else. They tasted awful. You don't know how bad something can taste until you've eaten fried toad. Uh-uh—"

The TimeBinder looked bemused. He hid his smile behind his hand, pretending to scratch his nose. When he looked over at Sawyer again, he said, "Something else besides the terrible taste of toads troubles you. And you want me to help you find a resolution, correct?"

"I don't know," Sawyer admitted. "I guess I just wanted you to explain something. What did you mean when you said that Finn and I didn't have the larger vision? Explain this larger vision thing to me."

This time Three-Dollar didn't laugh at Sawyer's ignorance. Instead he spoke calmly and patiently. "Lee told me how you tried to teach honor to Kask the Dragon. Do you remember how frustrated you became? The Dragon could think only of himself and his own honor; he didn't care about the rest of you or your survival."

Sawyer shrugged. "Dragons don't have a lot of intelligence. If a Dragon wants to complete a thought, he has to stand very close to another Dragon—whoever has the other synapse."

"Actually, Dragons have a great deal of intelligence," the TimeBinder corrected. "But most of them focus their attention so tightly that they never get the chance to exercise their very real wisdom."

"Really?" Sawyer looked over at Three-Dollar.

"I have it on the best authority." He tapped his halo. "I remember it well. But do you understand my point about the Dragon not caring about the rest of you?"

"Yes, I guess I do."

"You survived—you and Lee and all of the others—because you cooperated, right?"

"Mostly."

"Right. But the Dragon didn't get it—not like the rest of you. So he wouldn't cooperate. And the rest of you felt angry and frustrated, not just because he didn't cooperate, but because he didn't even understand the *need* to cooperate."

"And you think that Finn and I behaved as badly as the Dragon?"

"Badly? No. The Dragon didn't behave badly. He behaved exactly as a Dragon should have behaved. He couldn't have done anything else, because he didn't know anything else. And if you remember, the Dragon demonstrated an extraordinary capacity to learn better. When he finally did learn that he had misplaced his trust and his honor and that the Vampires had betrayed him, what did he do? He *created* a new allegiance for himself, an allegiance to an even higher standard."

"You didn't answer my question—"

"Do I think you and Finn behaved as badly as the Dragon? No, I think the two of you behaved worse. Much worse. The Dragon didn't know better. You did."

Sawyer could feel the heat of his anger rising, but he suppressed the impulse. It hurt his throat to swallow so much pride, but he forced it down anyway. "We didn't have a choice," he said defensively.

Three-Dollar snorted. "You had a choice. You chose not to acknowledge it."

Sawyer started to rise. "Thanks for your time, but I've already had enough abuse for today—"

The TimeBinder grabbed his arm and pulled him back down. "We haven't finished, Sawyer. You wanted to understand the *larger vision*. Before we can talk about that, you have to acknowledge the truth of your present vision. You and Finn have a focus almost as narrow as that of the Dragon. Just as the Dragons train themselves to focus only on their personal honor, you and your brother trained yourself to focus only on your own needs."

"So? Why shouldn't we? Who else would have watched out for us?"

"Sawyer, please—" The TimeBinder's voice remained calm and mellow. "I don't do this to hurt you. And I have a different purpose other than to sit in judgment of you. Understand, though, that you and Finn could just as easily have trained yourselves to live by a higher standard. The Dragon didn't have a choice in his training. You did. Can you understand that distinction?"

"I guess so. Yes."

"Good. Thank you. Because now you can begin to

learn. The Dragon had to break his training to learn the higher vision of cooperation with your makeshift band of escapees. Can you acknowledge the courage it took for Kask to do that? Because you would have to do the same—break your lifelong training—to learn the larger vision that I talked about with Lee."

Sawyer felt frustrated. "I hear your words," he said, "but they sound just like the same kind of words that everybody else uses."

"Yes, I guess they do. Let me try it another way. Can you accept responsibility for yourself?"

"I don't understand."

"Yes, you do. Can you accept responsibility for your own actions. Will you accept the consequences?"

"Uh—I already have. Oh, I see—yes, I guess I do accept responsibility for myself."

"Yes, you do. You've demonstrated that over and over again. Now, let's expand that vision. Can you accept responsibility for yourself *and* for Finn? Will you act as the cause of your lives, instead of the effect?"

"Cause? Effect?"

"Cause chooses. Effect lets others choose. Can you act as cause for yourself and Finn?"

Sawyer nodded. "Yes, I already do."

"Good. Now, think for a minute. Could you act as cause for the band of escapees you led out of the labor camp? Could you commit yourself to the success of that group?"

"We had no choice—"

"You could have gone your own way."

"No, we couldn't. We had to . . ." Reluctantly, Sawyer finished the sentence. "We had to stay with Lee, so he would lead us to you."

"You could have gone your own way. You could have chosen to let Finn die. Or you could have chosen to abandon the group. Or you could have—"

"Lee represented the Alliance of Life, so he had to commit himself to the survival of the others, so we had no choice, either, but also to commit to the success of the group—"

"My point exactly. Sometimes, in order to succeed

as an individual, you have to make sure that the family succeeds. Sometimes, in order to succeed as a family, you have to make sure that the tribe succeeds. Sometimes, in order to succeed as a tribe, you have to make sure that the nation succeeds. Do I have to go on? Sometimes you have to make sure that your people succeed. Can you commit to that? Can you accept that large a responsibility?"

Sawyer shook his head. "I can't even conceive of it."

"Yes, I know. But now that I've planted the thought in your head, you'll have to think about it, because it won't go away."

"I find it very hard to believe that people would willingly unite for a purpose as nebulous as you describe."

"I'll make it even harder for you to believe, Sawyer. Sometimes people will not only commit to the success of a larger group; sometimes they will even sacrifice their own personal goals to ensure that larger success."

Sawyer didn't answer that immediately. "It just seems so stupid to me," he said. "Why die for people you don't know? They don't care. Nobody cares. Nobody ever did—except Finn."

"I see," said Three-Dollar. And he did.

My Dinner with Zillabar

▫▫▫▫▫▫▫▫▫▫▫▫▫▫▫▫▫▫▫▫▫▫▫▫▫▫▫▫▫

A curious thought had occurred to Lady Zillabar. In space no one can hear you break the law. After some consideration she decided to wear the resultant smile on her public face, but simply not explain it.

She hissed away her maids and checked her appearance in a full-length mirror. As always, she demanded an impeccable presentation. Tonight she wore a scarlet shroud wrapped tightly around her entire body, leaving only her head free. She could barely move. Her maids would have to wheel her in, serve her, feed her, hold her glass to her lips for her.

She enjoyed the feeling of helplessness—while at the same time remaining totally in control. She enjoyed taunting her privileged guests with this performance. Perhaps she relished her insect heritage. She fantasized about hives and queens. She thought about all the workers who lived only to service the queen, all the drones who lived only to mate with her. The queen lay in her chambers. She spent her entire life in glorious dreamtime. She ate and grew fat. She mated and grew fatter. She laid eggs, eventually at the rate of two or three a day.

Lady Zillabar didn't particularly enjoy the last part of that fantasy. She knew that she had the responsibility to further the Zashti line. Sometimes she wished that she could avoid it, but she knew that when at last she finally did mate with some unfortunate male, the hormonal surge would carry her into a state of psychotic desires. She would want nothing else, but to eat and mate and lay eggs—and she would want nothing else until her reproductive storm began to ebb. With that in mind she knew that she had to firmly consolidate her authority *before* the storm clouds began to gather over her bed. Otherwise . . . events would sweep past her. She had to stop the Gathering; if she could do that, she could safely mate.

She thought about d'Vashti and laughed. She couldn't imagine him accepting her challenge. Without a challenger she could go for years without having to risk mating. Hm. Perhaps d'Vashti had done her a favor by arranging the death of Drydel.

Satisfied, she nodded to her maids. They maneuvered her gracefully onto a slanted board and wheeled her into the dining salon where her guests waited—the senior officers of her starship, all Phaestor, several of her most trusted personal aides, and the Dragon Lord. They stood as she entered and applauded the glimmering audacity of her gown. Beyond the windows the Eye of God

stared balefully, a wall of blazing light that colored everything in the salon with an unholy aura. She loved it.

The Dragon Lord waited respectfully at the end of
the table, his tail twitching patiently back and forth. Her
attendants wheeled her the entire length of the room so
she could greet him face-to-face.

"My Lady," he said, bowing his great head low
enough to look her straight in the eye. "You look good
enough to eat!" And then he laughed in that great boom-
ing rumble of his, loud enough to rattle the slender glas-
ses on the table.

Behind her Lady Zillabar could sense the shocked
silence of her officers. Too straitlaced to visibly appreciate a joke as vulgar as this without approval, they waited
for the Lady's reaction. Zillabar and the Dragon Lord exchanged a private smile; he enjoyed teasing her like this.
They had shared this joke before. At last, mindful of her
attendants and her officers, she allowed her amusement
to break through to the surface. She replied with coy
grace, "But, my Lord, you'll spoil your appetite for dinner."

"For such an hors d'oeuvre, I would gladly spoil a
hundred dinners, a thousand!"

"But, my Lord, while I would willingly do anything
in my power to offer you that pleasure, I fear that such
an act of generosity might also spoil *my* dinner—and I
would not have you bear such a stain upon your honor."

"As always, you think too much of me and not
enough of yourself, madam. If it pleases you to climb
onto my plate, I would not dream of stopping you. I will
happily bear any shame, any disgrace, for such a treat."

"Ah, my Lord Dragon, you do me such honor, I shall
surely swoon from delight. But, as you can see, my present attire makes such an act, no matter how much I desire it, impossible to implement. I lack the ability to
make any move at all under my own volition."

"Gracious madam, if you will allow me the honor of
touching your esteemed person, I would gladly place you
myself upon my plate."

"Oh, Great Lizard, as much as the thought of your
touch thrills me, I fear that such an action might appear

presumptuous and greedy, for you would leave little for the rest of my guests."

At last the Dragon conceded the point and put on his most sorrowful expression. "I shall remain forever disappointed."

"Not half as disappointed as I." Zillabar laughed in conclusion. "Eaten by a Dragon—who could wish for a more delicious death? You have me almost convinced to strip off this shroud and leap onto your plate right now. But, Great Lord, it occurs to me that you would not want to miss the entertainment I have planned for tonight's dinner, an entertainment in which I must play a particularly important role. You will appreciate its elegance, of that I have no doubt."

The Dragon Lord bowed. He lowered his huge head almost to the floor, then raised it again and towered over all the rest of the guests. Their banter concluded, the Lady hissed at her attendants, and they wheeled her around to the head of the table.

Entertainment

□□□□□□□□□□□□□□□□□□□□□□□□□□□□□

After the attendants had seated all of the Lady's guests at their places, the two elegant chairs at Lady Zillabar's left hand still remained empty. The Captain of the starship and several of the Lady's aides looked at the places with open curiosity. The Lady *never* allowed her guest list to unbalance her banquet table. The reputation of her hospitality, as well as the stories told about the sumptuousness of her sideboard, had spread throughout the Phaestor aristocracy; young Vampires all over the Regency aspired for an invitation to her table; so any gap in the seating arrangement could only provoke curiosity among the rest of the guests present.

Lady Zillabar waited until everybody had settled themselves, then nodded to one of her aides. The aide exited, and a moment later returned with a very chastened-looking Sawyer and Finn Markham. The young Vampire led them silently to the empty places, directing Finn specifically to the chair closest to Lady Zillabar. The two brothers looked at the exquisitely dressed table and the array of lustrous guests, looked at each other with reluctant agreement, and sat down warily.

"How *sweet* of you to join us," the Lady said ominously. "You don't look very well, Finn. I do hope you have the strength for this little celebration. I would hate to have your discomfort spoil anyone's evening. You will let me know if you begin to feel weak, won't you? Thank you." To the rest of her guests she announced, "Gentlemen, may I introduce to you two of the very best trackers in the Regency, Sawyer and Finn Markham. They have provided many useful services, and this dinner in their honor allows me to reward them in an appropriate manner."

While her guests applauded, she nodded to a pair of medical aides who had discreetly entered from the side. Immediately, they stepped to Finn's side, and while Sawyer watched in horror, one of them held Finn's arm and the other wrapped a medical band around it and connected an intravenous tap.

"You must promise me that you will eat well," the Lady said to him. "I would hate to have a stain on my hospitality. And besides, if you don't eat well, neither can I."

Already the servants had begun filling the wineglasses and placing delicately arranged trays of appetizers in front of each of the assembled guests. Neither Sawyer nor Finn recognized any of the meats, and neither felt immediately inclined to ask for annotation. While the other guests helped themselves, both of the men kept their hands politely in their laps.

The Lady Zillabar *tsk*ed in annoyance and nodded to the aides, who waited discreetly behind the two brothers. Without further ado, the attendants spread cloth napkins on both of the brothers' laps, and then, using silver serving utensils, placed an assortment of savories on the golden plates in front of each of them. Still, neither Sawyer nor Finn moved.

The Lady's most personal attendants now began to tend to her needs. One held a delicate goblet to her lips, allowing her to take just the faintest sip of the bright pink wine it held. The other placed a tiny sliver of blackened meat in the Lady's mouth. The Lady chewed delicately and swallowed. She glanced to the servant, and he placed another tiny sliver of meat on her tongue.

Sawyer and Finn exchanged a glance. Finn looked tired and haggard, but he held himself upright, refusing to let his weakness show in front of the Lady. Sawyer merely looked horrified. Whatever the Lady intended at this banquet, she could not possibly plan to let either of them survive. Not for long.

The Lady noticed Sawyer's expression then. She cocked her head curiously. "I fear that you have lost your appetite, Mr. Markham. Perhaps the chef has failed to prepare the food to your liking?"

"Uh—no, no. I don't doubt that your chefs have done their very best, madam." He pushed his plate away distastefully. "I just find it difficult to eat meat of such an uncertain ancestry. I can't help but wonder which of your former guests provided these particular savories."

The Lady's smile barely flickered. "You have such a remarkable way of looking at things. I confess that my palate has become so used to the elegance of my table that I often forget how others might perceive the fare served here. No matter," she said. "As long as your brother eats." She shifted her gaze to Finn and her eyes grew hard and cold. "*You will eat,*" she commanded him. She nodded to the servant behind Finn, who picked up a fork, speared a fragment of something dripping in red sauce, and held it up in front of Finn's mouth.

For a moment Finn thought to resist, but the attendant held something to the back of his neck, and he gasped in surprise. The fork popped into Finn's mouth and out again just as quickly. The attendant had obviously done this before. The next time the pale boy held the fork before Finn's mouth, he did not hesitate. He took the food quickly. Finally, reluctantly, Finn took the fork from the servant and began slowly feeding himself.

"Good," said the Lady. "Very good." The other guests at the table had watched this entire proceeding with elaborate interest. Now they too resumed their meal.

At the end of the table, the Dragon Lord enthusiastically plucked mayzel-fish[3] out of an especially large reinforced bowl with his bare talons and popping them happily into his gaping mouth. They looked like dead mice dipped in pond scum: soft, shapeless, and generally unpalatable. They also made terrible, disconcerting croaking noises. The Dragon Lord didn't seem to mind. He enjoyed eating them live. Sawyer almost felt sorry for the mayzel-fish; then he reminded himself where these fish had come from,[4] and he decided that they deserved what they got.

Sawyer turned back to the Lady. Her personal attendants had now begun feeding her some kind of squirming thing from a bowl full of squirming things. He didn't want to look, but he couldn't look away.

"Yes, Mr. Markham?" she asked.

"I—uh, hope you won't think me bad-mannered—"

"I would never do that," the Lady interjected sweetly.

"—but if I might presume to ask a favor of you. As you know, my brother suffers from a condition resembling tertiary blood-burn. . . ."

Lady Zillabar's laughter froze the words in Sawyer's throat.

"Oh, you poor dear. You have my profoundest apology. Of course, I should have explained this to you earlier. Kernel d'Vashti lied to you both. No antidote exists at all for your brother's condition." To the rest of her

---

[3]Especially imported for his pleasure from the Old City detainment on Thoska-Roole.

[4]Actually, a pretty good guess on Sawyer's part. One mayzel-fish looks pretty much like another.

guests the Lady explained, "Once again you see the problem we have with humans; they accept the wildest tales unfailingly. They always believe what they want to believe instead of seeing what actually lies before their eyes."

Before Sawyer could push his chair back and leap to his feet, Finn's hand came down on his arm, and even though Finn no longer had the strength to hold him in his chair, Sawyer got the message and restrained himself. "We've *seen* the lies before our eyes." Finn said for both of them.

As if she hadn't seen this exchange between the Markham brothers, nor heard Finn's remark, Lady Zillabar turned her attention back to Sawyer. "Besides, my dear, even if such an antidote existed, I wouldn't dream of offering it to your brother. It would *spoil* the taste." She added something in her own language, a command to her servants. Immediately, one of the attendants next to Finn bent to the intravenous tap on his arm and opened it. His dark red blood began sliding down the tube and into a silver goblet.

The brothers watched in fascinated horror as the servant closed off the tap and brought the goblet around to where the Lady Zillabar sat. The young Vampire held the cup to the Lady's lips, and she drank from it eagerly. When she had finished, she licked her lips appreciatively. Another servant approached and delicately touched a silken cloth to the corners of her mouth.

The Lady Zillabar sighed. "Ahhh. I enjoyed that." She looked at Sawyer and at Finn. "Finn, thank you so much. Truly, a delicious experience. I intend to have you share all of your meals with me. Oh, do have some more wine. I would like to get wonderfully drunk tonight." She turned to the rest of her guests. "Would anyone else like a taste?"

Dinner Thoughts

The Lady's guests laughed aloud at the delicious irony of her words—indeed, the whole nasty situation had a certain baroque charm. Only a Vampire could appreciate all the nuances of pain in the situation; only a Vampire would want to.

The Lady knew that the young Vampire males would whisper among themselves for months, spreading the tales of this evening's merriment. They would talk of the blood-red shroud that left the Lady helpless and vulnerable, and they would stimulate themselves to frenzies of lust as each of them imagined what grotesqueries they might perform if they could have her in such a helpless circumstance.

They would repeat her every word among themselves. They would laugh at her jokes and allow themselves to experience delicious thrills of envy and desire. And yes, of course, all of them would hunger for an invitation to her table. All of them would want to taste the blood of her next victim.

The Lady smiled at the thought. She wanted exactly this kind of story whispered among her admirers. For one thing, it would drive d'Vashti insane with rage and lust. She wondered how long she could keep Finn Markham alive. The idea intrigued her—how long would it take to drive Sawyer Markham mad? She would have to drink sparingly of Finn to make it work, but the enjoyment would certainly justify the restraint. Yes, she would give the appropriate orders immediately after tonight's meal concluded.

At the opposite end of the table, the Dragon Lord did not share the Lady's enthusiasm. He had enjoyed his earlier repartee with the Lady as an amusing conceit, a harmless flirtation wherein each of the partners gently tickled the other's sensibilities.

This shameless display of unrestrained blood-lust, however, he found extremely distasteful. Perhaps the Vampires found sport in the malicious taunting of the prey; it made him queasy. It reeked of dishonor. His progenitors had trained him to kill his meals quickly and cleanly. Additionally, he had always believed it the lowest form of dishonor to eat criminals. At least, in public. Destroying the distinction between criminals and prey befouled the prey and diminished the meal. It insulted the service of the one and exalted the other. No, eating the wrongdoer did not constitute an appropriate form of punishment. And it implied that the eater's hunger had grown so far beyond control that he *or she* had abandoned all pretense of dining as an art.

That he himself had only quite recently devoured an appallingly large human criminal did not affect this judgment at all. He could justify that matter easily enough in his own mind. That particular human had tried to escape, and he'd had to track her down personally. Once a Dragon enters into the pursuit of a fleeing animal, all the ancient Dragon instincts come boiling straight to the surface of his soul. The hunt cannot properly conclude until the Dragon has eaten the heart of the hunted. In such a situation, all arbitrary distinctions disappear.

Once having eaten the heart, the Dragon may also partake of the rest of the flesh, if he so desires. In this case the Lord of the Dragons had indeed desired. He had sated his hunger three times before abandoning the corpse to whatever predators waited in the dark red gloom beyond. . . .

Nevertheless, this situation wore a different face. To bring the criminal to the table and partake of his blood as a delicacy offended the Dragon Lord. Additionally, to taunt the prisoner for the entertainment of one's guests— well, maybe Vampires found amusement in that. Dragons did not.

After considering this matter for some time, the Dragon Lord at last came to a decision. He rose from his chair and excused himself from the table. The Lady barely noticed, so enraptured had she become with her jest. She did not see the Lord's grimace of distaste as he turned away and stamped heavily off to his own part of the vessel.

Along the way he stopped to address the ambitious young Captain Lax-Varney. "I do not want any Dragons at all assigned to Lady Zillabar's section of this vessel. Do you understand?"

"Sir?"

"I want no tales circulating among my Dragons. What they don't see, they can't discuss. Keep them all away from the Vampires' part of the vessel. If you fail me in this, I will eat your heart."

"Yes, my Lord." Lax-Varney hurried off quickly to give the orders.

Sawyer's Vow

ΩΩΩΩΩΩΩΩΩΩΩΩΩΩΩΩΩΩΩΩΩΩΩΩΩΩΩΩ

When the Vampires finally returned them to the cell with the others, Sawyer experienced a curious surge of emotion. He felt *glad* to see this tiny cramped cabin again. He felt *happy* to finally escape the Vampires' presence and return to the company of men—even men he had betrayed.

The lingering wake of this reaction puzzled him . . . and troubled him as well. Why should he feel anything for these people? He could only assume that he had become emotionally confused by the effect of Lady Zillabar's meticulously nasty treatment. He glanced around—

Sawyer saw the looks on their faces—Lee and Three-Dollar and Tuan—and caught himself abruptly.

Despite his rising fear, he asked the question anyway: "What happened to Drin and Tahl? Where did they go?"

"The Vampires took them," said Tuan. He added with quiet fury, "They said that . . . that Drin and Tahl would not return to us, but not to worry, the rest of us would join them soon enough."

Three-Dollar put a hand on Tuan's shoulder, comforting him as much as holding him back. He looked past him to Sawyer. "Do you know anything about that?"

Sawyer started to answer, but then—he couldn't help himself; the vision of the Lady's table, heaped high with platters of pale flesh, rose unbidden in his thoughts. He felt suddenly vomitous and barely made it to the sink in time—

When he straightened again, shaken and pale, he held up a hand to ward off the others' attentions and returned silently to his brother's wheelchair. He looked ashen.

Sawyer busied himself with Finn, helping him to his cot and covering him with a blanket. He ignored the questioning looks of the others and bent worriedly over his brother. Three-Dollar quietly pushed him aside and laid his hand on Finn's forehead. "He looks drained," he said.

"You can't imagine," Finn groaned.

Three-Dollar didn't answer. He peeled back the stocky man's eyelids and peered intently into his face. He took Finn's pulse and he looked at his tongue. Finally he examined Finn's arm and discovered the marks left by the intravenous tap. "I thought so."

"She has to kill us," said Sawyer. "She can't let us live to bear witness of her crimes against the Charter."

"So? What do you care?" asked Tuan bitterly.

Sawyer met his accusing gaze. He indicated the TimeBinder. "Why should he care about Finn?"

"Because I do," answered Three-Dollar without looking up.

"Well, then maybe I can learn to care too—"

"And why should we believe you?" Lee-1169 retorted.

"Don't believe me. I don't care if you do or not. I'll

act the same way no matter what you believe." He swallowed hard. "I won't let this crime go unavenged." But his words sounded hollow and ineffectual.

"Blankets," said Three-Dollar abruptly. "We need blankets to wrap him in." He pushed Lee away. "Go get every blanket in the cabin. Now!" To Sawyer he ordered, "You, get me some water."

The attack came upon Finn like a storm, sweeping across him in flashes of sudden hot chills and icy fevers. The sweat poured from his body until the sheets grew sodden. He shook and moaned and clutched himself in pain, writhing back and forth upon his cot. His flesh turned cold to the touch. They wrapped him in blankets and held him close, trying to push their warmth into his body by sheer strength of will alone. He wept in their arms, a shell of himself; his skin turned blue and pale. He fell so weak, he couldn't even lift his head to the water bag.

Sawyer climbed onto the cot next to his brother's and wrapped his arms around him. He began to weep in great heaving sobs. Finn remained powerless to resist, but his frantic eyes revealed how terror stricken he had become. At last William Three-Dollar and Lee-1169 gently pulled Sawyer Markham away from his dying brother. "He needs to rest—"

"No. I have to stay with him!" Sawyer insisted. "I'll stay with him to the end. I have to."

"Sawyer, shut up," said Lee. "Finn wants to talk."

Instantly, Sawyer ceased protesting. He sank to the floor and put his face close to Finn's. "Go ahead, Finn," he whispered.

With great difficulty Finn Markham managed to shape the words and force them past his dry, parched lips. "Sawyer—keep your promise. The promise that you made on Thoska-Roole. Don't let them cocoon me, Sawyer!"

Sawyer couldn't answer. He couldn't let his mind take the next step and the next. He couldn't allow himself to act as the instrument of his brother's death. He couldn't imagine what shape his life would take without his brother. But neither could he imagine his brother wrapped and hanging and waiting.

"Sawyer, please—" Finn grabbed his brother's arm and held on tightly. For a dying man he still had surprising strength. "You promised me!"

The tears poured down Sawyer's cheeks. "I know, I know. Oh, God, Finn! I don't want to do this!"

"You must—"

"I know—please forgive me."

"I love you, Sawyer. Please give me peace."

"I love you too, Finn. Listen to me—" He sniffed, gulped, caught his breath. And in that moment something happened to him. He reached inside himself and found an inner resource of strength that he had never known before.

He got angry.

He held his brother's hand and looked into his eyes and he said, "I promise you that this crime will not go unavenged!" And this time, when he said it, the words had the resonant and terrifying ring of true conviction— this time the words sounded like the death knell of the Regency. "I will not rest until I have destroyed the Lady Zillabar, and if necessary, the entire goddamned Vampire aristocracy!"

The other men in the room stared at Sawyer, astonished. They stood around him in a respectful circle, their eyes bright with the shared glow of his vision. His declaration sounded like a hundred thousand other desperate declarations made against tyranny—but he spoke it with the kind of resolve that troubled the sleep of tyrants everywhere. He spoke it as a man with nothing left to lose.

He looked down at Finn again for some sign of acknowledgment, but his brother had lapsed back into unconsciousness.

William Three-Dollar came over and pulled Sawyer away. "He needs his rest, son. Leave him for now."

Sawyer shook off the TimeBinder's large bony hands and sank to his knees next to his brother. He buried his face in his hands and began to cry again, great heaving sobs that left him out of breath and gasping.

Burihatin

◘◘◘◘◘◘◘◘◘◘◘◘◘◘◘◘◘◘◘◘◘◘◘◘◘◘◘◘◘

The tangled web of *otherspace* unfolded, shimmered, solidified, and begat a golden starflake of light.

The vessel sang as it spun gracefully toward the distant globe called Burihatin. *The Golden Fury* called to her sister ships across the emptiness, and she listened for their echoing cries. Then, at last, satisfied, she turned on her axis and dove downward toward the huge ringed world below. The starship still had many long hours of deceleration ahead. First she had to match orbits with the giant planet, then she had to match the orbit of the fourteenth moon.

Burihatin had an ethereal beauty. Not quite large enough to have become a star in her own right, she still loomed bright and golden. She radiated more heat than light; she gave off a lustrous warmth. The great planet swam brightly through the dark sea of space with her large family of satellites circling gracefully around her.

Forty satellites orbited Burihatin, some small enough to leap away from, others massing larger than some nearby worlds. More people lived on the moons of Burihatin than on all the other planets and moons circling Burihatin's primary. The giant ringed world reigned as a star system in her own right, co-opting even the authority of her primary.

The starship began correcting her trajectory to bring her into a parallel orbit with the fourteenth moon. As she approached, she began spawning an escort of Marauders. Some stayed close with the mothership, others sailed out adventurously, scouting, patrolling, and covering against any ship that might venture within missile-firing range.

Inside the big vessel the Lady Zillabar and the

Dragon Lord stood silently on the balcony above the command bay and watched as Burihatin loomed larger and larger ahead. The planet's size presented a deceptive appearance of proximity, when in fact they still had the better part of a day left before their scheduled disembarkation.

Finally, finding the continued silence intolerable, the Dragon Lord offered a solicitous courtesy. "I hope you have had a pleasant voyage, my Lady."

"Pleasant enough. And not without its tasty diversions."

The Dragon Lord nodded impartially. He did not appreciate the reference. He did not approve of dishonor, although he sometimes recognized it as a distasteful necessity; but if he could justify in his mind the occasional dishonorable act on behalf of the Regency, he still could not easily accept the casual discussions of same. He didn't want to have the precedent established that even small dishonors had attained the respectability of polite conversation.

The Captain of the starship came up to the observation deck then and bowed to the Lady and the Lord. He waited for their acknowledgments and then reported crisply. "We have announced our presence. We have experienced no resistance from the Burihatin patrols, and we expect none. However, with your permission I would like to modify our approach and keep the vessel orbiting at a safe distance until our Marauders have gone ahead and secured the area. I see no sense in putting you at even the slightest risk, Madame Zillabar."

The Lady nodded her agreement. "The resistance here will have heard about the death of Prince Drydel. They will have to have realized that the situation has accelerated gravely, and they might have just enough ambition to create a serious nuisance. Let us not grow overconfident on the eve of our triumphs. I concur with your decision, Captain. Besides, the extra delay means that I will have time for one more exquisite little dinner before disembarking." She waved the Captain away.

"I'll see to the arrangements," he said. He bowed and exited.

The Lady turned back to the Dragon Lord. "Would you care to join me?"

"I fear, madame, that I must regretfully decline. If I do not spend more time with my own warriors, they might begin to believe that I no longer appreciate their company. As much as I would enjoy the delights of your table, my responsibility to your safety must take precedence." He bowed.

Zillabar smiled sideways at him. "You don't fool me, you ravenous old lizard. I know that my eating habits disgust you—as your habits disgust me. But we need each other, and we tolerate each other, and we support each other . . . because without each other we each have nothing."

"My Lady," the Lord replied, towering over her even as he bowed his head. "I have far too much respect for your wisdom ever to dream of arguing with you. I shall look forward to seeing you again after your meal." He turned and lumbered away, leaving the Lady Zillabar studying his last words in her mind and wondering just how far she could depend on the loyalty of the Dragon Lord.

Plan B

Sawyer sat forlornly on the mattress that served as cot, his brother's head cradled in his lap. The others had withdrawn quietly to the opposite side of the room, from where they watched and waited in silence.

Sawyer carefully wiped the sweat from his brother's forehead with a damp cloth. His movements grew gentle and tender—and for a moment the two brothers appeared to have attained a small measure of peace. The yellow light of the cabin bathed them in a soft pearlescent glow.

At last Finn opened his eyes and looked up at his brother. "I think the time has finally come, Soy."

Sawyer nodded. He began pulling at the piping on the hem of his jacket, working at it with trembling hands. Finally he broke away a piece of the trim, unrolling it to reveal a tiny capsule. Without saying a word, he laid the capsule aside, where he could easily reach it.

"Before you go, Finn, let me say good-bye. Let me say thank you. Let me remind you of all the times you protected me, and—well, you know—took care of me. We always used to talk about how we wanted things different. I just want you to know that the way it worked out—well, I don't have any regrets. We did good. I wouldn't have wanted it any other way, okay?"

"Bullshit," grunted Finn, his voice barely audible. "You always wanted more. Even now you want more time."

Sawyer choked up. He couldn't think of anything else to say, so he merely said, "Thank you, Finn. I love you." Then he bent his face down to his brother's and kissed him gently on the lips.

"Sawyer—" Lee called softly from across the room, where he waited with one ear pressed to the door. "I hear them coming! The Vampires."

Sawyer picked up the pill and placed it gently in Finn's mouth. Then he held the water bag to Finn's dry lips and let him drink his fill.

Finn looked up at his brother and whispered, "Thank you, Soy." He closed his eyes and appeared to fall asleep. The tears began rolling down Sawyer's cheeks again, leaving streaks on his face. He held his brother close, cradling him gently against the night, and hummed a wordless lullaby.

The Vampires found them that way when they opened the door; Sawyer sitting on the floor of the cell and holding his brother close, while he sang softly to him and rocked him in his arms.

A Little History

🔲🔲🔲🔲🔲🔲🔲🔲🔲🔲🔲🔲🔲🔲🔲🔲🔲🔲🔲🔲🔲🔲🔲🔲🔲🔲

Giant Burihatin loomed like a great curved wall. The planet seeped a soft yellow warmth; magnificent storms swept across its surface, patterning its atmosphere with glorious chaotic swirls of color. Not quite large enough to ignite itself to stardom, it simmered in its orbit, circling its larger partner at a wary distance. Beyond, the primary star spread a bright blue blanket of light across the realms of space. Everything glowed.

Inside the Lady Zillabar's starship, inside her banquet room, the swollen globe of Burihatin provided a spectacular view. Its churning gas-scape stretched out before the broad windows of the chamber like a vast pink and violet ocean. Crimson swirls marked the passage of raging hurricanes, each one large enough to hold habitable worlds. The atmosphere seethed and glowed. Blue and white lightning flashed intermittently; the discharges sometimes spread visibly across the arc of the planet, rippling outward in a chain reaction of sparks and fury.

The ferocious storms presented an ever-changing, ever-constant dance of shape and color—much like the Lady Zillabar, whose own storms played across her surface in displays of gaudy decoration. What displayed on her outer countenance, however, rarely reflected the contours of her inner face.

Today the Lady wore an expression of absolute calm. She also wore an unrevealing shroud of ash-gray, the color of nothingness, cut by a bright diagonal slash of scarlet—the recognition of her office.

A noise distracted the Lady. She turned away from the balcony view and her contemplations. At the opposite end of the chamber, her insect attendants quietly ushered in her guests: the last known member of the Lee clone-family, number 1169; the TimeBinder, William Three-Dollar; his towering aide, Tuan; and the two troublesome trackers, Sawyer and Finn Markham. Finn sagged unconscious in a wheelchair; the attendants rolled him to the center of the room, then retired discreetly to the side of the room. Zillabar noted with amusement how Sawyer stayed close to his brother's side.

The others had also arrayed themselves protectively around Finn. She recognized the body language. The rebels had allied themselves with the trackers. Not that it mattered much. It would not affect the ultimate result of these affairs. But, still, she found their gallows-courage amusing. In the face of certain death, these pitiful creatures still behaved as if their actions might make a difference.

Zillabar moved languidly, unmindful of their hate-filled eyes. She crossed slowly over to Finn and touched his forearm, tracing a blue vein with delicate fingers. "Finn Markham, you have a delicious quality," she acknowledged. "Rough, crude, direct—but not without flavor. Sometimes the hard tastes have their own attraction." She smiled politely at the others. "I do not offer compliments like this casually. If nothing else, you may take some condolence in the fact that you have provided me not only with many pleasant hours of amusement, but also several very satisfying meals as well."

Turning back to Finn, she touched his arm again. "I believe that we have finally come to the end. You cannot possibly know how much sorrow that gives me. I have very much enjoyed our time together, and I truly regret that we will not share any more meals after this one, but you don't appear to have much strength left, and I really don't care to watch you linger. Besides, the flavor changes badly when you get down to the sediment.

"But please, Finn—" she whispered, pretending compassion. "Don't concern yourself after my welfare. I'll make do, somehow. I'll content myself with other diversions. Who do you think I should sample next? Your brother perhaps? Or should I save him for last? That possibility does provide a certain tangy symmetry. Yes, the last to go shall see all the others die before him. I wonder what TimeBinder tastes like; I know what Lee tastes like. No matter. Your brother will die alone, and I promise you, I will do everything I can to make it an *exquisite* death."

She motioned to her attendants, and they hurried over to tap the vein in Finn's arm. The dark blood flowed steadily into the goblet.

"A toast," said the Lady, raising the cup to her lips. Again she smiled at them, mocking their fierce determination with her liquid laugh. They couldn't take their eyes off her. Their expressions burned with intensity. "A toast—to those who serve the Regency. You should all feel honored. Just as the flavor of Finn Markham has brought pleasure to this sophisticated palate, so in turn will each of you provide that same service. I give you my sincerest thanks for your selfless sacrifices."

She drank deeply from the bowl, cradling it with both hands as she tilted the dark fluid across her lips, over her delicate forked tongue, and down her pulsing throat. The blood burned with a flavor she had never tasted before—peculiar, but tantalizing. It lingered in her mouth and left her with a haunting purple feeling. She licked her lips and wondered if she might allow herself another cup; this close to the bottom of the bottle, the flavor would almost certainly have overtones of death. She preferred her meals vigorous, not weak. And besides, a second cup might seem like shameless indulgence. Regretfully, she decided against it and handed the goblet to a faceless insect attendant.

She gestured for a settee and sank down onto it as it glided over to her. As the warmth of Finn's blood spread throughout her body, she cast a languorous, almost affectionate gaze across her guests. "You really don't appreciate the honor that this represents, do you? If only you knew your history better. Even you, Three-Dollar, have no idea of the high regard that the Phaestor have for their food species. You have always thought of us as cruel and uncaring, haven't you?"

Zillabar stretched herself luxuriously across the

couch. "But we do care. More than you know. You become part of us. We cherish you. We want to see you healthy and happy in your lives, not just because it affects the flavor, but because you will serve us more efficiently."

Three-Dollar inclined his head in a nod of polite deference. "I do know something of history. I would not presume to argue with your interpretation, but some of us have experienced the same events in a different light."

The Lady waved away his comment with a dainty gesture of irrelevance. "I grant you that some abuses have occurred, especially among the young and the reckless members of my species. But for the most part, you will find that we have only the highest regard for your people. You have accepted a holy burden on your shoulders." To the others' puzzled looks, she explained. "The Phaestor do not exist in an ecological vacuum. When we began, those who created us also created several bioform species for us to feed upon. Those species did not have the sentience to experience fear. Indeed, they felt only awe and reverence for us, their protectors. They bent their necks to us proudly and willingly; they gave their lives with such pleasure that the flavor of their blood sparkled in our mouths and invigorated our spirits. Or so I have heard," she added uncomfortably. It would not do to demonstrate too much familiarity with the flavors of bioform blood. Not even here.

"Unfortunately," she continued, "the war against the Predators lasted for many centuries, much longer than it should have. The logistics of interstellar war required many, many Phaestor. The Predators kept coming and coming, sometimes as many as two or three a decade. We had to stop them before they found and englobed the populated worlds, so we had to meet them in the deeps between the Cluster and the great wheel of the Eye of God. We had to wait long years in the darkness and challenge the Predators there.

"Do you know what that required—the ships, the crews, the long, almost suicidal watches? Can you even conceive of the courage of our brave Phaestor children?

The ships stayed on station for decades, the eggs thawed as needed; the children hatched in the most precarious conditions. They trained under the most rigorous of rules, no margins for error existed aboard the ships. But they served—without complaint. They served proudly. And we have all enjoyed the benefits of their sacrifices in the dark between the stars."

Lady Zillabar softened her tone. She brushed something away from her forehead, looked momentarily puzzled, then continued her discourse on the history of her species. "But for many years, the Predators came almost faster than we could meet them. We had to breed many young Phaestor for the battle, and regretfully, the needs of our defense outgrew our ability to maintain ourselves. We reproduced faster than our bioform cattle, and although we worked as hard as we could to build up our feedstocks, we realized early on that we would have to find alternate food supplies to sustain our health and our ability to breed.

"Courageously, your species—you humans and your uplifted companions, the dogs, the apes, and the others—your species volunteered to make up the difference in the blood-fall. You gave us your partnership so that we could fight the Predators together. You shared our victories. You still do."

The men looked unconvinced, and Lady Zillabar knew automatically what they thought. She answered it without their having to ask. "That we have not seen a Predator in centuries doesn't mean that we have vanquished them. Perhaps they still swarm across the Milky Way, breeding and spreading and smothering all the worlds they encounter. Perhaps one day they will again leap across light-years to the beckoning Cluster. Do we dare relax our defenses? Do we dare become complacent? I think not. The Phaestor still stand watch against the Predators, and those who benefit from our labors must pay us for our service. The transaction has no shame; we ask only life for life.

"We ask only your continued partnership."

Partnership

⬚⬚⬚⬚⬚⬚⬚⬚⬚⬚⬚⬚⬚⬚⬚⬚⬚⬚⬚⬚⬚⬚⬚⬚⬚⬚⬚

William Three-Dollar bowed politely. The tall red-skinned man had an angular grace that rivaled that of the Vampires themselves. He said, "My Lady, with no disrespect, your version of history differs significantly from mine. Perhaps the error lies with your perspective. Perhaps it lies with mine. Perhaps the truth lies somewhere in between, and perhaps indeed the truth exists in neither of our respective tellings. Nevertheless, it seems to me that your version of history contains a measure of self-serving inaccuracy that allows you to continue this fiction that we humans exist in partnership and that we should enjoy this relationship. In point of fact, we most emphatically do not."

Zillabar looked momentarily confused, but she recovered quickly and waved Three-Dollar's words away with one bejeweled hand. "Look out there. See the storms that sweep across Burihatin? You swim like a balloon-fish in the current. You have no idea of the forces that move you. You have no idea what lies beyond your ability to perceive. Your language doesn't even have the distinctions that would allow me to explain. You can't hear what I say, you can only hear what your perceptions allow you to hear."

Behind Three-Dollar, Sawyer and Lee exchanged a wary glance. Three-Dollar inclined his head curiously, as if listening to something else, then bowed politely. "Enlighten us, then. Show us what we do not understand."

Zillabar thought about standing up to face the impudent man, decided not to; she still felt the delicious warmth of Finn Markham's blood coursing through her veins; she didn't want to spoil the moment. She stretched out comfortably across the couch.

"I'll tell you part of what you don't know," she said. "We have found the taste of human blood and human flesh to have an invigorating effect upon our palates. Humans provide a very sweet addition to our diets, much more delicious than our original bioform prey. Humans breed faster and taste better. Many Vampires prefer the taste of humans, and correspondingly we feel much less pressure to restore and maintain our bioform herds as before. We would rather lessen the number of humans first. We do not enjoy your competition for resources.

"The matter of your sentience does not carry the same importance to us as it does to you; because from our vantage point you really do not have anywhere near as much sentience as you think you do. You have just enough rationality to understand the concept, but certainly not enough to achieve it.

"We plan to have a Phaestor governor on every Regency world before the beginning of the next cycle. All of the lesser species will soon serve our needs, and we will complete the process of restructuring the Dominion. Despite the untimely death of Lord Drydel—an event in which your participation will not go unpunished—our plans will go forward. I will lay many eggs—more than any other queen in history. And you humans will play an important part in that drama as well.

"Our experiments have proven that Phaestor boys grow faster and healthier when hatched in human hosts. So your species will provide another service to the Phaestoric Dominion. You will not only feed us, you will help us breed, and all the while you will help us reduce your numbers.

"From your feeble perspective, of course, this must appear as a terrible violation of your desperate urge to survive; but, when viewed from the larger frame of reference that we Vampires enjoy, when viewed from the greater historical perspective, this moment represents an extraordinary threshold of evolutionary opportunity. We approach critical mass. When it occurs, then . . . in one great leap, we shall cast off the past and reinvent the ruling intelligence of the Palethetic Cluster. Your feeble sentience will enhance that process, expressing itself ultimately in the joyous recognition of a self-designed, self-created godhood of Phaestoric consciousness. Gods *need* worshippers.

"The participation of humanity in this transformation of sentience exists as an evolutionary privilege never before granted to any intelligent species. I sometimes wonder how any intelligent creature would not eagerly wish to have such a partnership with the future. And equally, I sometimes wonder why you poor, pitiful things continue to demonstrate so much resistance to the inevitable course of life. As much as I try to understand the workings of your lesser minds, I remain appalled at the paucity of your imaginations, at your inability to accept that another species has earned its right to rule over you."

As if exhausted by this speech, the Lady sank back on her couch, again succumbing to the intoxicating glow of Finn's fresh blood. She had not realized how much she had needed this draught; she felt its effects much more profoundly than she expected. Perhaps the treatment in his blood had ripened much faster than she realized, or perhaps she had deprived herself too long of her own sweet red dreams. No matter. She would enjoy this one to the utmost. It would take a while before her ship slipped into orbit around Burihatin-14, and she had nothing better to do anyway. She felt woozy.

She lifted one hand to dismiss William Three-Dollar and the others, but before she could complete the gesture, the tall man began speaking to her. Both his words and his tone carried an ominous sense of danger. But she couldn't see how this pitiful man could possibly harm her. She listened in amusement as he said, "What you describe, Lady Zillabar, represents the most heinous violation of the Regency Charter since the original founders first crafted that sacred document. You have described a Vampire plan for racial war."

Zillabar struggled to sit up. "Ho!" she grunted. "Other races have abused the Vampires for centuries— this represents justice. We see it as a fair retribution."

Lee-1169 snorted then. "What else can we expect from a Vampire? You can't tell the difference between justice and revenge."

Zillabar shook her head. "You foolish man. In our language we make no distinction between the two concepts. Why should we?"

William Three-Dollar answered her. "If the Vampires have truly chosen to discard the charter and pursue this course, then the Regency has already collapsed. The Gathering of the TimeBinders represents the Cluster's only hope for true justice."

Zillabar laughed. "You pitiful little men. You think your demonstrations of bravado will make a difference? All of you will feed the holy transformation. I will mate and lay my eggs, and your veins will provide the wine of celebration." She tried to stagger to her feet, she wobbled as if drunk—she flushed with confusion, and a look of sudden understanding appeared on her face.

"What have you done?" she gasped. One delicate hand leapt upward, clutched at her throat. "You've tried to poison me—" She staggered to her feet. She had to support herself by holding on to the armrest of her couch. She tried to scream. "Guards—" but her voice came out as a pitiful croak.

She stumbled then, collapsing forward into Three-Dollar's waiting arms. Behind him Lee-1169 shouted, "Seize the moment!" He and Sawyer leapt. Three-Dollar turned Zillabar sideways in his grasp, pulled the dagger from her belt, and held it up to her throat, touching the silvery tip of the blade to the soft hollow at the root of her neck.

Lee grabbed the end of one of the hanging draperies framing the double doors of the main access, pulling it across and through the golden handles, tying it securely. Tuan pushed a couch in front of the servants' access door. Sawyer leapt sideways just in time to meet the Elite Guard of Vampires. A secret panel slid open, and a squad of pale boys in shining black armor came pouring through the opening.

Confrontation

Sawyer knew the truth of these children—selected for decoration more than for skill; he whirled on one leg, drop-kicking the first one into the room. He heard the fragile bones cracking as the boy slammed against the wall. Lee-1169 pulled the second one down with a vicious chop to the neck. Tuan scooped up a needle-gun that rattled across the floor, and shot the third guard in the chest, the fourth one in the face. The fifth guard ducked to one side, looking for an opening. The sixth guard stumbled into the cross fire and fell to the floor, writhing with a double set of wounds. By then Lee had a needle-gun too, and the two of them dashed back to flank Three-Dollar and Zillabar just in time before six Dragon Guards came bursting through the double doors like an avalanche of hardened flesh. Sawyer still scrambled for a weapon of his own.

The hulking lizards stopped when they saw the tableau before them: One knife held to Zillabar's throat. Two needle-guns held to her lolling head. She babbled incoherently. Against the walls the insect attendants twittered and fluttered uncomfortably. Without orders they wouldn't—*couldn't*—act. Sawyer rolled a fallen guard over; he plucked the gun from the dead Vampire's hand.

The Dragons stumbled to an uncertain halt. They hesitated.

Three-Dollar said, "If you shoot, she dies. Do you want that stain on your honor? Drop your weapons."

Still, they hesitated—

"Drop them or she dies!" Three-Dollar ordered.

Two more Dragons pounded into the room, colliding with the others. The Dragon Lord came in after them,

45

pushing to the front. Sawyer recognized him instantly; so did the others. He straightened up abruptly, bringing his weapon around to bear, already wondering if the smart-beam of the needle-gun had enough power to stop or even injure the great lizard. Maybe they could stun him. But what about the others?

Three-Dollar held the knife to the Lady's throat, tilting her head upward with it. "Tell your men to drop their weapons *or she dies.*"

Nothing about the Dragon Lord's demeanor betrayed his uncertainty, but he stood frozen in dismay. He had never even conceived of such an impossible situation as the one confronting him now. He stood like a rock while his brain raced.

As if to underline his point, Three-Dollar pressed the knife hard against Zillabar's unconscious throat. A single red drop of blood glistened for an instant, then rolled delicately down across her icy skin, leaving a dark angry stain.

The Dragon Lord hung his head in recognition. He gestured to his troops. "Put down your weapons. The safety of the Lady takes absolute precedence." The Dragons looked to him for confirmation. *"Do it!"* he roared suddenly. At least now he had a target for his anger. At least he could control his troops. The Dragons pointed their rifles to the ceiling, switched off the arming circuits, and locked the safeties in place. They dropped their heavy weapons to the floor with a loud clatter.

"Kick them over here," Three-Dollar ordered. "All of them."

The Dragon Lord nodded to Captain Lax-Varney—the soon-to-die failure, Captain Lax-Varney. The smaller Dragon saw no escape. He began reluctantly pushing all of the heavy rifles out toward the center of the room with his foot.

Sawyer shoved his needle-gun into his belt and stepped cautiously forward; he scooped up one of the cannons, grunting at its weight. "Holy shit. This thing could probably poke a hole in a small moon!" He pointed it at the guards. "Take off your armor now." He unlocked the safety on the weapon. It made a terrifyingly loud click. He punched the arming circuit. The weapon emitted a high-pitched whistle as it charged itself anew.

"If you fire that in here," cautioned the Dragon Lord, "you'll risk punching a hole in the hull of the ship."

"I doubt that," said Sawyer, "or you wouldn't have issued these weapons to your troops. Dragons do not have a reputation for either caution or intelligence. Take off your armor, all of you."

"A Dragon never takes off its armor," said the Dragon Lord, "and certainly not in front of a human."

"I wonder what the other Vampires will say when they hear that your refusal caused the death of Lady Zillabar." Sawyer fired a single precise shot. The sound of it crackled in the air like an explosion. And when the other Dragons looked around, Captain Lax-Varney tottered on his feet, a smoking hole sizzling in the exact center of his chest. Lax-Varney collapsed to his knees, clutching himself in pain, then laboriously struggled erect again. "No problem," he said, waving off help. "No problem. He has scorched my armor, nothing more." And then he collapsed again to the floor, this time to remain motionless. He looked dead. None of the other Dragons paid him any heed. They had already discarded him. Perhaps his death would satisfy the needs of honor. But probably not. The rest of them would probably have to die as well.

Sawyer reset the targeting on the weapon. "I'll fire the next shot at full power. At this range, who knows what effect that'll produce? I admit to considerable curiosity."

"You can't succeed, you know," advised the Dragon Lord.

"I have died five times over, m'Lord," Sawyer responded with a courteous nod. "At this point in life, my only interest lies in seeing how many others I can take with me the next time the opportunity arises. I should dearly like to have you accompany me to hell. Not every human arrives with a Dragon escort." He gestured with the rifle. "The armor, now."

"Never."

"Then you'll have the Lady's death-stain on your name!"

"Then I'll go down in history as the greatest Dragon of all." The Dragon Lord spread his legs wide apart. Still keeping his gaze focused on Sawyer, he hung his head low. His huge jaws parted, and a dreadful rumble came issuing from deep in his throat. The sound had a terrifying edge. The Dragon Lord's eyes took on a quality of frightening intensity.

Sawyer had heard stories about the Dragon roar of madness; he'd never actually heard it until now: the Dragon's death-warning. A Dragon would take the posture and let himself succumb to his emotions. He would stand and roar and build up his rage until it consumed him fully. When a Dragon did this, he became invulnerable to fear, to pain, to wounds of all kinds. When the madness finally overpowered him, he would attack and keep attacking until he destroyed the target of his rage or it destroyed him.

Breakout

▢▢▢▢▢▢▢▢▢▢▢▢▢▢▢▢▢▢▢▢▢▢▢▢▢▢

Sawyer knew he had to act quickly. He had to dissuade the death-rage before it erupted into a blind killing frenzy. He'd already seen an ordinary Dragon in action; he had no desire to witness firsthand the furies of the Dragon Lord. He cried, "Dishonor! Dishonor! Death-rage now will dishonor your name, your family, the Dragons, the office of Dragon Lord! Death-rage will dishonor all Dragons everywhere. Death-rage brings dishonor now!" He glanced back to the others.

"You shouldn't have asked him to take off his armor," Tuan said.

"Now you tell me." Sawyer turned his attention

back to the Dragon Lord. He didn't know if the giant beast had understood him or not. He didn't even know if the creature had heard his words over his own roaring.

He checked the charge on the rifle. Yes, he could bring the monster down if he had to. But if the Dragon Lord erupted in a berserk fury, so would his troops, and Sawyer knew he couldn't stop them all if they charged. But—

Without thinking, he slapped the controls of the gun, setting the beam for wide-angle, emergency discharge. He fired—

—the blast resounded throughout the entire ship. The defocused beam of the weapon leapt out, spreading a crackling blue nimbus across the entire arc of fire. The Dragons reeled as the smart-energy sought out its targets: their electronics, their augments, their nervous systems. They staggered under the impact; several of them collapsed to the floor. The Dragon Lord blinked, disconcerted, his death-rage interrupted, possibly broken.

—and still the spray of fire continued! Sawyer reeled under the strain of the weapon's fury. He had no idea that the Dragons had charged their weapons so high. They must have some kind of ultrapowered fuel cell that even he didn't know about. He should have suspected it by the effectiveness of his first shot. One by one the Dragons tottered and fell. It sounded like a forest collapsing around them. The crackling energy flickered over their bodies, hungrily drawn to the electrical fields in their armor, their spinal cords, their brains. It would not stop until it had discharged itself into those targets. The Dragons twitched where they lay.

—and then, finally, the weapon fell silent. Exhausted, depleted. Sawyer had pumped its entire reservoir of energy into the hapless Dragon Guard.

"Did you kill them?"

"Maybe. I don't think so. Dragons don't die easy." Sawyer threw the cannon aside and grabbed two more. One he slung over his shoulder, the other he hefted. He scrambled for an ammo belt. Tuan and Lee shoved their needle-guns into their shirts and did likewise, each one grabbing one weapon to use and a spare to carry. The rebellion had learned to gather weapons wherever they could, and old habits died hard.

Three-Dollar dumped Zillabar into Finn's lap, tying her in place with her own red diplomatic sash. He grabbed a cannon-rifle of his own and hung another one on the back of the wheelchair, plus several belts of extra charges. Then he pointed his weapon at those still remaining, set his beam on wide, and fired. Despite their armoring, the weapons couldn't withstand the assault. They melted into slag. Sawyer's ears began to hurt from all the noise.

"The bridge!" said Lee. "If we can seize the bridge—"

"Let's not get grandiose," said Sawyer. "Let's just get off this ship."

"This way." Three-Dollar pointed. He steered the wheelchair toward the door. "Sawyer, take the point. Lee, cover our butts."

The men circled the twitching Dragons warily. The seizures afflicting the great beasts had left them helpless in their own vomit. Their sphincter muscles had also relaxed, and they had fouled themselves with their own urine and feces. The horrendous stench filled the chamber. The rebels hurried out quickly.

Ahead, the brinewood-paneled corridor stood empty. An alarm clanged insistently, but no one came running to meet them.

"To the left," said Three-Dollar. "To the shuttle-bay."

Sawyer grunted and quickly headed left. The others hurried after, Tuan covering Sawyer, Three-Dollar steering the wheelchair, Lee dancing backward behind them.

Two insect attendants stepped out of a door. They looked surprised at seeing the men escorting Zillabar. They fluttered their claws nervously. "Get back!" Sawyer motioned them back into the chamber. The door slid shut behind them and the men hurried past.

"Why didn't you kill them?" asked Three-Dollar.

"Why kill slaves? They haven't hurt us."

Three-Dollar grunted.

"What does that mean?" Sawyer called back over his shoulder.

"You begin to show signs of a conscience, Sawyer. That does not bode well for your peace of mind."

Sawyer shook his head in annoyance. "Thanks for sharing that."

"To the right, now!" directed Three-Dollar. "This passage should lead directly to the shuttles." They ducked into a corridor that curved sharply around to the right, bending with the shape of the vessel's hull. "I don't like this," muttered Sawyer.

"They'll have no more visibility than us," said Tuan.

"I didn't mean the corridor," Sawyer replied. "This whole thing seems too easy. Why haven't they pursued us? No, this escape has too much convenience. It smells bad."

But even as he spoke, a squad of Vampires—more of the Elite Guard—came hurtling around the curve of the corridor ahead.

"You spoke too soon," called Lee.

Sawyer didn't waste time answering; he flattened himself against the wall and started firing immediately. So did Tuan. Bright blue fire punched through the Vampires' fragile bodies; it splattered off the walls. Screams and smoke and ricocheting pieces of metal and flesh filled the corridor. "Shit!" said Sawyer, and kept on firing. Wherever something moved, they blasted. Behind them Lee-1169 began firing steadily at attackers from the rear—Vampires or Dragons, Sawyer couldn't tell.

William Three-Dollar grabbed the Lady Zillabar's authority bracelet, yanking it off her arm. He began shouting quickly into it in the Vampires' own language: "Don't fire! Don't fire! They have the Lady Zillabar! They'll kill the Lady Zillabar! Don't fire! Stop all firing! Evacuate the shuttle-bay or they'll kill her! Do it now!"

Abruptly, the firing from behind them stopped; either Lee-1169 had successfully beaten back their attackers, or they had heard Three-Dollar's frantic message. Sawyer would have bet on the latter.

Unfortunately, whoever still blocked the passage ahead had not yet gotten the word. Intermittent fire still came splattering off the walls ahead of them. Sawyer ducked a ricochet. His skin stung sharply with the effects of the electric spray.

Three-Dollar punched up another channel and began grunting commands in the Dragons' own guttural language. "Don't fire! Don't fire! No dishonor. The Dragon Lord allows it. No dishonor! Let them pass! Save the Lady's life! Let them pass!"

A moment later the corridor fell silent.

"Come on," said Three-Dollar, pointing ahead. "Let's get into a boat before one of those damn reptiles starts thinking for itself."

The Shuttle

Halfway down the corridor another alarm went off. This one rasped with the sawtooth-edged note of ship security. Behind them they could hear the security doors slamming solidly shut, one after the other.

"Someone finally got smart," said Lee. The men ran as fast as they could toward the last door, the one leading into the shuttle bay. Sawyer fired ahead, hoping to disable the mechanism. The door hesitated—

Sawyer leapt through, then Tuan. The door hesitated again—Three-Dollar pushed the wheelchair into the bay and jumped through after it, with Lee close behind. The door slammed shut behind them.

Sawyer and Tuan moved into the long corridor cautiously, wondering how many Dragons and Vampires lay hiding in the passages that branched off to each side. Each tube led down to a different shuttleboat.

"Which one?" asked Sawyer.

"Any one," guessed Tuan. He pointed. "This first one?"

"No," said Three-Dollar. "If they've booby-trapped

any of them, they'll have rigged the ones closest to the door. Let's go forward. Lee, watch behind!"

Sawyer pointed to Tuan. "Watch how I do this." He unclipped the safety cover from the external launch panel, turned the arming key, and punched the red panel. The starship shuddered as the first shuttleboat leapt away. "Launch them all as decoys. They'll cover our escape."

They began working their way down the corridor, jettisoning each boat in turn. *The Golden Fury* reverberated again and again and again.

As they approached each access, Sawyer struck his cannon around the corner and fired down into the tube. The beam splattered painfully like a water-jet in a bucket. Already his fingers felt numb; his cheeks had turned red and blistered.

"Take this one—" Three-Dollar signaled. Sawyer approached the tube carefully. He stuck his gun around into the access—

"Don't shoot! Don't shoot!" someone called.

"Come out, slowly—"

A pale Vampire boy, hands held over his head, came crawling up out of the shuttle-tube. "Please, don't shoot—" he begged. His eyes flicked from one to the other, pausing only briefly on the unconscious form of Lady Zillabar before returning to meet Sawyer's. "Please let me go. I won't tell anyone. I promise—"

Sawyer hesitated. He looked to Three-Dollar. "We can't leave him here."

Three-Dollar looked unhappy. Behind him Lee-1169 scowled. "We can't take him with."

Sawyer made a decision. He motioned with his rifle. "Walk down to the end of the passageway. Stand there. Don't say anything. Don't do anything."

The boy nodded quickly, eager to please, and began backing away. He started to lower his arms; abruptly he reached behind himself—he ducked and rolled. Lee's shot narrowly missed Sawyer's head. He flinched sideways. The boy returned fire. Something splattered behind Sawyer. He ignored it and fired back. Another shot from Lee—the blue fire punched right through the Vampire boy, exploding him from the center outward. His right arm jerked away from his body with a needle-gun held tightly in its grip.

"Thought so," said Lee. "Vampires never beg."

Sawyer looked back to Three-Dollar. "Some Alliance of Life you've got." He stood up warily.

"This doesn't please me," Three-Dollar said bitterly.

"Where did Tuan go?" Sawyer asked.

Lee pointed at the passage opposite the one the boy had come from. "He jumped in there."

Sawyer looked into the tube and froze—Tuan lay on the floor, all charred and twisted. Three-Dollar stepped up beside him, looked, and turned away. A moment later Lee-1169 pushed them both aside. He didn't flinch. He merely nodded and said, "They'll pay for this one too. I promise it."

Sawyer bit his lip, wondering if he should add his vow to Lee's. Probably not. Lee might take offense, might feel that Sawyer had no right to vengeance here. So he just nodded, patted Lee once on the shoulder, and turned away. He didn't know how well the two men had known each other, what Tuan might have meant to Lee, and it didn't matter. Tuan had died in the service of the Alliance. In that, Sawyer realized . . . he had died for all of them.

"Come on," Three-Dollar said. He pushed Sawyer forward into the tube. He grabbed Lee too. "Let's get out of here before they decide to use sleepy-time gas." He steered the wheelchair quickly down the tunnel after them.

The access tube led down at a steep angle to where the hatch of the shuttleboat linked up with the hatch of the starship. Sawyer stepped into the boat cautiously. The cabin stood empty. The acceleration couches waited invitingly.

Three-Dollar pushed the wheelchair into the boat, followed by Lee, who quickly sealed and secured the hatch. Sawyer pulled out his needle-gun and nodded to Lee, who did the same. The two men moved forward toward the cockpit. The door popped open for them. Sawyer entered first, Lee came in right behind him. The two

Vampire pilots there immediately lifted their hands above their heads.

"Jettison this boat," Lee ordered. "Do it now."

The pilot shook his head. "I don't take orders from humans."

"Then go to hell," said Lee, and shot him at point-blank range. The Vampire's face imploded with the impact. Lee turned to the copilot. "What about you?"

The copilot hesitated. He licked his lips uncomfortably. "I—I—I'll do it." He started to turn around to the controls in front of him. Lee shot him in the back. He spasmed and slumped.

Sawyer looked to him, startled. "Do you know how to fly this thing?"

Lee shook his head. "Not really."

Sawyer pulled the two bodies out of their couches, laying them out on the floor. "Fortunately, I do," he muttered, climbing into the pilot's seat. "Go on, get them out of here." He started looking over the controls. "No telling what defense programs those two might have activated—"

"We don't have time to read the autolog," Lee snapped back.

"Do you want to kill me too, you bloodthirsty son of a bitch! What'll you do for a pilot then?" He reached up and snapped back the safety cover on the jettison control, armed the circuits, waited till they flashed green, then hit the large red panel. The shuttleboat thumped and clanged and then fell away into silence.

For a moment the bright glow of *The Golden Fury* filled all the windows of the shuttleboat. The view had a horrendous quality. They stared in awe and fear as the boat dropped swiftly away from the huge vessel's strangely silent gun ports and launchers. Sawyer's hands danced across the panels in front of him. The shuttleboat rotated. *The Golden Fury* slid out of view. He lifted his hands carefully away from the panel and studied the status screens.

"Come on!" said Lee. "Let's go!"

"I can't—not this close! Not yet. We'll trigger the automatic defenses."

"We launched decoys. They don't know which boat to aim at!"

"They will when our engines kick in. The longer we drift, the crazier their targeting computers will get."

"They won't fire on us with Zillabar aboard—"

"That depends on how many enemies the bitch left behind." Sawyer held up a hand for silence. "Shut up a minute. I need to follow this." He bent to the status panel again. Despite his anger, Lee held his silence.

Sawyer waited until the screen in front of him cleared. He didn't recognize all the notations. He'd never troubled to become proficient in the more arcane aspects of the Phaestoric language; but he knew enough to puzzle out the patterns. "All right," he said. "I think they've figured us out. The scanners have locked onto us as the last boat launched. We'll duck and cover—" He brought the boat around to a new bearing, sighted quickly, and punched for maximum thrust. The boat began accelerating straight for the rings of giant Burihatin.

"You didn't set a course."

"I didn't want to."

"Huh—?"

"If I had, they'd track it and project our destination. This will add to their confusion."

"They already know the only place we can go— Fourteen!"

"Right. But let's not make it easy for them to follow us down." Sawyer opened a transmission channel. "Attention starship, attention starship. We have the Lady Zillabar. If any ship follows us, if any ship attempts to intercept us, if any ship fires on us, we will kill the Lady immediately. And we will broadcast the manner of her death on all available channels, civilian and military. We will not repeat this warning." He switched off and swung around in his chair. He looked at the two bodies on the floor, then met Lee's angry gaze. "All right," he demanded. "Why did you shoot the second one?"

"The pilot refused. The copilot didn't. How far would you have trusted him?"

"Not very," Sawyer admitted.

Lee nodded. "Then you know why I had to shoot him."

"I just assumed you still felt angry about Tuan—"

"I have many different kinds of anger," Lee replied. "I've carried most of my rages for years. But my angers don't rule me. I'll avenge Tuan—and Drin and Tahl—at the appropriate time."

Sawyer shook his head. "I hadn't realized that the Alliance of Life sanctified so much killing." He said it sardonically.

"Do you think the Vampires would have given us any courtesy?"

"I didn't ask you about the Vampires. I asked about the Alliance of Life."

"Congratulations, Sawyer," Lee said, annoyance edging his voice. "You've accurately identified the moral dilemma at the heart of this struggle. The Alliance of Life works only when everybody agrees to it."

"Thanks for clearing that up," said Sawyer. "I wondered what justification you would use."

Lee's expression hardened. "Don't act the fool, Sawyer. The Vampires have sworn eternal enmity to all other species. What would you have had me do? At least you and I take the time to wonder about the morality of our actions."

Sawyer snorted. "I don't have to wonder about morality. I don't kill for ideology."

"Right. You kill for money."

"At least I can see a specific measurable result from my endeavors," Sawyer said quietly. He set the autopilot and pulled himself up out of the seat. He lifted one of the Vampire bodies. "Grab the other one," he ordered.

The two men dragged the dead Vampires into the main cabin of the shuttle. Three-Dollar had already secured the unconscious Zillabar in a couch; now he tended Finn Markham. The big man sagged in his chair, his features sunken and gray; he looked already dead. Three-Dollar looked across to them with a question in his face.

"No problem," explained Sawyer, indicating the bodies. "They died in the service of the Alliance of Life."

He started dragging the body of the pilot toward the doorway leading to the aft cargo bay, but abruptly Lee stopped him with a hand on his arm.

The clone-brother stepped silently past Sawyer, holding his needle-gun high and ready. "Wait," he mouthed. Sawyer and Three-Dollar exchanged a curious glance.

Lee approached the rear cabin door cautiously. He stepped to one side of it, then let it open. He hesitated, then threw himself diagonally into the aft cargo bay with military precision. Almost immediately, the ship reverberated with the bright electric sound of a needle-gun. Sawyer pulled his own weapon out—

Lee-1169 stepped back into the main cabin, a grim expression on his face. "No problem," he said, looking straight at Sawyer. "Another one dead in the service of the Alliance."

Perspective

□□□□□□□□□□□□□□□□□□□□□□□□□□□□□□

When Sawyer and Lee returned to the main cabin, they saw that Three-Dollar had opened one of the ship's two first-aid cabinets and had already installed Finn Markham in the coffinlike maintenance chamber.

Sawyer went straight to the head of the case and looked in at his brother. He stood there for a long moment studying the ashen face. When he finally spoke, his voice cracked with emotion. "Do you really think he has a chance?" he asked Three-Dollar.

"I honestly don't know," admitted the TimeBinder. "I've got him on a full blood-refresh, a liver-cleanse, spleen regeneration, and augmented bone-marrow functions. It can't hurt him. Maybe, if we can get him to Fourteen—"

"I've already said good-bye to him once," said Sawyer. "He—he always told me that if it ever came to *this*, I should pull the plug on him."

Three-Dollar put his hand on Sawyer's shoulder. "And he'd do the same for you, if he thought you had no chance."

"I—I just want to end his pain—"

"He can't feel anything now, Sawyer." Three-Dollar turned him away from the cabinet. "Look, maybe this just postpones the inevitable. And in that case, you have my sincerest apologies for prolonging his and your suffering. On the other hand ... well, I have a contract with the two of you, and I intend to collect in full."

Sawyer looked up sharply. "And you called us greedy—?"

"On the contrary." Three-Dollar grinned. "You'll find that the practice of greed takes on a whole new dimension when it exists in the service of ideology." The taller man smiled gently and rubbed Sawyer's shoulder in an affectionate manner. "Let me do what I can," he said. "He won't suffer. I promise."

Sawyer turned back to the case, feeling hopeful for the first time in days. He put his hands on the glass over Finn's head, as if to touch his brother's face.

Three-Dollar left him alone then. He checked on Zillabar's condition—she remained unconscious. The TimeBinder gestured to Lee. "Help me put her into the other maintenance cabinet."

"Huh! Why should we save her life?"

"Enlightened self-interest. She'll have more value to us alive than dead."

Lee looked unhappy, but he nodded his assent. "I'd just as soon toss her out the air lock."

"So would I," agreed Three-Dollar. "But what I want to do often bears little resemblance to what I actually will do. My heart and my head often have ferocious arguments about issues like this. It gives me terrible headaches."

Lee got the joke. He quit complaining.

Afterwards they adjourned to the forward half of the cabin, where William Three-Dollar began banging

around in the galley. "You want something to eat?" he
called back to Sawyer. The tracker still sat alone with his
brother.

"No thanks. What have you got?"

"I've got a goddamn well-stocked kitchen here. You
can have just about anything you want—" A pause. "No,
you won't want that. Or that. Or that either. Hm. We'll
have to jettison some of this stuff if we want to keep our
appetites for the rest." He tossed several unopened pack-
ages into the discard.

Reluctantly, Sawyer turned away from Finn and
went forward. Three-Dollar had unfolded a table and laid
out steaming plates of sliced meat, sausages, pickles,
steamed tubers, dipping sauces, and various unrecogniz-
able vegetables. "Eat, drink, and make merry," he said.
"Because somebody else has paid the bill."

"Lady Zillabar," snorted Lee.

"She'll have a good many hours of drooling unconsciousness before we present the check," said Three-
Dollar, seating himself. He folded his hands in front of
himself and bowed his head. Lee did likewise. In a qui-
eter voice Three-Dollar said, "For the gifts we have received in the past, we give thanks. For the gifts before us
now, we give thanks. For the gifts still to come, we give
thanks. Amen." He started passing plates of food around.

Sawyer sat down with Lee and Three-Dollar and
began picking at the food before him. After a moment he
looked up—the TimeBinder gazed at him with concern.
"What?" he asked.

"After we eat, let me run a medical scan on you.
Those blisters on your face don't look good. Do you have
any pain? Or numbness in your extremities?"

Sawyer shrugged. "I'll recover. I've had worse."

"Let me check you anyway."

Sawyer shrugged again, this time in assent. He
pushed some food around on his plate, then pushed the
plate away and leaned back in his chair. "That thing you
just said. About the gifts. And the thanks. Why did you
say that? And to who?"

Three-Dollar and Lee exchanged glances. Sawyer
couldn't read the meaning of it. Their expressions

seemed both amused and sad at the same time. Lee answered, "We call that a prayer."

"I know about prayers. I didn't think you believed in that nonsense—" Sawyer realized his gaffe too late. "I apologize," he said quickly. "I have no right to question your beliefs."

Three-Dollar held up a hand. "No, you have no reason to apologize. You only spoke your mind. Do you want an explanation, Sawyer Markham?"

Sawyer shrugged. "I'll listen."

The TimeBinder smiled wryly. "You have much more intelligence than your boyish countenance would suggest." He paused to take a bite of food, then continued thoughtfully. "We do not pray for the benefit of God. Whatever form God may take, that form remains unknowable to us. We cannot comprehend the shape of something greater than ourselves."

The tracker grunted. "Yeah, so?"

"If we cannot fathom the deity, neither can we fathom its plan, its purpose. Anything we might postulate—especially as it pertains to our own place in the universe—would probably express more vanity, more wishful thinking about ourselves, than holy truth."

"Right. So why pray?"

"We pray not for the benefit of God, but for ourselves. In all likelihood we can give nothing to God that God either needs or wants. And if God does need or want the mindless adulation of a species of naked apes, that God would certainly not deserve the respect of a species seeking intelligence, would it?" Three-Dollar smiled wryly. "Therefore, we speak our prayers for our wholeness, to remind ourselves of our place in God's universe. We restore our sense of perspective. We restore our relationship with the universe around us. And in that way, at least, we connect to God in the only way possible for us. Does that answer your question, Sawyer?"

Sawyer nodded slowly. He remained silent while he chewed over the information. Finally he remarked, "But all this depends on the existence of a God, doesn't it? How do you prove that?"

"You don't," said Three-Dollar, smiling with surreal finality.

"Well, then if you have no way of knowing if God really does exist or not, why pray?"

"Why take chances?" Lee-1169 grinned.

Three-Dollar held up a hand. "Why not?" he asked. "If the prayer provides a focus for individual meditation, does it matter if God hears it or not? The purpose still gets served. We restore ourselves and return to a sense of clarity about our purposes and goals. We enlarge our ability to function responsibly."

"Hm," said Sawyer. He pushed his plate away.

"Not hungry anymore?"

"Not for food." Sawyer excused himself and went back to the maintenance cabinet where his brother lay in repose. He sat down beside it, put his hands together on the glass surface, and lowered his head onto them. If he prayed or merely grieved, Lee and Three-Dollar couldn't tell.

Of Course

In the Lady's absence, confusion and panic ruled on the bridge of *The Golden Fury*. Her Senior Captain, and six of his junior officers, had already committed dishonorable suicide—rather than risk the wrath of the Lady's aides.

The Dragon Lord, still weak from the effects of Sawyer's assault, had to physically prevent the seventh junior officer from committing suicide. He held him aloft and roared in his face. "The Lady Zillabar will not tolerate any more acts of cowardice aboard this vessel, and neither will I! You may not kill yourself! You will immediately assume the responsibilities of the Captain of this vessel. I command it."

The young Vampire had never had a Dragon roar in his face before. Indeed, few Vampires had ever seen a Dragon's fury at such proximity and lived to tell about it. To his credit the officer not only did not faint, he retained full control of his bowels.[5]

When the Dragon Lord lowered him to the ground again, the new Captain of *The Golden Fury*, Commander 'Ga Lunik, swallowed hard, saluted nervously, and asked, "What do you bid, my Lord? Shall we pursue the boat?"

The Dragon Lord considered his strategy, muttering dull curses as he did so. He realized with annoyance that he had grown too used to having the opinions and advice of others. He had allowed himself to depend on the conversations of the Lady to bend and shape his own strategies. He resolved never to allow that weakness to overpower his own reasoning again. The Dragons would serve the Vampires on their own terms only.

He turned to the trembling Captain. "No. I think not. Order three squads of Marauders to pursue. Order them to track the boat at a distance. Do not approach it. In no way interfere with it. As long as those damned rebels have the Lady, we dare not give them reason to harm her." He added, "Keep all your other Marauders on alert."

"You have a plan?"

"A Dragon *always* has a plan," rumbled the Dragon Lord, turning away. He didn't have one now, but he would soon. Those who had caused this embarrassment to the Lady—and especially to himself and the Dragon Guards—would live just long enough to scream their regrets.

Captain 'Ga Lunik turned to his desperately depleted staff and began issuing the appropriate orders. Whatever would happen, would happen. He kept his expression bland. He would convey the Dragon Lord's

---

[5]In later days this young Captain would develop a reputation for incredible courage and fearlessness in the face of danger. In his own words: "What should I fear? If you can survive having a Dragon roar in your face, nothing else can touch you."

commands, maintain his personal discipline, and pray to die well. He could not see any other outcome for this disaster, no matter how he projected the course of events.

Shortly, he felt a faint series of thumps coming up through the deck beneath his boots. He counted them to himself. As each Marauder leapt away from the vessel, the clang of its departure reverberated upward to the bridge. Captain 'Ga Lunik turned to the main screen and watched as the tiny assault vehicles streaked off into the darkness.

Somewhere ahead, lost in the dark side of Burihatin, the shuttleboat accelerated recklessly. Perhaps they would recapture it. Perhaps not. Perhaps the Lady would die. Perhaps she would escape. Perhaps they would rescue her. No matter what, she would exact her retributions. He foresaw little chance of victory here, let alone survival. Therefore, he would die gallantly, as bravely as he could, to bring honor to his family name.

That decision made, he studied the course displays thoughtfully and considered strategy. The acting astrogator stepped up beside him to report quietly, "The signal from the shuttle's locator beacon remains strong. The Marauders will have no trouble tracking and closing." He indicated a screen. "According to the information relayed by the boat's system-analysis sensors, the Lady remains alive, but unconscious."

Captain 'Ga Lunik turned to report this information to the Dragon Lord, but the great lizard waved him away. "I heard," he said. "I think the rebels have made a stupid mistake keeping the Lady Zillabar alive. When she recovers her wits, keeping her restrained will become a very difficult task. Hmp. They would have shown more intelligence to kill her as soon as they got away. I would have done so. And," he admitted with disgraceful candor, "it would have made things a lot easier for everybody all around."

Captain 'Ga Lunik believed that discretion represented the better part of survival. He decided to ignore the Dragon Lord's seditious opinion. Instead he said, "My Lord, the Marauders have the advantage of speed, but the shuttleboat has a much longer range. The Marauders might intercept the boat, but they won't dare fire on it, not while the Lady Zillabar remains aboard. And if the Marauders can't fire, the boat will simply outrun them; they'll have to return."

"I don't expect the Marauders to catch them, Captain. I only want the rebels to believe that we pursue in earnest. It will keep them from making grandiose plans. They will head for Burihatin-14. Where else can they go? We will arrive there at the same time they do, and the locator in the boat will allow us to greet them where they land."

"What about the Lady?"

The Dragon Lord shrugged. "Perhaps she will learn some humility from this episode. This will teach her not to play with her food. . . ."

Directions

□□□□□□□□□□□□□□□□□□□□□□□□□□□□□

Already three million kilometers ahead, the shuttle dipped into the shadow of giant Burihatin and began decelerating, altering its course as it approached the outermost ring.

"We'll head directly across the rings," Sawyer said to Lee-1169 and William Three-Dollar. The three men had gone forward to the shuttle's cockpit to discuss their plans. They couldn't risk having the Lady Zillabar overhear their conversation. They had all heard stories about Vampires in "dreamtime." The Phaestor had the ability to remain conscious of everything that happened around them, even while comatose. None of them wanted to take the chance that Zillabar might still retain some awareness, despite her obviously drugged state.

Sawyer tapped the screen, indicating the schematic of the course he had plotted. "We'll dip below the rings, then above, then below. I want to make it hard for those damn Marauders to close with us." He pointed to the line of dots across the bottom of the display.

"They won't dare fire on us," said Lee. "And we have the range to outrun them."

"I know that."

"Then why not just head straight away as fast as we can?"

Sawyer studied the screens in front of him for a moment before he answered. "We need to shake them quickly. So we need to have them underestimate us. We have to make them think that we act in haste and stupidity. We have to act like scared rats for this plan to work."

"Hmp," Lee snorted. "I hope this plan works better than your last one."

"So do I. Finn and I spend too much time in jail." Sawyer finished programming the autopilot, locked it in, and swiveled around to look at Lee. "But this time we've got help."

"Huh?"

"Haven't you figured it out yet?"

"I have," said Three-Dollar. "The Dragon Lord let us go."

Lee leaned back in his chair and folded his arms skeptically across his chest. "You can't possibly believe that."

"I know the Dragons," said Three-Dollar. He tapped the silver band around his head. "I have a thousand years of memories, remember?"

"All right," said Lee, looking from one to the other. "Explain it to me."

"The moment we captured Zillabar, we dishonored him. Our success meant that he had failed to protect the Lady's safety. The fact that her own stupidity made her vulnerable to us doesn't mitigate his failure. The moment we seized her, his suicide became inevitable."

"But he went into a death rage," said Lee. "He would have killed us all—but not before we would have killed the Zillabitch. Correct me if I've figured this wrong, but that would have put an even bigger stain of dishonor on his family name. He would have had to commit immediate suicide, and probably all his heirs as well."

"You've extrapolated it correctly," Three-Dollar said. "At least, correctly by the best estimation a human can have about the way the minds of Dragons work. No matter what course of action he chose, either way he would have disgraced himself. At the core of it lies his failure to protect the Lady. We captured her—or we captured her and killed her. Either circumstance proves his ineptitude for the entire Cluster to see.

"So which course should he have taken? You or I, because of our commitment to the ideals of the Alliance of Life, would have acted to minimize the chances of death. But the Dragons don't think the same way that we do. The Dragon Lord chose the *greater* of the two disgraces—*death for the Lady while under his protection.*"

Lee scratched his head in confusion. He admitted sadly, "Perhaps I have too much enmity for the Dragons. Out of the fear that either understanding or respect would lessen my ability to hate them and my willingness to kill them, I have never allowed myself either to understand or respect them."

"And that," said Three-Dollar, reaching across the intervening space to tap Lee's chest with one bony forefinger, "explains why your brothers have died by the hundreds. None of you have allowed yourself to know your enemy well enough to use his weaknesses against him."

Three-Dollar's tone changed; he became a teacher again. "You need to understand this, my hot-blooded friend. The Dragons' thinking has at its core an incredible drive toward Armageddon. It overwhelms the thought processes of even the mildest of Dragons—if you can imagine such a thing as a mild Dragon. If a Dragon cannot win, it will lose in the most destructive manner possible: destruction for itself and for everything and everybody else within range. The knowledge of that terrible urge to violence has made many of the Dragons' opponents extremely cautious—as well as their employers.

"Zillabar became incautious," Three-Dollar said.

"The Dragon Lord must have seen her carelessness. The Dragons live for honor. They build their identities around it. The Dragon Lord had to have known the danger in which she had put him and all his heirs. He must have resented her profoundly for it. He would not have grieved over her death. Perhaps he even hates her. Whatever the case, he *meant* to take her down with him. He acted to pay back the disgrace."

"When I fired—" said Sawyer. "When I stunned the Dragons, I saved his life, and possibly his honor."

"That part I don't understand," Lee admitted.

"Falling in battle carries no stain," explained Three-Dollar. "The Dragon Lord had clearly made his choice. He had already stepped into his rage. Stopping a Dragon in his tracks, killing it or stunning it, does not stain the Dragon. It gives credit to the rival without taking anything away from the warrior. When Sawyer fired, he elevated himself in the Dragons' eyes—and us, by association—from annoying nuisances to courageous opponents. Thus the felling of the Dragon Lord does not stain him with the same disgrace as if he'd simply let us go."

Lee considered that for a moment.

Now Sawyer added a thought of his own, "The Dragon Lord *wanted* me to fire. He meant his refusal to take off his armor as a direct challenge. He *needed* us to elevate ourselves in his esteem so he could avoid his disgrace."

"But what about what you said a moment ago? About us having help?"

"The Dragon Lord needs us to look ferocious," Sawyer explained. "So he has to let us run wild for a while. This will alarm the Vampires. It will terrify them that humans can so openly thwart their authority. They will demand that the Dragon Lord act. Perhaps they will even expand his authority—at the expense of their own.

"I have no intention of disappointing the Dragon Lord. At this moment, it serves us to serve his purpose. But also I have no illusions about his ultimate goals either. As soon as our freedom brings him no more advantage, he'll squash us like mice. Our best hope lies in having him underestimate our ability to elude his forces. We shall demonstrate just enough cleverness to serve his purpose—enough cleverness to demonstrate our ferocity, but no more than that, lest we cause him undue concern or alarm."

Three-Dollar looked amused. "I see. And how much cleverness do you expect we'll need to demonstrate?"

"As much as we have and at least ten times more than that," Sawyer grinned. "We'll probably have to work overtime."

"Your contract doesn't allow for overtime, tracker."

"We don't get paid by the hour, TimeBinder. We get paid for producing results."

"Ahh," said William Three-Dollar, nodding in satisfaction. Abruptly, he raised a finger in concern. "Wait—" he said, a sudden thought occurring to him. "What happens if you overestimate how much cleverness you'll need?"

Sawyer shook his head sadly. "We'll just have to take that risk, won't we?"

Locators

□□□□□□□□□□□□□□□□□□□□□□□□□□

The shuttleboat dived through the outermost ring of Burihatin, ejected a wrapped package, and abruptly changed course. The package continued along the shuttleboat's original course.

Several hours later the first of the pursuing Marauders caught up with the ejected package, matched trajectories, carefully scanned the suspicious object, and finally brought it aboard. A few moments later, after examining the contents of the package, the pilot of the Marauder sent a coded message back to *The Golden Fury*. "The ejected package contained one of the boat's locator beacons—and the body of its copilot."

Several hours after that, the shuttleboat veered upward through the rings of Burihatin again. It ejected a second wrapped package and changed course again. The package continued along the previous course.

When the next pursuing Marauder caught up with and intercepted this package, a similar result occurred. The coded message sent back said, "The ejected object contained one of the boat's backup locator beacons—and the body of its astrogator."

Several hours later the shuttleboat again dived below the planet's rings. Again it ejected an object and changed course.

Eventually, a third Marauder matched trajectories with this package and brought it aboard. "The object contained the body of the boat's pilot and the second backup locator. In addition we found a message from the rebels attached. It says, and we quote, 'Recall all pursuers, or the next package will contain the body of Lady Zillabar, the cannibal.'"

On the bridge of *The Golden Fury*, this message provoked significant consternation among the Phaestor crew. The Dragon Lord, however, remained unfazed. "They don't dare," he remarked. "We still have them on our probability displays. We still track their course. If we gave the order to intercept, the Marauders could still catch them. This vessel could intercept them. If they kill the Lady, we will have them at our mercy within hours. This message—I don't believe it. They bluff."

"How can you have such certainty?" Commander 'Ga Lunik asked with temerity.

"I know humans. They don't think like Dragons. They don't think like Vampires. They fear death. They will do anything to avoid death or injury. They will fight for life even after life becomes hopeless and death becomes inevitable. They don't know how to die with honor. These humans . . . they have some courage, they certainly have a wild ferocity that deserves respectful caution on our part, and they have a surprising cleverness that does their species honor—but I do not think that they have the strength of Dragons when it comes to facing death. I believe that they will try to prolong their lives as long as possible."

The Dragon Lord turned to Commander 'Ga Lunik. "Tell your Marauders to keep tracking, but to continue to maintain discretionary distance."

"But, my Lord, they'll see the Marauders on their displays."

"I expect them to. We need to show them that we don't believe them, that they have no ability to fool us. Remember this, Commander 'Ga Lunik: youth and enthusiasm have no chance against age and treachery— especially when the youth and enthusiasm come from short-lived humans and the age and treachery come from an ancient Dragon."

"Yes, m'Lord. Thank you for the blessing of your wisdom."

The Dragon Lord grinned in appreciation. He rather liked the sound of that acknowledgment, especially as it came from the mouth of a Phaestor Commander. If only he could train the rest of the cannibalistic breed to such politesse.

Several hours later, his voice trembling with emotion, Commander 'Ga Lunik requested the presence of the Dragon Lord on the bridge. The Dragon Lord lumbered heavily along the wide corridors of Lady Zillabar's space-going palace, once again reminding himself how much he hated the Phaestoric self-indulgence and extravagance.

When he reached the bridge, Commander 'Ga Lunik led him to the large strategic display. He pointed at a blinking red dot coursing upward, away from the inner ring of Burihatin.

"What does that dot represent?" the Dragon Lord asked suspiciously.

"My Lord, I regret to inform you that the scarlet indicator represents the position locater implanted in Lady Zillabar's own person."

The Dragon Lord scratched himself thoughtfully. "We can pick it up at this range?"

Commander 'Ga Lunik nodded. "If they have attached an amplifier—not a hard thing to do—the signal could travel for many light-days."

"Hm," said the Dragon Lord thoughtfully. "I wonder if you haven't miscalculated, my young Captain. Perhaps they've killed the Lady after all. How unfortunate for you to have such a short, inglorious career."

"My Lord? The log will show that you advised me of this course of action. I followed your orders—"

"I should like to see you present that as a defense at your trial. I have always understood it that the Phaestoric aristocracy only gives orders, never takes them." He lumbered out, grinning.

Commander 'Ga Lunik stared after the departing Dragon. He mouthed a silent curse. Then he turned back to his waiting First Officer and ordered, "Tell the Marauders to intercept the object."

Escape

◻◻◻◻◻◻◻◻◻◻◻◻◻◻◻◻◻◻◻◻◻◻◻◻◻◻◻◻

Sawyer and Lee stood over the medical cabinet containing Zillabar's still-unconscious form, studying Three-Dollar's handiwork and grinning. The Lady would not only have a small scar under her right arm, but in the mirror it would appear as a TimeBinder's symbol: a circle with a sine wave across its center.

"I know that I display a foolish regression to infantile emotionalism to admit this," Three-Dollar said, "but I regret only that I could not have left the scar in the middle of her forehead. It would have represented an enjoyable demonstration of karmic justice. Ah, well." He sighed.

Among the many memories and experiences contained within the TimeBinder's headband, the skills of several brilliant surgeons remained vivid. William Three-

Dollar had artfully removed the Lady's implanted locator chip, connected it to an amplifier, wrapped it up with forty kilos of Vampire food—things no sane human would eat—and jettisoned the package before their last course change.

By now the boat had gone more than two thirds of the way around Burihatin's circumference, in a zigzag course that still led inevitably toward the fourteenth moon. On the display the course looked like the long way around, but Sawyer had a method to his madness. If he had guessed right, they had lost or confused most of their pursuit by now.

"We've found them all then, right? We have no more locator beacons aboard?" Lee asked.

Three-Dollar nodded. "To the best of my knowledge."

"And mine," agreed Sawyer. "I've scanned this boat, searched its programs, had system analysis look for all transmitters, audited all programming, and listened to six impossible hunches." He allowed himself a rueful grin. "If we have any more locators still aboard, they've earned the right to stay."

"In other words," said Lee, concerned, "we may still have a squad of Marauders on our tail?"

Sawyer nodded. "Perhaps—"

"How can you say that so coolly?" Lee's anger came up sharply. "Perhaps the Dragon Lord expects us to lead him to the TimeBinder of Burihatin. Maybe we missed a locater. Perhaps it only broadcasts intermittently. Maybe the Marauders only veered off to fool us into thinking that our plan has succeeded."

"Perhaps," agreed Three-Dollar. He put a calming hand on Lee-1169's shoulder. "And perhaps not. We'll know soon enough. We've already committed ourselves to this plan. We have to wait and see how it develops."

Sawyer scratched his head thoughtfully, then looked to Lee. "I agree with you that paranoia drives the Vampire thinking, but I honestly don't think they would have prepared every shuttleboat on the Lady's Imperial Starship for this kind of situation. The Phaestor have too much arrogance to seriously consider the possibility that

someone could capture a hostage on *The Golden Fury*
and use one of their own boats to escape. No," he concluded. "I doubt that the Vampires thought to prepare for
this circumstance."

"And what if you've figured this whole thing
wrong?" demanded Lee.

"Then you'll get a full refund," replied Sawyer.
"What else do you want? What else can I give you?"

Lee slammed himself back in his seat, disgusted.
Sawyer shrugged at his reaction. He looked to Three-
Dollar.

The memories of a thousand years usually confer a
good degree of wisdom on the wearer of the TimeBand.
Three-Dollar chose not to get involved. Instead he replied, "We need to choose a landing site. We still have
four hours before we obtain orbit around Fourteen." He
tapped his headband. "I've tried several times to contact
the TimeBinder of Burihatin. I'll keep trying, but I
haven't picked up any response."

"Don't worry," said Sawyer. "We'll find the
TimeBinder of Burihatin. We'll find him before the Lady
does, I can promise you that." His face became serious.
"I think I know a man who can save Finn. If anyone can,
Dr. M'bele can—if we can find him. But he hates the
Vampires as much as anyone, and he willingly serves
anyone else who shares that hatred. So . . . maybe he can
also help us find your missing TimeBinder."

Three-Dollar looked grim. "We don't even know if
the missing TimeBinder still lives."

"Don't worry. We found Murdock. We found you.
We'll find the TimeBand and anyone who's wearing it."
He allowed himself a bittersweet expression. "I always
told Finn I could work faster without him. Now I guess
I'll have to prove it."

Bad News Bearers

□□□□□□□□□□□□□□□□□□□□□□□□□□□□□□□□

This time Commander 'Ga Lunik handled it differently.

He selected his most junior aide—a pale neuter boy so frail looking that he seemed inadequate even to the task of carrying a simple message—and sent him back to the Dragon Lord's quarters bearing a casually scrawled note.

The Dragon Lord took the note from the aide, scowling in annoyance. He unfolded it clumsily and held it up before his tiny black eyes. In Phaestoric script—not Dragon—the note read: "I have information you may find interesting. At your convenience, I would appreciate your joining me on the bridge. Thank you. Commander 'Ga Lunik."

The Dragon Lord recognized the inherent insult. The boy. The note. The phrasing. Even the use of Phaestoric writing over Dragon script. Everything. He smiled inwardly. The child learned fast. Perhaps too fast.

Not a problem, he decided. The Dragon Lord looked down at the messenger, wondering if he should send him back with a reply or simply eat him. The latter action, of course, would represent extremely bad manners. On the other hand, considering the history of this whole voyage so far, the bizarre displays of the Lady and all the subsequent events that followed, the breach of etiquette that the accidental ingestion of a minor aide might represent would cause only a lesser embarrassment when compared with all the other much larger breaches of etiquette so far. The Dragon Lord eyed the child suspiciously, decided that the meal looked neither attractive enough nor plump enough to justify the trou-

ble it would cause, and allowed the Phæstor boy to return unharmed.

After a suitable delay—after several suitable delays,
each one long enough to represent a specific insult to the
Captain's authority—the Dragon Lord finally ambled out
of his quarters and forward to the great bridge of the Lady's Imperial Starship, *The Golden Fury*.

The balcony of the command bridge loomed high
above the main operations deck. The Dragon Lord
stepped boldly out into the center of the bridge and
waited. He had come to the bridge. He had come this far
and would come no farther. Commander 'Ga Lunik must
come now to him. He stopped. He stood. He struck a
pose. Squat and stolid, he waited.

And waited.

And waited. . . .

Commander 'Ga Lunik stood at the opposite end of
the bridge, drinking from a steaming mug. He listened to
the reports of his aides. He turned and studied the displays on the deck below. He turned back to his aides. He
issued several orders. He turned and noticed the Dragon
Lord waiting for him. He turned back to his aides and
chatted with them a while longer. He snapped his fingers
and an insect attendant scurried up. He handed the insect the mug and waved it away. He glanced at the displays below again, studied them for a long moment. He
conferred with a junior officer. At last he completed all
the many little tasks associated with running a starship
and ambled over to the Dragon Lord.

Commander 'Ga Lunik smiled at the Dragon Lord.
His expression revealed nothing of his inner face; it reflected only sincerity and concern. "Thank you for coming, my Lord."

"You have information?"

"As a matter of fact, we do. I thought you should
know. Our Marauders have intercepted the Lady's locator. Only the locator. Not the Lady. The rebels have . . .
removed it from her body."

"They have *touched* her? They've laid hands upon
her flesh?"

Commander 'Ga Lunik kept his expression neutral.

"I would presume so, yes. I cannot imagine any other way to remove the locator without a physical extraction."

The Dragon Lord snorted in fury. "They have soiled the Lady's purity! Will their heinous offenses never cease?" He stamped around in circles, lashing his huge tail back and forth. For several moments he gave one of his very best performances of offense and rage. When he finally came to a stop, he noticed that few of the Phaestor crew members had reacted or even bothered to look up from their instruments.

The Dragon Lord realized with chagrin that the Vampires had not accepted his performance as genuine. Indeed, apparently they had even expected him to demonstrate his rage. He hadn't fooled them at all. Hmm. He considered killing a few, but the moment for that urge had already passed. He allowed his anger to subside and turned back to the waiting Captain of the starship. "What else?" he demanded.

"With the loss of this last locator, we can no longer track the course of the boat. Our probability display shows an ever-expanding sphere of possibility. Within two hours we will have to assume that they have landed on Burihatin-14."

"Yes," acknowledged the Dragon Lord. "We will have to assume that, won't we?" He roared once in annoyance, just to see if 'Ga Lunik would flinch. It worked; he did. The Dragon Lord felt a little better. But not much.

This latest bit of news represented a serious setback to his strategies. He had meant to discomfit Zillabar, not endanger her. He had never considered her in real danger while they still maintained the ability to track her. Now the damned rebels had actually escaped! And Zillabar's safety had become more than problematic. Suppose they injured her further. Suppose they killed her—?

The Dragon Lord groaned inwardly. The recapture of the rebels and the rescue of Zillabar would require a major effort. Dishonorable suicide began to look inevitable again. The Dragon Lord did not like that thought at all. He knew of too many tastes that he had not yet sampled, too many things he had not yet had the chance to eat.

He snorted and turned to Commander 'Ga Lunik. "Recall all your Marauders, except those that can get to Fourteen faster. Set an immediate course for Burihatin-14. We need to arrive there as soon as possible."

Commander 'Ga Lunik stared at the Dragon Lord blandly. "My Lord, perhaps you have forgotten. The Phaestor do not take orders from the Dragons. I give the orders aboard this vessel. And I have already given all the orders on this matter which I consider necessary and appropriate." He bowed gracefully. "Thank you for giving me the opportunity to advise you. You may return to your quarters now. Your continued presence on the bridge may present a distraction to my crew." Commander 'Ga Lunik turned crisply and strode away without waiting to see the Dragon Lord's reaction.

The Lady MacBeth

ꚸꚸꚸꚸꚸꚸꚸꚸꚸꚸꚸꚸꚸꚸꚸꚸꚸꚸꚸꚸꚸꚸꚸꚸ

Aboard the starship *The Lady MacBeth, otherspace* appeared as a glorious blur of light and color. The entire ship glowed with energy, within and without. As beautiful as the omnipresent FTL aura appeared, it annoyed the hell out of Star-Captain Neena Linn-Campbell. She strode angrily up the keel-corridor of *The Lady MacBeth*, swearing every step of the way to the Operations Deck.

Two aides followed her—Ota, her bioform First Officer, and Robin, her android copilot. "I won't have it!" she exclaimed. "I won't have this ship run like a third-class freebooter freighter."

"But, Captain—our registration *lists* us as a third-class freebooter freighter," said Robin, keeping her voice and expression neutral.

"So what? That doesn't mean we have to act like it. I want us to represent ourselves as a first-class ship, inside and out, top to bottom, bow to stern, forward and aft, with no one and nothing left out, goddammit! This damned FTL shimmer curdles the milk. It wilts the lettuce. It fatigues the polyceramics. And it gives me migraines! I want the fluction-bars recalibrated. I don't care how many goddamn times Shariba-Jen has to do it. If we have to flush every last assembly valve in the entire system, then that's what we'll do. And I want it done before we break orbit from Burihatin-14. God knows what an undamped FTL-effect will do to a cargo of five-week pfingle eggs."

"Allow me to say this again, Captain. I have my doubts about the rating of those eggs—"

At that moment Gito, the ship's engineer, turned out of a cross passage ahead of them. Seeing the Captain and the look on her face, he thought to step back quickly; but he acted too late. Captain Campbell stopped him with a roar. "Gito! Can you hear it? Can you see it? The hyperspace injectors have begun making that pocketa-pocketa noise again!"

"Yes, Captain. I can see it. I can hear it. And I promise you, Shariba-Jen and I will find the problem and fix it." Without missing a beat he added, "May I ask you when you will find the time to continue our contract renegotiation?"

"When you and Jen complete the repairs to this ship, then we'll talk. Why should I discuss shares in the corporation with an engineer who can't keep an *otherspace* field in tune?" Catching sight of the robot crew member behind Gito, she added, "Oh, and Jen—I see you! Don't you try to hide! I want you to see to the food processors again! The orange juice still has a nasty blue tinge. I thought you said you fixed that."

"Yes, Captain. I'll see to it immediately. But if I might echo Gito's concern, perhaps we might have more attention to some of these things if we felt a sense of financial partnership as well as spiritual—"

"No, goddammit! No! I will have no discussions of partnership of any kind unless and until every damn doohickey and thingamabob on this bucket works correctly! You will not get your way through blackmail, greenmail, whitemail, or any other kind of mail! Prove your worth and then we'll talk! You think I don't know what the lot of you have done! Put this ship right, or I'll shove the lot of you out the goddamn air lock and drag this thing home myself!" She stormed ahead, leaving the rest of the crew gaping after her, unable to reply. Ota, a LIX-class bioform, followed without comment.

Gito and Shariba-Jen exchanged looks. "Come on, Jen," said Gito. "Let's go 'prove our worth.' Let's see if she likes it when the toilet tickles her every time she squats to pee."

"I wouldn't advise that," recommended Robin. "Perhaps we should rethink our strategy."

"Nah," said Gito. "The crazier she gets, the more advantage we have." He grinned and hurried off, followed by the expressionless robot.

Robin shrugged and hurried after Ota and Captain Campbell.

The Captain climbed up through the Operations Bay, onto the Ops Deck, and from there up to the Command Bridge, swearing a blue streak that spanned seven different languages, including the Old Tongue, Diplomatic Phaestor, Dragonic, Neo-High German, Interlingua, Interstellar Binary, and Object Pascal. Ota followed, without comment and without apparent understanding. Nevertheless, several of the Captain's more colorful euphemisms left the bioform distinctly uncomfortable.

aptain Campbell flung herself into her Command Seat unhappily. "Idiots, thieves, and imbeciles. They attack us from without. They attack us from within. Thank the stars I've never allowed myself to trust another person long enough to let him, her, or it, get close enough to do any real damage. We'll hire a whole new crew if we have to— and that includes you too, Ota. Don't you give me that look. Okay, yes, so I rescued you from a death worse than fate on Thoska-Roole. Don't let it go to your head. I can just as easily jettison you and all the rest. I have a business to tend to. I didn't turn in my Guild Insignia so the rest of you could get rich by feeding off the bones of my flayed corpse. I expect a little loyalty, a little unity, a little cooperation, goddammit. And what do I get? Malfeasance, nonfeasance, incompetence, and unreasonable requests! This has all got to stop! What do I have to do to get things back to normal around here anyway?"

"You could start by lowering your voice," suggested Ota. "The paneling on the walls has begun to blister."

Neena Linn-Campbell gave her First Officer a skeptical look. "I thought bioforms didn't make jokes."

"Only in self-defense," Ota replied.

"All right," Campbell said. She damped her anger and slowed her words. "Talk to me."

"Have you considered the possibility of bankruptcy?"

"No. I did that once. I didn't enjoy it. I don't want to do it again." Then she stopped and looked at Ota with sudden graveness. "We do have other alternatives, don't we?"

Ota held up a hand and rotated it in a gesture of uncertainty; palm up, palm down, palm up again.

Neena Linn-Campbell raised an eyebrow. "That bad, huh?"

"We have assumed more debts than we should."

"Mm."

"We've missed too many opportunities, Captain. We missed several chances to pick up charters on Thoska-Roole—"

"You may remember, we had *other* concerns at the time."

"I don't question that, Captain, but—"

"What would you have had me do—risk having the ship seized?"

"No, ma'am. I just wanted to point out had we picked up those cargoes, they would have covered the cost of this jump. The failure of the Zillabar charter to pay their fees in full, plus our failure to pick up paying cargo for the jump back to Burihatin has left us in a serious debit situation. In addition, the failure of Sawyer and Finn Markham, and Lee-1169, to rendezvous as promised has left us with passengers aboard who cannot pay for their passage as expected—not to mention the fact that we remain heavily invested in pfingle eggs that currently sit aging in a Burihatin warehouse."

Ota shook her head unhappily. "I don't see a way for us to escape this financial trap. Freebooters working without Guild Insignia don't command the same kind of rates as Guild licensed vessels. It worries me."

"We've experienced worse," Captain Campbell said.

"Not in my memory," Ota reported.

"Mm. You might have a point there." Abruptly, she shook her head. "Look, if we can deliver the pfingle eggs before they hatch, the payment for that cargo should resolve our problem."

"I wish I shared your certainty, ma'am. I don't trust our supplier to have actually sold us three-month pfingle eggs. I'd sure hate to have them hatch while in transit."

"We'll stash them in the aft cargo bay and monitor them continually. If we detect any undue activity, we'll jettison the whole cargo."

Ota remarked blandly, "I have heard that once the first pfingle hatches, the rest will hatch within thirty seconds. That would mean blasting open the aft cargo doors in a deliberate act of explosive decompression. Shariba-Jen has informed me that while such an act would entail considerable risk, and in fact might cause significant structural damage to the stern of the vessel, we should have a fairly good chance of surviving an emergency jettisoning of the cargo. But only, of course, if we can detect the hatching of the first egg in time."

"Mm, yes." Captain Campbell considered that. "I wonder if we might install the whole thing in an external bubble. Would that give us an additional margin for error?"

"I'll have to ask Shariba-Jen, as well as EDNA."

Star-Captain Campbell sagged in her chair. "I had no idea that it would cost so much to shake free of Regency interference."

"It would have cost us more to maintain our Guild membership."

Star-Captain Campbell looked to Ota, surprised. "I had no idea that you thought that way. I thought you disagreed with my decision."

"On the contrary, Captain. You just never asked me for my opinion."

"Well. Thank you."

"Besides, as a freebooter, it offers the rest of the crew the opportunity to renegotiate our profit position with you."

Captain Campbell stared at Ota for a long moment. "*Et tu*, Ota?"

Ota nodded meekly. "You have always encouraged me to express more independence."

Captain Campbell closed her mouth. She held her hands up in front of her in a broad gesture of deference and respect. "Then I have only myself to blame." She turned away abruptly. "EDNA? You have something to say?"

The ship's mind answered softly. "We will arrive at Burihatin in eleven minutes. We should begin preparations to drop out of *otherspace*."

Neena Linn-Campbell nodded. "Do it," she ordered. "Me and my big mouth."

"Pardon?" asked EDNA.

"Nothing."

The Fourteenth Moon

Burihatin's forty moons took their light from the star and their warmth from their gigantic parent. With patient tending several of them had attained environments capable of supporting life comfortably.

The fourteenth moon had a sizable ocean of nearly fresh water, a thick, breathable atmosphere, and lush forests girdling its equator. It would have enjoyed a reputation as a garden-world, had it not also had unpleasantly warm seasons, a gravity high enough to cause serious

heart spasms, and a radiant sky of sulfurous yellow. Most
visitors, and many inhabitants, wore biomedical monitors
and personal gravity-suits on the surface of the captive
world.

The inhabitants of Fourteen called their world
Dupa—named after Dupa the Peril, a nasty goblin of
some forgotten ancient mythology. In the same pantheon,
Burihatin represented the monster that lived under the
world. Seen from the surface of Dupa, Burihatin loomed
as an oppressive presence, alternately lambent and
gloomy, as Dupa swung patiently around it.

The great disk of the world-monster filled the sky
like a threat, by turns appearing as a descending ceiling,
an impenetrable wall, and even a terrifyingly distant
floor. Burihatin the beast lurked too large and too close
for the inhabitants of Dupa to believe that the sky of
their world also presented an access to the stars. Sometimes it shone as a disk, sometimes as a half sphere,
sometimes as a crescent, and sometimes only as a great
blackness in the void—and always with the sharp line of
the rings cutting brightly across its hemisphere. At this
moment Burihatin appeared as a half world, split almost
equidistantly into portions of darkness and light.

Beneath this lowering sky, unbroken forests of blacktrees sprawled across the continents. Like one gigantic
creature, the lush vegetation wrapped itself around the
land in a constricting strangle of sprawling limbs. The
trunks of the great trees curled around and upward, de-
fining huge dark spaces within the body of the forest.
The leafy canopy of the woods hovered over all, almost a
separate ecology unto itself, a dark ceiling covering everything so thickly that the forest floor remained un-
touched by the light of Burihatin's sun. Below, the magic
of the weald took on a somber, unholy quality.

Strange creatures prowled through Dupa's bleak
shadows, howling mournfully as they moved through the
forests. Creatures of all sizes and shapes leapt and slith-
ered and crawled and fluttered and slunk through the
gloom. They chittered and shrieked and hooted and
groaned. They hunted and killed and fed and fought

and died. Some of them even lived long enough to mate and raise the next generation of breeders and feeders.

Tiny clusters of domes lay spotted across Dupa's continents. Most of the major cities and towns sprawled out in the rocky barrens, well away from the predators of the forests. Only a few tiny settlements huddled among the towering blacktrees; their safety came *from* the jungle and the separation they maintained from the larger cities. In the cities the Regency still held most of the authority. In the jungle . . . no one did. For many inhabitants of Burihatin, the dangers of the jungle remained preferable to those of the Regency.

Now—a single antigrav sled came racing across the roof of the forest. Slicing its way through the air only a bare two meters above the canopy of the jungle, it left behind itself a wake of swirling leaves and waving branches. The escapees and their hostage sat grim-faced behind the clear windshield of the open craft. The air screamed past them, whipping viciously at their clothing.

"Take us higher, dammit!" Lee shouted to Sawyer. "You'll hit something!"

"We have to stay low, so they can't scan us. I know this world. The Regency has got spyfrogs everywhere."

"Well, then—take us lower! Let's drop down to the forest floor. They can't monitor us there. You can weave in and out through the trunks of the trees."

Sawyer looked to Three-Dollar. He inclined his head to indicate Lee-1169. "What kind of medication have you got him on? And where can I get some? Did you hear what he just suggested? I should have hallucinations so bizarre." Looking back to Lee, he said seriously, "What you suggest won't work. The last person who tried to drive an antigrav sled through the blacktrees left a smear a half kilometer long."

"Well . . . I don't like this at all," replied Lee. "It scares me. It feels unnecessarily dangerous."

"I've done this before," Sawyer said. "Trust me."

"The last time we trusted you, we all ended up in jail."

"Everybody makes mistakes," Sawyer answered back. "You did when you trusted Finn and me for the first time. Now we have to get you out of the mess you made for all of us when you did that."

Lee blinked. He shook his head. Sawyer's logic remained unassailable and bizarre. He turned away grumpily. He couldn't win this argument. And he didn't want to distract the man while he needed to keep his attention on the task of piloting the antigrav sled.

Sawyer called back to Three-Dollar. "Check the helmet on the Zillabitch."

"She can't see a thing," replied Three-Dollar. "I doubt she can hear much either."

"Good," said Sawyer. "Time to zig again." He swung the sky-raft hard to starboard, bringing it directly on course for the distant wall of half Burihatin that filled the horizon. The sharp angle of the planet's rings demonstrated their latitude on the moon. Sawyer grunted and pointed ahead. "Do you see that?" he asked Lee. He indicated a towering plateau that reached up out of the forest like a gigantic monolith.

"We'll land there?" asked Lee.

"We'll stop there."

Lee glanced sideways to Sawyer. "It doesn't look very secret to me."

"You have an astute eye," Sawyer remarked drily.

Lee scowled. Sawyer's refusal to provide clarity about their destination had begun to seriously annoy him.

Sawyer backed off on the throttle then, slowing the sled to an easier pace. He took it lower, allowing the craft to brush the very tops of the trees, weaving gently around the taller protrusions of vegetation. "All right," he said, calling to Lee and Three-Dollar. "You've heard of the unnatural protrusions of rock that dot this part of the continent, the columns called Dupa's Warts? We head for the easternmost wart. Except for that singular distinction of Dupagraphy, it has no other distinguishing quality. The other columns farther west hold the honors of height, width, and size, both greater and lesser than this one. This wart cannot even represent an average of all the warts. It has no distinction at all except its location. Nevertheless, it has some use to us as a landmark."

Lee nodded. "That I can understand. We start from there and fly a certain distance in a certain direction, right?"

"Nope. Sorry. We land there and abandon the raft. I'll program it to head north for an hour, then take itself down into the trees as low as it can, find a place to park, and wait for a recall signal."

"And what do we do?"

"I don't know about you, but I intend to empty my bladder."

"And after that?"

"I'll have something to drink, so I can empty it again at our next stop."

"Do you never answer a question honestly?"

Sawyer pretended to consider the question. "Even if I told you what we had to do next, you wouldn't believe me. So I choose not to waste the words."

Dissatisfied, Lee turned away, grumpily. "You don't look happy," he remarked to the TimeBinder.

"Neither do you," Three-Dollar replied blandly.

"Does this tracker's intractability bother you as much as it bothers me?"

Three-Dollar patted Lee gently on the shoulder. "No, it doesn't. Indeed, I envy you in that. I have a much larger and darker worry." His face became uncommonly glum. "I've tried continuously since we landed. I've listened and listened across all the bands." He lowered his head sadly. "I cannot detect the presence of a TimeBinder on this world. The TimeBand still remains here on Dupa, I can sense that much, but no one wears it. I fear that Zillabar's agents may have finally succeeded in assassinating the TimeBinder. Perhaps they have even obtained custody of the TimeBand. If so, then we may have lost our last hope." He let out his breath in a somber exhalation. "I cannot think of any other explanation. When a TimeBinder dies, his successor puts on the band immediately. If the band remains unworn, perhaps that means that it lies waiting for Zillabar to claim it."

The Messenger

□□□□□□□□□□□□□□□□□□□□□□□□□□□□□

Otherspace unfolded. A tiny ship shaped like a water-melon seed came spitting out of nothingness. It shot through the darkness of realspace toward the distant jewel of *The Golden Fury*, decelerating only at the last possible moment.

The speedboat Marauder came alongside the much greater starship, waited for the security scanners to complete their various tasks, then slid easily into a docking port. Transfer tubes connected themselves. Things clanged, hissed, wheezed, puffed, and banged, all in the process of linking, securing, and testing the connections. The intelligence engine of the larger vessel accepted the responsibility of equalizing the pressures and the flavors of both enclosed atmospheres, and additional noises became noticeable as this occurred. Shortly, the process concluded and the intervening hatches slid open. A single black-clad Phaestor youth came climbing out of the vessel.

He spoke to no one. He nodded perfunctorily to the commander of the docking crew, but exchanged no pleasantries and offered no gossip. He kept his face carefully blank. He handed over his security pass without comment and waited patiently while the representative of the Elite Guard confirmed his identity. At last the security officer handed the pass back and nodded him through.

The channel to the anteroom opened to a personal security scanning chamber. From there the messenger obtained access to the main body of the vessel. He carried a security case and strode directly through to the command center of the Imperial Starship.

Upon arriving at the command bridge, he saluted

the officer on duty and asked for an immediate audience with the Captain. The vessel's executive officer reported blandly that Captain 'Ga Lunik still remained in dreamtime.

The messenger did not react to the unfamiliar name. He merely stood on the golden balcony and waited.

"Will you take refreshment while you wait? We can offer you a delicious variety of spices. On the orders of Captain 'Ga Lunik, the Lady's kitchen has become available to all of her senior officers."

The messenger ignored the offer. "I have a message that the Captain will wish to hear immediately."

"Perhaps you didn't hear me," the executive officer replied. "Captain 'Ga Lunik lies in dreamtime. We have orders not to disturb him."

"Disturb him anyway," replied the messenger.

The executive officer debated with himself whether or not to argue the point. Before he could decide, the messenger added, "Do so on the direct authority of a representative of Kernel d'Vashti."

"Very good, sir." The executive officer felt relieved not to have to make this decision himself. He nodded to his assistant to take command and hurried off immediately to the Captain's chambers.

Very shortly Captain 'Ga Lunik appeared on the command bridge. He looked irritable and uncomfortable. He seemed ready to kill something. Seeing the messenger, he advanced on him furiously. "Why do you wake me? Have you no manners? Don't you appreciate the value of dreamtime? Especially the dreamtime of a superior?"

The messenger remained stiff and unbending before 'Ga Lunik's obvious anger. He simply held out the security case before him. "Your thumbprint, sir?"

'Ga Lunik scowled, speechless. The rudeness of this youth startled and annoyed him. He studied the boy's face with more than casual interest. Perhaps he had underestimated the strength of character displayed here. He suppressed his displeasure and thumbed the recognition panel. It flashed red for a moment as the security device conferred with the starship's computer, requesting confirmation that the bearer of this thumb actually held the office of Captain aboard the Lady's Imperial Starship. After a moment more, the panel flashed green and the security case popped open.

'Ga Lunik reached in and pulled out a sealed document. He broke the seal on the papers and glanced at them quickly. His eyebrows lifted momentarily. He handed the papers to his waiting executive officer. "You will need to begin making preparations for this immediately."

The executive officer took the papers and read them immediately. He nodded and turned away, quietly issuing orders through his headset.

"You should look at the recorded greeting as well," the messenger suggested to 'Ga Lunik.

The Captain of *The Golden Fury* looked into the security case again and withdrew a set of coded information cards. He sorted through them, selecting the one with the yellow seal of the Regency on its face. He stepped over to a reader and laid it flat on the plate.

Immediately, a holographic image of Kernel d'Vashti appeared before him. "Captain," he said, "greetings. Thank you for the hospitality you have shown my messenger. Your courtesies will not go unrewarded."

'Ga Lunik glanced sideways at the messenger, wondering briefly if the boy had shared d'Vashti's bed recently. If so, that might explain the other's concern for the welfare of the young officer. 'Ga Lunik reconsidered his plans to have the child's head sent back to d'Vashti without any accompanying note.

"Captain, you will please do me the great honor of informing the Lord of the Dragons that a great fleet of Marauders stands ready to move out. We have assembled at the final staging area. I have sent this messenger ahead so that you may prepare adequately for my arrival. He carries all appropriate instructions."

d'Vashti's image bowed, then added, "I would not presume to intrude upon the Lady Zillabar's privacy. I know how much she cherishes her time alone. Nevertheless, when the appropriate moment arises, I would appreciate it if you would convey to her my sincerest good wishes for her comfort and happiness. I look forward to seeing her again, and I will bring her many delicious gifts. Again, thank you."

The image of d'Vashti faded away.

'Ga Lunik remained motionless, staring sourly at the space where only a moment previously the Phaestor Lord had arrogantly stood.

"You have a problem?" the messenger observed.

"No," said 'Ga Lunik.

"I would have guessed otherwise," the messenger replied smugly. "From the look on your face, it seemed as if you did not welcome this news."

"You have no idea what the expression on my face represents," 'Ga Lunik said testily, but he knew the messenger had observed his reaction accurately. He snapped his fingers for the attention of his executive; the officer stepped quickly to his Captain's elbow. Without taking his eyes off the messenger, 'Ga Lunik said, "I regret to inform you that you have failed to please your master. His written greetings instruct me to dispose of you as I see fit." To the executive officer he said, "Have this rude boy executed immediately."

"Sir—?" gasped the messenger.

'Ga Lunik cocked his head curiously at the other's protest. "You demand an explanation? You may have it. I do not always kill the bearer of bad news, but in this case . . . the bearer *smirked*." He gestured, the executive officer gestured, and two security officers stepped up to escort the messenger away.

"d'Vashti won't like that," observed the exec.

'Ga Lunik nodded knowingly. "If events continue to occur in the present as we have observed in the past, then I do not expect that either you or I will remain alive long enough to incur the brunt of d'Vashti's displeasure. At least this sends him a correspondingly nasty message in reply. I will not die without honor."

Having expressed that much candor, 'Ga Lunik resumed his authoritarian bearing and ordered, "Go. Summon the Dragon Lord to the bridge. Let him hear the bad news next. At least I can enjoy watching the play of expressions on his ugly face. He'll probably react with as much enthusiasm as I did. Now for sure he'll have to find Zillabar immediately. This gets more and more interesting."

As the executive officer started away, 'Ga Lunik added an afterthought. "Oh, and one more thing. Mobilize our own Elite Guards. Issue them the strongest weapons we have—weapons that can kill Dragons, if such an event should become necessary."

"Yes, Captain." The exec bowed respectfully and hurried off.

Dupa's Wart

Sawyer and Lee struggled with the medical cabinet containing Finn, lifting it carefully off the antigrav sled and lowering it to the rocky surface of Dupa's Eastern Wart.

Then . . . distastefully, they removed the silence helmet from Zillabar's head and helped her down from the sled. Zillabar, still in shackles and restraints, hissed at their touch and pulled away so violently that she slipped and tumbled, falling painfully onto the rocks and rolling dangerously close to the edge of the precipice.

"Whoops!" said Lee. "She almost saved us the trouble." He looked to Sawyer. "Listen, if we decide that she has to die—I want to do it."

Sawyer shook his head. "After what she did to Finn, I have first dibs."

Three-Dollar stepped between the two men. "No. If she has killed the TimeBinder, I will take her life. . . ."

Both Sawyer and Lee turned to stare at him. Sawyer spoke for them both. "I thought TimeBinders didn't believe in killing?"

Lee asked the question even more directly. "What about the Alliance of Life?"

Three-Dollar shook his head. "You didn't let me finish. And after I take her life, I will take my own because I'll have betrayed my own principles."

Sawyer and Lee looked at each other, confused. They exchanged shrugs and then went to retrieve the Lady Zillabar from her unceremonious sprawl in the dirt. Sawyer bent to the lady and grabbed her arm tightly, jerking her upright to bring her face level with his. He slapped her hard across the face with the back of his other hand. She spat at him. He slapped her again, this time harder. "I slapped you the first time to get your attention. I slapped you the second time to let you know that I expect you to behave like a lady. If you cooperate, we'll treat you with courtesy. If you treat us with contempt, we'll disgrace you so badly that even your own people won't want you back. I promise you that my imagination knows no bounds when it comes to obscene behavior. Lady or pig—you choose."

She considered his words without apparent emotion. She studied his eyes. "How can I behave like a Lady if you insist on acting like a barbarian?"

"I don't know how to behave otherwise, my Lady. You do." Sawyer looked at her quizzically. "Or do you?"

In answer she turned her back on him.

Sawyer grabbed her by the arm and walked her roughly back to stand next to Finn's medical cabinet. He looped her chains through one of the handles of the casket, locking her to it. "You put him in there," he said. "You'll help carry him."

"We walk from here?" Lee asked.

"Only a short way." Sawyer turned to the airboat and locked in his evasion program. He activated it and stood back. The boat hummed and lifted. Sawyer and Lee pushed it off the edge of the precipice. It dipped toward the jungle below, caught itself, and then began sliding away across the sea of dark leafy trees.

Sawyer checked on Finn's condition, then switched on the cabinet's local antigrav field, and the four of them—Sawyer, Lee, Three-Dollar, and Zillabar—each grabbed a handle at the corner. Sawyer shook his head at the unlikely committee that they formed, allowing himself a sardonic reaction to the way the whole situation had developed.

He pointed toward the faintest hint of a trail. "We go down that way—"

The trail, a narrow path of dirt, led down over the edge of the cliff; someone had painstakingly carved it out of the naked rock, all the way down. It spiraled uncomfortably around the face of the wart, sometimes wrapping around the curve of rock, sometimes cutting back and forth across the sheer cliff face. In many places they could only proceed single file, an almost impossible task with Finn's casket between them. Had the cabinet not had its own levitation panels, they would have had no choice but to have left it on top of the rocky pillar.

Every so often Sawyer glanced back to monitor Zillabar's behavior. Curiously, she had become impassive, neither cooperative nor disobedient. She had withdrawn inside herself and reacted not like the haughty queen he had grown used to, but instead as emotionlessly as an insect attendant. She had become a zombied shell of her former self.

Sawyer wondered if she had gone mad. He had heard of such things—of Phaestor aristocrats subjected to such hardship, perversity, or sheer indignity that they willed themselves to death. They simply withdrew from their own lives and let their bodies wither away. Sawyer worried about it. This did not bode well.

He worried about the Lady's near-catatonic behavior. On the one hand, it made her much more manageable, but on the other hand it gave them much more to worry about. Or did it? Did her demeanor even matter anymore? They had not yet decided among themselves what they should do with her.

They didn't dare return her to the Phaestor aristocracy. The Regency would demand immediate revenge. The incredible offense of taking the Lady Zillabar hostage demanded horrible punishment. The Vampires would run amok on a dozen worlds, killing and feeding on every human they could find.

On the other hand, as long as they kept her hostage, the Vampires and Dragons would scorch the land bare in their search for her. They would wreak every bit as much violence in their search for the Lady's captors as they would in retribution after they found her. The situation held no victory for humans. They had a Vampire by the horns. They couldn't let go of her, they couldn't hang on.

No, the more Sawyer thought about it, the more he felt sure that they would have to kill her—disgrace her and then kill her. They would have to disgrace her so badly that her own people would not want her back. The thought made him smile grimly. The Lady certainly deserved such a fate. He wouldn't shed any tears over her.

He began to brood over suitable destinies. Perhaps they could allow a family of pig-men to pay two caseys a piece for the opportunity to fornicate with her. . . .

No. He didn't want to insult the porcines.

Besides, if any species became known as the singular agents of the Lady's downfall, the rest of the Phaestor would hunt that species into extinction. No, he wanted something disgraceful, but unpunishable. Something brought about by the Lady's own actions, if possible.

Sawyer couldn't think of anything. It frustrated him because it belied his image of himself as a clever man. "Well, we could always stuff her into a black hole," he muttered in annoyance. "That has a certain implosive charm to it. If only we could send the rest of the Regency there with her."

The thought echoed in his head for a long moment.

Reluctantly, he began to realize the truth of it. The Regency would not allow the Lady's kidnapping to go unpunished. It had seemed like a good idea at the time—a Plan B that allowed Sawyer and Finn and the other rebels a chance to escape the Lady's delicious hospitality; but in retrospect it now became apparent that, like it or not, Sawyer and Finn would have to lend their talents to the rebellion. They had no choice. At the moment they took the Lady captive, they had guaranteed that the Regency would invest all of its resources in their destruction.

He remembered his vow, the one he had made in the Lady's prison cell, and it left him uncomfortable. *"I will not rest until I have destroyed the Lady Zillabar, and*

if necessary, the entire goddamned Vampire aristocracy!"
He'd said it in anger at the time, but now he realized he
might actually have to live up to those words. Perhaps he
shouldn't have spoken with such certainty. The universe
had apparently listened and believed him and had con-
spired to put the Lady Zillabar in his power. Now he
would have to do what he promised.

"I don't mind having an enemy or two," Sawyer said
to himself. "A little controversy makes life interesting—
but I think I've become an overachiever. This will *not*
make Finn happy. Hm. Maybe I won't tell him. . . ."

A Lesson in Manners

Eventually, they descended into the canopy of the unbroken forest. The path continued to wind around the face
of the cliff, only now the leafy ceiling shaded them, and
the many smells of the jungle became a rich soup of fra-
grance. At last they came to a broken shelf carved out of
the side of the column. It lay sheltered beneath a dark
overhang, almost a cave. Here the path ended against
solid rock.

Lee stopped in annoyance. "Now what?" he demanded.

Sawyer said, "First we put Finn down; then we
rest." He eased the casket down to the ground and
switched off its levitators. He bent to the controls to
check on Finn's condition; it had not changed, but he remained there with his brother for a long moment.

Three-Dollar leaned against the cabinet. He looked
tired, but not exhausted. After a moment he noticed that
Zillabar hadn't moved. He tugged on her sleeve and
guided her to a similar rest.

"What happens next?" Lee demanded from Sawyer.

Sawyer turned away from the medical casket. "We still have a long way to go," he said. "We'll need our strength." Sawyer shrugged out of his backpack. He pulled out a ration-bar and began unwrapping it. He bit off a mouthful and began chewing it loudly. When he noticed that Lee still waited for him to answer, he gestured with the rest of the bar. "I suggest you do the same."

Lee turned around, frustrated. William Three-Dollar stood behind him, offering him another ration-bar. "Sawyer knows his business. Eat." The TimeBinder turned then to Zillabar and offered her a packaged meal. The Phaestor Queen appeared not even to notice the gesture. The TimeBinder waved his hand slowly in front of her eyes. She blinked, but she didn't focus.

Three-Dollar looked to Sawyer with a question on his face.

Sawyer nodded in response. "I see it." He shook his head as if to say it didn't matter one way or the other.

"Her welfare remains our responsibility, Sawyer."

"If you think I'll donate a pint of blood every time we sit down to rest, you've got another think coming."

"I didn't mean that."

"Then what did you mean? What would you have us do?"

The TimeBinder didn't answer. Instead he took a ration-bar, unwrapped it completely, and placed it in Zillabar's hand. "You must eat something. You must keep your strength up."

Zillabar sat motionless and unmoving. Her grip loosened and the bar slipped from her fingers.

Watching this, Sawyer grunted in annoyance. "You don't understand the Vampires very well, do you?"

"I understand them better than you. I have most of their history right here," Three-Dollar responded, tapping the TimeBand around his forehead.

"But you haven't seen them as I have," Sawyer replied. He eased himself to his feet, crossed to Zillabar, and stood in front of her. He picked up the fallen ration-bar from the ground and handed it to Three-Dollar. "Hold this," he said. Then he slapped Zillabar hard across the face.

She blinked. "Don't do that," she said. But her expression remained unchanged.

Sawyer pulled his arm back to slap her again. Three-Dollar grabbed it and held him back. Sawyer jerked his arm free and glared at the TimeBinder. "You have to speak to them in their own language!" he said. He slapped Zillabar a second time, even harder than before.

She started to lift a hand—Sawyer knocked it away and slapped her again.

"This gives you pleasure!" Three-Dollar accused.

"Damn right it does!" Sawyer snarled back. "But even if it didn't give me pleasure, I'd still have to do this. Consider it a job benefit that I get to beat on Vampire women!" He slapped the queen again.

Finally, at last—

Zillabar rose haughtily to her feet, her eyes glaring, her hands curled into defensive claws, her lips curled back from her teeth, her face contorted in rage and fury. *"How dare you lay a hand on me, you filthy barbarian beast! How dare you even presume to touch the sacred flesh of a Regency aristocrat! I'll have you filleted alive and served to the rats who eat the garbage of the street!"*

Sawyer ignored her rage. He took the ration-bar from Three-Dollar and held it out before her. "Eat. If you don't eat this, I'll cram it down your throat until you choke to death on it. If you ever again try to refuse an order from me or any of my companions, I'll strip you naked and parade you through the center of the dirtiest back alley of Pig Town! You'll do exactly what we tell you, or you'll discover the true meaning of dishonor—and you'd better believe it when I tell you that I know dishonor."

"I believe it," she replied haughtily.

"Yes, you should. I learned it all from watching Vampires at work and at play. I know what happened at Drydel's secret villa. So does Lee—and half a dozen other witnesses. So don't give me any more of your disgusting arrogance. You and your kind have no higher role to play than the stingflies that suck a man's blood in the forest. In my eyes you live as a parasite, sucking the blood of others and giving nothing in return but death, disease, and despair. If you died right now, I'd dance on your corpse and sing a song of disgusting fornication. I know more than a few. But we need you alive and you'll stay alive! If you try again to will yourself to death, I promise you, you'll live to regret it a long long time."

The Lady Zillabar glared at him, but she took the ration-bar from him and bit into it savagely. She never took her eyes from his. She didn't have to speak, but Sawyer knew exactly which part of his anatomy she dreamed of tearing off with her teeth. He turned away, half in disgust, half so she wouldn't see how visceral a reaction she had triggered in him.

Three-Dollar followed him to the other end of the casket, where Sawyer pretended to busy himself checking on Finn. "You look like a man who has swallowed a live toad," he said softly. "Twice."

Sawyer glanced away, glanced down, glanced finally back to Three-Dollar. "All right, yes. I have. I did. I said I liked slapping her. I lied. I wanted to get even with her more than anything in the universe. And now that I have her here—in my power, under my control, where I can finally take my revenge against her—I see that I don't like myself for what I've done or what I want to do to her in the future. And I blame you. Until I met you, I didn't have to worry about scruples or conscience or things like that. I could just do the job and collect the money. And if occasionally the universe offered me the opportunity for revenge, I could consider that a bonus.

"Now, however, I find myself thinking dangerous thoughts—that even beating up on a Vampire bitch who deserves it, who earned it fairly, who would kill us all in an instant if she could, carries no honor; only the stain of brutality and barbarism. You did that to me, you son of a bitch. You took away my pride in myself as a cruel bastard. You've destroyed me, you know."

"I don't think so," said Three-Dollar. "If anything, I've given you the opportunity to reinvent yourself."

"Oh, great—sure. What shall I turn into next? A poodle-boy?"

Three-Dollar grinned at the thought, but shook his

head blandly. "No. I expect you might make a wonderful TimeBinder someday."

"Huh? Who? Me? You've lost your mind, 'Binder."

Three-Dollar patted Sawyer on the shoulder. "Don't worry about it. I have no intention of dying anytime soon. And I haven't yet decided to name you as my heir." He walked away, leaving Sawyer staring after him, wondering if the old man had just made a joke or a prediction.

Blacktrees

"All right," said Lee. "I've paced this shelf long enough. I can't find any secret passages, entrances to caves, hidden stairwells, or anything else. Where do we go from here?"

Sawyer grinned. "You didn't look hard enough."

"Huh?"

The tracker pointed at the wall of jungle. Lee glanced at it without seeing, then looked back to Sawyer. "Yeah? So?"

Sawyer looked annoyed. "Look again."

Lee still didn't see it.

Sawyer took him by the arm and led him to the edge of the shelf, where the huge branch of the closest blacktree reached out to form a curving avenue down into the leafy darkness.

"That?" asked Lee, incredulous.

"That," confirmed Sawyer, blandly.

"We walk . . . ? Into the jungle?"

"Uh-huh. We walk. Into the jungle."

"But— . . ." Lee pulled away abruptly. "That might work on Thoska-Roole, where the only predators you need to worry about wear police uniforms, but this—"

The clone-brother couldn't find the words to express his discomfort. "Do you know what things lurk in that blackness? I've heard stories of prowlers and growlers and bears—of beasties and goblins and long-legged things that go bump in the dark. I've heard of killer swarms and trap-door spiders, carnivorous shrike-vines, and even feral Chtorrans. People tell stories about pythons the size of shuttleboats and slithering panther-sharks and—and—... I don't know what else. And you want us to just walk down into *that* unprotected and vulnerable?"

"Yes," agreed Sawyer. "Do you have a problem with that?"

"Uh—" Lee blinked. After a moment he managed to say, "I think one of us has a communication disorder."

"And the other one has an unreasonable terror of the dark," Sawyer replied coolly. "Which one do you want to lay claim to?"

Lee stopped as the meaning of Sawyer's words sank in. "Cowardice? You accuse me of cowardice?"

"Of course not. I've seen you in battle."

"Then what—?"

Sawyer held up a hand. "A coward would refuse to proceed. A courageous man just needs to know the nature of his fear before he confronts it."

Lee took a step back, incredulous. "That won't work. The Lees did not raise many fools. Or let me say it another way. The wise man studies the odds before he lays down his bet. I don't feel like wagering my life against these odds."

Sawyer nodded with understanding. "I hear you. We'll have to proceed without you then."

"No. We'll have to find another way. Or another destination. We'll go back up and recall the boat. We'll fly. We don't need to see this M'bele of yours, We can connect with the rebellion here on Dupa. I have some sources of my own—"

Sawyer shook his head. "We can't fly to M'bele. I have no idea where he lives. This jungle highway provides the only access to him." He advanced on Lee angrily. "Listen to me. We don't have time to argue over this. If you can't summon up the strength to confront a

few miserable nonsentient appetites, then you sure as
hell can't summon up the strength to confront the Regency and its millions of sentient Phaestoric hungers!
Now demonstrate the courage that you keep speaking
about or stay behind. Choose and choose now. We have
no more time to waste."

Sawyer stepped over to Finn's coffin and switched
on the levitators. He looked to Three-Dollar. "If you
want to come with me, then let's get moving. Otherwise
I'll leave you behind, and I'll get Finn there on my own."

Three-Dollar nodded. He nudged Zillabar and she
stood up again; she had abandoned her mask of hostility.
Now she walked proudly, like a queen. Sawyer noted the
change in her attitude. That the Lady had now regained
her presence meant that he would have to take extra precautions; it meant that she had begun planning ways to
manage the course of events to her own advantage again.
He grunted and strode over to where she stood.

He examined each of her bindings carefully. None
showed any signs of tampering; that worried him even
more. Finally he looked into her eyes. She stared back at
him with equanimity. "If you try to escape, I'll kill you—
and I'll let the scavengers of pig-town feast on your remains. And I'll have pictures of your final ignominy
distributed to every inhabited world in the Cluster. Do
you understand me?"

"You will do as you must," she replied. "I will do as
I must."

"I didn't ask you for a lesson in behavioral science,"
Sawyer snapped. "Do you understand me?" He lifted a
hand as if to strike her.

She glanced at his hand, then returned her pale, dry
gaze to his. "I understand you. Obviously, you don't understand me."

In reply Sawyer spat sideways. He checked to see
that the others had taken their places at the handles of
the coffin and then gave the command to move. Moving
carefully, they stepped out onto the broad expanse of the
blacktree's limb and began following it carefully down.

The branch of the tree presented itself as a broad
curved highway; occasional subbranches curled up off it,

big enough to look like independent trees themselves. They bent outward, forming wide pathways across to other branches. Sawyer led them past the first three branches, then had them cross a leftward-curving limb that stretched out over a deep gap in the forest canopy. "Don't look down," he cautioned.

Zillabar kept her eyes steadily forward. Three-Dollar glanced down once and didn't react. Lee couldn't help himself—he had to look, and instantly regretted it. He couldn't see the ground below at all. It lay hidden in gloom, but what he could see presented such a horrifying sense of their height within the forest canopy that he involuntarily gasped and clutched the levitation casket beside him.

"I told you not to look," Sawyer called from ahead.

Lee gritted his teeth and followed the others. The branch on which they crossed seemed as wide as any mall or starship corridor—but the fact of its unprotected height made it seem much more terrifying to him. The clone-man wanted to drop to his knees and crawl along the length of it; but his pride overwon his fear, and he began picking his steps carefully. Beside him, on the other side of the casket, Zillabar snorted in contempt.

"Fuck you with a pig's dick," Lee replied, and forced himself to match her haughty steps. Zillabar smiled to herself.

At last they reached a place where the branch lay across another horizontal highway, and they lowered themselves down onto it. This limb sprung from another blacktree, and they followed its leisurely rise upward to a wide basin-like gnarl, where Sawyer directed them to rest again. They had come close enough to the roof of the forest that the dingy light of the day actually sparkled through the green, blue, and black leaves above. The minty smell pervaded the softly glowing air.

Sawyer paced the gnarl as if looking for something. It curled around them like an amphitheater, and he stepped up onto the wooden berm and began pacing off a measure. He stopped, scratched himself, looked around—"No, I can't have made a mistake that stupid," he said. He paced back the other way. He stopped again and stared up into the branches.

He climbed back down from the height of the gnarl and stood next to the casket, looking frustrated. He scratched his chin thoughtfully. He rubbed his cheek with the flat of his hand. He wiped his nose. He scratched under his arm. He scratched his head. "I could use a bath," he remarked to no one in particular.

Three-Dollar looked at him blandly, patiently.

Lee-1169 did not have the same manners as the TimeBinder. "Have we reached the end of your plan? Or have you simply run out of ideas?"

Sawyer looked at him sharply, as if offended. He replied with an almost haughty tone, "Neither. Some things have changed here. I need to remember what to do. Leave me alone to think." He didn't wait for Lee's reply, but strode to the opposite side of the wide gnarl. He gave it a frustrated kick, then turned and leaned against it, folding his arms across his chest. "Damn!" he said to himself. "I wish I had Finn here to talk to—"

Abruptly, he realized what he had said—and the horror and grief flooded in on him anew. He didn't know whether to rage or cry. He lowered his head and bit his lip, trying to hold back the tears welling up in his eyes. This whole thing—he hated it. Frustrated, he gave up. He crossed to the casket and put his hands on the glass over his brother's unconscious face, as if to touch him, as if to wake him. "Finn," he whispered. "Please—I need you now. I spoke in error when I said I thought I could work faster without you. I can't. I need you."

Remembrance of Things Vast

□□□□□□□□□□□□□□□□□□□□□□□□□□□□

Finn didn't answer. He remained unconscious, and Sawyer feared that Finn would never answer him again. He looked at the readouts on the casket and saw that Finn's condition remained unchanged from the last time he had looked, and the time before that, and the time before that too.

Sawyer stood there for a long moment. He knew that Three-Dollar and Lee and Zillabar stood watching him, waiting for him to act. Each of them had their own thoughts and reactions to his ... failure.

What had he missed? What had he forgotten here? What had he never known? Why hadn't he paid closer attention the last time they'd come through here? He remembered that Finn and M'bele had—

He stopped. He straightened. He turned around. He stared.

The others looked at him with curiosity, startled by his sudden alertness.

Sawyer climbed slowly back to the top of the gnarl. He paced along the ridge, not counting, just looking. Eventually, he found a small, shallow depression. "Aha. I knew I'd found the right place. I don't make *stupid* mistakes."

Sawyer opened the front of his trousers and began urinating into the depression. The yellow stream splashed away in warm spatters. He stood there, letting it flow and flow. He filled the depression in the berm until it overflowed, then forced himself to stop while he still had fluid left in his bladder. The rank smell of his urine reached his nostrils then and made him wonder what he'd eaten recently. Abruptly he remembered the food in the shuttleboat and shuddered uncomfortably.

He sealed up his pants again, jumped down off the berm, and returned to the others. Zillabar looked offended; he'd expected nothing less. Lee had a scornful expression on his face. Three-Dollar remained unmoved. Sawyer made himself comfortable at the head of the medical cabinet and waited.

He didn't have long to wait. Very shortly, a sound came from the leaves above. The others didn't notice it at first; it sounded like the wind. But Sawyer knew what to listen for, and he recognized the steady rustling of something moving through the canopy above. So when the *thing* came screeching down from the trees, he betrayed no surprise. He did enjoy watching Lee-1169 flinch. He noticed with annoyance, however, that Zillabar had not reacted at all. She had heard the creature's steady approach as surely as he had.

The beast had silvery fur, almost blue. The slight sheen of color glittered even here in the shadowy gloom. Large and flat, the creature had no head. Its eyes—all six of them—stared out from the center of its body, spaced equidistantly around its puckered mouth. It had long, ungainly arms, one at each corner; each arm ended in a bony, clawlike hand. Breathing slits opened and closed along its sides. The creature looked like the hybrid progeny of an ape, a spider, and a nightmare.

It had dropped down from above, swinging on a leathery brown vine. It scuttled along the berm until it came to the depression that Sawyer had urinated into. It lowered itself over the puddle as if sniffing. It hissed and backed away several steps, turning itself around and elevating that part of its body that Sawyer assumed operated as its hindquarters. It opened its cloaca and aimed a jet of oily dark fluid at the offending puddle of Sawyer's urine.

Sawyer glanced over at Lee. The clone-man's eyes had gone wide—with terror or amazement, Sawyer couldn't tell. He took a step sideways and whispered, "Don't move. Don't say anything. Put your gun away. The natives call it a spiderman. It won't hurt you if you don't hurt it—and believe me, you *don't* want to hurt it."

The creature finished its task and backed away,

whirling again and raising itself up on three of its legs to glare at the humans and the Vampire, as if waiting.

"My turn again," Sawyer said, and climbed back up onto the berm. He walked around the entire arc of the woody gnarl, all the while making snarling and snorting noises at the silver spiderman. "Kiss my rose red behind, you feeble excuse for a fright wig. Eat my shit." He made horrible noises and waved his arms around in the air. He knew the creature couldn't understand how he maneuvered on two legs only—the silver spiderman hissed, but took two cautious steps backward.

"Don't you scream at me! I don't believe in you either!" Sawyer bellowed. As he approached the disputed depression, he stamped each footstep as hard as he could. "I claim this territory. Not you! You can't pee here! I pee here! Your pee smells like flowers! MY PEE SMELLS LIKE PEE SHOULD SMELL!" He knew the beast could not possibly understand his words, but it certainly understood his intent. It scuttled away another ten steps.

Sawyer opened his trousers again and finished the job he had started earlier. He forced the urine from his bladder so that it spattered away all traces of the darker oil of the spiderman. Then he took a few steps back to allow the other to sniff the depression again.

The spiderman approached cautiously, periodically pausing to raise itself up to look at Sawyer. At last it reached the fresh urine and lowered its face close enough to sniff. It started to turn itself around, as if to repeat its previous performance, but at that point Sawyer charged three steps forward, shouting, "Don't you even think of it, or I'll have your silvery pelt for a rug, you stinking slime-bag excuse for a primate!"

It worked. The creature scuttled away, startled. It raised itself up, stared, blinked, then rolled over on its back and waved its long bony arms in the air for a moment.

"Good," said Sawyer. "You have enough intelligence to see it my way."

The spiderman folded itself into a sitting position and waited.

Sawyer stepped away from the stinking depression and faced Three-Dollar and Lee. They both looked amused. Sawyer returned their looks with a cockeyed grin. "Sometimes you just gotta speak to them in their own language." Abruptly, catching the motion of the spiderman out of the corner of his eye, he whirled and advanced again, stamping his feet, waving his arms, and screaming, "Oh, no, you don't, you filthy little flea-bitten bag of hair! You come near my hole and I'll feed you to the nearest Vampire, and if you don't believe me, I've brought one with me!"

The spiderman scuttled back away again, this time farther than before. It made a rude noise and settled itself down to wait. Sawyer glanced down to Lee. "I gotta do that. I haven't any piss left. Sooner or later, it'll get the point."

Lee spread his hands in a gesture of confusion. "You wanna explain it to me? I don't get the point."

"He has to claim this as his territory," Three-Dollar said.

"But why?"

"Because he has to."

Sawyer strode back and forth on the wooden crest of the gnarl, strutting and posturing for the watching spiderman.

"Does that thing have any intelligence?" Lee asked.

"Just enough to know that it shouldn't try to pee in my hole," Sawyer called back.

"I don't get it."

"Don't worry about it," Sawyer reassured him. "I know what I have to do."

Sawyer's pacing took him away from the depression in the wood and then back again; each time he went a step farther away from it than before. The spiderman watched him warily. It folded itself and refolded itself and finally folded itself a third way. It made funny little snuffling noises that sounded vaguely unhappy.

At last the spidery creature gave up. It unfolded itself and leapt off the gnarl toward a nearby vine. It caught the vine, swung in midair for a moment, then scrambled up into the leafy canopy above, where it disappeared.

"I win," announced Sawyer. He dropped down into the center of the gnarl and rejoined the others.

"Now what?" asked Lee.

Sawyer scratched his cheek. "We wait and see if the little bastard believed me."

The Elevated Railroad

□□□□□□□□□□□□□□□□□□□□□□□□□□□□

For a long while nothing happened—long enough for Sawyer to begin to wonder if perhaps he had failed to convince the spiderman of his sincerity in the matter.

Then, suddenly, everything happened at once. Silvery spider-things began dropping out of the canopy all around them, dropping down on vines, swarming down tree limbs, and just plain falling down from the branches above. They shrieked and screamed and snorted; they scrambled and scuttled and scrabbled around the humans, the Vampire queen, and the medical cabinet, touching, probing, exploring, pinching, sniffing, and generally making the most hellacious nuisances of themselves.

But even in all the confusion, a pattern of activity began to emerge. Dropping down from the leaves above came a hand-built platform, a rough basket of interwoven vines and planks—a crude gondola with a wooden floor and netted sides. Despite its inelegant appearance, it hung from silken strands, and Sawyer could see the glint of metal in its fastenings.

The spidermen surrounded them, pushing them, pulling at them with their narrow bony fingers, tugging them toward the basket. At first Lee reacted with a measure of revulsion, Three-Dollar with curiosity, Zillabar with annoyance, but at Sawyer's urging they relaxed and let the silvery spider-things guide them to the clumsy-looking craft. When they came for Sawyer, he stood by the medical cabinet and refused to move. Instead he switched on the levitators and began pushing it along toward the hanging basket. Almost immediately, the hairy spiders got the idea and helped him along.

As they lifted it up onto the planks of the platform, they appeared to express surprise at its light weight. They chittered and chattered among themselves, but if they had a language, Sawyer couldn't tell. He couldn't recognize any meaning in their sounds. Sawyer climbed up into the hanging gondola with the others and hooked one arm through the woven net enclosing it. "I think you'd all better find something to hang on to. This ride has some rough moments."

A handful of spider-things climbed onto the net of the gondola with them; another handful climbed up to the top of the rigging and began worrying at the cables. Almost immediately, the gondola jerked and swung—it hesitated, swinging backward and forward for a moment with a sickening motion—and then it swung away from the gnarl, across the branch, and out over the edge of nothingness.

Lee-1169 screamed.

The gondola dropped down the cable into the blackness of the forest for the longest moment, spider-things clambering all over the netting, screeching and moaning as the basket slid and rolled, bucking through the air. They seemed to fall forever.

Lee stopped screaming long enough to catch his breath. He clutched at the netting and held on as tightly as he could; his eyes bespoke his terror. Three-Dollar looked a little pale himself. Only Zillabar seemed able to maintain her poise. Sawyer looked up and saw a near-invisible wire running rapidly through a set of silvery wheels. The gondola raced down along it at a terrifying speed. It seemed faster even than the airboat that had brought them racing across the roof of the jungle. Sawyer recognized the illusory quality of the experience, but it did not mitigate the lump climbing up into his throat.

They slid through darkness, through shafts of silvery-blue light, through great empty spaces and narrow corridors of vegetation, over the broad stretching branches of the blacktrees, between the huge upright curls of the sublimbs, through the veils of greenery and vines—they slid down the wire so long that Sawyer began to doubt that they would ever find a bottom. He leaned sideways to see if he could see the bottom of the forest, but he saw only branches and limbs, leaves and vines, extending all the way down, disappearing finally into a blue hazy gloom.

And then—at last—the descent began to ebb, and they careened along horizontally through a great open vault of emptiness. Blacktrees above, blacktrees below, blacktree limbs all around—and yet they flew through an impossible cavernous green realm. Birds soared beneath them—and above them as well. Sawyer grinned with glee, enjoying the view. Lee abruptly turned to the side and heaved the better part of his recent meal out into the air; it spewed away in an impressive arc. Sawyer suppressed a laugh; he'd done the same thing once. Three-Dollar reached over and gave Lee a sympathetic pat on the knee. Zillabar just snorted.

Now their momentum began swinging them up and up and up. The little car climbed steadily through another realm of blacktree limbs; their speed began to burn off slowly as they rose up the wire. Ahead, the giant wall of a stupendous blacktree loomed like an impassable barrier. Sawyer eyed it diffidently; he knew they couldn't hit it, but the sense of impending impact gave this part of the ride an alarming flavor.

The gondola jerked slightly as the motors connected to the pulleys kicked in. They lifted steadily toward the tree, toward an outstretched limb—the gondola rattled as it passed close under the limb, and then, just as abruptly, they began dropping away again—this time in a new direction. They dropped only a little way this time and began rising again almost immediately.

Gradually the ride assumed its own mad rhythm of sudden drops and long free swoops; and the momentum of each fall ebbed into gentle rises, then sharper rises and motorized acceleration, followed by the rattling of the pulleys as they rode across the supporting structures; and then, once more, they would drop away into the deep gloom below. The wire zigged and zagged its way through the forest, and the riders of the cable car soon lost all sense of direction. They held on tightly and plunged out of the darkness behind into the darkness ahead. Most of the time gravity pulled the gondola along the wire, but every time the rate of travel fell below a certain speed, the motors kicked in—especially every time they rose toward another supporting blacktree arm.

They traveled this way for what seemed like an eternity. The forest around them grew darker and closer and ever more menacing. Things howled in the distance, other things hooted in reply, and once—just as they passed beneath a great overhanging limb, something very close by *grunted* with a distinct sense of annoyance. The spidermen clambered around the gondola, seemingly oblivious to the comfort of the passengers. Several of them hooked their claws into the nets, folded themselves into sacklike things, and appeared to fall asleep.

Sawyer envied them. If he remembered correctly, this part of the journey would take the better part of a day. He had no idea how far they had to travel from Dupa's easternmost wart. He had no idea where they would eventually end up. He wondered if perhaps M'bele had the cables periodically restrung, and moved himself about the forest at will.

Eventually, the last light of day drained out of the jungle around them. The reflected glow of giant ringed Burihatin provided no relief. They raced on in utter darkness. Sawyer tried aiming a light ahead, but the narrow beam of the spotlight revealed little, only a flickering of leaves; when he set the spread of the beam to a wider dispersion, the light became dissipated and worthless. And so they rocketed on through unseen terrors and possibilities, with nothing but intermittent noises punctuating long empty silences to give them any clue to their surroundings.

Sawyer must have slept. He didn't remember falling asleep, or even waking up again, but when the light be-

gan returning to the Burihatin gloom, it didn't seem to
him as if enough time had passed to make a full night.
He glanced around the gondola. Three-Dollar seemed
lost in meditation. Lee slept fitfully. Zillabar—wide
awake—studied him with evil cunning.

"You will die soon," she said softly. "Already your
aura has turned black. Death enshrouds you. It follows in
your wake, taking all who travel with you, creeping ever
closer with each new life it feeds upon. Soon it will have
taken everyone but you—and then it will take you as
well."

Sawyer nodded in agreement. "Yep," he said. "I've
often thought that myself. But it doesn't worry me. I'll
see your death first. That will give me more than enough
satisfaction for one life. I'll meet death gladly after that."

"I didn't think you believed in the Alliance of Life,"
she said smugly.

"I don't believe in anything," Sawyer replied without feeling. "Neither do you."

"I believe in the Phaestor," Zillabar said. "The
Phaestor don't need to hide behind an ideology. Our hunger and our children provide all the ideology we'll ever
need."

"You prove my point. You believe in nothing. Even
more disheartening, you've also just explained why the
Alliance of Life can never work," Sawyer admitted.
"While the Phaestor still live to feed, partnership among
all the sentient races remains impossible."

"Not true," said Zillabar. "The Regency represents a
working partnership. The Phaestor provide direction; everyone else provides . . . meat."

"Thank you for clearing that up," Sawyer said. "The
next time I have to wreak violence against a Vampire
bitch, I won't bother to let the issue of my conscience
stand in the way." He scooted himself around so he
wouldn't have to look at her anymore.

It almost worked. He could still feel her eyes upon
his back.

"You will die, you know. Badly. You will beg me for
mercy. But you won't get it. Because Vampires have
none. Remember that."

Waiting for M'bele

□□□□□□□□□□□□□□□□□□□□□□□□□□□□□

And then, abruptly, the hellacious ride came to an end.

The gondola slowed as it rose, approaching the high crest of an arching branch—but instead of rattling underneath it and rocketing away in a new direction, the cable car rose up above the branch and jerked uncomfortably to a stop. They swung back and forth for several moments, bouncing in the air like a child's toy. The spidermen swarmed upward into the leaves and disappeared. After a moment the gondola jerked and began lowering unsteadily down to the surface of the branch.

The travelers found themselves on a large wooden gnarl, almost identical to the one at their departure point. Indeed, Sawyer had no way of knowing that they *hadn't* traveled in some great circle only to return to the exact same tree. They pulled the medical casket from the gondola, and their travel packs as well. As soon as they took the last of their belongings from the cable car, it jerked upward into the leaves and vanished. So did the spidermen. No evidence remained of their journey at all.

They stood alone on the wide gnarl—one tracker, one clone, one TimeBinder, a Vampire Queen, and an unconscious man in a medical chest. Above, a thinning in the forest canopy allowed beams of dappled sunlight to filter down in shades of pale, hazy blue. Below, the distant foliage fell away in ranks of darkening color. To one side, a great veil of purple vines glowed with speckles of wet reflection; to the other, a blacktree limb as huge as one of Dupa's Warts filled their view.

At least a hundred people had died to bring them here. Sawyer sagged down onto a rounded upswelling of the gnarl. He ached. His stomach hurt. And even though he stood on a solid surface again, his body still insisted that the world around him remained unsteady.

Lee-1169, even more unhappy looking, glared across at him. "All right," he demanded. "Now what do we do?"

"Anything you want. Eat. Sleep. Defecate. Urinate. Get on each other's nerves. Try not to kill each other." Sawyer added, "Oh, yes—and for enjoyment we'll watch Zillabar squirm at the indignity of her treatment." He grinned. "In other words . . . we wait."

"I see. And just exactly *what* do we wait for?"

"To see if M'bele will greet us—or kill us."

"You mean, you brought us here all this way—and you don't know what kind of reception we'll get?"

Sawyer nodded. "M'bele knows how to hold a grudge."

"What kind of a grudge?" Lee demanded.

"The usual," Sawyer admitted.

Lee threw his hands up in disgust. "I should have known." He glared around for someone to commiserate with, found no one, glared at Zillabar, turned at last to Three-Dollar. "*You* should have known! Why did you expect that these two trackers could do anything for us? They can't do anything without leaving behind a trail of dead bodies and bad debts."

"At least that makes them easy to follow," remarked Three-Dollar blandly.

"All right." Lee turned back to Sawyer. "Tell me the rest. How much do you owe M'bele?"

Sawyer shrugged eloquently. "Enough. But hardly enough to justify killing a man, let alone two—especially when one of them already lies dying in a medical casket. I figure he can't afford to let Finn die, or me, or he'll never stand a chance of getting repaid."

"And what if you've guessed wrongly?"

"Why, then, very shortly none of us will have much to worry about at all, will we?" Sawyer allowed himself a sardonic smile. "In the meantime, sit back, get comfortable, and enjoy the view. The blacktrees of Dupa have a reputation for peace and majesty throughout the Cluster.

You have a rare opportunity here to see them in their natural unspoiled condition."

"I've seen all the blacktrees I care to see, thank you, unspoiled or otherwise." Lee made a growling sound and turned away in frustration.

Sawyer shrugged. "Suit yourself."

Three-Dollar's gaze remained on Sawyer. His eyes had a depth of understanding that Sawyer found difficult to resist. He tried looking away, but every time he looked back, Three-Dollar still studied him.

"What?" Sawyer demanded finally.

"Nothing."

"Not nothing. You keep looking at me. You have a question, don't you?"

Three-Dollar conceded with a nod. "Despite the fact that you don't think M'bele will help us, you still brought us here. Why?"

"Why not?" Sawyer sighed and admitted, "I couldn't think of anywhere else to go. I just have to hope that the pheromone for revenge doesn't overwhelm his lust for remuneration. M'bele has the talent that we need. Do you have a better idea?"

Three-Dollar went blank for just the quickest of instants; then he returned. He shook his head. "I have memories. But only a fool stores his past in the future. In the meantime this horse has obviously chosen its own path."

"This *horse?*" asked Sawyer.

"A creature of ancient mythology," the TimeBinder explained.

"Ah," said Sawyer.

Listening to them, Lee-1169 made a sound of derision. "Whatever he says, it doesn't matter. Nothing else will happen here until it happens."

Three-Dollar smiled in agreement. "You have the makings of a true master, Lee. You have finally realized that the universe operates at its own speed."

He just had time to finish the sentence. And then . . . it happened.

And Another Thing

□□□□□□□□□□□□□□□□□□□□□□□□□□

First, the air began to tremble. Very faintly. Then the sound became louder and more pronounced—not a sound as much as a feeling. A dark, low feeling. Then, abruptly, something came rumbling up from below, climbing up the perpendicular limb of the close-by tree.

The thing had a lumpy shape, like a cluster of different-sized bubbles all stuck together, and it had multiple arms and graspers. It walked itself up the surface of the tree, each separate arm reaching, grabbing, hooking, pulling in turn. It looked like a vertical centipede tied in multiple knots and with cancerous protuberances bulging from its body at odd angles.

A thousand separate eyestalks swiveled around to gaze at the waiting travelers; several thousand others continued to survey the vast forest above, below, and around them. A bevy of spotlights lit up then, fingering the visitors in their bright focus. Sawyer stood up and faced the machinery. He bowed extravagantly and announced, "Sawyer and Finn Markham, at your service. I bring friends"—here, he paused to point to Lee-1169 and William Three-Dollar—"and I bring a gift." And this time he waved his hand to include Zillabar. The Vampire Queen's countenance remained unreadable.

The machinery did not react. Not immediately.

Lee looked to Sawyer, a question in his eyes. Sawyer shrugged. Lee looked to Three-Dollar, a different question in his eyes this time. The TimeBinder shrugged as well. Lee did not look to Zillabar.

A moment later the machinery reacted. Weapon ports began opening, and at least a hundred separate devices turned around to point themselves at Sawyer's party.

"Uh-oh ... ," said Lee. "Somebody guessed wrong—"

Sawyer kept his expression blank. He scratched his eyebrow and thought about the possibility of a bath. He sucked his teeth, looked down at his boots, and considered several other things he might say and the wisdom of saying them. He looked again to the cameras. "I think you should open up, M'bele," he said disarmingly. "We could talk about two hundred and sixty-two thousand, one hundred and forty-four caseys."

"Three hundred thousand caseys!" a sonorous voice boomed in reply.

"Not by my accounting!" Sawyer shouted back angrily.

"I have included the interest," the voice intoned drily.

"Usurer!"

"Thief!" M'bele continued. "By the rights of Dupa, I should shoot you now and have done with the whole nasty matter."

"You do and you'll miss one of the best opportunities I've ever brought you!"

"The last opportunity you brought me cost me a fortune. I can't afford too many more of your opportunities, Sawyer. You'll bankrupt me. Begone!" And then, a moment later, the voice said in a kinder tone, "I thought you said that Finn came with you."

"He did."

"I don't see him."

Sawyer stepped to one side and indicated the medical casket with an unhappy gesture. "He needs your help, M'bele. If you don't help him, he'll die. And if he dies, you'll never get your money."

"The money has no meaning to me," said the voice. "I consider it only a means of keeping score in the greater game of life. What ails him?"

"Blood-burn."

"I have no cure for blood-burn. No one does."

"I know what causes it."

Despite itself, the voice replied, "What causes the blood-burn?"

"A Vampire's bite."

"I have no cure for Vampire bites either."

"I brought the Vampire with me."

"Hmp." The voice fell silent.

"I need your help," Sawyer said.

The voice did not respond.

"Don't make me beg. Please, M'bele. I have no other hope."

Still no response—

Abruptly, a huge hole popped open in the great gnarl of the blacktree. A tall man, heavyset, and with skin so dark it gleamed purple, came striding angrily out. Shiny kinks of white hair framed his head, and his eyes burned with a deep, unresolved anger. M'bele pushed past Lee and Three-Dollar and went directly to the head of the medical casket. He carried a black case.

"All right, yes, yes. Shut up, Sawyer. Let me see him—" He bent to the readout screens and studied them, all the while making nasty little noises of empathy and disgust. "Oh, good God. How in the hell did this happen to him?"

"I told you—"

"I don't know why I should trust you, Sawyer. I don't know why *anyone* should trust you. I heard how you betrayed the TimeBinder of Thoska-Roole."

Three-Dollar stepped forward then. "Excuse me," he said. He tapped the TimeBand around his forehead. "I wear the TimeBand of Thoska-Roole. Will you trust my word? Will you save this life because I ask you to?"

M'bele hesitated. Several emotions flickered rapidly across his dark face. Finally he snorted in exasperation. "You make it hard for a man to hold on to his anger, you know that, don't you?"

Three-Dollar merely smiled blandly.

Abruptly, M'bele looked around to Sawyer and Lee. "Well, don't just stand there, you stinking idiots! Help me get him into the lab!" He pointed to Zillabar. "Not you—you stay right there."

"Don't you have a brig or cell you can lock her up in?" Lee asked.

"Let her wait out here," M'bele retorted. "Where can she run to? The jungle will eat her alive. And if she does try to escape, we'll have one less problem to worry about. No, consider it a test. Let's see how much intelligence a Vampire really has."

"I don't like it," said Sawyer.

M'bele pointed at the huge machine still hanging on the tree. "All right. I'll have the poppet watch her. If she takes more than ten steps in any direction, we'll have to send her home in a plastic bag."

Reluctantly, Sawyer accepted M'bele's wisdom. He bent to switch on the levitators, and they pushed the medical casket down the ramp and into the living flesh of the gigantic tree.

Dragon's Layer

The Burihatin starport sprawled across a rocky tableland. Starships lay like beached sky-whales in shallow cradles scattered in a seemingly haphazard array across the broken terrain. Connection tubes snaked over the surface leading from each cradle back to a sprawl of domes and spheres that overlooked them all.

The first dawn slid across the yellow landscape—the glow of amber Burihatin's dayside suffused the sand and rocks and scraggly, patchy vegetation. The parent world appeared now as a crescent, and its reflected light gave little useful illumination. Later, however, when the great beast had climbed well past zenith, the second dawn would bring a brighter day to the land. The bright pinpoint of Burihatin's primary would etch the landscape with a stark blue radiance.

Above, the sky began to rumble with ferocious energy. The rumble grew louder and even more compelling. It became a multifaceted roar, shrieking with notes all up and down the spectrum, beyond the ranges of hearing, both above and below. The ground shook—and a gleaming squadron of golden vessels came screaming over the horizon.

They coasted to a stop and drifted past the starport toward the great flat landing zone beyond. The Marauders came gliding gently down to the tarmac as graceful as feathers, each one stopping where it touched down—all of them arriving at their final rest in the same perfect formation they had demonstrated in the air.

Almost immediately the doors of the vessels popped open, the ramps dropped down, and the surviving members of the Elite Dragon Guard came pouring out of the ships like an avalanche of flesh, cascading across the ground and forming up into ranks of terrifying splendor.

Even before the last of the Dragons had come down the ramp, a bevy of ground cars came speeding directly across the landing zone, hurtling to a halt before the largest of the landing craft. Gray-uniformed officials—all human—leapt from the vehicles, hurrying to line up at the base of the ramp. They looked pale and frightened.

When the last of the welcoming committee had taken his place at the end of the line, the great door of the landing craft popped open and the imperious figure of the Dragon Lord came waddling heavily down to the ground; his tail lashed behind him in restless anger. Two of the waiting officials exchanged nervous glances.

The Dragon Lord surveyed the line of waiting humans with a contemptuous snarl. The two senior executives stepped forward quickly. "We welcome you to Burihatin-14, Your Excellency. We hope you will have a pleasant stay, and if you require any service at all from us, you need only—"

The Dragon Lord held up a hand. "I want the starport sealed off. Nothing lands. Nothing leaves. Nothing moves."

"But, Excellency—that would paralyze the economy of the planet. We couldn't possibly—"

The Dragon Lord didn't even wait for the man to finish. He opened his jaws wide, lowered his head, and bit the man's head off, spitting it sideways across the tarmac, where it bounced and rolled an incredibly long distance. The man's body spurted blood from the neck for one frozen terrifying moment; then it toppled diagonally to the ground, the blood still pumping outward in a bright red flow.

The second official gulped and said quickly, "We'll seal the port immediately, Your Excellency, no questions asked!" He thumbed his communicator to life and began issuing orders at a frantic pace.

The Dragon Lord held up a hand. The man paused. "Just a moment—" he said to his communicator. "Yes, Excellency?"

"Dangerous rebels have captured a Vampire Queen and brought her to this world. We have some idea where they landed, but they may have deceived us. My warriors will scour every settlement on Dupa if they have to. They will start with this starport. They will also report to me about any interesting cargoes that they find . . . so if any of your officials have allowed any traffic in contraband, I would suggest for your own sake that you have it confiscated immediately."

"Oh, yes sir, absolutely, Excellency. I don't think you'll find a hair out of place here. We run a very clean port. Absolutely—"

The Dragon Lord didn't hear the man—or perhaps he simply didn't care to listen to any more prattle. He turned away with a casual wave of dismissal. As his tail whipped around, several of the starport officials leapt to get out of its way; two didn't make it in time—they went flying across the ground.

And then the Dragon Lord turned back again, his nostrils flaring. "I need a car," he said in a voice of imminent doom. "I see no other cars here! Did you forget to order vehicles for me and my warriors?"

The executive's eyes rolled up in his head. He keeled over in a dead faint, falling to the ground in a limp gray bundle.

M'bele

□□□□□□□□□□□□□□□□□□□□□□□□□□□□□

M'bele's house had no rooms, no doors, no windows—it existed as a winding network of tunnels that curled up and down through the flesh of the blacktree. All around them the sinewy cables of the tree slowly pulsed with life-giving sap. Here and there, great spaces opened up within the limbs and branches and multiple trunks.

Lights hung everywhere, but the maze remained unfathomable to the strangers. Very quickly, they became lost in the tunnels and simply followed the dark man down and around and up again. At last they arrived at a cavernous room filled with medical gear and equipment. Several scanning tables stood side by side, and with Sawyer's help M'bele quickly slid Finn onto the nearest one. Seeing Finn's ashen color, he pursed his lips thoughtfully, then turned away to the nearest workstation.

By the time the dark man completed his medical scan of Finn Markham, his expression had gone through several grim transformations. Finally his face just closed down and his eyes became unreadable.

He swiveled away from the bank of displays and sighed. He let his head sink down on his chest in exhaustion. After a moment he looked up at Sawyer and said, "Your brother has the worst case of tertiary blood-burn I've ever seen. I don't know a medico in the Cluster who could help him. How the hell did you bastards end up in this situation?"

Sawyer explained quickly. "d'Vashti bit Finn—and then promised us the antidote if we'd track down and deliver the TimeBinder of Thoska-Roole. Then the Zillabitch refused to provide the antidote, so we helped William Three-Dollar escape."

M'bele scowled. "You guys never did stay bought."

"She betrayed us!"

"Good. Now you know how it feels." M'bele turned angrily back to the displays and studied them again. "I still don't like you, Sawyer. But I want you to know that my anger over our previous business dealings has nothing to do with what I have to say to you." He took a breath and lowered his head in resignation. "I wish I knew more. I don't know what I can do for Finn except ease his final passing."

A noise made them all turn around. A nine-year-old girl, wearing only an ankle-length smock, stood in the opening of a small nearby tunnel, sleepily rubbing her eyes. She looked from one person to the other in confusion. "I heard talking," she said. Her speech had a clumsy, indistinct quality. Sawyer's eyes narrowed as he studied her. He looked to Three-Dollar, who nodded almost imperceptibly.

M'bele dropped to his knees and scooped the child into his arms. "Nyota. You promised to stay in bed."

"I heard talking," the girl repeated. She looked around the room, wide-eyed. Her expression had a dull, glassy quality, as if nothing she saw quite made sense. As if she existed in her own simpler reality.

M'bele kissed her once and held her tightly. "You shouldn't have gotten out of bed. You know the rules."

Nyota nodded solemnly. "Uh-huh."

"All these people will disappear by morning, just like any other bad dream. I promise."

Nyota's eyes kept wandering from one face to the other. "But I heard talking."

"Excuse me a moment," M'bele said curtly, and disappeared up into the tunnel, carrying the child with him.

For a moment none of the men said anything. Finally Sawyer glanced to Three-Dollar. "She has no soul—?"

Three-Dollar shook his head. "No. She has a soul. Every human does. But apparently she doesn't have the intelligence to animate her body as you and I might deem appropriate. But don't judge him too quickly, Sawyer. M'bele might carry a heavier burden than most parents, but he carries it well."

"Parent?"

"Do you remember what I spoke to you in Zillabar's prison? Of a time when humans brought their own children into the world? M'bele has done just that."

Sawyer stared at the empty tunnel in disbelief. "I cannot imagine M'bele as a mother—how can you know that about him?"

"Not a mother, a *father*. And I can see the relationship expressed in everything he does, the way he looks at her, the way he holds her, the way he speaks to her, the way he protects her from us."

"From us? We wouldn't hurt a child—"

Three-Dollar raised an eyebrow. "How many Vampires have you killed? How many Dragons have you killed? How many other lights have you snuffed out to bring us here? I cannot blame M'bele for having fears for his daughter's safety around you."

Sawyer puzzled at Three-Dollar's words, but he couldn't quite connect them all the way. He felt trapped by his language, as if a thought fluttered helplessly around in his brain, unable to express itself, unable to leap out into the air, because he lacked the words to speak it. He turned away in frustration; he went back to the table where Finn lay bathed in amber light.

M'bele returned then, looking grim.

Sawyer glanced up, looking at the dark man with somber new eyes. "May I ask you something personal? The child? She came from K'fai's womb—?"

M'bele's face hardened further. But he answered Sawyer's question curtly. "K'fai passed away four years ago. No one else knew of the child until now. She has never seen another human until now. I have no idea how she will react to you."

Sawyer shuffled his feet, embarrassed. "Forgive me. I apologize for intruding on your privacy. Perhaps we should leave—"

"And Finn? What will you do about Finn?"

"You said you had no hope. If you have no hope, then neither do I."

"No. I didn't say that. You *heard* that, but I didn't say it. I said I didn't know of a medico in the Cluster who could help him."

"Then you can help him?"

"I said I didn't know enough to help him. I didn't say I wouldn't try. If he has nothing to lose, we can still take desperate measures. I've already begun transfusing his blood, cleaning it as best I can. That'll buy him some time, but I don't know if I can save him, Sawyer. I honestly don't know. But I can promise you this much—if he dies, he won't die in vain. I know this offers you only small comfort, but I'll learn everything I can." He scratched his head as he studied the displays again. "The Vampire woman—why did you bring her with you? I never knew you to go jogging with an anchor before."

"We needed to bring Zillabar," Sawyer said. "We couldn't leave her behind."

"Zillabar!" M'bele came shooting out of his chair. "Do you mean to say that you brought Zillabar here? The Dragons will burn the forest to a cinder if they have to. They'll track her here! How dare you? I have a daughter! You've risked my life in the past, but now you've gone too far. You've endangered my child!" The dark man turned darker with rage.

Sawyer waited until M'bele's anger began to ebb. He held up his hands in an apologetic gesture. "I didn't know you had a child. And besides, we took precautions. We destroyed all the locators. We put down in Salut Minoh, we traveled to the Eastern Wart by sled, which we then sent away. They have no way of knowing where we went."

M'bele remained unconvinced. "And you think you acted intelligently? The Dragons will start their search in the tunnels of Salut Minoh. They always do. Don't you think they know something about the trade in contraband by now? Don't you think they know where the smugglers go?"

Sawyer nodded and smiled impishly. "You should listen to the news channels more often. Apparently, one of the tunnels will shortly collapse. We may hear of a terrible loss of life. The Dragons will have much to mourn. What else would you like to know?"

"At best you bought yourself two days," M'bele snorted. "They'll kill every person on the planet if they have to. The Dragons know the locations of at least three of my nests. I suspect they may know more. They know that you've dealt with me in the past. You've effectively destroyed my investment here." He turned to Sawyer with an odd look on his face. "You realize, of course, I'll have to charge you for my losses."

"Add it to my bill."

"I already have. How do you feel about indentured servitude?"

"I think you'll have to buy my contract from the Alliance of Life, but other than that, I've already resigned myself to a lifetime of reparations."

"Damn!" said M'bele. "And I had just begun to develop a real fondness for this place." He grunted and shook his head. "Y'know, it would make my life a lot easier if I just got on the channel and turned you guys in. Perhaps I could collect a big reward."

"If you lived, yes. But do you really think the Dragons would let a human claim the honor of rescuing the Vampire Queen?"

M'bele grunted an unhappy acknowledgment. "At least your logic hasn't failed you, even though your emotions have." The dark man considered his possibilities, and which loyalty would best serve his own interests. He did not have to consider for too long. He knew the Vampires too well. "All right," he said. "At least I can finally discover how the blood-burn immobilizes its victims." After a moment he added softly. "But damn! I wish this had happened to almost anybody else but Finn. I *liked* Finn. I'll miss him a lot more, Sawyer, than I'd miss you—"

"Thanks for your affection," the tracker said. His voice sounded odd.

"Anytime," M'bele replied bitterly.

Sawyer sank to a chair. He had given up hope three times already. He had let himself rekindle that hope three times. He sagged where he sat, drained and empty and close to a total breakdown. The anguish showed in his every move. M'bele had his back to Sawyer and did not see the effect that his words had had on the distraught man.

Exhaustion and grief overwhelmed Sawyer. He had hoped for too much, had spent every last bit of energy getting his brother here to M'bele's secret laboratory. He had finally run out of ideas and run out of strength, both at the same time.

Remembrances of Things Vast

▆▆▆▆▆▆▆▆▆▆▆▆▆▆▆▆▆▆▆▆▆▆▆▆▆▆▆▆

William Three-Dollar spoke then. Actually, he made a sound like an exploding gasket, halfway a scream of rage and a burst of frustration. Everyone turned to look at him.

"I know something," he said.

M'bele, Sawyer, and Lee waited for him to go on.

"I have difficulty speaking this," Three-Dollar said. He licked his dry lips uncertainly. "TimeBinders often know things that they should not discuss. Sometimes people don't want to hear them. More often other people don't want them said. Sometimes we take our own oaths of confidentiality. To reveal this might threaten the existence of the Regency, but—"

"Do go on," M'bele said.

"—but we have already committed ourselves to attend a Gathering with the express purpose of dissolving the Regency's charter and breaking the back of the Vampires' power. So here I stand, struggling with my own dilemma. Do I break this trust or not?"

Sawyer glanced up from where he sat. "Should we care?"

"I have to make this decision," Three-Dollar said. "I have to assume the responsibility and speak what I know.

The information may save your brother's life." He explained softly, "We have a contract. Your lives in exchange for your service. You provided service and gave us our escape from the custody of the Vampires. I must keep my part of the bargain and give you back your lives."

He stepped over to the console that displayed the progress of Finn's transfusion and studied the schematics and readouts. He began speaking softly to the computer, giving it careful instructions.

After several moments he stopped and turned around to the others again. "The Regency has an ancient history. Most people don't know it, because the Phaestoric aristocracy has little interest in having this knowledge widespread. It might encourage people to ask too many questions. Sit," he said. "Get comfortable. This will take a few moments.

"To understand the beginnings of the Regency, you need to know the reasons for the initial desperate pilgrimages out here to the Palethetic Cluster. A long time ago we all lived in the Eye of God—that great whirl of light that looms over the entire Cluster. So very very near and yet so many years away. We lived in only a corner of God's eye, but we had already begun to spread in all directions. At that time we had not yet created the many different species that we know today. At that time humanity stood alone, a single race.

"Now I will tell you the great *shame* of humanity. In those days, just like now, great wars often raged for centuries; men fought against men, often for no apparent reason ... except perhaps that the men who ordered other men into battle had the range of their ideals set for small.

"As humanity expanded its boundaries, so did we expand our capacity for finding new things to argue about, new reasons to scourge each other's cities and worlds. You may appreciate this, Sawyer—the Vampires have no claim on horror. Humans will always hold the record for atrocities because we wrought them on ourselves, over and over and over again.

"As we grew more powerful—not wiser, just more

powerful—our capacity for war finally outgrew our ability to control it, and a holocaust of unprecedented scale and ferocity broke out. This terrible great war raged across the western arm of the spiral, wreaking havoc and destruction that went far beyond the mere devastation of civilizations; it destroyed whole star systems. A chain of supernovas marked the fiercest battles. Worlds disappeared in cosmic fire. The waves of deadly radiation blasted outward one after the other, like ripples of a firestorm. The seething energy scoured planets for hundreds of light years in all directions for centuries afterward, and even today, all these many millennia later, those waves of energy still blast outward.

"In the silence that followed, the survivors knew that they could not allow this atrocity to ever occur again. The best way to prevent a repeat, the survivors believed, lay in the creation of weaponry so terrifying that no possible enemy would dare risk having it unleashed.

"So, of course, the next round of violence astonished even those who had created it.

"To this day places exist in the Eye of God where time and matter no longer obey their own laws. Burning things still lurk in the darkness to trouble the sleep of distant astrophysicists. Eventually, the wars subsided, but the damage remains.

"The absolute worst of the nightmares, the predators, still exist. Nearly indestructible, these incredibly vast, deceptively frail planet-killing webs still hide in the black places between the stars. They drift silently, hungrily, looking for new worlds to feed upon.

"Yes. *Humanity created the predators.*

"Sometimes TimeBinders argue about the responsibility of this knowledge. Some of us argue that the fault belongs only to a brutal subset of the race, that those of us who did not create the horror should not whip ourselves with shame and regret. Indeed, those who hold that position also believe that we should hate the ones who created the weapons that drove us from our ancient homes. But other TimeBinders believe that attitude a dangerous one; it allows us to think again in terms of *us* and *them.*

"Some of us believe that it doesn't matter which branch of humanity created the weapon, we all share responsibility in the matter. Before the last predator dies, our species will have killed every life-form in the Eye of God. We may very well stand throughout time as the most voracious, destructive, verminous form of life ever spawned in the universe. Quite a triumph, no?

"Some of us believe that we cannot hide from our own history. We must own it to transcend it. Otherwise we condemn ourselves to repeat it."

Sawyer waved it away with a frustrated gesture. "So how will any of this save my brother's life?"

Three-Dollar looked to M'bele. "Do you see how limited our vision remains? We take the grandiose and reduce it to our most personal concerns. 'What does it mean to me?' In this room we have enough hatred to reinvent the predators. Don't try to deny it. Listen to yourselves speak. You all have someone or something you want to kill. What difference does it make on what scale you operate?"

The three other men in the room remained silent and shamed.

Three-Dollar continued, "Every time I see a death, I feel hatred too. But I don't have to act on my hatred. Do I?" He added, "If I acted on my hatred, I might initiate a process that would destroy the entire Cluster."

The others looked up sharply at this. "What do you mean?" M'bele demanded.

"Nothing," said Three-Dollar, waving it away with a hand. "I spoke from exhaustion and anger and frustration. Let me"—he wiped his forehead, then continued quickly—"let me get back to our real purpose here. At the first gathering the survivors of the exodus from the Eye of God created the Regency to protect the Cluster worlds from the Predators. We created the Vampires and the Dragons. When I say 'we,' I speak from my memory, of course. My TimeBand carries the lives and the wisdom and the experiences of more than three hundred individuals already.

"We created the Vampires. They don't like that knowledge widely known; but we did create them. We wanted a hunting pack that could go out into the dark between the stars, waiting there forever if they had to. We gave them cunning, longevity, intelligence, hunger, and ruthless ferocity. We gave them the ability to turn themselves off for long periods of inactivity so they could wait and wait and keep on waiting without ever feeling frustrated; we gave them dreamtime as a compensation, to keep them focused, to keep them from going mad.

"We created better than we knew. But we didn't know that at the time. We believed we had done well. The Vampires went out into the great emptiness between the Eye of God and the Cluster and patrolled for Predators as ruthlessly as we had hoped and dreamed they would. The Vampires became our first line of defense against the scourge."

"And we created the Dragons too?" asked Lee.

Three-Dollar nodded. "We gave them Dragons for their protection. The Dragons needed some wit, some cunning; but mostly we created them to give the Vampires strength where they needed it most. The Vampires themselves have a certain physical fragility that makes them extremely vulnerable—as we have all seen. But in compensation their intelligence and control over the Dragons makes them formidable opponents in any battle—as we have also discovered to our great regret." He shook his head. "I don't have to tell you the rest. You've seen it yourselves. Over the generations the Phaestoric aristocracy has expanded its influence across the entire Cluster. Their internecine warfare has fragmented the peace and brought the Regency to the brink of civil war. The family fleets have already begun gathering to move against the remaining free worlds."

Sawyer stood up then and confronted Three-Dollar. "But what does any of this have to do with my brother?" He had a profound anguish in his voice.

Three-Dollar tapped his head. "I have the knowledge of the Vampires' creation stored in my TimeBand. I have the memories of the men who designed their genome. Yes, the line of TimeBinders extends even *that* far back. The Vampires began on Thoska-Roole. You didn't know that, did you?

"Only three TimeBinders chose to carry the memories of the people who created the Vampires: the TimeBinders of Willowar, Thoska-Roole, and Burihatin. The Willowar headband disappeared years ago. We think the Vampires have it. Now the Burihatin TimeBinder has also disappeared; what's happened to that TimeBand?"

M'bele interrupted thoughtfully. "Perhaps the Vampires fear that the knowledge of their creation also carries with it the potential for their destruction."

Three-Dollar nodded. "The Vampires fear everything. The builders designed the Vampire mind-set to include a substantial degree of paranoia. Considering the foe they went out to confront, paranoia represented a valuable survival trait." He stopped. "I must violate a trust. I've sworn a sacred oath never to reveal information that compromises the integrity of the Regency. But as we stand here, the Regency has already begun to rip itself apart. Does my oath still carry weight, or do I have a larger duty to the future that even now struggles toward realization?"

"You promised to help save my brother," said Sawyer.

"Yes, I did. And that fact troubles me so greatly that I have already considered suicide three times over. You have me trapped in a dilemma. Do I break the small promise or the big one? Do I keep my word or save a life? What commitment will I keep? The commitment to the Alliance of Life, which exists only as an unrealized ideal—or the commitment to the past, which has endured for over six thousand years?"

"You keep the commitment that will save my brother's life," said Sawyer. "Because that exists as a specific, measurable result—a demonstration of the truth of the Alliance of Life."

"Yes, I know that," said Three-Dollar. "But you don't know the size of the oath I will have to break to keep that promise."

"You speak accurately," said Sawyer. "I don't know—and I don't care. Tell M'bele what he needs to know. Tell him now, while we still have a chance. Don't make me argue. Don't make me beg. I expect better from you."

Three-Dollar sank to a chair and began speaking.

Remembrances of
Things Half-Vast

□□□□□□□□□□□□□□□□□□□□□□□□□□□□□

"The microorganism that causes the blood-burn lives in the blood and saliva of male Vampires. The creature has a symbiotic relationship with its hosts. When injected into a body, the phage produces a paralyzing enzyme. A large injection will produce paralysis within minutes. With a small injection the paralysis will take much longer and will occur as a series of increasingly severe attacks, a condition we call the blood-burn. In either case the same result occurs. The victim falls into a paralytic coma.

"Depending on the metabolism of the victim, the paralyzing enzyme produces a repertoire of varying effects. First, it softens the blood and the tissues for the Vampire's delicate palate. Second, the enzymes also act as a preservative so that the prey survives for a long, long time in its cocoon. This allows the Vampire to feed at leisure.

"The female Vampire has no poison in her bite, but she does have the same immunity to the enzyme that the male has. This means that Vampires cannot hurt each other with their bites—although I will admit that unsavory rumors of cannibalism among the young males continue to persist—never mind that; the males cocoon the victims and present them to the females to earn the right to breed. The TimeBinders have kept this a secret to protect the Vampires from biological enemies."

A look of understanding appeared on Lee-1169's face. "That explains the gift of the dog-children." To M'bele, he explained, "Lady Zillabar brought six dog-children back from Dupa; she gave them to Lord Drydel. One of them escaped. We found the other five cocooned in a barn in the Lady's private nest. I understand it now. She didn't bring the gift for Drydel's pleasure alone; she brought them to him so that he could give them back to her ready to eat!"

Three-Dollar nodded in agreement. "You have most of it, Lee, but not all of it. She intended the children as a *mating gift*. She gave Drydel the children so he could present them as a wedding feast. The male enzyme prepares the female for mating. If the female accepts the gift and feeds, then her body becomes receptive to that male's sperm. Zillabar intended to mate with Drydel and begin laying her eggs. Your attack on the nest and the death of Drydel destroyed her carefully worked out plan. You have cost the Lady dearly."

"But what about Finn then? What did she intend with him?"

"Letting Finn Markham walk around with the blood-burn in his veins represents an act of extraordinary cruelty on her part. I suspect that even she did not realize her own unconscious purposes; by keeping him alive, by drinking his blood, she also made herself receptive to d'Vashti's advances. She knows she must breed soon. But she did speak truthfully to you when she told you that no antidote exists. Why should the Vampires expend any energy in helping their dinner avoid the plate?"

Sawyer seemed to shrivel at this news. The color drained from his face. He sagged where he stood.

Three-Dollar added perceptively, "But at least she spared him the fate she obviously planned for you, Sawyer. She would have had you bitten and infected, and you would have hosted her eggs. After they had hatched in your paralyzed, but still-living body, the grubs would have eaten their way out."

Sawyer barely heard him. "Stop trying to cheer me up," he said. "I don't think I want to hear any more."

But M'bele's eyes flashed with insight and sudden enthusiasm at this news. "I understand why you told me this," he said perceptively. "Humans deliberately created the Vampires. From our own flesh, correct? That suggests to me that we can also duplicate their immunity to the paralyzing enzyme."

Three-Dollar acknowledged this with a nod. "But do you understand that this knowledge would also represent a significant threat to the stability of the Regency? I swore an oath of loyalty when I put on the TimeBand; so did nearly three hundred others before me who wore this same TimeBand. This could bring down the Vampires and the Regency, because it would allow . . . humans to create a vaccine that would make it impossible for the Vampires to feed."

M'bele considered that fact. "My heart fills with sorrow at the prospect," he admitted. He allowed himself another two seconds of intense heartfelt sorrow, then headed for the door. "Now let's get that bitch in here and get a sample of her blood!"

Rights

□□□□□□□□□□□□□□□□□□□□□□□□□□□□□

Lee and M'bele brought a helmeted Zillabar down to the laboratory and secured her to a scanning table. The Vampire Queen cursed them with every step. M'bele ignored her. Lee glanced to Sawyer. "May I slap her?"

Despite himself Sawyer shook his head. "Not unless she gives you a reason. Unnecessary cruelty serves no purpose here."

Lee grinned. "We'll make a believer out of you yet."

M'bele had already begun working feverishly. Three-Dollar offered to help, but the dark man shook his head. "No thanks—I've got my own system here. I appreciate your assistance, but you'd only get in the way."

M'bele's fingers danced across the keyboards in front of him. He shouted commands at the computer. He peered anxiously at the readouts, and at one point he even leapt into the air, shouting in delight. "Gotcha! You little bastard!" He came down laughing. "Okay, now let's see if I can take you apart. Let's see what makes you click—"

A moment later he called Three-Dollar over. "Look." He pointed. "See these cells here? They look like T cells, but these structures have no relevant counterpart in the human genome. Let's see what happens if we construct a model of its effects." He added, "We've suspected for a long time that Vampire blood has antibodies in it that neutralize the effects of the blood-burn. The disease doesn't affect the Phaestor, but the aristocracy has never let any medical organization explore that anomaly. Now, perhaps—" He stopped, studied a pattern on a display, altered it, studied it again, performed other esoteric calculations, and watched as the display re-formed itself again. The process seemed agonizingly slow to Sawyer, who stood apart and watched.

M'bele's focus darted here and there across his work space. He danced through the images like a man possessed. "I don't know how long this will take," he called over his shoulder. "The whole problem could crack apart like an egg; it might resist like an anvil." Abruptly he turned and explained. "Look—if the Phaestor have a true symbiosis with the phage, I don't think I can save Finn. He'd need a Vampire's metabolism to survive the infection.

"On the other hand . . . if these modified T cells can actually neutralize the microorganism, then maybe . . . just maybe I can find a way to duplicate that process in Finn's body. If that doesn't work—we'll look to see what we can do to disable the paralyzing enzyme so that the effects of the phage become irrelevant. And if that doesn't work, we can always try linking their blood systems in a shared circulatory system and let Zillabar's liver clean Finn's blood. Hm. We'd have to run multiple cleansings in both directions, but maybe we can temporarily transmute Finn into a pseudo-Vampire. I have the intelligence engine processing the possibilities now. All three avenues have promise."

"You can't do this," Zillabar said abruptly. She had such venom in her voice that all four of the men stopped to look at her. "You may not take my blood without my permission. That violates my rights under the Charter of the Regency."

M'bele considered her objection for half a second. "Lawyers, Vampires—they only complain when someone else does the bloodsucking. The hell with you. Sue me."

"I claim my rights—under the Regency or under the Alliance of Life, whichever you serve."

Sawyer retorted quickly. "She has no rights. She took Finn's blood without permission—"

"You had a fair contract," said Zillabar from the scanning table. "You did not fulfill it."

"Yes, we did!"

"When you killed Drydel, you forfeited your claim!"

"We didn't kill Drydel. One of your own Dragons did that!"

"The Dragon traveled under your jurisdiction."

"Nobody controls a Dragon."

"I demand an arbiter!"

This brought silence to the room. The men looked at each other uncomfortably. None of them could imagine refusing her request. Even though the Vampire aristocracy had already betrayed Regency justice so many times as to turn the phrase into a hated mockery of itself, the respect for tradition still held true for those who remembered their own ideals.

M'bele turned to Three-Dollar. "You must assume the responsibility of arbitration here. Anything else would prove fatal to Finn Markham. A TimeBinder has the legal authority under the Regency, and presumably also under the Alliance."

Three-Dollar nodded. "You may have your arbitration," he said to Zillabar. For a moment his eyes glazed over as he consulted his memories and the hundreds of thousands of precedents stored within. Then he focused again. "After giving this matter considerable thought," he said, "I find in favor of Sawyer and Finn Markham. I have logged my decision and will register it with the Authority at the earliest opportunity." To M'bele he said, "You may proceed."

M'bele looked at Three-Dollar, visibly surprised. "You mean that? We can do this?"

"I can cite precedents extending as far back as ... *Shadow v. Kiki.* Drawing blood has many meanings under the law, but the antecedents of this case remain clear. Additionally, the benefit that may occur as a result of discovering a cure for the blood-burn justifies the discomfort given to an agency that may in fact serve as part of the cause of the disease. I can cite several relevant precedents for that decision as well, but it would please me just as much to establish a new one here that restricts the rights of the aristocracy in matters of public health. Go ahead, Doctor."

M'bele grinned and turned to his work. Once the process had begun, he turned quickly to Sawyer Markham, grasping him by the shoulders. "Listen, old friend. Many researchers even better than I have done a lot of research on the problem of the blood-burn; most of that research proved fatal to the patient. I can't promise that this will turn out any different, but at least I have access to information that no one else has ever had, and I have the engines here that can use that information wisely. I promise you, I'll do my best. Now, leave me to my work. This will take time."

Sawyer nodded. He broke away from M'bele and stepped over to Finn's still form. He touched his brother's arm and stood there for a moment, just looking at the ashen skin and sunken features of the dying man. Sawyer lowered his face to Finn's ear. "Listen to me, you son of a bitch," he whispered. "I need you. Don't you dare die on me. You promised me you would always stand by me. Don't you break your promise now—not now when we have a chance of making some *real* money."

Recriminations of Things Half-Asked

□□□□□□□□□□□□□□□□□□□□□□□□□□□□□□

Three-Dollar took Sawyer by the arm and led him away up the tunnel. "Lee will guard your interests, I promise, but leave the man alone to work. You've gotten what you came for. I broke my oath, three times over, to repay your debt. Now you need to get some rest—"

Realization came to Sawyer suddenly. "Wait a minute," he interrupted. "You didn't tell us everything. You left something out. You would not have broken your oath as easily as you did unless you had some larger reason. Don't for a minute think that you fooled me."

"I have no idea what you mean," Three-Dollar said blandly.

"Yes, you do." Sawyer straightened and looked the TimeBinder directly in the eye.

"I think your emotions have carried you a little far afield, tracker-man."

Sawyer shook off the accusation by acknowledging the truth of it. "All right, yes, I admit it. My emotions have carried me to some pretty wild extremes in the past few days. But my intelligence didn't go on vacation. I heard what you said—*and I heard what you didn't say.* I might not know everything about your Alliance and your oath and your history, but I do know when I hear a lie."

"I didn't lie to you."

"No, you didn't lie directly. But you lied by leaving something out. What did you leave out, you son of a bitch? Tell me the larger reason why you betrayed the Vampires. It has to do with the missing TimeBands, doesn't it?"

Three-Dollar's eyes looked suddenly old and weary. "We have no contract, Sawyer. You have fulfilled your responsibility. I have fulfilled mine to the best of my ability. You have no right to demand anything more than you've already received. I may have to destroy myself and this TimeBand—"

"Oh, no, you don't. You don't get away that easily. You'll need my help getting to the Gathering. That'll cost you the truth. So we do have a contract, after all. This time you pay first. Tell me! What did you leave out?"

"If I tell you," the TimeBinder asked, "then will you commit to serve the Alliance until the completion of the Gathering? Will you help me find out what happened to the missing TimeBand? And your brother too, if he lives?"

"That contract doesn't have balance. What else do I get out of it if I help you?"

"You'll have the opportunity to fulfill the rest of your vow. You'll get to help bring down the Regency."

Sawyer considered the offer. "I like that," he admitted. "I don't usually make deals without Finn's advice and consent, but considering the circumstances ... I guess I'll have to make an exception this time. Done." He held out a hand.

Three-Dollar shook it solemnly. "All right. I'll tell you what you want to know. But it won't make you happy. It certainly won't give you any peace of mind."

"Go on—"

"I wish I didn't have to reveal this to you. No TimeBinder should ever have to reveal this information to anyone, I find it that appalling, but this will tell you exactly why we *must* call a new Gathering."

William Three-Dollar cleared his throat and spoke with great reluctance. "I carry in my TimeBand one part of the knowing how to construct a Predator seed. Every TimeBand carries a separate piece of the puzzle, holographically encoded. Seven TimeBinders represent the critical mass necessary to restore the complete hologram. That means, Sawyer, that any seven out of thirteen TimeBinders could decode the knowledge of how to create a Predator."

Sawyer's eyes widened. He took a step back in horror. The fear crept up his spine. "My God. That explains why Zillabar wants to capture TimeBinders. She wants to build new predators. But why—?" He held up a hand. "Wait a minute. I've got it. She wants to renew the mandate of the Phaestor to protect the Regency, doesn't she?"

"Yes," agreed Three-Dollar. "I believe that you have accurately assessed the situation. Somehow Zillabar has discovered the secret of the TimeBands." He smiled gently. "Most people believe that we function only as a cultural memory, a curious, but otherwise unnecessary, access to past ages. We allow that fiction to maintain because the truth would not serve anyone. But our real purpose has a much darker flavor. We serve as custodians of the most dangerous knowledge humanity has ever possessed. We've deliberately kept ourselves to different worlds to make it difficult for anyone to reassemble the knowledge, even ourselves. But now"—he spread his hands widely in regret—"this Gathering will give us the opportunity to destroy this knowledge once and for all—or to destroy the Regency instead."

"I vote for the latter," said Sawyer glibly.

"You don't get a vote," Three-Dollar reprimanded him. "Only the TimeBinders do. We will probably decide to destroy the TimeBands altogether. At least I see no *other* solution."

The TimeBinder strode away from Sawyer, looking like a man facing a death sentence. For the first time Sawyer found himself feeling *sorry* for him.

Starport Blues

▢▢▢▢▢▢▢▢▢▢▢▢▢▢▢▢▢▢▢▢▢▢▢▢▢▢▢▢▢▢

The pinpoint glare of Burihatin's primary cast an actinic light sideways across the harsh terrain of Dupa's rocky flats. The landscape looked like a desert with scattered patches of tundra. The eastern half of the sky blazed.

Later in the day the whole dome of the firmament would ache with the blue blaze of the sun. Dupa had too many faces, too many seasons, and too damn many kinds of weather to suit Star-Captain Neena Linn-Campbell's tastes.

Clad in her crisp black uniform and looking like the Angel of Death, she came striding out of the glare of dawn and into the offices of the starport Adjutant, wearing an expression of determination that served as its own warning. Following in her wake came Ota, *The Lady MacBeth*'s bioform First Officer, carrying a thick sheaf of customs and security documents. Following behind Ota came the starship's Chief Engineer, Gito, the high-gravity dwarf. And behind him, at a leisurely pace, came the (recently retired) Arbiter of Thoska-Roole, Justice Godfrey Daniels Harry Mertz.

The Assistant Executive Aide to the Office of the Senior Secretary to the Vice-Adjutant of the Burihatin-14 starport wore a nondescript gray suit and a matching expression. He sat behind a high desk on a high dais and looked down his long nose at the petite form of Neena Linn-Campbell. He had his multicolored hair brushed back and then up so that it curled forward over the crown of his head. A bright gold chain hung from one gaudy earring, wrapped itself several times around his neck, then reached back up to connect to the other gaudy earring. All in all he presented himself as a startling apparition.

Neena Linn-Campbell didn't even blink. She nodded to Gito, who grabbed her by the ankles and lifted her up to stand on his shoulders. She reached across the desk, grabbed the Assistant Executive Aide to the Office of the Senior Secretary to the Vice-Adjutant by the neck chains, and yanked him forward—*hard*—shoving the barrel of her needle-gun firmly up his left nostril.

She looked him straight in the eye and said, "Now, tell it to me again, this time face-to-face. We must have had a faulty communication channel, because it sounded like you said that no cargo could leave this planet until the Dragon Lord had inspected it."

"*Fnrkle,*" replied the Assistant Executive Aide to the

Office of the Senior Secretary to the Vice-Adjutant of the
Burihatin-14 starport.

"I didn't understand that," said Star-Captain
Campbell. "It sounded like you said *'fnrkle'* this time."
She nodded to Ota, and the LIX-class bioform carefully
placed the entire sheaf of documents and clearances on
the desk of the Assistant Executive Aide to the Office of
the Senior Secretary to the Vice-Adjutant where he could
just barely see it over the end of Captain Campbell's
needle-gun.

"G'flrkn'igl," he said.

"I see," said Captain Campbell. "So may I assume,
then, that you spoke in error before?" She shoved the
weapon farther up the man's left nostril, heedless of the
high cost of reconstructive surgery here in Dupa's
outerland.

The man held his delicately manicured hands high
in the air, helpless. He couldn't nod, he couldn't speak,
and he couldn't even successfully faint.

"I need you to stamp these papers," Linn-Campbell
said.

"Gnrsh."

"I didn't understand you clearly. Did you say 'yes-
gnrsh' or 'no-*gnrsh*?' Think clearly before you speak. A
great deal depends on your answer—"

At that moment a door in the back wall of the office
popped open, and a short, round man, with a much less
flamboyant appearance, came waddling out, beaming and
bustling with an air of enthusiasm and efficiency.
"Neena," he called jovially. "It delights me to see you
again. As always, you look beautiful. Please do come into
my office and let me offer you some chocolate." He
glanced at the man behind the desk and remarked,
"Goodness, that looks uncomfortable. Fergle, do take that
stupid thing out of your nose before you hurt yourself.
Neena, come in, come in."

"It thrills me to see you again too, Puckie,"
Campbell muttered, reholstering her weapon. Gito lowered her to the ground, and the whole party followed her
into the round man's office.

"All right," she said. "How long? Three days? Five?"

Puckie held up his hands. "Let's attend to first things first. Oh—and in the future, please have a little more care how you treat my associates. Fnorley has only just joined this division and has very little experience with methods as direct as yours." He added politely, "Do you want cream or butter in your chocolate?"

"Save the chocolate. It makes Ota's face break out. And besides, I know where you get your syrup. I wouldn't drink that crap if you promised me immortality. It took me a year to get the taste out of my mind last time. Why don't you let *me* supply you?"

"Ah, would that I could—" Puckie said, spreading his hands wide. "But the aristocracy controls the trade of luxury beans—as they control everything around here. All right, at least I've tried to put on the appearance of manners. Someday you'll surprise me and respond with courtesy and I'll drop dead of a heart attack."

"Let's hope that such an event occurs soon, Puckie. Perhaps your successor will realize that the commerce of this port sustains the economy of this world. I have pfingle eggs in a warehouse here, getting older by the minute."

Puckie held up a hand. "I wish I could step outside this minute and watch you and your ship ascend into the sky—never to return. You always bring me more problems than you resolve. But this time, dear lady, I believe that neither of us can resolve this particular dilemma. The Dragon Lord has instructed my superiors that he will scourge this starport if he has to—and he will certainly do it if we disregard his instructions to lock everything down. Dupa remains under a complete state of emergency. Surely you've heard what's happened?"

"The problems of Vampires don't concern me," Neena Linn-Campbell said. She knew what events Puckie referred to—the kidnapping of Zillabar—and furthermore, she had enjoyed hearing not only the news of the Vampire Queen's disgrace, but also a great deal of additional salacious gossip circulating through the underlife of the port, with much more enthusiasm than considered appropriate for an officer of her rank. To say that Captain Campbell despised the Lady Zillabar would demonstrate an insufficiency of language comparable to calling the Dragon Lord's breath foul smelling.

"Actually," corrected Puckie, "the problems of Vampires do concern you. Until the Dragon Lord locates the Lady Zillabar, no ship will leave this field. If any ship attempts to flee the port, he'll have it blasted from the sky. You my, if you wish, choose to ignore this warning, and I will regretfully place roses on your grave—assuming that we can find any ̣ ̣es of you big enough to bury. I would not recommena that you try." He extended his hand graciously. Captain Campbell did not take it. "In the meantime I suggest that you enjoy the sights of Dupa. I know of many fascinating tours—up the Yangle River, perhaps, to see the flowering islands; or maybe you would appreciate two weeks of touring the black-trees on the back of a trained fawn, always an exciting journey; but I think you should try my personal favorite, an excursion to Dupa's Warts—"

"Fold it, Puckie," Captain Campbell said. "Who do I see about getting an exception? And how large a bribe will I need to offer?"

"You'd have to see the Dragon Lord," Puckie replied blandly. "But the last three freebooters who tried . . . the Dragon Lord ate them." His expression darkened in regret. "Perhaps if you had a Regency Crest or a Spacer's Guild Insignia, he might consider advancing the date of inspection for your vessel, but I doubt that—"

Puckie should have known better than to suggest this latter course. After all, he had known Neena Linn-Campbell long enough to have a clear sense of her behavior. Indeed, he had even provided assistance to her during the notorious brinewood affair.[6]

Fortunately, Ota and Gito and Harry Mertz finally proved able to pull a furious Captain Campbell off his throat and out of his office before she inflicted injuries on the hapless little man severe enough to require serious medical attention and a federal warrant for her arrest.

---

[6]For details, see *Under the Eye of God*.

"If you need anything else . . . ," he managed to gasp, but the door had already irised shut after them. Puckie rubbed his throat painfully and considered taking an early retirement. This job no longer provided as much fun as he had originally believed it would.

Discovery

□□□□□□□□□□□□□□□□□□□□□□□□□□□□□

Warrior-lizards of all castes had spread out across the surface of Dupa. They ranged from the ice caverns of the storm-wracked poles, to the rocky headlands, where the basalt underpinnings broke through the granite crusts of the continents. They prowled the desert tundra and made desperate feints into the towering blacktrees. They probed the oceans with sonar bombs, bio-searched the orbiting stations three times over, and even—despite their own better judgment—deep-scanned the acid tunnels of Salut Minoh.

On the third day of the search, one of the tunnels of Salut Minoh collapsed disastrously, triggering cave-ins throughout the historic complex of caverns. The unexpected series of implosions instantly killed a squad of twenty Black Destroyers and imprisoned another thirty beyond any hope of rescue. Nevertheless, additional units rushed immediately to the area—not in any vain attempt to save their fallen comrades, but in a larger effort to determine if the Lady Zillabar's landing craft lay buried beneath the megatons of rock.

Unfortunately for Sawyer's carefully crafted plan, one of the units heading toward the tunnel disaster accidentally drifted off course and flew directly over Little Crater Wreak, the smallest of three brine-filled dimples in the rocky desert south of the Lesser Blacktree Spiral. While the Dragons did not expect to find any evidence of the abandoned shuttleboat this far from any major blacktree spine, they had routinely left their scanning devices running. So when the main display beeped and registered a large unaccountable mass of alloyed metal, the pilot of the sky-sled decided to investigate. He swung the craft around for another pass over Little Crater Wreak.

Although he did not believe the scanners had detected anything more unusual than a minor masscon anomaly, the pilot still felt that caution represented the better part of survival. This particular act of survival eventually gained him a bonus, a promotion, and a chance at the semiannual mating games.[7]

Sawyer Markham had not expected the shuttleboat to remain undiscovered for long. Had he known how quickly the Dragons had located it—whether by luck or by intention—he would have felt extremely chagrined. However, his remorse would not have lasted long, because the next part of his plan went off exactly as he had expected. Both the shuttleboat and the craft attempting to lift it out of the briny Wreak exploded with a very satisfying flash and fury.

When the underlings finally dared to relay this news to the offices of the Dragon Lord, they discovered that the destruction of the landing craft and lifting sled had both occurred as the *smaller* explosions of the day. Fortunately, the bearers of this bad news retained enough presence of mind to send in their dispatches anonymously. Several of them actually survived the resultant pogrom.

---

[7]Unfortunately for the lucky pilot, when he reached the mating games, he overestimated both his skill and his luck. He miscalculated in the second round of combat with the neural whip-sling, earning himself respectful applause from the audience and a beautiful burial site.

The Choice

▭▭▭▭▭▭▭▭▭▭▭▭▭▭▭▭▭▭▭▭▭▭▭▭▭▭▭▭▭

M'bele brought Sawyer back to the chamber in the blacktree where Finn lay unconscious, still caught in a state of suspended metabolic process. Sawyer started to go over to his brother, but M'bele held him back. "Wait," he said. "I have to talk to you."

"You can't help him," Sawyer guessed. "Right?"

M'bele frowned. "If you already know what I have to say, then why should I bother saying it?"

"I apologize," said Sawyer. "I'll shut up." He shut.

"I think I may have something," M'bele said. "It will require the transmutation of your brother's metabolism. The intelligence engine thinks this will work. All of the models that we've run show that it *should* work. But I have never placed my faith totally in models, because if you've accidentally left something out of the model, then it can't function as an accurate representation of the situation, can it? And the result that it predicts will have no relation to the problem you want to solve."

"Would you translate that into my language, please?" Sawyer said drily.

"I have no way to test this," M'bele said grimly. "I have no way to prove that this will work. I think it will work, but I can't guarantee it. If I've made a mistake in my thinking, it might very well kill him. You do realize that, don't you?"

Sawyer nodded. "We've always had that possibility hanging over our heads. If we don't try this, he'll die anyway."

"Yes, but you need to understand something else. If he survives, he will probably begin demonstrating certain unsavory aspects of Phaestor behavior, especially in

149

the area of diet. He may have cravings for certain foods—"

"He'll turn into a Vampire?"

"I don't know," M'bele admitted. "Maybe. Maybe not. And maybe after he stabilizes, we can begin bringing him back. I have no idea."

"So I have to choose between death and Vampirism for Finn, right?"

M'bele nodded unhappily.

Sawyer felt his stomach knotting painfully. "Nothing you say offers me any certainty." He glanced up at M'bele. "Would you use this treatment on your daughter?"

M'bele's eyes shaded with pain. "I would not have let my daughter live this long under such a death sentence. I would not have subjected her to the suffering that you have inflicted on Finn in your desperate attempts to save him. I hope he'll forgive you someday. The question here has nothing to do with me, Sawyer Markham, or with Nyota. It has to do with the life you want to return to Finn. Will he thank you for this life or curse you for it? Do you want to save him for himself, or for yourself? You regard his life as too precious to lose— but what do you think he would say if he could speak to you now? What would he choose for you if you lay on that table and he stood here? You need to put aside your own desperate hungers here."

"You think I should let him die?"

"No. I didn't say that. If he survives, his blood may provide a universal serum for the blood-burn. If he survives, he could serve all humanity as a healer. But if he survives, his life may also have a disproportionate amount of pain and difficulty because of his condition."

Sawyer hung his head. "Almost—I almost let him go. I almost came to the edge of the thought that I should release him peacefully. And then you said that last thing. About healing. And I realized that I have a larger duty that goes beyond what happens to Finn and myself. You see . . ." Sawyer's voice caught as he admitted it; he found it embarrassing. ". . . I've made a new deal with Three-Dollar. I've . . . promised to serve the Alliance of

Life. And because I made the deal on behalf of Finn and myself, I have to choose to return Finn to life." He looked deep into M'bele's eyes. "So let's stop wasting time and do it."

M'bele nodded in agreement. "Good. I thought you would see that possibility." He grinned. "I hoped you would make that choice."

"Really?"

M'bele grinned. "Of course. I want to see if this will actually work. And I'd rather have it fail on one of you two than on someone I really care about. You don't think I've spent all this time and effort because I like you two, do you? And besides, you now owe me five hundred thousand caseys. I have a better chance of collecting if Finn survives."

"You said three hundred thousand before—!"

"You don't think I give my medical services away for free, do you? Finn's treatment will cost you heavily— even with your usual courtesy discount."

Sawyer followed M'bele over to his workstation. "What courtesy discount?" he demanded. "You haven't shown us any courtesy at all. You never do."

"I didn't kill you on sight, did I?" M'bele tapped in his password and authorized the intelligence engine to begin the transmutation of Finn Markham.

"Hah! You call *that* courtesy?"

"Hell, in this neighborhood, Sawyer, most people would call that downright affectionate." He stepped away from the console. "There," he said. "We've made the commitment. Now ... we wait."

"For how long?"

"For as long as it takes. Until he dies—or until he gets up from that table and punches you in the face."

"I wouldn't mind that," Sawyer said. He crossed to the table and put his hand on Finn's cold arm. "At least he'd do it out of love—"

No Time for Sorrow

CCCCCCCCCCCCCCCCCCCCCCCCCCC

After two days had passed, Finn's condition remained unimproved. Despite M'bele's constant attention and repeated treatments in which his blood flowed through Zillabar's liver and then back again, the tracker's condition stayed the same. M'bele looked sleepless and frustrated. He even admitted aloud how mystified he felt. "I don't know," he said. "It should have worked by now. Maybe Finn's condition has deteriorated worse than we realized. Maybe I've done something wrong. I don't know what else to do."

Sawyer had to remind the dark man of his own instructions. "Remember? You said we had to wait—until he dies, or until he gets up off the table. Let's just wait."

"That presents a problem. We can't stay here much longer," M'bele said. "The Dragons will find us if we do. They have some very sophisticated equipment for searching the jungle. I'd rather move him now than later."

Three-Dollar spoke up then. "We should decamp then. Besides, Sawyer has a debt to pay, and you don't need his assistance. I do." To the tracker he said, "We must locate the TimeBand. Prove to me that you have the tracking skills you claim. Find the missing TimeBand. Take Lee with you. If you get to starport, ask an Informant. The rebellion uses Informants a lot. I'll give you my passwords."

"I don't want to leave Finn."

"You can't help him by standing around. You can help all of us—including yourself—by finding that missing TimeBand."

Sawyer started to shake his head, but M'bele

grabbed his arm. "Listen. We have to assume that you've already compromised this tree house—"

"I promise you, we didn't."

"Do you want to bet Finn's life on it?"

Sawyer hesitated. "All right. I see your point."

"Thank you. Now listen up. I've got robots to move my equipment; the poppet can carry the rest of us to a more secure location; and I'll have the spider-things re-string the railroad. Don't worry, this will work. I've always followed the teachings of Saint Rah."

"Eh?"

"Keep prepared to move fast—you'll have to at least three times in your life." M'bele turned to Three-Dollar. "Get Finn back into that medical casket, and put him on maintenance. Use the program in the red workstation. I'll get Nyota dressed. Sawyer, you and Lee should leave immediately. The spider-things will take you back to the wart if you want to recall your sled. Otherwise, they can take you almost anywhere else in the forest. You have no idea how widely the railroad reaches."

"Let me say good-bye to Finn, first."

"You say more good-byes than anybody I know, Sawyer," grumbled Lee.

"I've never lost a brother before," Sawyer snapped right back. "Forgive me if I don't know how to do it right."

Sawyer's words struck home. Lee had lost over two thousand brothers. His expression crumpled. "I apologize, tracker. Your loss may not have the same weight of numbers as mine, but the pain of it must feel every bit as large to you. I lost all of my family; you risk losing all of yours. In that we share the same experience. You have my sympathies."

"Thanks," grunted Sawyer. "Maybe we can both learn from each other." He crossed to the medical cabinet again and spoke softly to his unconscious older brother. "Listen, big bro', I know you can hear me. Get up off your lazy butt and help me, will you? I signed a contract and I can't do it alone." He gave Finn a soft, affectionate punch on the arm and added very softly, "Besides . . . I love you." Then he walked out the tunnel after Lee.

M'bele watched them go with a sad expression on his face. He bent close to Finn and began whispering in the big man's ear. "Listen to me, you big stupid meatball. Listen up and listen good—I know you can hear me. You have to get off this table, and you'd better do it damn quick, so you can start paying me what you owe me."

Now M'bele's voice became even more intense. "Do you think Sawyer will survive on his own? Do you think he can make it yet without you? If you die, your little brother will probably follow right behind you knocking on the gates of hell. That fool will do something to get himself killed damn quick without you around. Do you want that to happen? I don't think you do.

"So pay attention, and I'll tell you what you have to do. Get your flamethrower. You know the one I mean. Yeah, you got it. Get your flamethrower. Unlock the safeties. Arm that sucker. Now I want you to start in your left arm and work your way through every vein and artery of your body, torching the virus wherever you find it, blasting away the enzymes. Just clean out everything that doesn't have your name stenciled on the ID plate. Up and down the arteries, Finn, in and out of all the veins. Don't forget to clean behind your capillaries. Get in there and scourge the bloodstream. Yeah, I know that you don't like hard work, but this work satisfies you. The more you do it, the better it feels. Good, good—keep it up, Finn—"

The big man on the table hadn't moved at all, but M'bele paid that no mind. He spoke to Finn Markham as if coaching an athlete on the field. He gave him detailed instructions, a road map to every part of his body. He detailed the trip, and he told Finn where to go and what to do to burn out the invading phages. "You know how to do this, Finn—I've given you the Vampire weapon. Use it. And don't worry about running out of fuel. Use your anger. Your anger will keep you going forever. Your anger will make you invincible in this battle. Keep it up, Finn, keep it up."

When he finally straightened and turned around, he

realized that William Three-Dollar, the TimeBinder, stood directly behind him, watching him curiously.

M'bele shrugged. "I'll use whatever I need to use. Even sympathetic magic. I'll use every goddamn brand of medicine I have. If I have to rattle beads and feathers over him and dance around a bonfire stark naked while chanting prayers to the great god Ghu, I'll do it. I'll find something that'll work . . . unless this bastard really does want to die."

The Dragon's Net

◻◻◻◻◻◻◻◻◻◻◻◻◻◻◻◻◻◻◻◻◻◻◻◻◻◻

After two days of full self-expression, most of the Dragon Lord's anger had finally begun to subside along with the related death tolls. While his rage had created no small amount of consternation among those who served him, it also served to inspire his (surviving) troops to an extraordinary level of diligence. And as an ancillary benefit, cooperation among the local authorities as well as among the native civilian population increased dramatically.

Nevertheless, Zillabar's whereabouts still remained unknown.

The discovery of the landing boat at Little Crater Wreak had at least provided some clue as to where the kidnappers might have taken Zillabar. Assuming the kidnappers had used the shuttle's antigrav sled for their escape, they could not have gone more than fifteen hundred klicks in any direction from Little Crater Wreak. South of the Wreak lay only desert; north and west, the blacktree forest sprawled across the planet's equator.

The Dragon Lord paced around his quarters for a bit, thinking this out. He did not think they would have gone the full range of the sled. Probably they had landed somewhere within the fifteen-hundred-kilometer radius.

He studied the wall-sized map. A scattering of small settlements lay haphazardly across the southern plains, none of them large enough to present a serious candidate for inspection, but—he didn't dare overlook any possibility. He wondered about that. Perhaps the rebellion had somehow established a base in some tunnel complex?

No. He didn't see how they could have constructed anything bigger than a pig-wallow without the Regency's satellite scanners noticing the ground activity. Still . . . the conditions at most of those outposts remained so primitive that they seemed the last place anyone would look. Therefore, he'd have to spend valuable time and resources on a full search of each and every encampment out there—seventeen villages and one hundred twenty-three individual farms. How many more of these stupid humans would his men have to kill? He didn't mind the killing, of course, but the Vampires might find it politically difficult. Hmm. In that case he might just as well have them all killed and claim that the Vampires gave the orders. The thought made him smile—every death makes some carrion-feeder happy, and many deaths make a Dragon Lord ecstatic.

He grunted in satisfaction and turned his attention to the blacktree sprawl.

His hunting instinct told him that the jungle represented an impenetrable problem—not just for the hunter, but for the prey as well. He studied the display without expression, seeking out features within the great dark mass. If the rebels had headed simply for a set of coordinates in the forest, then the Dragon Guard would have to search every kilometer of jungle, scanning for anomalies.

On the other hand, if they had headed toward some landmark . . . then his troops could focus their search on high-probability areas. Unfortunately, the blacktree forest contained very few landmarks, just a scattering of warts, a few lakes, and not much else. Even the widest rivers remained hidden beneath the pervasive blue canopy of the trees.

The warts.

The Dragon Lord extended one long claw and

touched the dimensional representation of a small towering monolith. Within the range of the sled, only seven warts stood out, and four of them lay at the far northwestern edge of the sky-sled's range. While he wouldn't rule those out, most likely the sled would have headed toward one of the other three, all of which stood significantly closer to Little Crater Wreak.

Hmm.

How far from a wart could a human travel?

He expanded the image of the warts and studied them thoughtfully.

The warts provided access to the jungle canopy. From there . . . the Dragon Lord had the intelligence to recognize that he could not make any estimation at all of what might lie beneath the trees. Nevertheless, he could arrange for squads of Raptors to visit each of the warts and explore them thoroughly. If they found evidence of a landing, they would have a new center for their search.

Yes. He turned away from the map and began hissing orders. His aides scurried to obey. He smiled inwardly. He rather enjoyed the increase in efficiency that occurred every time he allowed the free expression of his rage. He'd have to do it more often—if he could figure out a way to keep the casualty rate at a sustainable level. That might require some thought.

In the meantime he hoped that the rebels had provided the Lady Zillabar with a perfectly dreadful time. It didn't matter to him. She deserved it. She'd earned it fairly. And whatever political realignment eventually came of this event, the Dragons would benefit either way. Whether required to extract revenge on the perpetrators or to provide increased security for a host of fearful Vampires, the Dragons would still end up holding more power in the Regency than ever before. The Dragon Lord had actually begun to appreciate the opportunities provided by this rebellion. He wondered how long he could keep his troops from locating her. . . .

A small red lizard came scampering into the room excitedly. It saluted, bowed, and flung itself to the floor at the Dragon Lord's feet. "I have great news, Your Excellency. This will please you immensely!"

"Someone has found Zillabar?" He tried to hide his displeasure.

"No, sir. Even better than that! We've found a large cache of pfingle eggs in a warehouse at the northern starport. You will want to inspect them immediately, won't you, sir?"

"Why, yes ... I will. What a thoughtful gesture. Lead me to this bounty immediately—"

Tracking

□□□□□□□□□□□□□□□□□□□□□□□□□□□□

Under cover of dawn M'bele's antigrav sled came out of the forest and onto the open plains below the northern slopes of Mount Whillma, a long-dormant volcano whose tinder cone reached high enough into the sky to wear a mantle of white snow all year round.

Sawyer Markham and Lee-1169 drove the airboat around the southern foothills of the volcano and finally headed up into a river-carved canyon toward a distinctive rocky bluff called the Devil's Penis. From there they abandoned the course of the river and struck out westward, roller-coastering over a series of jagged escarpments that thrust upward like knife blades. Finally they dove down into the steepest of canyons and followed south along its narrow zigzag course until its red walls fell away to either side and it opened onto the empty marshlands on the northern edge of the Krislov Gulf.

Avoiding the open water—antigrav fields dissipate badly over large bodies of water—they turned west again until they came to the Devil's *Other* Penis, striking upward from a rocky patch at the southernmost edge of a small blacktree tangle. From there they headed northwest until they came to the Somewhere River, a great muddy sluice of water, wide, sluggish, and black. They followed the river northward, up into the rolling plains of the Northern Wasteland. When they came to the shallow delta where Twisted River fed into Somewhere, they veered off in a northeastern direction and followed Twisted River all the way up into Twisted River Canyon at the base of the Great Stone Glacier, a black basaltic outcropping that stretched northward for several hundred kilometers.

The dark walls of Twisted River Canyon closed around them uncomfortably. Beneath them the deep waters rushed and tumbled past them in a broken southward course, often with patches of rough-looking white water punctuating placid open stretches and fast-moving narrows. The sky-boat wobbled and slid precariously above the coursing foam, and Sawyer had a difficult time keeping it steady while he tried to follow the sharp twists and turns of the canyon. Twisted River Canyon enjoyed no small amount of fame for the haphazard way it wound itself downward through the Great Stone Glacier.

Up until this point Sawyer and Lee had seen little sign of human habitation anywhere in their travels. Indeed, they had planned their course so as to deliberately avoid all settlements and the allied risk of calling attention to themselves. Now, however, as they came upward through the canyon, they began seeing small encampments here and there—scattered stone bungalows, desperate-looking farms clutching at steep slopes, and once even a small fishing village. Some of the people glanced up at them. No one waved. Most turned away. Around here sky-boats often meant Dragons or Vampires. They could not expect a friendly reception if they landed—only distrust and skepticism.

At last they came to a place where the Twisted River widened into a dark, brooding lake. Sawyer aimed the airboat high and accelerated ferociously across the lake, applying power until the levitators began whining and threatening to stall. The boat skipped and slid above the water like an ice cube on a hot metal surface. Lee screamed once in protest, but Sawyer ignored him and concentrated on steering the unruly boat with short, vicious kicks of power. They coasted nervously toward the opposite side where a scattering of ruined buildings stood. The clone-brother swore quietly and glared at him until Sawyer brought the boat safely over land again. The difference in control became immediately obvious and both men relaxed—but only Sawyer grinned. Lee went silent and resentful.

Sawyer brought the airboat around, and they circled the shattered compound for several moments. From the air the settlement revealed little. Whatever destruction had happened here, the events had not occurred recently, but neither had they occurred in the distant past. The scorch marks on the walls still looked fresh; the rubble of the fallen buildings had still not softened. But no bodies lay on the ground either.

"No TimeBinder lives here now," said Sawyer. He brought the boat down in an easy descent, parking it gently in front of the ruined villa. He grunted in annoyance, then fished around behind himself for a portable scanning unit. Pulling it out, he powered it up with a dejected expression on his face. "I don't expect to find anything here," he said, and climbed down out of the sky-boat. Lee followed him, carrying one of the cannons they had liberated from the Elite Dragon Guard.

Blowing out his cheeks in disgust, Sawyer explored the entire villa. Whoever had done this had known their business well. The attack had come from several directions simultaneously. Someone had snuck up on this place under cover of night, surrounded it, seized it quickly, searched it methodically and thoroughly, then blasted it when they didn't find what they sought. At least ... it looked that way to him.

The fact that no bodies lay anywhere in the compound could mean one of two things: The attackers had taken everyone prisoner—or the dwellers in this compound had already evacuated when the attack occurred. Sawyer hoped for the latter. He and Lee walked back to the antigrav sled glumly. They had found exactly what they had expected to find. Nothing.

"But we do know one thing," Sawyer said. "The TimeBand survived. Three-Dollar can feel its presence somewhere on the planet. That means that somebody escaped." He turned around slowly, surveying the surrounding terrain. "How did they do it?" he asked of no one in particular. "How did they do it?"

"How would you do it?" Lee asked.

"I don't know—it would depend on where I most expected the attack to come from. But I wouldn't do the obvious."

Sawyer walked away from the ruin and climbed up onto a small hill to give himself a better vantage point. To the northeast the land sloped upward steeply. To the northwest Twisted River tumbled down out of the canyon. To the east lay a gentle downhill slope and a narrow inlet of water. He motioned to Lee, and they both headed back to the sky-boat.

A moment later they lifted up into the air, swung the boat around, and headed out toward the hidden neck of water. Almost immediately, he spotted it. "There," said Sawyer. He brought the sled down on the rocky shore of the lake near a small deserted pier. No other structure stood nearby.

"You think they had a boat hidden here?" Lee asked.

"It certainly looks that way," Sawyer said thoughtfully. He turned around slowly, then pointed at the hill behind them. "Look at that—" He began trudging up the slope toward a small opening cut into the rock. Lee followed quickly. Sawyer shone his light into the tunnel. It headed back in the direction of the ruined villa.

"A secret passage?" said Lee.

"If we can discover it this easily, it doesn't seem like much of a secret, does it?" Sawyer asked. He headed back down the hill to the pier. "If you had a boat hidden here, where could you go with it? Into the lake? No. Anyone could see you on the lake. So you'd have to follow this inlet—but to where? It looks like a dead end to me."

He clucked his tongue thoughtfully. A TimeBinder would not make stupid mistakes. A Dragon might assume that all humans lacked the intellectual range of Vampires—but neither would a Dragon realize that a TimeBinder had access to six thousand years of human memories. No, he couldn't believe that the Dragons had caught the TimeBinder unaware.

He tried to imagine what he might have done in the same situation.

He tried to imagine himself a TimeBinder, tried to envision all the memories that he would have, as clearly as if he had experienced the events himself—tried to extrapolate the wisdom that such memories would comprise.

He couldn't do it.

He couldn't imagine what such a state of mind might feel like.

It bothered him.

He'd never thought about TimeBinders before. Perhaps he should have. That thing that Three-Dollar had said—about naming Sawyer as his heir—those words still rattled around in his memory, like some annoying insect making scraping sounds in the dark.

Sawyer began to play with the idea, standing in it as a possibility.

If you had no weapon except the memories of six thousand years, you still had the advantage of knowledge. Indeed, it would change your whole way of thinking so dramatically, that . . . the way you thought would appear as something alien to everyone who didn't think the same way—and that would mean everyone, because only thirteen TimeBands existed.

Sawyer realized it like a flash. The importance lay in the knowledge—in the 'Band. The person of the 'Binder has no relevance. A TimeBinder would choose death rather than allow the TimeBand to fall into the wrong hands. The answer seemed immediately obvious to him—the same answer would not occur to a squad of shortsighted Dragons ordered to bring back the 'Binder.

The 'Binder gives up his identity when he first puts on the TimeBand. He sacrifices his personal past in order to carry the cultural past. The TimeBand exists as the true TimeBinder. It speaks through the body of the person wearing it. Sawyer thought about that for a long moment. Putting on the TimeBand must produce an extraordinary transformation in the wearer. He becomes a different kind of human. If the identity of the individual disappears, then so would all of his concerns about personal survival.

Knowing that the Vampires intended to kill *any* wearer of the TimeBand, the TimeBinder would have realized that he must hide the 'Band to keep it safe. Perhaps he had taken it off and sent it away. Then he could have put on a decoy TimeBand and gone willingly with the Dragons. This would have allowed the bearer of the real TimeBand an opportunity to escape. However long it would take the Vampires to realize that they did not have the real 'Band, that same length of time would allow the carrier of the TimeBand to disappear almost anywhere on the planet.

Sawyer sucked at his teeth as he considered the idea. The more he thought about it, the more logical it seemed. The TimeBinder couldn't hide. The TimeBand could. Something had definitely happened to the TimeBinder; they couldn't know what; but the TimeBand had just as certainly taken a different course.

Sawyer turned to Lee. "Forget the boat dock. They put it here as a decoy. Whoever escaped did not go downriver to the nearest settlement. If anyone escaped from here, they went over the mountain to starport. They went the hard way."

Lee-1169 frowned and shook his head. He didn't see it. Sawyer nodded at him. "Yes."

"Why? Why do you think so?"

"Because I do. I'd do it under the same circumstances, and I have to assume that the TimeBinder has at least as much intelligence as I do." He headed down the slope toward the waiting antigrav sled. "Come on. Let's go to starport."

Pfingle Eggs

∎∎∎∎∎∎∎∎∎∎∎∎∎∎∎∎∎∎∎∎∎∎∎∎∎∎∎∎∎∎

Imagine:
   A warehouse.
   A high-security warehouse.
   A self-destruct, high-security warehouse.
   A self-destruct, high-security warehouse containing thirty-three metric tons of industrial-grade pfingle eggs.
   Thirty-day pfingle eggs.
   Rapidly incubating, thirty-day pfingle eggs.
   A warehouse full of pfingle eggs, sealed for inspection by the High Lord of the Elite Dragon Guards of the Regency of Terra in the Palethetic Cluster.
   A self-destruct, high-security warehouse containing thirty-three metric tons of rapidly incubating, thirty-day, industrial-grade pfingle eggs that belonged to Star-Captain Neena Linn-Campbell, of the freebooter vessel, *The Lady MacBeth*, pride and property of the Shakespeare Corporation, duly registered on forty-three worlds of the Palethetic Cluster.
   A sealed warehouse of pfingle eggs, representing a potential gross income of five million caseys if delivered to the right market before hatching.[8]

---

[8]Connoisseurs rate pfingle eggs by size, by species, by grade, and by how many days until hatching. Pfingle eggs enjoy considerable immunity to cold; refrigeration only delays hatching, it does not prevent it.
   Most gourmands prefer their pfingle eggs as ripe as possible; but at the same time most gourmands also consider it very bad luck to remain in the proximity of pfingle eggs when they hatch. In the interests of safety, most experts recommend the rapid consumption (or destruction) of any egg rated at less than ten days. Most (surviving) governments require the destruction of pfingle eggs on the fifth day before hatching.
   This requires some explanation. Pfingles travel in swarms. Large swarms. On their home planet the natives often use swarms of pfingles as war weapons, secretly

If deliverable.

The bulk of the warehouse sat deep in the ground, cut from the rock and layered over with three meters of rehardened stone. Star-Captain Neena Linn-Campbell arrived at the entrance like a flaming Valkyrie. She came striding angrily across the northside supervisory catwalk and into the office that overlooked the cavernous interior of the underground chamber. Half the crew of *The Lady MacBeth* came running after her, not certain whether they would have to join the fight or protect another poor innocent from the Captain's wrath—

Captain Campbell slammed the doors of the office open and advanced furiously on Robin. The android woman stood in charge of cargo handling; only moments before she had sent an anguished call to Captain Campbell. Now, despite her training, she stood trembling with uncertainty—like something caught between two opposing forces of nature.

"What do you mean?" Neena Linn-Campbell demanded ferociously. "What do you mean—'We have Dragons in the pfingles'!"

Helpless to speak, somehow Robin managed to point to the window of the office. Captain Campbell crossed to the window and looked down. "Oh my dear Lady of the Skies!"

Not just Dragons—but *the Dragon Lord himself*!

Down below, the huge green warrior-lizard strode hungrily up and down the aisles, sniffing the cases and

---

smuggling ripe eggs into their enemy's most valuable cities and installations. Some terraformers use industrial-grade pfingles for clearing continents.

Despite this, pfingle eggs enjoy a widespread popularity throughout the Cluster. With proper handling and preparation, a talented cook can prepare pfingle eggs in any of a thousand different delightful ways, including raw pfingle pie, pfingle soufflé, poached pfingle, roast pfingle stew, and even candied pfingles. Indeed, throughout the Cluster, millions of people consider unhatched pfingle eggs a regular and important part of their diet. At 3500 calories per egg, a pfingle egg represents a significant part of the daily protein requirement for many species.

As a result, a cargo of pfingle eggs has a profit/investment ratio high enough to bring tears of joy to even the most jaded accountant. Averaging two dozen eggs per kilogram, one metric ton of pfingle eggs should realize eighty-four thousand caseys on the open market. Freebooters regard pfingle eggs as one of the most profitable cargoes a starship can carry—as well as one of the most dangerous.

leaving great wet puddles of drool in his wake. As Neena
Linn-Campbell watched, the Dragon Lord pulled open a
case of eggs and stuck his great snout deep into its interior. When he pulled his face out again, his mouth
dripped with pieces of eggshell, yellow fluid, white ichor,
and green gobbets of pfingle flesh.

"I'll kill that slime-eating, flatulent, pig-faced, toad-
sucking, egg-stealing, scum-bucket wart on the ass-end of
the Regency's lowest garbage—"

Gito and Shariba-Jen exchanged glances with Ota;
they readied themselves to grab the Captain if she made
even half a move toward the door. The Dragon Lord had
already killed and eaten a score of starport officials and
at least half that many freebooter Star-Captains.

But Captain Campbell had passed beyond rage. Her
swearing petered out in a futile, ineffective stream. Helpless, she stared down in horror at the terrible scene below.

Standing in the aisle, the Dragon Lord grunted in
happy satisfaction. He chewed at length. He swallowed
loudly. He grinned with delight. He opened his mouth,
revealing three rows of gigantic teeth. He tilted his huge
head back and roared in delicious glee. "I love ripe
pfingle eggs!" he screamed. The warehouse shook with
the force of his cry. The echoes ricocheted around and
around, rattling windows and causing the floors of the office to bounce uncomfortably.

Ota, the LIX-class bioform First Officer shuddered
and looked to her clipboard. "I estimate that every egg
he eats costs us 6.5 caseys; 3.5 for the egg, three more in
overhead." She flinched in response as the Dragon Lord
sank his head eagerly into the case again, as if she could
hear the money disappearing down his sucking gullet.

"I *like* these eggs!" the Dragon Lord shouted to his
aides. "These will please the troops. Oh, yes—these will
make me very popular among the ones who have survived." His aides began dancing in the aisles, whooping
and shouting happily. Several of them even bravely
sniffed the containers themselves, leaving their own puddles of drool on the floor.

"Maybe we could bill the Regency . . . ?" Ota offered.

"We'd have a tough time collecting," Robin opined.

"We wouldn't have to present the collection warranty here. . . ." Gito suggested.

Captain Campbell scratched her left eyelid thoughtfully. Still staring at the horror below, she held out her hand sideways. "Give me the clipboard. I'll do it."

Ota surrendered the manifest unhappily. Captain Campbell swallowed hard and walked over to the droptube. "Don't anybody do anything stupid," she cautioned. "Let me do it." She entered the tube and dropped gently out of sight.

As she stepped out onto the floor of the warehouse, Captain Campbell finally began to realize the true size of the Dragon Lord. He stood five meters high, and his tail massed more than some of his aides. He shone with ebony armor, and several of his claws stretched longer than her arms. She watched as he ripped open another case, shoved his great snout eagerly into it, and began crunching ecstatically through the eggs—wrapping, padding, and all, he obviously didn't care.

Star-Captain Campbell then did one of the bravest things she'd ever done in her life. She held out the clipboard to the Lord of all Moktar Dragons and asked politely, "Please initial this, Your Excellency." She had to ask three times before the monster noticed her. At last, however, he blinked and swung his great head around to look at her in surprise. She repeated her request and held the clipboard out to him. Around them, she noticed, the other Dragons—all sizes—had stopped to watch this transaction.

The Dragon Lord reached down slowly and took the clipboard from her. He brought it up to his eyes and gazed at it for a long moment without reaction. He turned his head this way and that, looking at the invoice first with one eye, then the other. At last, puzzled, he said, "This requisition seems to authorize payment for these eggs. Who authorized it?"

"I believe you did, or perhaps someone in your offices, my Lord." Star-Captain Campbell bowed.

The Dragon Lord shook his head. "No, I would have remembered such an authorization. For one thing—" He frowned. "You have quoted a price three times higher than the Regency will pay. Ten caseys per egg? The Dragons never pay that much. We pay ten caseys per crate. Yes, I believe your adjutant or whatever you call it must have made a mistake in the price here. Let's correct that and I'll happily sign for this cargo."

"Umm . . . no, I don't think so, my Lord. That price might apply on any of the worlds where pfingle-swarms mate naturally; but here, where pfingle eggs exist only as an imported commodity, certain ancillary costs drive the price up enormously. I apologize for the inconvenience, of course, but I couldn't possibly accept less than . . . oh, say, nine caseys per egg."

The Dragon Lord crunched the tiny clipboard in his gigantic claw, allowing the pieces of plastic and metal to rain down on Captain Campbell. "No, I don't think so," he said bluntly.

"Um," said Captain Campbell. For the first time she began to wonder if she would survive this conversation. She thought about apologizing—for half a nanosecond—then decided against it. She would not show weakness to this thief, no matter how much larger he loomed. She stared up at him defiantly, expecting at any moment to receive an individualized tour of the digestive system of a Moktar Dragon.

But the taste of pfingle eggs had taken the edge off the Dragon Lord's quickness to anger. He felt too pleased with himself right then to kill anyone. He wanted to gloat. And besides, he preferred a larger audience for his horrific deeds—he needed witnesses other than his own underlings to properly spread the word.

"Let me explain something to you," the Dragon Lord said in a voice that sounded like an avalanche turning cold. "As a Regency officer I have the right of first refusal on all necessary supplies in times of planetary emergency. Such as now. I also have the right to set a fair price. I have offered you a fair price. You have rejected it. If necessary, I can appropriate what I need without recompense. I will do that now."

Captain Campbell pointed at the window of the overhead office. "I have an Arbiter watching this entire proceeding, my lord. I will file a claim of unlawful seizure if I have to. I would not like to embarrass the Dragon Guard by bringing such a charge, but I will if I have to."

The Dragon Lord glanced upward, identified Harry Mertz at the window—Harry waved and offered a weak smile—then the Dragon Lord glanced back down to the captain of the *Lady MacBeth*. He grinned widely. "You know how to play this game well," he acknowledged. "But, unfortunately, not well enough."

"My Lord?"

"My inspection of your cargo has turned up an interesting anomaly. I don't think these eggs carry a correct rating. These eggs do not taste like thirty-day eggs. They taste like ten-day eggs. I believe someone has falsified the labels on these crates in a deliberate act of ecological sabotage. However, we have discovered the danger before any damage occurred, and I will graciously arrange the immediate destruction of this cargo and spare you the additional expenses you would otherwise incur. We can call it even, correct?"

"I thank you for your consideration, my Lord. I appreciate the demonstration of how you earned your reputation for justice and graciousness; but please let me do the honors. I will take custody of these eggs immediately and—with your permission—remove them from the surface of Burihatin-14."

The Dragon Lord shook his head. "The law requires mandatory destruction. Usually by incineration. If I let you take custody, I would have no way of knowing for certain that you would satisfy the conditions of the law. I couldn't let you put yourself in jeopardy that way."

"I will drop the eggs into the sun—"

"A fine promise indeed," the Dragon Lord acknowledged. "But what if you decide to believe these incorrect labels and attempt to deliver your cargo somewhere? No, I couldn't let you endanger yourself and your crew. You would have more than ten days of travel to the nearest market. Even if you did get there before the eggs exploded, they would still present a major danger to the buyers. No, I could not allow the possibility of that occurrence. I would have failed badly in my duty to protect the various peoples of the Regency." The Dragon Lord lowered his head in a great bow. "Therefore, I must declare this cargo a total loss and seize it in the name of the Regency."

"You leave me no choice, my Lord, but to express my admiration for your wisdom, your thoughtfulness, and your incredible ... incredible ... appetite. For justice, I mean."

"Thank you, Star-Captain. I hope our next encounter will please both of us as much as this one has."

"Yes," Captain Campbell agreed. "I will bring great hopes to our next encounter. You may definitely count on that."

She kept her smile firmly in place as she returned the Dragon's final bow. She backed away, bowing and scraping, bowing and scraping. As she stepped back into the drop chute, she stopped bowing and started swearing slowly and quietly, all the way up.

"Those filthy, egg-sucking, Vampire-toady, scaly-skinned, scum-sucking, lawyer-loving, degenerate spawn of a sand-bellied, dirt-crawling, black-slime, mud-deviled ..."

Star-Captain Neena Linn-Campbell knew how to swear in nine different languages, including binary code. Star-Captain Neena Linn-Campbell could have continued swearing for six days straight without repeating herself. Star-Captain Neena Linn-Campbell could have raised blisters at two hundred meters with just an angry glance. Star-Captain Neena Linn-Campbell's language could have shattered glass and crippled strong men. Star Captain Neena Linn-Campbell's language represented a life-threatening danger to animals and small children.

Star-Captain Neena Linn-Campbell readied herself for a full expression of her feelings. She stopped just long enough to take a breath. . . .

—at which point Ota clapped her great furry paw over Star-Captain Neena Linn-Campbell's mouth and, with the help of the rest of the crew, dragged her quickly out of the warehouse before she set off the emergency sprinkler system.

Chapter Eleven

Outside, the bright actinic sunlight cast harsh shadows through the dusky glow of Burihatin. The day seemed both lazy and hard at the same time. It matched their mood. They all felt a need to act immediately, but they also felt the profound emptiness and despair of their situation. Each of them—Gito, Robin, Shariba-Jen, Harry, Ota, Star-Captain Campbell—reacted in a different way.

Curiously, Captain Campbell's behavior seemed the most muted. Once they had gotten safely away, Ota removed her hand from Captain Campbell's mouth. Neena Linn-Campbell didn't react to the offense that Ota had committed. She just stood silently, showing no emotion at all. The others watched her curiously.

At last Captain Campbell looked up. She looked to Ota with a strange expression. "The Dragon has put us out of business. Hasn't he?"

Ota nodded. They had hocked the entire corporation for this cargo.

"It should have worked," said Robin. "We planned it perfectly. Everything. The market price, the delivery costs, the transportation time—we should have cleared three million easily—" And then she added, "If only that damn bitch, Zillabar, hadn't forced her charter on us, none of this would have happened. We could have done it. I know it—"

Captain Campbell ignored Robin's litany of if-onlys. "What about our insurance?" she asked Ota.

"Canceled. We forfeited Guild insurance when you turned in the Insignia."

"Mm. I thought so." She kicked at a nonexistent

rock and started heading back toward the starport. The others followed dejectedly in her wake.

"How long have we got?" Gito whispered to Robin.

"Well, the Captain Campbell I used to know," Robin whispered back, "would have already had a new cargo secured by now, and we'd lift as soon as we could seal the hatch. Any legal servitor with a warrant would find only an empty launch cradle. We'd work our way back up, somehow. But"—she shrugged helplessly—"as long as the lockdown at the port remains in place, we can't leave. These warrants may actually get served. Hmm . . ."

She thought about it a while longer. "On the other hand, with the lockdown in place, the servitor's office doesn't have to rush. They know that no one can lift, so why bother hurrying?" A thoughtful frown crossed her face. "I wonder if Captain Campbell has realized the same thing I just did. Some circumstances mandate immediate clearance from a starport. An outbreak of Meazlish Plague, for one—"

"That sounds a little extreme to me," Gito said in a gravelly voice.

"We'll have to research this, I think."

Up ahead Captain Campbell still walked alone. The day had turned abruptly dark as the pinpoint of the sun disappeared below the red rocky hills at the edge of the close horizon.

Harry Mertz, (retired) Arbiter of Thoska-Roole, hurried to catch up with her. He didn't speak, he just walked beside her in an act of comfort and support. If she had anything she needed to say, he would provide the ears to listen.

After a moment Captain Campbell said something, too soft for Harry to understand.

"Say again?" he asked.

She repeated it, this time louder. "I want revenge."

Harry nodded. "I can understand that. You need to know, however, that revenge does not produce satisfaction."

"In this case it will."

"Your anger speaks for you now. Remember the

words of the Zyne Masters. Revenge does not demonstrate enlightenment."

"So? When did I say I wanted enlightenment?"

Harry bowed his head in acknowledgment. "I stand
corrected."

"Good."

They walked a while farther in silence.

After a little longer Captain Campbell said, "So you
think I shouldn't want revenge, right?"

Harry nodded.

"All right. I don't want revenge. I want justice. Tell
me the difference."

Harry grinned. "In this case none. You want the
pain spread around equally. That serves as justice for
most people."

Captain Campbell looked at the old man sideways.
Did he really mean that? She caught the impish twinkle
in his eyes, and her features relaxed into a momentary
smile of appreciation. "Yeah," she agreed. "I got it."

They trudged on.

"It still doesn't solve my problem," she admitted.
"But at least now I know what I want and why I want it."

"Captain—?" Ota the bioform came trundling forward to walk along her other side. "I really do need to
report something else to you." Harry fell back a polite
half step.

"More bad news?"

"Sort of. I think. For someone. Anyway."

Captain Campbell looked at Ota, surprised. The
bioform rarely hedged its language. "Go ahead," she said.
"I have no more anger left in me—at least not for a
while."

"Um. After you went down to confer with the
Dragon Lord, I did a terrible thing."

Captain Campbell raised an eyebrow. "Ota? What
did you do?"

"Well . . . when I saw that the Dragon Lord would
not negotiate in good faith, I reset the cargo-management
program of the warehouse computer. I changed all of the
temperature controls from refrigeration to incubation. I
doubt the Dragons will notice, with all their heavy insu-

lated armor, but the eggs most certainly will. I expect the eggs to hatch sometime within the next thirty hours."

Captain Campbell didn't react immediately. She pursed her lips and frowned as she considered the image of thirty-three metric tons of industrial-grade pfingle eggs hatching all at once within a self-destruct, high-security warehouse. After a moment she shuddered. "I had no idea you had such a potential for . . . vindictiveness."

Ota replied, "I didn't do it out of viciousness, Captain. I just asked myself what you would have ordered me to do."

"Uh-huh, sure." Captain Campbell grinned. Ota's great furry expression remained as placid as always. After a moment more of uncomfortable empathy, Ota faded back to walk beside Harry.

Harry Mertz remembered a much older conversation, one that had occurred in the stygian depths of a Regency prison. He glanced sideways to Ota and said quietly, "You once told me you had no intention of getting involved."

Ota shrugged. "They filled my cup with vinegar. Three times over. How could that not involve me?"

Keep On Tracking

▱▱▱▱▱▱▱▱▱▱▱▱▱▱▱▱▱▱▱▱▱▱▱▱▱▱

South of starport, where the red rocks crumbled brokenly into the briny waters of Slug Lake, a less official community had sprung up. Here, clinging to the sides of the cliffs, carved into the bluffs, perched precariously on top of escarpments, or jammed into the spaces between two upthrusts of land, a haphazard collection of shanties, shacks, and tumbledowns had grown like a cancerous animal. The community alternately clustered and sprawled, with rough-hewn ways barely connecting each part with every other. Multiple piers extended out over the edges of the lake. Occasional towers climbed up out of the water, with tendrils extending onto the land. The smoke of industrial plants and cooking fires collected in an odorous brown haze that hung permanently over the village, giving everything a gangrenous smell of rotting flesh, sewage, brine, and sulfur.

The inhabitants called it Porginara. Everyone else knew it as Pig Town.

Where starport lay heavily under the Authority of the Regency, Pig Town gave its allegiance only to the banknote. Everything in Pig Town had its price. Those who came here usually did so with a specific purpose, a specific end in mind.

While Pig Town may have lacked much of the resources or versatility of larger communities, like MesaPort on Thoska-Roole, the intent remained the same—to provide access to commodities and services not generally available elsewhere. A ruggedly independent trade in darkside goods had grown up here and after several hundred years still stubbornly resisted all attempts to control or eradicate it.

In Pig Town you might not find exactly what you wanted—but you would certainly find someone who knew where you could get it. If you could afford it.

On the afternoon in question, two aristocratic fops wandered into Pig Town on an excursion of obvious curiosity. They strode arm in arm, chattering gaily, pointing, and taking pictures of everything that didn't glower at them. Few of the natives of Pig Town paid them any serious attention. Tourists from the nearby starport often came down to the shores of the lake to sample the more vigorous life of Porginara. As long as they left some money behind, no one paid them too much attention.

Had anyone paused to give them a serious inspection, he would quickly have noticed that neither of the men wore clothes that fit them very well, and the uncomfortable mix of color and garment suggested either an ignorance of style, or a deliberate flouting of convention. Their cloaks did not match their boots, their

breeches caught and bagged in all the wrong places;
their vests betrayed the bulges of too many weapons.

An even closer observer would have also noticed
that these two fops didn't even like each other very much
and most of their banter seemed forced and deliberate.
Indeed, they exchanged most of their words through
clenched and gritted teeth.

"I don't like it here," Lee whispered to Sawyer.
"This place has a bad reputation for violence. Even
Death travels in pairs."

"You want the goddamn TimeBand?" Sawyer whispered back. "Then we need to find an Informant. Now
quit your damn bellyaching and let me do my job."

"Can't we do it somewhere else? I don't think the
residents of Pig Town feel very kindly toward human
tourists."

"Don't take it personally. They hate everybody
equally. What do you expect from porcines?" Sawyer
grabbed Lee's arm and pointed. "There. That green
banner."

He led his companion across the broken plaza toward a small round structure, festooned with green banners, silken veils, and velvet drapes. They ducked into it
quickly and found themselves in a room of dark blue and
green light that came filtering down through a stained-
glass ceiling. More silks hung all around—they hung in
tatters and shreds and gave the chamber a feeling like
the inside of a spider's nest. In the center of the room sat
a small, low table. Around the edges sat gray, featureless
lumps.

Lee took one look around and reacted in dismay. He
wrinkled his nose at the musty smell and tried to wave it
away.

"You've never visited an Informant before, I take
it?"

"I've never had need of their services," Lee said.
Then he admitted, "Actually, I don't believe in Informants."

"They probably don't believe in you either," said
Sawyer. "Sit over there on that gray lump."

"Lump of what?"

"The Knaxx spin great bales of silk, which they sell to the unwary. Sometimes you'll find an unpleasant surprise inside all the windings. But don't worry, you can sit on it safely." Sawyer seated himself on another great gray lump.

Lee lowered himself tentatively onto the mass of silk threads that Sawyer had pointed him toward and found it surprisingly comfortable. He allowed himself to relax only slightly. "You've come here before, haven't you?"

"Once or twice," Sawyer admitted.

"Do you trust this Informant?"

"I trust Informants," Sawyer said obliquely.

"What do you mean by that?"

"I've never known if I've ever spoken to the same Informant twice. Nobody does. They all look exactly the same."

"Don't they have names?"

Sawyer shook his head. "They have no identities at all. I've never heard of a way to tell one Knaxx from another. I don't think they can do it themselves. Apparently, they consider it rude to ask. If you even raise the subject, they get up and walk away."

The curtains at the back of the room parted then, and the creature known as the Knaxx[9] stepped out into a beam of amber luminance. Lee's eyes widened at the sight. He stiffened where he sat. The creature had a short fat body; it glistened with chitinous scales that re-

---

[9]Of the three true alien species known to humanity, the Knaxx remain the most mysterious. Humanity discovered them on multiple planets of the Cluster, although the Knaxx have never demonstrated any evidence of the necessary technological ability to build starships. As humanity spread through the Palethetic Cluster, so did the Knaxx, shipping themselves and their eggs on human cargo vessels.

The Regency tolerates their existence. They cause no harm to their surroundings and do not interfere in Regency affairs; apparently, they prefer to observe silently the activities of humans and other allied species without interacting to any great degree.

The Knaxx have resisted all attempts to study them in depth. According to the best assessment of Regency experts, the Knaxx evolved from insectlike hive creatures. Whatever one of them knows, all of the rest of them seem to know it immediately too. No one has yet discovered how they do this, but this particular ability has made them very useful throughout the Cluster as buyers and sellers of information of all kinds. Most starports usually have a scattering of Informant booths around their fringes.

flected back a metallic sheen. Glittery-green and shiny all over, the Knaxx had huge multifaceted eyes that covered the greater part of its head. Instead of a mouth it had a cluster of short mandibles surrounding a curled proboscis.

Sawyer leaned over and touched Lee's arm gently. "Relax. They only eat fruit. They just look like . . . well, what they look like." Sawyer did not know if a Knaxx could take offense. He didn't want to find out now.

The creature did not speak. It eyed both of the men without apparent expression or reaction. With one bony arm, black and hairy, it reached into the folds of its garment, a vestlike affair, and extracted a small white bowl, which it placed in the center of the table before them.

"What do we do now?" Lee asked.

"We ask our question," Sawyer explained. "Then we start putting money in the bowl. When we've put enough money in the bowl, the Knaxx turns the bowl over and answers the question. Unfortunately—"

"What?"

"Well . . . sometimes the Knaxx answers in riddles. Sometimes indecipherable riddles." Sawyer poked Lee. "Go ahead. Ask."

Lee puffed out his cheeks and blew. He cleared his throat. He looked at the Informant. The Informant looked back at him. He swallowed hard and said, "My companion and I need to find someone. We want to find the person who wears or carries the TimeBand of Burihatin-14. Whoever has the TimeBand, we want to locate that person." He glanced to Sawyer. "Did I say that clearly enough?"

Sawyer nodded. "Go ahead. Start putting money in the bowl.'

Lee reached into his cloak and pulled out a sheaf of bills. He began peeling off notes—the Knaxx watched impassively—but before Lee could lay them in the bowl, the creature put its clawlike hand over the top of the bowl.

"What does that mean?" Lee asked.

"I don't know. I've never seen an Informant do this

before. Maybe it means that it won't answer the question. Or can't." The two men traded puzzled looks.

Abruptly, the Informant spoke. It had a voice like a soft whistling breeze, sibilant and blurred. They had to strain to make out the words. "Now you should pray."

"I beg your pardon?" Sawyer asked.

"Say your prayers," the Knaxx repeated. Then it got up and left the room, leaving them alone with the table and the empty bowl.

"What do you think that meant?" Lee asked.

Sawyer scratched his head. "I think . . . it meant that we should say our prayers."

"Doesn't it worry you?"

"Everything worries me these days."

Mixed Signals

Captain 'Ga Lunik watched the fleet of landers approach *The Golden Fury* with mixed emotions—fear and loathing. The return of the Dragon Lord to the Imperial Starship had come much too soon for his taste, but he recognized the inevitability of it.

The Dragon Lord had not acknowledged his request for information about the search for Zillabar. That meant that the search for the Imperial Queen had still not turned up any trace of either the Lady or her captors. The embarrassment of failure would make the Dragon Lord a ferocious passenger indeed, and Captain 'Ga Lunik did not look forward to welcoming a troop of disgruntled Dragons back aboard his vessel.

He knew the Dragon Lord would not tell him everything that had occurred down on Burihatin-14; but the Vampires had their own resources of information, and Captain 'Ga Lunik had used them to determine that the

Dragon Lord had savaged the economy of Dupa badly
enough to require several generations of serious repair
work to undo the worst of the havoc. Dragons did not
have a reputation for patience. Furious at the lack of immediate results, the Lord of All Moktar Warriors had assumed a lack of cooperation on the part of the natives
and ordered grievous retributions. Over a hundred small
towns and cities had disappeared from the maps of Dupa.

While Captain 'Ga Lunik understood the *rationale*
for the Dragon Lord's actions, in the long run such offenses served only to annoy the natives, instill greater resentment than fear, and make the job of peaceful
governance that much more difficult.

Additionally, the Dragon Lord had expanded his orders to keep the starport sealed. Now, if any ship tried to
run the blockade either *in* or *out*, the Marauders would
intercept it. If the Captain of the intercepted vessel refused to allow boarders, the Marauders had orders to destroy the vessel without questions. Captain 'Ga Lunik
expected horrendous repercussions from that decision—
especially after the second or third vessel disappeared in
a bright nuclear flash.

He pondered his own future with a less than san-
guine apprehension. The bad news had not yet finished
arriving, and he did not particularly relish the thought of
attending the confrontation about to occur.

Another starship—even bigger than *The Golden
Fury*—had arrived at Burihatin and brought itself alongside. He had recognized it immediately: *The Black
Destructor*, Kernel d'Vashti's Armageddon-Class battle-
wagon, the largest military ship in the Palethetic Cluster.
Kernel d'Vashti had already signaled his desire to meet
with the Lady Zillabar at her earliest opportunity.

Captain 'Ga Lunik had not known how to answer
this appropriately. He had spent long moments pacing
the bridge of his vessel, considering what he might reply
to d'Vashti's request. Should he inform d'Vashti of the
circumstances of the Lady's abrupt unavailability? He
didn't like that idea; he knew what happened to bad-
news bearers. He'd done it himself. Should he attempt to
discourage d'Vashti without revealing exactly what had

happened? That course of action seemed equally inappropriate. When d'Vashti found out—as he most certainly would in a very short matter of time—he would not have very good feelings about the author of obscure messages.

After a bit more cogitation, Captain 'Ga Lunik hit upon a dangerous, but ideal, subterfuge. He signaled d'Vashti that, "In respect to the Lady's present circumstances, all those who seek an audience with her must present themselves first to the Lord of All Moktar Dragons."

Yes. He liked that solution best. It took him out of the cross fire.

Maybe.

Coincidentalism

"I don't know what it means," Sawyer said again. His frustration rose with every repetition. "I've never heard an Informant say anything like that before."

"Well, figure it out! You said you knew Informants. Show me some of your famous expertise!"

"Maybe it means exactly what it means! Maybe we should find a temple and say our prayers." Sawyer felt helpless. He'd never come up against a problem like this before. "Y'know, sometimes the Knaxx *don't* speak in riddles. No wonder nobody understands them."

"And maybe it means we have *no* chance at all," Lee suggested. "Maybe the Knaxx meant that the situation has passed beyond the point of simple hopelessness into a state of total annihilation." Lee grabbed Sawyer angrily. "Do you have any more good ideas?"

Sawyer shook off Lee's frustration. "I think we should try saying our prayers—" He looked around. "There," he pointed.

"What?"

"Across the square. I see a House of Random Happenstance."

Lee raised an eyebrow at him. "Coincidentalism?"

Sawyer's expression turned into one of conviction. "The one thing I do have certainty about—Informants do not make mistakes."

"Of that," said Lee, "I still remain unconvinced."

Sawyer didn't bother answering. He just grabbed Lee's arm and began pulling him across the plaza toward the House of Random Happenstance, also known to those who worshiped regularly within its walls as the Temple of Intentional Coincidence.[10]

The temple presented a simple appearance. Four whitewashed walls stood apart at a distance of thirty meters, forming a perfect square. The walls stood unconnected to each other, and their thick white surfaces remained unbroken by doors. Pilgrims entered at the open corners.

Sawyer and Lee entered the temple respectfully. No ceiling covered the space within, a complex roof of silk banners hung from the tops of the walls; the thin cloth rippled in the soft breezes of the ringed Burihatin dusk.

Here and there Coincidentalists of all species, but mostly porcines, consulted various oracles of meditation. Sixty-four low tables lay arranged in a pattern of eight rows by eight; worshipers bent over several of them, casting complex hexagrams with yarrow stalks and coins. The process began with the writing of an important question on a scrap of holy parchment; then the pilgrim burned the parchment in a dish of incense while waving fifty sacred yarrow stalks through the smoke. Then the questioner would begin sorting the stalks in a complex it-

---

[10]Coincidentalists believe that the universe does not commit accidents.

Everything has a purpose. Everything has a reason. It only looks happenstance because we don't understand the larger flows of the universe. According to the higher realms of the Coincidentalist philosophy, we achieve happiness by being a part of that flow instead of resisting it.

In the larger scheme of things, Coincidentalism seems no sillier than any other religion. To its credit its practitioners have produced some extraordinary, if unduplicatable, results.

eration, which would eventually result in a remainder representing two lines of the final pattern.

Every set of iterations produced two more lines of the total pattern, one line grew from the past, the other from the future. At completion the practitioner would have before him two separate patterns; one represented the events that had formed this moment, the other represented the events that would grow from this moment. The patterns reached out through time, in both directions simultaneously.

To the mendicant the seeming randomness of the process represented an access to influences outside the realm of human control. Believing that nothing occurred randomly, that everything occurred as part of a much larger set of connected events, this process of nonspecific consultation allowed the Coincidentalist to determine the specific flows that affected his life. Because he served as the focus of events at the selection of the yarrow stalks, the randomness that occurred around him represented the actual flows of his own local condition; thus he would receive precise information from the greater cosmos about his own place in it—if only he knew how to interpret it. Fortunately, a wide variety of texts existed for the interpretation of the patterns, drawing complex meanings from the shape of every line, broken or unbroken.

Coincidentalists believed that the entire careful process gave them a cross section of universal intention as precise as any measured by an electron chamber. The consultant's fate sat, poised like a bubble in delicate balance, between the past and the future. The hexagrams gave him information about the shape of each. By consulting the texts about the hexagrams, the petitioner could make himself aware of the greater flows of the universe. He could then choose to direct his efforts either with or against those currents.

Or so the Coincidentalists believed.

For serious questions the rituals of the hexagrams took the better part of a day to cast and even longer to consider. In such cases most Coincidentalists would meditate on the meanings of their hexagrams for at least seven days before making a commitment to action. For lesser questions, however, the entire process often took only a few moments.

The most devout Coincidentalists preferred the hours of either dusk or dawn for their consultations of the oracle. As Sawyer and Lee watched, several pilgrims finished their consultations, gathered up their belongings, and left. Other pilgrims entered and took their places at tables within the square. A low level of activity remained constant throughout. Around the edges of the tables, small groups of men stood around in knots, actively discussing the finer points of random happenstance. Several wore gray robes, indicating that others had recognized their expertise in the matter and conferred upon them the acknowledgment of rank.

Suddenly, a wail of despair interrupted the quiet ruminations of the temple. Not too far from where Sawyer and Lee stood, a wealthy-looking porcine merchant stood up from the table where his hexagrams lay before him. He took out a broad knife, uttered a loud cry of anguish, and plunged it into his heart. His dark red blood immediately soaked his shirt front. For an instant his face registered panic, then peace—then he sank to the floor and died.

The other petitioners stared for a moment, then returned to their own meditations. The fate of the merchant did not concern them. One or two of the porcines standing on the edges of the square, however, wandered over to study the hexagrams that the fallen merchant had left on his table. They shook their heads and shrugged, then wandered away. The hexagrams themselves presented a neutral face; the petitioners gave them meaning by the questions they asked. Shortly, several novices in brown robes entered the temple and removed the body. Others stayed behind just long enough to clean the bloodstains from the stone.

"Does that happen all the time?" asked Lee.

Sawyer shook his head. "No. I've seen worse."

"Well, now what do we do?" Lee turned to Sawyer. "I don't consider suicide a viable option."

"Neither do I," Sawyer agreed. He took Lee by the

arm. "Now we walk. Around the edges of the square. Six steps at a time. Then we stop for a count of six. Then six more steps and we stop again. When we've completed six circuits, we turn around and go the other way. When we've completed six circuits in reverse, we leave."

"I see," said Lee. "And this will solve our problems?"

"No, you don't see anything at all," said Sawyer. "Let me finish telling you how it works. As you walk around the square, you meet people—"

As if to demonstrate the point, they found themselves stopped in front of a huge porcine woman. Lee wanted to hold his nose against the unpleasant smell of her sweat. The woman had a small female child with her. She looked at Sawyer and Lee with a sour expression. "I need to find a buyer for this child; she won't obey. Can you help me—?"

The two men looked at the child; it had a sad, bedraggled expression. They both felt sorry for it, but neither wanted to assume the responsibility either. They shook their heads. The porcine woman snorted in disgust, spattering them with a fine spray, and waddled past, dragging the hapless child by the arm.

"As I said," continued Sawyer, as if nothing untoward had happened, "as you walk around the square, you meet people. Sooner or later you'll meet someone who can give you assistance. Or you'll assist someone else with his or her problem, and out of that you may find the solution you need."

"And you believe that?"

Sawyer shrugged. "Whether I believe or not, it still works." To Lee's look, he added, "Trackers learn a lot of different things. You learn to use whatever works."

Lee looked unconvinced.

Sawyer added, "I had a wild childhood. I ran away once. I lived with a group of Trancers—until Finn caught up with me and took me home. I got curious how he found me. He told me. I told him how he could have done it better. So he made me a partner. He never asked me to change. He just asked me to use what I had. I figured what the hell, I liked solving interesting problems.

I guess I had more luck than I realized. Finn found me before I got in too deep."

Lee considered that for a bit. They completed their first circuit in silence. They exchanged greetings with one or two other petitioners, but neither they nor the others pressed for further conversation. Finally Lee said, "I always knew my family. We had brothers everywhere, all ages. I never had to worry about my identity—I had already stepped into it. You have a relationship with your brother that I never had with any of mine—oh, don't get me wrong. A clone-family has its own closeness; but the closeness grows out of a common identity. All members share the same Self. You and your brother, you had to create closeness for yourselves; you could just as easily have chosen not to. I find it difficult to . . . understand. But I don't disparage it. Not anymore."

"Thank you," said Sawyer. "You do me honor with your words. I hope someday I can return the honor a thousandfold."

"Thank you," said Lee.

They walked on in silence, occasionally looking around at the other pilgrims, studying them and wondering which if any might present themselves as a possible solution to their problem. "Y'know," said Lee. "I find this interesting, but I don't think it'll help us. I really don't believe in coincidence. And I don't think we should either expect it or depend on it."

Abruptly, they came face-to-face with an older woman—human; she looked terribly afraid. She wore a green robe and had stringy gray hair. She had no shoes on her blackened feet. She looked haggard, as if she had not rested in days. She held a bulky travel sack close to her chest. She looked from Sawyer to Lee and back again. "Can you help me? I have . . . a method for madness."

Lee started to shake his head and move on, but Sawyer held him back. "You haven't eaten, have you?" he said to the woman.

She shook her head. "I don't remember when I ate last. It doesn't matter. I've come such a long way. The Informant said to come here. For three days I've walked the circuit, but no one can hear me. I think—" She shook her head as if to clear it. "Some people have fed me. Will you help me?"

"We'll feed you," Sawyer said abruptly. "Say nothing else. Come with us now." He and Lee guided the woman quietly out of the temple and into the shelter of a nearby café. Sawyer signaled a servitor and ordered a pitcher of cold refreshing juice, plates of gentle-berries, savories, and other soft foods. He tended the woman solicitously. "I think we can help you," he said. "And you can help us."

Lee stared at him in puzzlement the whole time. Finally he leaned across to Sawyer and whispered, "Why do you do this? We didn't come here to feed beggars."

"Open your eyes and take another look, dummy," Sawyer whispered back. "This woman has just answered our prayers."

Azra

□□□□□□□□□□□□□□□□□□□□□□□□□□□

She had served the TimeBinder of Burihatin-14 almost all of her life. Three separate bodies had worn the TimeBand during the period of her service, but she served the TimeBinder regardless, not the person.

One night the TimeBinder had shaken her awake and given her desperate, but precise, instructions. "Azra, tonight you must perform the single most important task of your entire life. Take this box. Go to starport. You'll have to walk. No one will find you if you take the old Superstition Trail. Stay away from settlements. Don't talk to anyone. I'll give you a list of names and passwords. Memorize them. If you can't find any of these people at starport, then go to the Informants and tell them this: The TimeBinder has freed the TimeBand. Tell them that the 'Band must not fall into the hands of the Regency and that the 'Binders will repay them handsomely for their assistance in this service. Ask them to help you get the TimeBand to the Gathering. If necessary, open the box and show them what you carry. But don't allow anyone to put the TimeBand on. If they do, you must kill them. No one must put the 'Band on except someone chosen by the other TimeBinders. Do you understand all this?"

Azra nodded sleepily.

"Repeat it back to me."

She did so, stumbling only once in her recitation.

Satisfied, the TimeBinder hugged and kissed her. "Promise me that you will do this. I cannot begin to tell you the importance of what you do. I must know that you will not fail."

Azra straightened, as if offended. "You do not need my promise. I have served the TimeBand for three times as long as you have worn it. If you think to doubt me now, then you shouldn't trust me with this task or any other—regardless of its importance."

The TimeBinder nodded, as if shamed. "I apologize, Azra. My fear overwhelmed my wisdom. Here, take this and go."

The TimeBinder took off the headband then, placed it in the wooden box, and handed it across to Azra. "Go now, before either of us stops to consider how impossible a task I have given you."

Azra dressed quickly. She took down her travel sack, placed a knife, a canteen, and as much hardbread, cheese, and sausage into it as she could carry, took the wooden case the TimeBinder gave her and two small purses of coins, and walked out of the TimeBinder's citadel, knowing that she would never return.

She had to walk more than three hundred kilometers to starport. It had taken her almost a month to cover that distance. Nobody stopped her on her journey. Occasionally, she had seen other travelers on the road, but she kept away from them, even to the point of hiding in the tall weeds when they passed. Once Dragons had stopped her; they took her sausage and her money; they did not examine the contents of the wooden box. The TimeBinder had predicted correctly. Nobody would suspect an old woman who looked like a beggar.

The latter part of her journey she'd had to survive on roots and berries and the occasional small animal, which she roasted by the side of the road. She'd drunk ditch water and chewed on bits of hide to stave off the pangs of her own desperate hunger. When she reached starport, she could find none of the people whose names she had memorized. They had all disappeared in the Dragons' pogrom. Despairing, she hid in alleys and lived on garbage. She went to the Informants. For a week they told her nothing. Then one of them had told her to say her prayers, and she had spent three days walking the circuit of the House of Random Happenstance.

She told none of this to Sawyer and Lee. Instead she drank and ate hungrily while they watched her thoughtfully. She did not know if she could trust these two strangers, but the hunger gnawed at her belly like a rat. She couldn't remember the last time she had eaten this well. She didn't think it would violate her promise to take care of her own welfare. After all, how could she keep her promise if she didn't refresh herself periodically?

Her eyes darted from one man to the other—from the tracker to the clone. She didn't know these men, but she knew their type. If the Dragons found them, they'd kill them—and anyone with them.

She had already made up her mind. As soon as she finished eating, she would bolt from this place. She already knew a hundred different places to hide in the rat's warren of Pig Town. She knew a thousand different ways to get to her hiding places. If they followed, she'd elude them.

Lee started to whisper to Sawyer, but Sawyer shushed him. Instead he turned to Azra and spoke gently. "I see that you've come a long way. I see that you carry the weight of hunger and thirst as well as the heavier burden of . . . a method for madness. I think the time has come for you to lay down that burden?"

For the first time Azra looked up expectantly. "Why do you think that?"

"I see Dragons everywhere. I think that we will soon see . . . a time for treason."

Azra studied the plate before her without looking up, but her voice took on a harder edge. "And if you predict right," she asked slowly. "What then?"

"We all need to learn where our courage lives. Indeed, I believe that you can help us. I believe that you carry . . . a case for courage."

Azra's eyes widened. "Who told you to say that?"

Sawyer glanced around the plaza. He saw no one suspicious near, but he still didn't trust their surroundings. He leaned across the table and whispered, "We have an acquaintance who wears a most interesting piece of jewelry." Pretending to straighten his hair, Sawyer brushed his fingers from one temple to the other, as if in illustration. "He's come a long way, looking for an old friend. But the old friend has disappeared. Perhaps you might have some information?"

Azra reached into her travel sack and pulled out a large, flat wooden box. She put it on the table between them. "You may look," she said.

Sawyer and Lee exchanged glances. Sawyer licked his lips nervously. Lee turned around to survey the empty plaza. Neither Dragons nor Vampires lurked anywhere in his vision; but he didn't feel reassured. Anyone could have hidden a hundred cameras to spy down on the dealings in the shops around the plaza. Behind him Sawyer rubbed his forehead with the heel of his hand, debating with himself whether or not he could risk opening the case.

Finally his curiosity won out. He unlatched the chest and lifted the lid just enough to slide his hand into the darkness within. Something cool and metallic *tingled* there. Sawyer swallowed hard. He put on an expression of disgust and annoyance. He withdrew his hand, closed the lid, and latched it shut. He pushed the case back toward Azra. "I apologize," he said. "I thought that you and I might have helped each other. Apparently, I made a mistake. But here—let me give you some money for your trouble." He passed some bills across the table. "Here, that should buy you a week's food and lodging at the Inn of the Red Flower. Perhaps we will even see you there, as we may have some business in that neighborhood soon."

Sawyer stood up quickly and pulled Lee to his feet as well. "Come, my friend. We have dallied too long here and wasted the best part of the evening. Let us go seek some real entertainment and some fancier prizes."

"But, what——?"

"Shut up, stupid. You've drunk too much again. Why, look. You can hardly hold yourself erect. Will I have to carry you home again tonight?" Sawyer grabbed Lee's arm firmly and drag-walked him into an alley.

"I don't have to put up with this——"

Sawyer pushed Lee swiftly up against a nearby stone wall, putting his hand carefully around the clone-brother's throat. "Don't. Talk," he said. Then, just as quickly, taking on the pretense of a penitent lover, he fell into Lee's arms and put his lips close to the other's ear. "The woman can take care of herself. She'll have to. The spies of Pig Town watch us, not her."

"Then she——"

"She has the TimeBand, yes." Sawyer looked into Lee's face with a grin. "Now, what did you say before about not believing in coincidence?"

A Meeting of Minds

Kernel d'Vashti stepped out of the connecting tube between the two starships and into the private greeting chamber where the Dragon Lord waited. The great warrior lizard shifted his weight from one foot to the other, and his tail lashed uneasily. Captain 'Ga Lunik and several officers waited to one side. d'Vashti ignored them and headed straight for the Dragon Lord.

He didn't even bother with formal greetings. He walked directly up to the Lord of All Moktar Dragons, putting himself immediately below the great creature's head, an uncomfortable position for himself—but a painful position for the Dragon Lord as well. The monster had to arch his neck back to tilt his head downward far enough to see the Vampire military lord.

d'Vashti waited until the Dragon's gaze had found him and then addressed the huge reptile in an extraordinarily casual tone. "I've heard the most *amazing* rumor," he said. "I couldn't possibly give it credence, except I've heard it from six different sources. Perhaps you know the rumor I mean?"

The Dragon Lord grunted and cleared his throat. He said nothing else.

"Well, then let me enlighten you. According to this . . . this astonishing news, several of the Lady's 'dinner guests'—including the trackers, Sawyer and Finn Markham, and the TimeBinder of Thoska-Roole— somehow broke free of their bonds, captured the Lady, overpowered a troop of Dragon Guards, seized a landing shuttle, evaded a squadron of Marauders, landed undetected on Burihatin-14, escaped into the blacktree jungle with the Lady Zillabar as hostage, and have managed to elude the crack search teams of the Elite Dragons for more than seven days."

d'Vashti laughed at the outrageousness of the story; but his laughter had a nasty edge to it. "Don't you agree," he said to the Dragon Lord, "that the story has such an air of impossibility that only a deranged prankster would dream of repeating it? Indeed, the first time I heard it, I found it so amusing that I insisted on sharing it with the entire bridge command of my ship. But"—His expression darkened—"the most curious thing happened. We kept hearing the same story. We heard it from one source, and then we heard it from another. We heard it repeated as if people actually believed this tale."

d'Vashti paced back and forth in front of the silent Dragon Lord. "We heard that the Dragons had sealed the starport. We heard that Dragons had run amok on the surface of Dupa, killing and eating thousands of civilians. We heard that Dragons found the Lady's lander at the bottom of Little Crater Wreak, and it blew up in their faces. We heard that the Dragons behaved so stupidly that even the Lord of All Moktar Dragons had prepared himself for dishonorable suicide."

d'Vashti stopped his furious pacing and looked sideways and up at the Dragon Lord. "Now, I don't believe any of these tales. But I would certainly hope that if any of them have any truth at all, then certainly the last one—the part about the dishonorable suicide—should also carry significant weight. Wouldn't you agree?"

Around the edges of the room, Captain 'Ga Lunik and his officers had gone pale. They expected mayhem to occur at any moment. Yet they saw no convenient way to beat a diplomatic retreat.

The Dragon Lord did not answer d'Vashti immediately. He chewed thoughtfully for a long moment, as if dislodging a forgotten piece of gristle from the rear part of his jaw. His tongue prowled around between his teeth, searching for the item. Finding it at last, the Dragon's gaze returned unenthusiastically to d'Vashti. The great warrior-lizard seemed almost surprised to find the Phaestor aristocrat still waiting for an answer to his earlier question. "I wonder what Vampire tastes like," he said.

"I wonder what Dragon blood tastes like," d'Vashti retorted. "You don't scare me, you overgrown toad-suck. My family raised yours out of poverty. A thousand years ago your ancestors wallowed in their own shit while mine had already won their positions in the Regency. So don't give me your supercilious arrogance. What we gave you we can just as easily take away. If necessary, I'll see you wrapped in the skins of a hundred lawyers and buried in an unmarked grave beneath the worst sewage of Pig Town, and you'll never get to paradise. So don't mess with me, fella. I haven't even started on you and your incompetent, bumbling, walking stink-bags that dare to wear the insignia of the Regency. You have raised ineptitude to a new low!"

The Dragon Lord waited until d'Vashti started to run down. He sucked his teeth thoughtfully and asked in a gravelly roar, "Have you quite finished, you little pissant?"

d'Vashti ignored the Dragon's rudeness. He took a few steps back so he could stare up into the Dragon's eyes more easily. "Do you realize the importance that the Lady Zillabar represents to the future of the Regency? With a proper mating she could invigorate the aristocracy with a hundred thousand new young lords. With her you and I will hold the reins of power throughout the entire Cluster. Without her you and I lose everything—but I promise you this . . ."

d'Vashti's voice came down an octave. His listeners had to strain to hear what he said next. Even the Dragon Lord lowered his head respectfully. "If I go down, I will see you go down before me. In flames. I will see that your name will carry the greatest stain that any Dragon ever bore. Dragons from now until the end of time will curse you and all your offspring. I will put such a curse on your name that no one will even dare to kill your children out of mercy, for fear that such a kindness would stain them as well. Your children will carry your shame as their own, and their children, and their children, from now until forever. Every Dragon who carries even the barest hint of your genetic heritage will carry the stain. Do you understand what I tell you? Even after I have ground your bones to dust and scattered them over the garbage dumps of a thousand worlds, I will still devote my remaining days to thinking up ways to add to your shame. Not even if you groveled and begged for my forgiveness for a thousand years would I relent—"

d'Vashti never completed the sentence. He never had the chance. The Dragon Lord moved then. He took several quick steps back and lowered his massive bulk to the floor, flattening himself into a mountain of abject green flesh. Captain 'Ga Lunik and the others scampered backward to get out of his way. The Dragon spread out his great arms and legs in a vast spread-eagle sprawl and let out a mournful howl toward the ceiling.

"Kill me now, then!" he demanded. "If you truly believe these calumnies and lies, then kill me now! Disgrace me, disgrace my name, disgrace my children! Go ahead! I'd rather bear that disgrace and any other disgrace you care to name than try to defend myself against the malicious little gossips of others. I will not dignify these stories. To do so gives them credence. I will not give that satisfaction to the enemies of the Regency. Kill me now. I accept your penalty." The Dragon Lord fell silent, his head pointing across the floor gazing mournfully at d'Vashti.

d'Vashti stood on the same level as the monster's gaze. He stared directly into the great lizard's eyes. Without hesitating he walked carefully forward, right up to the Dragon's mouth. He could feel the hot breath of the beast like the wind from the open door of a furnace. He placed one booted foot directly on the end of the Dragon's snout, leaned forward, and rested his arms on his knee. "Listen to me," he said to the Dragon Lord. "I don't care how many villages you burn, and I don't care how many humans you eat, and I don't care what other crimes and foulnesses you commit along the way. I want Zillabar and nothing else. If you can't do it, I'll get someone who can. Tell me now why I should let you go on."

The Dragon Lord howled. "You have my loyalty, d'Vashti. You have always had my allegiance. I will not rest until you achieve the honor of fertilizing the Lady's eggs and bring forth the next generation of proud Phaestor aristocrats. I will redouble my efforts. I will do whatever necessary for you to have what you want."

d'Vashti took his foot off the Dragon's snout, unimpressed. "I worry when someone gets that effusive in their loyalty," he remarked. "It makes me want to hire an extra food-taster." He kicked gently at the big beast's jaw. "Get up. You make me sick."

The Dragon Lord rumbled deep in his throat. He levered himself awkwardly back to his feet. "I share the same feelings about you, bloodsucker," he grunted.

"Good," acknowledged d'Vashti. "Then we understand each other perfectly."

Evasive Maneuvers

Legend has it that when night falls across Dupa, strange things happen. Birds talk, cats walk on their hind legs, the machines whisper with strange noises, and even the very bricks in the walls huddle closer in fear.

However, those who spend their time near starport know that the stuff of legends compares poorly to the events that occur in the gloomy underside of Pig Town. Southwest of starport, where Pig Town evaporates against the broken rocks of the Crumble, residents have occasionally claimed to see willowisps, ghosts, trolls, goblins, and other grotesques. Of course, no one believes that supernatural beings actually prowl the edges of the night, but at the same time, only the foolhardy go out into the darkness to investigate.

In truth the monsters of the Crumble have a much more mundane existence. Most have day jobs and retreat to the broken slabs of the Crumble only for activities they prefer to keep hidden from the Regency authorities. Here, beyond the casual crimes of Pig Town, the serious explorer will find the big-money crimes that juice the underground economy of the planet—especially the smuggling of contraband goods. If Pig Town serves as the free market for starport, then the Crumble serves as its wholesale supplier. Every freebooter in the sector knows of the Crumble, and a thousand other places just like it on a hundred other worlds.

Beyond the Crumble, the Trail of Fear leads past the abandoned mines of the ancient Calico Corporation, and from there north and west into the Valley of Broken Dreams. A few reclusive settlements lie up the valley. Beyond them scattered lights occasionally become visible, suggesting the presence of either hermits or pirates. Few have gone to investigate. Fewer still have come back to report.

On this night, however, neither Sawyer nor Lee chose to venture anywhere near the Crumble, the Trail of Fear, the Valley of Broken Dreams, or anywhere beyond.

Instead they walked—seemingly at random—northward through the streets of Pig Town, eventually staggering back up into starport. They continued to wander in a haphazard manner, pausing here and there for the occasional drink or snack, then eventually maundered back toward Pig Town, almost as if by accident. By now it seemed as if they could not pass a tavern or a café without stopping to sample its wares, and if any Regency authority followed them, he would have long since developed a severe case of indigestion and sore feet. Nevertheless, the tracker and the clone continued on.

To any casual observer they appeared as two drunken fools, oblivious to both the virtues and the dangers of the town around them; that same casual observer would not have seen what happened to the three mugs who tried to separate Sawyer and Lee from their purses. Just as well, for it would have spoiled the carefully crafted illusion they had worked all evening to create. The two did not return to their hostel until the hour of the roach. Already the first faint glow of the primary had become visible beyond the distant horizon. Several habitués of the residence eyed them suspiciously as they entered.

They bumped their way down the long narrow hall, all the way to the back of the building, hanging on to each other for support, loudly whispering words of endearment and affection, kicking the door to their room open with boisterous promises of additional pleasures to come, and tumbling loudly onto the bed, which creaked alarmingly. Sawyer planted a big wet kiss on Lee's mouth as he kicked the door to the room shut—

Almost immediately, he leapt up again and secured it while Lee slid the bed sideways to reveal an opening that led down into the basement of the establishment. Hurriedly, they made their way down the narrow steps and secured the sliding platform with the bed on it above them. "Don't for a minute think that I meant any of that," Sawyer said, wiping his mouth.

Only the dimmest of lights allowed them to see the scattering of boxes, chests, and discarded furniture. Lee began making his way toward the back of the cellar. "Trust me," he replied. "I did not enjoy that, I will never do that again, and the next time you suggest a disguise for me, I would rather portray a corpse than your lover."

"Uh-huh. Sure. Then how come you kept asking me to dance with you at the last three bars we stepped into?"

"How come you said yes?"

"Politeness!" snapped Sawyer.

"Politeness?" replied Lee, with incredulity. "I only did it out of consideration for you! I didn't enjoy it either. I just thought that you—never mind! Help me with this."

"Yeah, yeah—uh-huh. I invented the perfect disguise for you, and now you claim you didn't have a good time."

"Yeah, you invented it for yourself—" Sawyer put his shoulder to a seemingly immobile crate, while Lee counted bricks. He found the one he sought, pressed it, then pressed another one, two up and three over. The crate slid sideways, revealing another downward tunnel. Quickly, they dropped down into it, then pressed the panel that slid the heavy-looking crate back.

"Have you got the light?"

"Yeah, wait a minute. There—"

Vision returned with illumination, but they could still see very little. Narrow and cramped, this brick-lined tunnel cut sharply downward. Lee led the way. They had to proceed slowly, walking stooped over and single file. The steep slope made it difficult for both of them to keep their footing. Worse, the passage stank of mold and other less appealing animal odors.

"Do you suffer from claustrophobia?"

"Claustrophobia?"

"A fear of small, dark, tight places."

"Not yet. But give me another five minutes of this . . ."

They proceeded downward, mostly in silence, occasionally grunting or cursing when one or the other would slip. When Lee fell, Sawyer would trip or stumble over him. When Sawyer fell, he sometimes toppled forward, grabbing Lee and pulling him down too. As a result both of their vocabularies began to enlarge. Sawyer taught Lee a few choice phrases in the Phaestoric conversation of manners, in exchange for several equally profound sentiments in the pre-diaspora old tongue.

After a while the tunnel leveled off and turned sharply to the right. They followed it around through a series of uneven zigs and zags.

"Have you lost your bearings yet?"

"A long time ago," Sawyer replied. "I have no idea how far we've come or in which direction."

"Wait a minute—" said Lee. And then he fell silent.

Sawyer realized that Lee had stepped into a new kind of space. He approached cautiously. "Stay there!" said Lee, holding up a cautionary hand. "I don't want to lose the tunnel we came out of."

Sawyer peeked forward. He found himself looking into a six-sided room. A new tunnel opened up in each wall.

"They might get past the bed," said Lee. "They might get past the basement. They won't get past this. But neither will we if I don't remember correctly." He began reciting a childish counting rhyme as he turned round and round the room. With each beat he pointed at a different tunnel. With each rhyme he reversed direction. Sawyer watched patiently, keeping absolutely still so as not to distract the clone.

The first time he finished, Lee ended up with his hand pointing directly at Sawyer.

"Wanna try that again?" Sawyer grinned.

Lee nodded. "I plan on doing this until I get the same tunnel three times in a row. We can't afford to get this one wrong."

Four recitals later Sawyer suggested, "You know, a thought has occurred to me—"

"All right," said Lee exhaustedly. "Tell me your thought."

"I've watched you. All five times. You didn't make any mistakes. Maybe ... we should turn around and go right back up the same tunnel. Maybe when we go up the tunnel, we come out in a different place."

Lee considered the idea. After a bit he announced, "You've exhausted either your wit or your intelligence. I haven't decided which."

"Do you have a better idea?"

"I hate it when you say that."

"Do you want to try a different rhyme?"

"Never mind," said Lee. "Let's try it your way. Maybe we'll meet a Dragon on the way down, and I can stop worrying when I'll die."

"You can die anytime you want to," Sawyer said. "I won't miss you. Give me the light, I'll lead." He stepped out of the tunnel to turn around and immediately headed back into it.

Lee followed him into the tunnel. "Yeah, I guess I can say now that I've had just about every experience necessary to a complete life. Including getting kissed by a drunken tracker."

"Congratulations. I've never had that experience. Many will envy you."

"Not bloody likely."

"You keep complaining, and you won't have to wait for a Dragon. I'll kill you myself."

They followed the tunnel upward to where it leveled off again and into the same bizarre series of uneven zigs and zags that had confused them so badly before.

Suddenly Sawyer stumbled up against a dead end. He bumped his head against the hard rock and cursed in annoyance. Lee bumped into him from behind, and he banged into the rock a second time. "Watch it, dammit!"

"Why did you stop?"

"We've come to a dead end."

"Oh," Lee said. "Look up."

Sawyer angled the light to illuminate the roof of the tunnel. He saw two bare-metal handles. He started to reach for one of them—

"Don't touch them!" shouted Lee.

—Sawyer drew his hand back as if stung.

"Give me the light. Grab one handle in each hand, turn them both ninety degrees; clockwise or counter-clockwise, it doesn't matter. Then pull down."

"What happens if I pull them down without turning?"

"According to what M'bele told me, you'll detonate the explosive charges under your feet."

"Right," agreed Sawyer. "Turn the handles *first*"—he did so carefully—"then pull down." The handles, and a surrounding slab of rock, came sliding down from the ceiling. The whole became the footing of a thin metal ladder. Sawyer pulled it all the way down until it locked into place. "Got it," he said. "Do we climb it now, or do we have to do something else?"

"Climb it," said Lee. "Let's get out of here."

Safe House

At the top of the ladder they came to a metal lid. Sawyer pushed on it without luck. Then he banged on it in anger, and someone lifted it away. Bright yellow light blinded him immediately, but strong hands came reaching down to pull him out of the hole in the floor, and a moment later Lee came climbing up after him.

"What took you so long?" asked M'bele.

"Lee wanted a third dance," muttered Sawyer, brushing the dirt off his cloak. "Did she get here all right?"

"Hours ago."

"Good." Sawyer looked around the chamber. He saw a more comfortable room than he expected. "What kind of a hideout have you got here?" He reached up and touched the hewn-rock ceiling with wonder.

M'bele led them into a larger room. Here they

found more comfortable furnishings and plates of waiting refreshments. This room also lacked windows; apparently, they still remained far underground. "You and your brother never knew me as well as you thought you did," the dark man said. "In my business a wise man always keeps at least three safe houses to escape to. Call me foolish, but the habit remains ingrained from my days as a rejuvenation-spice smuggler."

"Nice place," Sawyer nodded.

"I never thought I'd need to use it again," M'bele admitted. "But then, when I considered the quality of my business associates, keeping it ready seemed like a necessary act of foresight."

"I love you too." Sawyer shrugged out of his travel cloak and looked to M'bele. "Did you talk to her? Did she say anything?"

"She almost didn't make it. She gave the Burihatin TimeBand to Three-Dollar and collapsed. We put her to bed. We'll talk to her when she awakens. Physically, she'll recover. Emotionally, I don't know. Something happened to her during her journey. I think someone or some*thing* attacked her. I find it hard to believe she made it here at all."

Sawyer sank down onto a bench, wiping his forehead, allowing the relief to flood over him. "All day long, all night long, we kept staggering around the goddamn city, not knowing if anyone followed us, not knowing if our performance had an audience—all the while wondering if she'd understood my words, fearing that the Dragons might still find her, terrified that she'd hide from us and we'd never find her again. I think I need an easier line of work, one that doesn't put so much strain on my emotions."

M'bele glanced past Sawyer's shoulder, to someone standing in the door behind him. Sawyer didn't see the look. Then another voice spoke. "Hmp. I guess I'll have to choose for my next partner someone with more endurance."

For a moment the voice didn't register on Sawyer—and then he leapt to his feet and turned around in astonishment. He grabbed his brother with an overjoyed look on his face; Finn Markham grinned right back at him—still weak, still pale, but *standing* and *conscious*! Sawyer couldn't speak; the emotions rushing through him nearly toppled him with their power. Tears of joy came pouring freely down his cheeks. He grabbed his brother hard, holding him in his arms as tightly as he could—

"Easy there, little bro'. Don't break me—"

"I couldn't break you if I tried. I think we'll have to rename you 'Finn the Unkillable.' " He held his brother at arm's length to look at him, studying his eyes, his face, his smile. "You still look like hell, you big piece of leather."

Finn held on to Sawyer too, as much for support as affection. "You don't look all that great yourself—dancing and drinking all night without me. Didn't I teach you better than that?"

"I had a duty to perform—" Sawyer started to reply, then gave up. "Oh, the hell with it. You look so good to me."

"I still have a long way to go, kiddo. M'bele says it'll take multiple treatments. Fortunately, we have Zillabar. I'll drink her blood for a change."

"That sounds fair to me." They both laughed gently.

"You did good today." Finn remained holding on to his brother. "You did good in getting me to M'bele. Three-Dollar told me what you did. You make me proud."

Sawyer couldn't respond to that easily. The words wouldn't come. So he just smiled and kept on smiling. "I—I—can't lose you. Not yet."

"Let me sit down now," Finn said. "You've just used up my entire reserve of energy." Sawyer helped his brother to the bench, and the two of them sat side by side, holding each other up for a while.

"I just have one question for you, Sawyer," Finn said. "I told you to give me a suicide pill. You promised me. But here I sit. I still live, I still breathe. What happened, you stupid git? Can't you do anything right?"

The New TimeBinder

Sawyer looked around the room. Three-Dollar, Lee, and M'bele stood grinning at the two trackers, sharing the emotions of their reunion.

"All right," he said. "What happens now?"

Three-Dollar sat down opposite them. He looked exhausted. "We've had a long talk about that. The TimeBinder of Burihatin has freed the TimeBand. She did this without choosing her successor—"

"She?"

Three-Dollar nodded. "By tradition a woman always wears this TimeBand."

"Did the Vampires get her? Did they kill her?"

Three-Dollar looked momentarily unhappy. He really didn't want to address Sawyer's question, but he answered it anyway. "She committed suicide, rather than risk capture."

"Oh," said Sawyer. For some reason the news filled him with a terrible sadness. He'd never met the woman, he didn't even know her name, but he did know the kind of loyalty she had inspired in the people around her. He felt as if he shared some of their loss. He looked at Three-Dollar. "You must feel particularly sad."

"Yes. And no," replied the TimeBinder of Thoska-Roole. "I have memories of a thousand losses. More. Another death does not add significantly to my burden of woe. But, yes, I do feel a great despair at the news of a TimeBinder willingly relinquishing her crown and dying. But even as I grieve, I also feel a shared sense of pride that she could honor her commitment so profoundly."

"Well . . . if it helps any," said Sawyer, "you have my sympathies and my assistance."

"Thank you," said Three-Dollar. "And later, perhaps, when I have time to grieve in fullness, I will appreciate your condolences more than I can express right now. At the moment we have other concerns that demand our attention. The Gathering, for instance. We have to have a TimeBinder from Burihatin. We can't conduct our business with an incomplete number."

"Can't you just choose one?" Finn asked. "You have the authority to do so, don't you?"

"I do and I don't. By that I mean I have the moral obligation to further the continuity of the TimeBand. And the thought has already occurred to me that the woman Azra has earned the right to wear the 'Band. She has served it all her life. But the 'Band carries with it an emotional burden that can crush the unwary soul. And with each life that gets added to it, the burden becomes greater." Three-Dollar rubbed his eyes wearily. "A TimeBinder must choose as his successor someone who has the personal strength to deal with the weight. I don't know anyone here that I can trust."

Now M'bele spoke up. "And we don't have a lot of time left. We have to ship out tonight. I've booked a charter. Don't worry—I'll add it to your bill."

"I thought the Dragon Lord sealed the starport."

"He did. But I found a freebooter with a reputation for breaking blockades. Additionally, the Dragon Lord went up last night, and without him here the security net has begun to unravel. The Dragons have spent the day gorging themselves on anything that moves. By morning most of them will have gone torpid. We may never have a better opportunity."

"We can't go—" said Three Dollar. "Not yet. We need a new TimeBinder—"

"We can't wait—" replied M'bele, his anger rising.

"Daddy?" a childish voice interrupted the discussion. "I can't get it off."

All eyes in the room went to the door—to M'bele's nine-year-old daughter, Nyota. And to the shining band she wore around her forehead.

"Daddy?" she said, her expression crumpling into tears. "I can't get it off! *And it hurts!*"

M'bele reached her just as she collapsed into his arms.

"Oh, shit," said Lee.

M'bele reached for the TimeBand. Three-Dollar stopped him—the two men glared at each other across the whimpering girl. "If you try to remove it," Three-Dollar said, *"you'll kill her!"*

"I can't leave her in pain!"

"It won't last. In a moment she'll stop crying. Just hold her. Wait." The two men stayed like that while Nyota wept between them. Three-Dollar looked stricken. "She always wanted to touch my 'Band. She kept asking if she could wear it. I didn't realize how attractive she found it. I didn't think. Oh, God. What have I done? How can I beg your forgiveness?"

"What the hell do you mean?" M'bele said. "Explain yourself. As soon as she stops crying, you'll tell me how to take the band off. No harm done—"

"You don't understand, do you? She can't take the TimeBand off. *Ever.* If she does, she dies. I thought I made that clear when I told you what happened to the TimeBinder of Burihatin. Your daughter has taken her place." Three-Dollar stroked her head compassionately. The girl's crying had begun to ease. His eyes met M'bele's again. "At least she's solved part of our problem. Your world has a new TimeBinder. We can go to the Gathering now."

The Transformation

Rage came to M'bele first.

But before he could speak, before he could express it, Nyota opened her eyes and looked up at her father with a new understanding. "Father," she said, putting her hand on his cheek. Her voice had suddenly taken on an ageless quality. Whoever lay there in his arms, she no longer existed as the Nyota he had tended so carefully for nine precious years. Now she spoke as if from a mountain six thousand years high.

"Father, please don't fill yourself with anger. My pain has ended. I have gained the . . . wisdom to appreciate the love that you've given me all your life. This TimeBand has given me a greater gift than I ever dreamed possible. Please share my joy at this moment?"

M'bele's eyes filled with tears. He did not know what to say. He let go of his daughter as if she had suddenly turned into a monstrous thing. The child remained in Three-Dollar's arms as her father cast about the room, looking for something, anything, on which to focus his anguish.

Awakened by the noise, Azra came into the room, looking first dazed, then surprised, and finally joyous. She dropped to her knees before the child. "I prayed for this," she said. She looked around to the others. "Not *this*," she explained, pointing to Nyota, "—but *this*." She pointed to the TimeBand. "I serve the TimeBand. Without a wearer I have no life. I prayed that the TimeBand would find a new wearer, one who would need me as much as I need her." To M'bele she said, "Your child speaks the truth, doctor. Destiny has blessed both your lives."

M'bele shook his head in denial. "No, no—I cannot have this. This—this *thing* has a monstrous quality. I knew my child. I tended her. I kept her safe from fear and harm. I've spent nine years paying the price for my mistake. I'll spend my whole life if I have to." To their puzzled looks he explained "Her . . . handicap. It occurred at birth. I delivered her. I made a mistake. I thought I knew everything. I didn't know enough. I hurt her. She lost her ability to . . . think like others. She became *simple*. But at least, with her simpleness, she had *peace*. It seemed almost a fair enough trade. But now—this thing has stolen even that from her. She'll never know peace again."

"Father—" Nyota sat up. Her eyes had become focused and clear. "I don't want peace. Now that I can see farther than ever before, now that I can see the alternative, I *choose* this destiny. Please don't rage. Please accept it. Please realize that you have gained the daughter you have always wished for. I've seen the look in your eyes. I know how deeply you've hated yourself for your long-ago mistake. Father, I forgive you. Please forgive me now for choosing this blessing, and give me back your love!" She held out her arms imploringly.

M'bele tried to resist. He could not. He fell to his knees in front of her and grabbed her tightly and held her close; great weeping sobs racked his body. "I've lost my little baby," he said. "I don't know who or what I've gained in return. Please forgive me for feeling this way, but—I can't help it."

Nyota pulled back and met her father's gaze. "This will give us both greater happiness and greater pride. I promise you."

M'bele's eyes shrouded. "I hear you. I hear your noble words. But I don't know if these words come from my little girl or from the TimeBand. Nyota waited like an empty cup. This *thing* has not only filled her up with strange new words and manners, it has replaced the simple part that spoke to me as a daughter."

"No," said Nyota. "I know it looks that way to you. I know you cannot help but feel a great loss. But please believe me, father—two separate parts have now become one. Neither has replaced the other. Each has taken on the flavor of the other. Please give me the chance to show you."

"I have no choice," said M'Bele. "You've done something I thought would never happen. You've become greater than me. I don't know how to live with this, but I've become unnecessary."

Nyota didn't answer that. She couldn't deny the fact. They both knew that a TimeBinder existed independently of her family. Despite all her protestations of love and devotion, they both knew that a childish curiosity had irrevocably transformed both their lives.

M'bele let go of his daughter, and again the anger grew in him. He turned away from her and his gaze fell on Sawyer and Finn. "Why did you two have to come back into my life? Haven't you done enough damage?" He looked beaten and weary. "I want you off my planet and out of my life. I never want to see the two of you again as long as I live."

Sawyer and Finn exchanged a troubled glance. "We never meant to bring you sorrow," said Finn. "You've given me back my life, and we've taken away a large part of yours. We'll go. . . ." He made as if to rise.

Three-Dollar stepped over and pushed him back down onto the bench. "All of you, shut up!" he said, with as much anger as Sawyer had ever seen him express. "Not a one of you has any understanding at all about what has happened here!" He turned to M'bele. "Speaking of empty cups, your pain has filled yours. Would you rather have your daughter a simpleton again? Would you condemn her to that when she finally has a chance to make a difference for her people? You wallow in your own pain when you should celebrate the fact that your daughter has the strength of soul to wear a TimeBand without dying. Yes, she could have *died*! I've seen that happen too. I carry the memories of seventy deaths that this TimeBand has experienced."

The TimeBinder towered over the doctor. "We have a job to do. We have to go to the Gathering and we have to leave now. The First Officer of the freebooter vessel waits for us, even while we stand here yammering at each other. Now, do you want to argue? Or do you want to save your world from further ravages by the Dragons?"

M'bele hung his head. Not in shame. Not in resignation. He accepted the TimeBinder's words, and he held his fury. Somehow he would bank the fires, leaving the resolution of this moment for another moment yet to come.

"Good," said Three-Dollar. "Everybody get your things and let's go." He stepped into the other room and returned with an LIX-class bioform following him. Sawyer, Finn, and Lee looked up in surprise as Three-Dollar said, "Ota will give us instructions on how to get to the

hiding place of the landing boat that will take us up to
The Lady MacBeth."

Sawyer looked to Lee. "I seem to remember you
had something to say about coincidence?"

Lee just shook his head in disbelief.

Away

M'bele led them to another room, this one with darkened
windows. One by one he led them down a hallway,
through a narrow door, and out into a dark alley where a
large covered sled waited. Sawyer brought Finn out in a
wheelchair and secured him carefully. Lee came out to
help. The two of them looked up at the open sky above
and exchanged embarrassed grins.

"I thought we still lurked safe underground."

"I share your embarrassment. Me too."

Lee took the wheelchair back in and brought out
next a bound, gagged, and blind-helmeted Zillabar. They
placed her beside Finn, who grinned at the Vampire
broadly. She couldn't see him, but her nostrils flared as
she sniffed the air. Finn leaned close to her and whispered, "How nice to see you again, Lady." He patted her
on the leg with undue familiarity—just to see her stiffen
in anger.

Azra brought Nyota out. Three-Dollar and M'bele
followed. Ota climbed into the front of the sled, next to
the robot driver, and said, "Take us away, Jen."

The sled pulled away from the back of the House of
the Charitable Sisters, and out into the street. Sawyer
looked out the back of the truck just long enough to see
that, for all of their traveling underground, they had
ended up exactly across the street from their starting
point, the Inn of the Red Flower. He wondered about

the size of the nest of tunnels underneath Pig Town and made a mental note to ask M'bele someday—assuming that M'bele would ever speak to him again.

Shariba-Jen steered the van carefully, always avoiding the main highways. As soon as possible he struck out overland, lifting the vehicle westward over the Crumble and into the broken fissures of Short Rock Canyon. They traveled without lights, but the lack did not bother the robot. Jen expanded the range of its sensors and navigated across the dark landscape by the heat evaporating off the rocks. That, plus his inertial guidance system, gave him all the information he needed to keep the van from splattering up against a sudden upthrust of stone.

Abruptly, Shariba-Jen turned the van northward and accelerated rapidly. "Now what?" said Sawyer. He climbed forward to peer between Jen and Ota's shoulders. The forward window remained impenetrably dark, but the readouts showed the robot taking the van uncomfortably high.

"I believe a Dragon-boat has caught our scent," said Jen politely.

"Robots don't believe anything," Sawyer grunted. "Either we have pursuit or we don't."

"We do."

"Great."

"Don't worry," said Jen. "I've already contacted the landing boat—"

"We've got lights behind us!" Lee called forward.

Sawyer glanced back. Three sets of beams came slicing up through the air. "Aww, shit." To Jen he said, "I thought you said *one* Dragon-boat."

"It looked like one, until they split apart. One— three—does it make a difference?"

"Yes!"

"Stand by," said Jen.

"They've started firing at us!" shouted Lee.

"Warning shots," said Jen. "They don't dare—"

Abruptly, the van shuddered violently as a disruptor beam splattered off the bottom of its antigrav field. Sawyer swore as his head bounced against the roof. "Will you start taking this seriously?"

"Stand by," repeated Jen.

Before he had even finished speaking the words, a flash of light illuminated the night behind them. Sawyer caught a quick glimpse of something coming apart in fast flying fragments.

"How did you do that?" he demanded.

"I have friends in high places," Jen said. The robot struggled to keep the van steady in the air. "Stand by—"

The second Dragon-boat disintegrated in a fiery blast, this one closer than before. The van bounced in the air as the shock wave overtook them. From behind, Lee started swearing furiously. "Why do you hate me so much, Sawyer? What have I ever done to you?"

"You forgot my birthday," Sawyer replied. To Jen he said, "Can you evade the third boat?"

"I have to hold a steady course to give our friends a chance to target them. Uh-oh, it looks like he figured it out. He turned off. Well, we can't win them all. But he'll probably tell his friends about us. Stand by—" he said.

"For what?"

"For immediate pickup—"

Suddenly, the whole front window of the van lit up. Close above them Sawyer saw the underside of *The Lady MacBeth*'s largest landing craft. The van rocked in the downpush of the shuttle's powerful levitators. Then, as it pulled forward, Sawyer saw the open hatch of the aft cargo bay looming directly ahead.

"Oh, no—" he said. "You don't really think—"

But before he finished the sentence, something large and hard clanged against the van's roof. "Gotcha!" Jen said triumphantly. The van swung up inside the shuttle, the cargo doors came swinging up beneath it, and the sudden rush of acceleration pushed them all back in their seats—all except for Sawyer, who tumbled backward onto the floor as the shuttle climbed up into the sky.

Acceleration

□□□□□□□□□□□□□□□□□□□□□□□□□□□□□

The shuttle pilot obviously had less concern for her passengers than she did for her trajectory. She stood the ship on its tail and boosted at full acceleration. Sawyer heard Finn cry out in pain. Nyota and Azra too. Even Ota, in the forward seat, grunted. "I apologize for the inconvenience," Shariba-Jen said crisply. "This will nullify all attempts at pursuit by ground-based Dragon-boats. It will also make interception by orbital Marauders extremely difficult."

"And what happens when we reach orbit and try to dock with the starship—?" Sawyer gasped from the back. "The Marauders will surely catch us then."

He didn't think the robot had heard him, but Jen answered with efficiency. "Again, not a problem. We have no intention of docking in orbit. *The Lady MacBeth* will meet us before then."

"Say *what*?"

"*The Lady MacBeth* will match our velocity in the upper reaches of the atmosphere and take the shuttle aboard the same way the shuttle picked up the van."

This news left Sawyer even more incredulous. "I don't believe I just heard what you said. Your Captain has either no brains or no sanity. We'll vaporize!"

"Logic suggests that I agree with your estimation. However, Star-Captain Neena Linn-Campbell has proved adept in similar tactical situations. This maneuver has worked almost every time we've needed to use it."

"Almost . . . ?"

"The one time it didn't work, the blame lay with an inexperienced pilot," Shariba-Jen acknowledged. "We don't have that problem today. You may relax with a confidence rating of seventy-three percent."

"Seventy-three percent, huh?"

"And rising, even as we climb."

"Why does this not fill me with excitement?" Sawyer asked of no one in particular. "I met your Captain on Thoska-Roole—" he offered. "A real charmer."

"Thank you," said Jen, oblivious to the sarcasm. "Stand by."

"Now what?"

"Free fall."

"What—?"

"The orbiting Marauders expect us to achieve escape velocity. On the contrary, we will shortly cease accelerating as if we intend to fall into a ballistic trajectory heading back down to a hiding place somewhere on the surface. This will confuse both ground and space observers."

As if on cue the acceleration cut out abruptly, accompanied by gasps of shock and discomfort from most of the van's passengers. Sawyer pushed himself up off the floor, bounced off the ceiling, and pulled himself forward again. This time he strapped himself into a forward seat.

"Don't panic," Jen said. "*The Lady MacBeth* has already descended into the atmosphere to catch the shuttle just as it approaches the top of its arc. The whole maneuver requires very precise timing. Even as we speak, I continue to monitor the trajectories of both vessels. So far you have nothing to worry about."

"Uh-huh. I don't have a lot of confidence in this method of escape, you know."

"Oh, we'll get away with it. We did the last two times we had to do this maneuver."

"Right. And pretty soon someone will figure out this trick and prepare for it. Then what will your Captain do?"

"Statistically, that should happen the next time we try. And I believe the Captain has already figured out how to use that very expectation to fool anyone who thinks to outwit us."

Sawyer shuddered. "This woman thinks like I do.

How do I get off this ship?" Despite himself he had to ask. "All right. Tell me the awful rest of it. What happens when *The Lady MacBeth* grabs the shuttle?"

"We accelerate straight up again. The orbital Marauders will try to match course and intercept us, or at least get close enough to fire missiles or beams, but I don't think they'll have either the speed or the maneuverability to close the gap in time. We have the advantage of range. Stand by." The robot added, "This one may cause some discomfort."

"Thanks for the warning—" Sawyer started to say.

Something CLANKED outside the van, outside the shuttle that had caught them. For a moment nothing seemed to happen; then they felt themselves turning upward, and a great pressure pushed them all back in their seats. It went on and on and on. Sawyer found it hard to breathe, and after several painful lifetimes he began to wonder how much longer the crushing acceleration would continue. He might have passed out; when he came to, the acceleration still pushed him back in his seat, but nowhere near as fiercely as before.

"Stand by," said Shariba-Jen one more time.

The acceleration stopped abruptly. They hung in free fall for several terrifying seconds. Then the artificial gravity kicked in. Sawyer felt sore and aching all over his body. He felt as if several Dragons had just given him a customized beating.

Shariba-Jen raised its voice. "Welcome aboard *The Lady MacBeth*. Please follow me to the salon. We have made every arrangement for a comfortable journey for each of you. Hurry along, please. The Captain would like to have the ship secured as rapidly as possible before the transit to *otherspace*."

Ota picked up Lady Zillabar and tossed her unceremoniously over its shoulder. Shariba-Jen picked up Finn Markham a lot more carefully. Sawyer, Lee, Three-Dollar, M'bele, Nyota, and Azra followed uncertainly. They climbed out of the van, and then out the now-reopened cargo doors of the landing shuttle, and found themselves in the large docking bay at the stern of *The Lady MacBeth*.

"Hey?" asked Ota of Shariba-Jen, pointing back at the shuttle. "We have to return that rental truck before the end of the week."

Shariba-Jen shook its head. "We'll have to do it next trip. I don't think Captain Campbell will let us take it back now." He turned around to their passengers. "This way please. Hurry along—"

Reunions

□□□□□□□□□□□□□□□□□□□□□□□□□□□

For a while the salon of *The Lady MacBeth* looked like bedlam as old friends greeted one another.

Kask, the rebellious Dragon, grabbed Sawyer with both his foreclaws, the closest a Dragon had ever managed to an affectionate hug, and honored him for his adventures in escaping from the Lady's starship. Ibaka, the dog-child, bounced up and down on Kask's great shoulder, demanding a full recounting of the entire tale, excitedly questioning every detail. Robin, the starship's de facto medico, insisted on taking Finn down to sick bay and installing him in a maintenance tube so she could monitor his condition. Arl-N, the tall, spindly man who had escaped from the detainment at MesaPort with Sawyer and Finn and Lee, kept shaking each of their hands in turn; his delight lit up his whole face. Three-Dollar and M'bele tried to confer quietly with Captain Campbell about appropriate accommodations for their hostage, the lady Zillabar—Captain Campbell demonstrated something less than enthusiasm at the return of the Vampire Queen to *The Lady MacBeth*. Azra and Nyota, both wide-eyed, stood and stared in amazement. Gito, the high-gravity dwarf and Chief Engineer of the starship, stood apart and grumbled. Beside him, Arbiter Harry

Mertz nodded sagely at the bizarre collection of crew members and passengers aboard the vessel.

"I've seen a lot of refugee ships," he remarked. "But never any like this." He shook his head bemusedly. "I intend to enjoy this journey. I'll probably get rich from all the fees I'll collect hearing arbitrations. I expect to hear the first complaint before the last passenger falls asleep tonight."

Gito turned to him and said, "That reminds me. Captain Campbell has postponed the renegotiation of our contract again. Do we have legal recourse?"

Justice Harry Mertz smiled to himself at the accuracy of his prediction. "Sometimes I just don't know my own strength."

Sawyer managed to pull Captain Campbell aside long enough to ask her, "We've got Marauders on our tail, don't we?"

"We did." Captain Campbell scratched her ear as she listened to a private report from EDNA, the ship's intelligence engine. "Two of them blew up mysteriously. The other three won't get close enough to blow up." She looked at Sawyer blandly. "Don't worry. We have at least an hour before the next attempted interception. I've got to get all you folks settled and strapped in before then."

"What about *otherspace*? Why haven't we gone into transit already?"

"This close to a gravity well?" Captain Campbell looked at Sawyer as if astonished at his foolhardiness. "Just what do you use for brains, tracker? If we tried anything that foolhardy, we'd shred the vessel."

"I beg your pardon? You have the audacity to say that—after that little escape maneuver off of Dupa?"

"We only take *calculated* risks," Campbell said stiffly. "Go take a look in the engine room and then tell me how you feel about *otherspace*."

At first Sawyer didn't realize the import of her words. Then it sank in. "*The Lady MacBeth* has a singularity stardrive? Good God!"

"You have a problem with that?" Her eyes narrowed and her expression hardened. "Would you like to visit the air lock instead?"

"No, no, not at all," he protested. "I apologize. Forgive me for my stupidity. Perhaps I misremembered what I'd learned about stardrives. I'd heard that singularity drives have . . . uh, sometimes demonstrated a notorious finickiness, a tendency to collapse the surrounding vessel. I suppose that some people get nervous in the proximity of a pinpoint black hole and just can't accept the reality of a very tricky piece of applied physics at faster-than-light velocities. I know I have a great deal of trouble with it myself, and I studied *otherspace* mechanics once." Sawyer began to feel embarrassed. His mouth seemed to have taken on an embarrassing life of its own.

Captain Campbell allowed herself the slightest of smiles. "You may relax," she said. "I don't take responsibility for what other singularity vessels have done. But this one will not go *fwooop!* anytime in the near future. Not while I have anything to say about it."

Sawyer nodded politely. "I find that very reassuring. Thank you, Captain. I'll certainly feel a lot better about this voyage now."

"Good!" Captain Campbell patted his arm and smiled sweetly. "Oh, by the way—you do know that I'll have to bill you for that missed rendezvous on Thoska-Roole. We had a great deal of trouble arranging that, you know."

Sawyer gritted his teeth. "I had hoped we could talk about that. . . ."

Captain Campbell remained smiling. "We just did."

"Um . . . right. Thank you."

"Whatever else we can do to make your journey as pleasant as possible, don't hesitate to ask me or any of my crew members. Now, if you'll excuse me—" She nodded and made her way forward.

Sawyer stared after her, puzzled. Had she made that last statement in earnest, or had he detected the slightest bit of mockery in her tone?

Damn! But he did find her attractive. *Very* attractive.

Challenge

☐☐☐☐☐☐☐☐☐☐☐☐☐☐☐☐☐☐☐☐☐☐☐☐☐☐☐☐☐

Aboard *The Golden Fury*, a bright red messenger lizard came running to the Dragon Lord's quarters with an urgent message.

Sensors showed a freebooter vessel trying to break the blockade. Furthermore, the suspect ship, *The Lady MacBeth*, had brought the Lady Zillabar to Thoska-Roole on her last journey; her Captain had since resigned from the Spacers' Guild and (according to reliable intelligence on both Thoska-Roole and Dupa) had sworn vengeance against both the Lady and the Regency. Captain Neena Linn-Campbell had also helped several rebels escape from Thoska-Roole, including her own First Officer. "We also have reason to believe that she harbors considerable resentment against the Dragon Lord over the recent confiscation of a warehouse full of prime pfingle eggs."

The Dragon Lord didn't need to have it all explained to him. If the rebels who'd captured Lady Zillabar needed a freebooter willing to break the blockade, Captain Campbell certainly met the necessary requirements of skill and rebelliousness.

As the Dragon Lord stumped heavily toward the bridge of the starship, the little red lizard continued to brief him on the situation. "*The Lady MacBeth* performed several unusual—and extremely dangerous—upper-atmosphere maneuvers to retrieve her shuttleboat and evade the orbital Marauders. She has a singularity stardrive, so she'll need to get quite a ways out of the gravity well before she can risk a transit to overdrive. Captain 'Ga Lunik has anticipated your orders and already put us on an interception course."

The Dragon Lord grunted. At the moment he cared

less about the fate of Zillabar, or even of the possible interception of the freebooter. Getting free of the oppression of d'Vashti pleased him more. Someday Dragons would no longer have to kneel before Vampires. He hoped to live long enough to humble d'Vashti himself.

It could happen. He had deliberately fostered the rebellious Alliance of Life by carefully not targeting its leaders for many years; and as a result they had taken Zillabar out of the picture for him. Perhaps soon they would take down d'Vashti—and the Dragons could assume their rightful role of leadership over the Cluster. Who else had the strength to rule? If history taught anything, it taught that strength *always* ruled.

The Dragon Lord entered the command level of the bridge of *The Golden Fury*, looking almost pleased. Captain 'Ga Lunik even advanced to meet him and brief him directly, a sure sign that the politics of the situation had begun to improve again. "We've powered up, but we have so much more mass than the freebooter that it significantly affects our ability to maneuver and accelerate. Nevertheless, they have to get away from the gravity well before they can risk a transit. Our best calculations suggest that we will overtake them in ten minutes. We have a very short window of opportunity, but we have an excellent chance to put a tractor beam on them."

"Good," rumbled the Dragon Lord. "Let's take them alive. It will suit both of our purposes to have this triumph."

"An excellent thought," agreed 'Ga Lunik, careful not to assign it the credential of an order, or even the value of a suggestion. He had learned this lesson well and would give the Dragon Lord nothing to take home again except the barest of victories, one that would suit his own purposes as well.

'Ga Lunik stepped over to the astrogational display and studied the sweeping curves, lines, and shaded triangles. Despite *The Lady MacBeth*'s rapid approach into the ellipse of possible interceptions, *The Golden Fury* had the advantage of position. They did not have to overtake *The Lady MacBeth*. Rather, the freebooter vessel would do most of the overtaking itself; the Imperial vessel needed only to use its forward position to maximum advantage, making it impossible for the smaller vessel to elude their greater power and weaponry. The freebooter ship could not change course to avoid them without losing valuable time and distance and making itself even more vulnerable to interception; they had no choice but to accelerate fiercely ahead.

'Ga Lunik turned to his executive officer. "Signal *The Lady MacBeth*. Tell them to shut down their engines immediately. We intend to intercept, board, and inspect. Tell them we will destroy them if they resist."

A moment later a very embarrassed executive officer returned to report to his Captain. "I regret to inform you, sir, that they have rejected your signal."

"What did they say?"

"I would prefer not to repeat it on the bridge of an Imperial Starship, sir."

"Tell me anyway."

"Sir—" The exec looked very uncomfortable.

The Dragon Lord stumped over angrily to loom over them both. "Speak it!" he roared to the exec.

"Yes, sir." The exec cleared his throat. "The captain of *The Lady MacBeth* says, and I quote this, sir, she said, 'Tell your lizard-sucking Captain and his egg-stealing Dragon Lord that they can go straight to the handmaiden's hell where they both belong."

'Ga Lunik kept his outer face bland. He avoided looking at the Dragon Lord, but he could tell by the sudden rush of hot breath on his back that the Dragon Lord had not appreciated the sentiment either.

"Did you tell them that we would destroy them if they resisted?"

"They said—" The exec swallowed hard. "Captain Campbell said, 'Go ahead.' Actually, she said, 'Go ahead, you pig-brained, thieving, Regency whores.' She also said, 'We have the Lady Zillabar. Fire on us at your own risk. If you take any hostile action against this vessel, we will kill her immediately—' " The exec stopped himself, took a breath, and started again. "Actually, she said, 'We will kill the bitch painfully and then self-destruct. Do not approach under any circumstances.' "

Captain 'Ga Lunik considered the import of this message for three long seconds, wondering if he had just reached the limits of his ability to wend his way through the labyrinthine politics of the Regency. He turned around and looked up at the Dragon Lord behind him. "I have always appreciated the value of your thoughts, Your Excellency. . . ."

The Dragon Lord grunted without thinking. "So what? If she dies, she dies. Perhaps she has outlived her usefulness to the Regency."

"My Lord—?" 'Ga Lunik's face went pale with astonishment.

"You heard me!" the Dragon roared. "Who do you serve? The Lady or the Dragon? Or do you wish to kneel to d'Vashti's sons the rest of your life?"

'Ga Lunik considered his alternatives. None had promise. But clearly, the Lady Zillabar had somehow lost her influence. Without her, d'Vashti's power would crumble too. In the vacuum that would surely follow, a new leader would have many opportunities to rise to power. Who better than the loyal commander of the Imperial flagship? Hm, yes.

'Ga Lunik turned back to his exec. "Intercept them. As soon as you have them in range, grab them with a beam. Pull them in. If they fire, hit them with low-level disruptors. Don't breach hull integrity—and watch out. They've got a singularity stardrive. Don't bobble their fluction. I don't want a pinpoint running loose."

"Yes, Captain."

"Oh, and one more thing," 'Ga Lunik added. "Send this signal. Whatever harm befalls the Lady Zillabar, every person aboard that ship will experience the same thing, ten times over. A hundred. A thousand." Privately, he added, but no matter what else happens, *I intend to personally break the spine and drink the blood of that insolent bitch, Captain Neena Linn-Campbell.*

Interception

◻◻◻◻◻◻◻◻◻◻◻◻◻◻◻◻◻◻◻◻◻◻◻◻◻◻◻◻◻◻◻

Standing on the bridge of *The Lady MacBeth*, Star-Captain Neena Linn-Campbell chewed on a nail thoughtfully as she considered her options.

Unfortunately, she had no options.

The mechanics of acceleration, vector, and trajectory made interception inevitable. The laws of physics had a certain irrevocable nastiness. If you stepped off the top of a cliff, sooner or later you would bump up against a very unpleasant and very hard fact; sudden changes in velocity or direction, while theoretically possible, carry an impossibly high price in practice.

She had gambled that *The Lady MacBeth* could out-maneuver and outrun the orbital Marauders, and she had won that gamble. She had gambled that *The Golden Fury* would not pursue, or that its position would prevent it from mounting an effective interception. She had lost that gamble. The great Imperial Starship had powered up almost immediately for interception. In only a few moments more, the final confrontation would occur.

Her crew stood at their posts and waited for her decision. Ota, the pandalike First Officer; Robin, the android exec and astrogator; Gito, the high-gravity dwarf and Chief Engineer; Shariba-Jen, the robot who didn't need a title and simply performed every job required of him—all of them represented a responsibility that she had never acknowledged with words, and certainly never in their presence; but she held her commitment to their welfare as sacred as she held her commitment to the profitability of the Shakespeare Corporation. They trusted her with their lives. In return she held no higher priority.

She didn't dare let Zillabar live. Once restored to power, Zillabar would take the most ferocious revenge against her and everyone else aboard *The Lady MacBeth*. On the other hand, so would the Dragon Lord. She really had no choice. As a dead freebooter, at least she could deny them the luxury of revenge. "EDNA," she said. "Stand by for self-destruct, on my command."

"Aww," said the intelligence engine, petulantly. "Not again."

"This time I mean it."

"Sure, Captain—just like you meant it all the other times."

"Do you have a better idea?"

EDNA didn't answer.

"I thought so. If anyone from *The Golden Fury* attempts to board this ship, or if they attempt to disable us, I will give the final self-destruct authorization. Additionally, I grant you authorization to destroy this ship within sixty seconds of my death or at the forcible removable of myself or anyone else currently aboard. Unless I countermand the order. Have you got that?"

"Don't I always get it? Do you prefer a specific method of dissolution?"

"The usual."

"Hm." EDNA considered that for several thousandths of a second. "I believe that *The Golden Fury* intends to intercept us, connect with a tractor beam, and board us with armed troops. In such an event a deliberate malfluction of the singularity would also destroy *The Golden Fury* and all aboard her. My sacredness of life programming demands that I request a specific override command from you before I can activate such a self-destruct sequence."

"Right," said Neena Linn-Campbell. She rubbed her ear and frowned. "I grant you full authorization to override all your sacredness of life routines if necessary to destroy this vessel and any other vessel in close proximity, including all hostiles. This order shall remain in effect until one of two events occurs—either I countermand it directly, or you execute the self-destruct. After executing the self-destruct, you may reenable your sacredness of life routines."

"Aye, aye, Cap'n." After a moment EDNA reported, "*The Golden Fury* will have us in range of her tractor beams within three minutes."

Captain Campbell looked to her crew. "Does anyone object to my decision? Does anyone here wish to surrender?"

Ota looked to Robin. Robin looked to Gito. Gito looked to Shariba-Jen. Shariba-Jen looked back to Captain Campbell. "Did you intend that question for anyone on this bridge, Captain?"

"Thank you," said Neena Linn-Campbell. "I appreciate the acknowledgment."

"Acknowledgment, hell," grumbled Gito. "I just don't want to end up on the Dragon Lord's plate."

"Ota, take the Conn. I'll go tell our passengers."

As Captain Campbell entered the main salon, she felt a dull *thump* that resonated throughout the starship. "I assume you all felt that," she said. "The Imperial Starship, *The Golden Fury*, has caught us in a tractor beam. We will attempt to make it as difficult as possible for them to reel us in, but you may expect that they will clamp on to this ship within the hour."

Sawyer and Lee both started to protest. William Three-Dollar stood up alarmed. Finn, still looking weak and frail, shook his head vigorously. Azra held Nyota tightly on her lap; M'bele stepped close to his daughter and put a hand on her shoulder. Ibaka wept in fear, but the Dragon Kask picked the dog-child up in his huge hands and cradled him gently. Arl-N stood resolutely still.

She held up a hand for silence. "I have made a decision," Captain Campbell said firmly, "based on my situation and my knowledge of your situation. If they try to board us or disable us, this vessel will self-destruct through a singularity fluction. That should also destroy *The Golden Fury* at the same time, a result that may afford some of you some comfort. We have informed them of our intent; I don't know if they believe my threat or not. They have underestimated all of us in the past. At this point, though, I would expect that they will try to take us under tow and return us to orbit around Dupa."

She allowed her exhaustion to show. "If that happens, then very quickly we will have a standoff. A state of siege. If they believe my threat to self-destruct, they won't dare try to board us or disable us. We can't give up. We know that. On the other hand, they can't let us go without making the Regency look ineffective. The standoff can continue only as long as we maintain air, water, food, and associated life-support functions. They will get stronger with time. We will get weaker. Whatever advantage we might have in such a situation will erode quickly. In this case both sides have a Dragon by the tail. Neither can hang on. Neither can let go. Therefore"—she ran a hand through her hair—"I will not let the siege continue more than twenty-four hours. I'll set a deadline. If they don't release us, we'll trigger the fluction."

Harry Mertz spoke first. "We have no chance at all, then?"

Captain Campbell shook her head. "I don't believe in miracles. Although occasionally I've had to depend on them. You might pray. If anyone aboard believes in the power of random happenstance, you might want to cast some hexagrams now. Beyond that—" She shrugged, helplessly. "If anyone else has any ideas, let's hear them."

No one spoke. Even the two TimeBinders remained thoughtful and silent.

"I thought not." She went to the rear wall and opened a hidden panel, revealing an impressive brace of weaponry, enough to start a small war. "If by any chance the plan fails and Dragons and Vampires somehow gain access to this vessel, feel free to defend yourselves appropriately."

Lee and Sawyer and Arl-N moved first to the cabinet. They began selecting equipment. Sawyer noticed Finn waving weakly at him and pulled down a small hand weapon that his brother could manage effectively in his still-weakened condition. Lee passed out weapons to the others, leaving out only Nyota and Ibaka.

Even Three-Dollar took a rifle, though he seemed to have a different purpose than the others. If it became necessary, he intended to destroy the Time-Bands. First Nyota's, then his own.

Captain Campbell returned to the bridge slowly, finally feeling her age.

As she stepped out onto the command deck of her vessel, she felt the *clang* of the first grapples. She grabbed hold of the railing with both hands and hung her head in despair. She bit her lip and waited for the sound of a docking tube connecting to the aft air lock.

The Pfickle Pfingle of Pfate

Seemingly motionless, *The Golden Fury* hung silent in space, with the tail end of *The Lady MacBeth* held firmly in its tractonic grapples. A long, thin docking tube extended, matched sockets with the air lock of the much smaller vessel, and connected to the harness ring with a solid set of clicks and thunks. Air filled the tube, and it inflated with a *whoosh*, becoming purposefully erect.

A moment later a squad of slender lizards scooted across the intervening space and pried opened the outer air-lock hatch. Then they waited.

The image of the Dragon Lord appeared on the main screen of the bridge of *The Lady MacBeth*. He appeared at his full height of fifteen meters. Captain Campbell noted idly that the camera had photographed him from a low angle, so as to make him look even bigger. She reached out to her console and dialed the image down to a much smaller size. A one-meter-high image of the Dragon Lord roared at her. She amused herself by resynthesizing his voice as a high-pitched squeak.

"You have sixty seconds to surrender," the image nattered at her. "My troops stand ready to peel back the inner door of your air lock."

Neena Linn-Campbell stepped forward, lifting her arm to show the object she held in her hand. "Take a good look at this, you noxious little fart! Do you recognize a dead man's switch? If I let go of this, the intelligence engine of this vessel will trigger a singularity fluction in the pinpoint black hole that we use for power. Approximately four seconds after that, your ship and mine will cease to exist. Everyone aboard both vessels will likewise cease to exist. Instead we will leave a sphere of rapidly expanding radiation. If your nasty little lizards touch my air-lock door, I'll toss this across my bridge, far enough away that I will have no chance for second thoughts."

The Dragon Lord snorted his contempt. "If you think to threaten me with lies and tricks, it won't work. However, you should know that I have removed myself from the luxury of *The Golden Fury*, specifically to deny you the opportunity to wreak havoc against the body of the Lord of All Moktar Dragons. You may destroy the Lady's Imperial Starship. I could not care less. The worlds of the Regency will happily tax themselves to excess to build a new replacement. They will remember your name with gratitude for the opportunity you will soon give them. Myself, I watch from a safe distance, so that I might report your actions honestly."

Captain Campbell looked quickly to Ota. Ota inclined her head slightly toward the tactical display. A great golden blip represented *The Golden Fury*; a smaller red dot connected to it represented *The Lady MacBeth*. Several smaller blips indicated tactical Marauders coasting in matching orbits, more than ten thousand kilometers distant. One of the blips blinked steadily—the source of the Dragon Lord's broadcasts. Captain Campbell gave no sign of acknowledgment. She dropped her eyes to her own display. She noticed that the tractor beam had finally cut off, leaving only the grapples holding them in place. Good.

Captain Campbell turned back to the viewscreen. "I expected an act of cowardice from you," she replied. "Thank you for not disappointing me. A real Dragon would have stood unafraid on the bridge of the flagship.

Perhaps your troops will someday honor your courage in song and story. I look forward to hearing your courage celebrated. In the meantime maybe you can tell me something—which end of the Dragon produces the most noxious noises and odors? I confess an inability to tell the difference anymore."

On the forward screen the shrunken image of the Dragon Lord opened its mouth to answer. Abruptly, the beast closed his mouth. Puzzled. He opened his mouth. He closed it again.

Curious, Neena Linn-Campbell dialed up the size of the image again.

The Dragon Lord looked . . . *distracted*. As if something peculiar had bitten him on the ass. Something had.

"Ota, did you see that?"

"Yes, Captain, I did."

"What did it look like to you?"

"It looked like a pfingle, Captain."

"It looked like a pfingle to me too."

Now the Dragon Lord turned away from the viewscreen and began lashing frenziedly at something. At a lot of somethings.

"Ota, I don't understand this," Captain Campbell said innocently. "Why would the Dragon Lord carry a swarm of live pfingles onto his ship? I can't think of anything more dangerous."

Ota kept its face blank. "I can't imagine any good reason, Captain. Perhaps he had a large cache of pfingle eggs aboard? Perhaps he misjudged their ripeness?"

"An excellent hypothesis," Captain Campbell agreed. She sat down in her command chair to watch, dialing up the image to full size.

Unfortunately, the performance did not last long. Very shortly the image winked out and the carrier beam cut off. On the tactical display the blinking blip had fallen out of formation.

"Hm," said Captain Campbell blandly. "When I pray for miracles, I don't mess around, do I?" She sat back, grinning. "I rather like the way that one turned out." She punched up a different channel. "Ahoy, *The Golden Fury*. Captain Campbell of *The Lady MacBeth* here."

A distracted Captain 'Ga Lunik appeared on the main view screen. "I can't talk to you now," he said. "That goddamned Dragon brought thirty metric tons of pfingle eggs aboard my ship. Ripe pfingle eggs!"

"Goodness," said Neena Linn-Campbell. "Ota, I do believe you calculated correctly. That bastard on Dupa sold us two-month eggs instead of three-month eggs. Thank goodness we found out before we hurt ourselves."

Ota replied, "Thank you, Captain. I appreciate the acknowledgement."

Captain Campbell turned back to the viewscreen. "Captain 'Ga Lunik, I've heard that industrial-grade carnivorous pfingles have quite an appetite when freshly hatched. You certainly understand that I can't risk my vessel in such close proximity to yours while you have this particular problem. I will have to disconnect your docking tube now, and we'll have to continue this discussion another time—"

Captain 'Ga Lunik still had enough presence of mind to think of revenge. "I'll take you with me, you bloody damned witch!" To someone else he screamed, "Open the inner door of their air lock. Let them have pfingles too!"

"I don't think so." Neena Linn-Campbell tossed aside the dummy dead man's switch. "EDNA, blow the docking tube and take us out of here. Fast." Something suddenly went BANG in the back of the ship. Neena Linn-Campbell nodded in recognition. The blast of the hidden explosive charges on the outer air-lock door resonated throughout *The Lady MacBeth*, creating an extremely satisfying impact. In her mind's eye she saw the docking tube writhing away from the back end of her vessel, spilling a horde of gasping lizards directly into the vacuum of space.

"Sealing the outer air-lock doors," EDNA reported. "Status: minimal damage, requiring less than thirty hours of repair and testing. Shariba-Jen will tend to it during *otherspace* transit." A moment later EDNA added, "We have full acceleration. We will reach a safe transit distance within two hours."

Captain Campbell almost didn't hear it. The signal

from the bridge of *The Golden Fury* continued. The crew stared in horror at the devastation occurring on Lady Zillabar's Imperial Starship. The pfingles swarmed across the bridge, the Ops Bay, the Ops Deck, the Command Deck, ravenously attacking every organic thing they encountered.

"Save this," said Ota to Shariba-Jen. "We'll want to show it to the others later. In particular, the Lady Zillabar will have to see this."

Captain Campbell turned around to see Justice Harry Mertz standing behind her, thoughtfully watching the distant carnage. She raised an eyebrow at him. "Yes?"

"You cut it a little close there, didn't you?"

She shrugged. "To tell the truth—I honestly didn't plan that one, but it does have a certain rough justice. He who lives by the pfingle, dies by the pfingle." She studied the tactical display thoughtfully. "Do you know that pfingle eggs can survive hard vacuum?"

"Really?"

"Really." She nodded. "I don't think anyone will ever want to board *that* ship again. They should push it into the sun. I would. I wish we had the time to do it ourselves."

Justice Considered

▭▭▭▭▭▭▭▭▭▭▭▭▭▭▭▭▭▭▭▭▭▭▭▭▭▭▭▭

Otherspace.

Time and distance and form became abstract concepts. *Otherspace* defied the mind's ability to rationalize. Think of nothingness. No. Don't think of the *concept* of nothingness. Think of nothingness. You can't. Not for long. The human mind cannot think of nothingness; it traps itself automatically in the conceptualization of it. The human mind will retreat in horror from those things it cannot reduce to convenient symbols—infinity, nothingness, death. And *otherspace*.

It doesn't matter. The human mind doesn't have to think about *otherspace*. Lethetic intelligence engines can do most of the appropriate thinking for humans. These powerful constructed sentients make it possible for ships to transit between realspace and *otherspace* and back again. And *otherspace* makes it possible for a vessel to journey from one star to another in a simple matter of days.

But aboard the starship time still passes—and because the human mind abhors nothingness, it needs activity to fill the days of travel.

Fortunately, aboard *The Lady MacBeth*, no lack of activity existed.

First of all, they had to consider the Zillabar problem.

As with all serious discussions, before the participants held their formal discussions, they first held their *informal* discussions. The conversations had a peripatetic quality, wandering from the ship's mess to the salon, to the cabins, back to the salon, and finally back to the ship's mess, where they careened ominously toward an unpleasant resolution.

Star-Captain Campbell sat in on these discussions, listening more than talking. The two TimeBinders, William Three-Dollar and Nyota, both offered anecdotes and precedents from their memories. Justice Mertz had opinions on the law. Lee and Sawyer and Finn had strong ideas about justice, regardless of the law.

At one point Harry caught Three-Dollar looking at him strangely—as if he recognized him from somewhere. "I have a memory of you, but I don't know why."

Harry shrugged it off. "We live in a small galaxy." But Three-Dollar continued to study the man with curiosity.

Kask and Ibaka, an inseparable pair now, also joined this discussion, neither quite sure why the humans needed to debate these issues, but certain that they too had a right to participate in any decision made here.

Over a cup of spice-tea Harry Mertz finally spoke

the question for all of them. "What do we do with the Lady Zillabar? What kind of status will she have at the Gathering? Should we treat her as a guest or as a prisoner of war? A diplomatic representative? A hostage? Whatever we decide will very likely affect the outcome of the Gathering. The possibilities for a disastrous legal precedent worry me."

"Wait a minute," said Finn in a voice so low that at first the others didn't hear him. Sawyer had to hush the rest so Finn could speak. "Maybe the aftereffects of the blood-burn still cloud my thinking, but won't the Gathering have the authority to set aside all old precedents, if necessary? I don't think we should automatically assume that we'll determine the final outcome by any action we take toward the Lady. And—" He coughed once, waved away Sawyer's solicitous assistance, then nodded as if to allow Sawyer to finish his thought.

"And, besides," said Sawyer, "both Finn and I believe that we should act in the spirit of justice, regardless of what the law says."

"Hm," said Harry. "An interesting concept, that."

"You don't agree?" Sawyer confronted him across the table.

"I agree that we want justice," said Harry, "but when we also agree to abandon the law, which must serve as the guideline for justice, we take away the only protection that we have of administering justice fairly. And yes"—he held up his hands as if to ward off Sawyer's further accusations—"I know how people have used and misused the law to thwart justice rather than create it. I know it better than you, my friend, Sawyer."

"Let's get back to the issue of Lady Zillabar's status," Captain Campbell said. "I need an arbitration on this. The Lady could charge me with accessory to kidnapping, piracy, I don't know what all, if we don't resolve this before the Gathering."

Sawyer giggled abruptly, and Captain Campbell glared at him. "Why do you laugh, tracker?"

"You destroyed the Lady's Imperial starship. I think that makes any lesser crime irrelevant. If Kernel d'Vashti catches up with us, he'll hang us all as conspirators. If we make it to the Gathering, they'll call us heroes, the opinions of the Phaestor notwithstanding. The context will determine the interpretation of our actions much more than any other consideration."

"I think you spend too much time watching cheap entertainments," Captain Campbell replied. "Only in stories do people get to escape the consequences of their actions. In the real world somebody always has to clean up the mess."

"Usually lawyers," grinned Harry.

Sawyer shuddered.

"You don't agree," said Harry.

"The way I remember it, lawyers got us into this mess."

"I appreciate the jaundice of your opinion."

"You think so? I challenge you to demonstrate that a lawyer can solve a problem for once instead of creating one."

"Eh? I don't understand."

"The more we talk, the more confused the situation gets. The Vampires nearly took Finn's life. According to M'bele, he still could die. He needs Zillabar's blood—at least four more treatments, maybe more. Who knows how many more?"

"So?"

"So what happens if you declare her a guest? Or a diplomatic representative? She'll have the right to refuse access to her blood. And she will. And what if Finn dies as a result? Would you call that problem solving?"

"I see," said Harry. He looked to Captain Campbell. "According to space law the Captain has final authority aboard her vessel. I can offer my opinions, but unless the aggrieved parties specifically hire me to arbitrate, my opinions remain without weight. Perhaps I should solve this problem by deferring to the legal authority of the Captain and let her make the decision."

"I'll settle it easily. Take all of that bitch's blood you want."

"You see," said Harry. "That presented no problem at all."

"Very funny," said Sawyer, "but you know as well as

I that you didn't solve anything. As long as you keep talking about the Lady's status, you continue to endanger Finn's treatment. Somebody has to contract for an arbitration in this matter. And you'll have to make a decision."

Captain Campbell nodded. "Sorry, Harry, but I think the tracker has a point. Even though I hold authority aboard this ship, anything I might decide would hold no legality the moment any of us step out the air lock. The TimeBinders both have vested interests and cannot claim impartiality. You, however, have both the credential and the experience, and more important, any ruling you might make would remain binding even beyond the termination of this voyage."

"Shit," said Harry.

"He sees my point," Campbell explained to the others.

"I assume, then, that I may interpret this as a request for me to assume the responsibilities of a formal arbitration."

"You may," agreed the Captain.

Harry stroked his chin. "Does anyone disagree?" He looked to Three-Dollar and Nyota and M'bele.

All three nodded their assent. "We want you to proceed."

"All right," said Harry. "On your own heads have it—" He began slowly, "We have several matters here. First off, the brothers Markham versus the Lady Zillabar, representative of the Regency. Secondly, Lady Zillabar versus the brothers Markham on a civil charge of kidnapping. We'll have to consider those two actions as appeals, seeing as how Three-Dollar has already ruled partially on them. Thirdly, Lady Zillabar versus *The Lady MacBeth*, accessory to the kidnapping, destruction of private property, terrorism. Finally, the issue of Lady Zillabar's status aboard this vessel. Ordinarily, I would disqualify myself, because I too have some history with the Lady, but because of the urgency of this case, I will take extra steps to keep my personal feelings from coloring my decisions."

Captain Campbell spoke up immediately. "I can't

believe you. I saved your life—how many times over, old man—and you demonstrate your gratitude by making me a defendant? I asked you for an arbitration—and now you make charges against me and my ship?"

Harry held up a hand. "Dear Lady, you have asked me to make law, not friends. The two have no relation at all. When you ask for justice, you should remember that she carries a double-edged sword."

"Gito—" Captain Campbell called into the galley. "Do you remember the name of the last lawyer we shoved out the air lock?"

Harry Mertz leaned back in his chair, frowning and pursing his lips. He cradled his cup of spice-tea—still steaming—and inhaled its vapors deeply. "After some consideration," he said, "it seems appropriate to me to dismiss the charges against Captain Campbell and *The Lady MacBeth*, without prejudice. We needed to consider the charges so as to demonstrate that this court has neither prejudice nor favoritism for either party in the matter."

Captain Campbell folded her arms, satisfied. "I can accept that. Go on."

"You need to understand this, Captain. Your threats did not influence my decision. I do not threaten that easily. Let me explain the reasons for my decision to dismiss the charges." He grinned at her and continued. "The actions of the Regency in relation to this vessel so transcended the boundaries of law that you had no choice but to act as you did in response. Therefore, while this court would find your actions objectionable under normal circumstances, the greater crimes committed against you mitigate all charges of piracy, terrorism, etcetera, and I hereby publish a summary dismissal of any Regency warrants based on those charges. Additionally, this court awards you five million caseys in damages for the confiscation of your cargo on Burihatin-14 and an additional five million caseys in punitive damages; such sums to come from the Regency treasury accounts administered on behalf of the Dragon Lord and Lady Zillabar."

"Thank you," said Captain Campbell politely.

"Don't thank me. You'll probably have some trouble

collecting that debt. Especially if the Gathering succeeds in dissolving the Regency."

"If the Gathering succeeds in dissolving the Regency, a lot of my other debts will magically disappear with that bastard government. Approximately eighteen million caseys' worth. So either way, I'll come out ahead."

Justice Harry Mertz smiled in satisfaction. "Good. Now, as to the other matters, we'll have to reconvene with the Lady Zillabar in attendance, at which time I will hear arguments from both sides. I expect to make a decision on all matters before we reach the Gathering."

Considered Justice

Justice Godfrey Daniels Harry Mertz, wearing a white robe, entered the salon from the bridge. He waited until Ota announced, "Oyez, oyez. All rise before the Honorable Justice Harry Mertz, Arbiter of Thoska-Roole, and Chief Officer of this court." The room rustled with movement as the various attendees shuffled to their feet.

Harry straightened his crisp new gown and grinned appreciatively at Robin and Shariba-Jen. The two had spent several feverish hours sewing an appropriate robe for Harry. Because the workings of justice required a certain amount of ritual and ceremony in order to convey the importance of the process, Harry had not simply requested the robe and certain other props—he had *demanded* them as necessary. He knew that he could not risk having the proceedings look haphazard or slipshod in any way. He couldn't allow any of these matters to arrive at the Gathering incomplete.

Harry seated himself at the forward end of the ship's brinewood salon. Glancing around, he grinned. "I've worked tougher rooms, but never one as pretty as this." He tapped the bell on the makeshift desk in front of him and announced, "The session has begun. We will now consider the first case on the docket, the matter of the brothers Markham versus the Lady Zillabar, in reference to a contract to locate and secure the personage of the TimeBinder of Thoska-Roole, in return for which the Lady or her representatives would supply a cure for Finn Markham's affliction, the blood-burn. Now, let's see—" Harry shuffled through the documents on the table before him, sorting his notes for the fifteenth time, then looked up again.

Sawyer and Finn sat at a table on the right side of the room, Zillabar sat stiffly on the left. Harry nodded and glanced back to the papers in his hands. "I see that the TimeBinder of Thoska-Roole has already made a previous ruling on this case. The Lady Zillabar has contested that ruling. I shall regard this hearing, then, as an appeal for total reconsideration." He looked to the Markhams, he looked to Zillabar. "Do all parties here recognize the authority of this court?"

Sawyer and Finn nodded. The Lady Zillabar remained dispassionate.

"Lady Zillabar?"

She glanced up slowly. "I don't recognize your authority over me," she said quietly.

"Unfortunately, that defense won't work here. Aboard a starship the Captain has ultimate authority and has delegated that authority to me to reach a just solution to certain problems that need resolution before we reach our destination. Whether you recognize the authority or not, under Regency law I have it." He tried to resist the impulse to grin. The Lady Zillabar had once tried to strip him of his title and whatever ceremonial authority it had carried. Now he had all the authority and more that she had tried to deny. The situation here tickled his sense of karmic retribution. He covered with a cough, hoping to hide even the slightest sense of a smirk. He didn't succeed.

Zillabar snorted. "I do not have appropriate representation," she said.

"I recognize the limited skills available here. However, you have access to EDNA, the ship's lethetic intelligence engine, and the court will appoint either William Three-Dollar or Nyota M'bele to assist you with appropriate case precedents and advice."

"I will represent myself, thank you—"

"As you wish."

"—but I want you to put it on the record. I do not believe I can get a fair hearing in this venue."

Sitting off to one side, Captain Campbell couldn't help smirking. "You don't like having the situation reversed, do you?" she said to Zillabar. In the back of the salon Gito laughed aloud and Kask rumbled good-naturedly. Lee snorted derisively.

Justice Mertz rapped his gavel lightly. "Uh-uh-uh-uh," he said. "Captain Campbell, if you do that again, I'll have to ask you to leave. This court will not tolerate any disrespect."

"Yes, Your Honor. I apologize." Chastened, Campbell sat back in her chair and folded her arms across her chest.

To Zillabar, Harry said, "I recognize your objections. I promise you that this court will make every effort to see that you receive every consideration that the law demands. Conversely, if the final ruling goes against you, this court will also make every effort to see that you receive every punishment the law demands. If you wish to offer terms for a settlement before we get into the details of the case—or if the brothers Markham wish to make an offer—the court will gladly allow that."

Harry looked to Sawyer and Finn expectantly. The brothers Markham shook their heads. "We have nothing to offer."

The judge turned his glance to Lady Zillabar. "Do you wish to offer a settlement?"

She returned his gaze stonily. "What I wish to offer," she said, "I don't think you would allow."

"Perhaps not," Harry agreed. "Let's get on with it, then. To speed this matter, we'll proceed with informal court rules. Please state your case."

The Lady Zillabar stood up and said, "I have a simple case, Your Honor—" She inclined her head in a slight nod at the words *Your Honor.* Harry couldn't tell if she intended the gesture with respect or sarcasm. "—I wish to halt the illegal draining of my blood."

Her words drew a sharp reaction from the audience gathered in the rear of the salon. Lee-1169 hooted out loud. Arl-N guffawed. Kask roared. Ibaka chittered and pounded his chest. The sight of a Vampire—especially *this* Vampire—protesting a blood-draining had a delicious irony to everyone in the chamber, most of whom had suffered sorely at her hands in the recent past.

After a moment or two of this Harry picked up his gavel and rapped it lightly on the table. "Order, order," he demanded. "We will have order. The court recognizes that many of you have strong feelings about this plaintiff. Nevertheless, we will not allow the rude behavior of anyone in this chamber to compromise the integrity of the proceedings. You will maintain decorum." The room began to settle down immediately. To Lady Zillabar, Harry said, "I have some experience with the circumstances of this case. The brothers Markham agreed to provide services, which they did—"

"They reneged."

"Only after you did. Nevertheless, they did locate and secure the personage of William Three-Dollar for you. So they fulfilled their part of the contract. You and your representatives agreed to provide an antidote or cure for the blood-burn. You reneged on your part of the contract. Do you wish to offer any explanation or mitigating circumstances?"

Lady Zillabar glared at Harry. She knew what he meant. She knew she didn't dare risk it. She shook her head curtly.

But Harry refused to take her head shake as an answer. "Correct me if I've made a mistake, but I had heard that you considered the Markhams' part in the death of Lord Drydel as a factor in your decision not to honor your part of the contract. Perhaps we should discuss that for a bit? I have several witnesses to that affair here; it might cast additional light on this matter. Although it represents a diversion from the main direction of this case, I think the circumstances of Lord Drydel's death belong in the public record, don't you?"

"No, I do not," said the Lady Zillabar dispassionately. "I still carry my grief as a private affair. I do not want the wounds reopened, and I request the court's understanding in this." Underneath she seethed. She couldn't possibly allow any public acknowledgment that Lord Drydel had violated the Regency Charter at her private feeding grounds.

Harry smiled gently. "Well, yes—as you wish. Perhaps another time, then." He glanced back at the papers before him. "So, then, we may correctly assume that you never intended to honor your part of the contract at all, did you?"

Lady Zillabar didn't reply.

"In earlier testimony Sawyer and Finn Markham both stated that you told them you had deceived them about a cure for the blood-burn, that it didn't exist. Would you like to clarify that statement now?"

She shook her head slowly.

Sawyer and Finn exchanged a confused glance. Why didn't Lady Zillabar try to argue or explain the facts? By acceding these points so easily, she gave her case away. Even Harry Mertz seemed puzzled. He glanced around the room, as if looking for an answer, then back to Zillabar again.

"All right," he said. "You leave me no choice but to rule against you. You made a contract with the Markhams; they kept their part of it, therefore you must keep your part of it. That no antidote exists does not mitigate the debt. You may not use that as an excuse for nonpayment. Because you allowed the Markhams to believe that an antidote existed, you committed a fraud, and this court must take steps to repair the damages wrought by your deception. Let me note here that the Markhams discovered on their own the possibility of a treatment or cure for the blood-burn that would require your physical cooperation. Because you represented yourself as the source of a cure, this court finds that you must make yourself available for Finn Markham's continued blood-cleansing treatments." He tapped his gavel and added,

"Ruling for the defendants. Lady Zillabar's blood now belongs to Sawyer and Finn Markham for the purposes of Finn Markham's continued treatment for as long as necessary to obtain a permanent state of good health for Finn Markham."

"I expected nothing less from you," said Lady Zillabar.

"Madam Zillabar," Harry said, "I believe you have not yet seen the whole picture. Sawyer and Finn Markham now have a vested interest in keeping you *alive*. It has not escaped my attention that some of the other passengers and crew members aboard this vessel heartily wish you dead. You now have two very dedicated bodyguards who will not allow that to happen. Here or anywhere else."

"You'll forgive me if I don't find much consolation in that news, Your Honor." She remained standing at her table. "I would now like to appeal your ruling on the grounds that it represents a cruel and unjust punishment."

Harry laid down his gavel and stared at her. "All right," he said. "Let's hear it."

"I have no choice but to recognize the authority of this court. Reluctantly, and under protest, I have done so. Reluctantly, and under protest, I must also accept the court's ruling. You consider it justice that the Markhams use my body to extract a cure that I allegedly promised. Fair enough. At least as far as it goes—"

"As far as it goes—?"

"Does the court also demand that the Markhams extract this punishment at the expense of my good health?"

"Dr. M'bele has assured me that he has every concern for your welfare—"

"Your honor, with all due respect—I believe that I know much more about Phaestor physiology than a backwoods juju man. The fact remains that the present course of this treatment threatens my life."

"I don't see how—"

"Then I'll explain it in terms that even you can understand. This treatment drains my strength, without replenishing it. Dr. M'bele and the Markhams have denied me access to an appropriate diet for my metabolism."

Justice Reconsidered

▢▢▢▢▢▢▢▢▢▢▢▢▢▢▢▢▢▢▢▢▢▢▢▢▢▢▢▢▢

"I beg your pardon?" Harry Mertz stared across the salon of the starship, wondering exactly what kind of legal quagmire he had just stepped into.

Lady Zillabar explained calmly, "Your ruling allows them to systematically starve me to death. Without my regular diet I will gradually weaken and die. I request that you expand your ruling to mandate that the Markhams must *guarantee* my continued good health."

"Hm," said Justice Mertz. "Would you please give me the punch line on this? What exactly do you want the court to do?"

"Thank you." The Lady nodded. "I wish the return of my property, for one." She turned and pointed directly at Ibaka, the dog-child sitting contentedly in the hands of Kask the Dragon. "That pup belongs to me. While I do not have it here, I do have a bill of sale to prove that I purchased him and his littermates on Burihatin-14. The Dragon who holds him witnessed the purchase. Furthermore, that same Dragon served as an attendant for the pups during transit and delivery, so he can confirm my claim to ownership."

At these words Ibaka began whimpering and squirming in Kask's hands. The Dragon began rumbling deep in his throat.

The Lady ignored them both. "I see that the pup has gained quite a bit of weight since I last saw him. He would sustain me for many days, certainly until we reached the Gathering, at which time I feel confident that I can find many other sources of appropriate nourishment. In the meantime, since you have already established the precedent that you will take one person's

243

blood to guarantee another's welfare, then I demand the return of my property so that I may use its blood to guarantee my welfare."

"*Oy vey*," said Harry quietly. He put his head in his hands and asked himself why he had ever accepted this particular honor. Wearily, he picked up the gavel and began banging on the desktop. "Order, order," he demanded. The uproar in the salon did not subside. "Order! Goddammit! I'll have order in this court, or you'll all take a one-way trip out the nearest air lock!"

At the back of the chamber Kask rose to his feet, holding the dog-child close to his chest. "By the great god Ghu, you will not have this child!" he roared. "I swear on my honor as a Moktar Dragon that no harm will come to this dog-boy."

Harry looked to Zillabar, annoyed. She smiled sweetly at him and reseated herself to wait for order to return to the courtroom. Lee-1169 stood screaming incoherently at Zillabar. Sawyer and Finn had begun shouting arguments at Harry; they turned to Three-Dollar and repeated their words. Nyota wept and wailed in Azra's lap. She resisted all attempts by M'bele to pick her up and comfort her. She beat at his chest. Even the normally placid Ota had taken on a menacing air.

Finally Harry turned to Captain Campbell. "Would you do something, please?"

Captain Campbell motioned to Shariba-Jen; the robot raised its voice to a level several decibels *above* the threshold of pain and shouted, "EVERYBODY SHUT UP."

It worked. They shut and stayed shut. Astonished at the depth and range of Shariba-Jen's voice.

"Thank you," Jen said.

"Thank you," Harry repeated. "Everybody calm down. Just because the Lady makes a demand does not mean that the court has to grant it." He looked unhappy, but he continued. "On the surface, yes, it does appear that the previous ruling sets a nasty precedent. However, this court finds that ruling specific to the nature of Finn's disability and without relevance to Madame Zillabar's current claim.

"Yes," he acknowledged, "the situations do have a certain similarity, but let us not let the similarity blind us to alternative possibilities. While no alternate source of treatment exists for Finn Markham's condition, I think that we can certainly find several excellent alternate sources of appropriate nourishment for Madame Zillabar. As Madame Zillabar has traveled aboard *The Lady Mac-Beth* before, it seems likely that Captain Campbell retains more than a passing familiarity with the Lady's needs."

To the Phaestor Queen, he said, "Without ruling directly on the preexistent claim of ownership, this court cannot allow you to advance your claim to the dog-child's blood. For one thing, the child may have witnessed several serious violations of the Regency charter that we may wish to investigate later. For another, your claim to his blood does not give you the right to kill him to collect. Therefore, I must dismiss this petition as invalid. Additionally, I will leave open the possibility for Ibaka to bring a claim against you and the Regency for involuntary slavery."

"Hmpf," said Zillabar. "I care little for the feelings of prey. Food does not get to have opinions."

"Yes," said Harry. "We all know your opinion about the opinions of others. However, you have raised an interesting issue that this court feels compelled to examine—the question of the dog-child's ownership. If you wish, we can settle this now. On the other hand, if Madame Zillabar prefers to wait and raise this issue again at the Gathering, I feel certain that we can reach a resolution there."

Justice Mertz looked directly at Zillabar. "Once again, however—and at the risk of upsetting you—let me inform you that should you bring any such claim to bear at the Gathering, the courts will also demand evidence about the fate of Ibaka's siblings. I will insist on that myself. This will of course involve reopening the question of Lord Drydel's activities at the time of his death, so at this point, if you wish to avoid that unpleasantness, I recommend that you reconsider your claim to the person of Ibaka."

"Other than the fact that you have just legalized the theft of my property," Zillabar retorted, "I have little interest in the dog-child." But she nodded in resignation. "All right. I relinquish my claim to it. But I wish to go on record that your actions here confirm what I already suspected—that I cannot expect fairness from this court."

"On the contrary, madam, this court has strained itself mightily to treat you with every courtesy and consideration possible."

"Yes, and in the meantime I die of hunger. You have the gall to call that consideration? I cannot eat the manufactured food on this ship. It tastes foul to me. I need blood. Real blood. Warm and hot. Human blood, preferably, but bioform blood will do nicely too."

Harry looked to M'bele, who nodded. So did Three-Dollar, and even little Nyota.

At this Sawyer Markham stood. "Your honor—this affects your previous ruling. If the Lady doesn't feed, she won't have the strength to save my brother. She has to have food—"

From the back of the room Kask roared again. Lee started screaming at Sawyer, "Now you take her side? Now we see how long a Markham's commitment lasts—"

Reconsidered Justice

▯▯▯▯▯▯▯▯▯▯▯▯▯▯▯▯▯▯▯▯▯▯▯▯▯▯▯▯▯

Justice Harry Mertz couldn't remember the last time he had seen such a great game of "Let's Have An Upset" in a courtroom. And . . . it did not escape his attention that the Lady Zillabar looked extremely pleased with herself as the argument raged around her.

About the time the head of the gavel broke off, Harry stopped trying to call for order. Shariba-Jen had hollered three times, and no one had paid attention.

Harry shrugged and stood up and prepared to leave, but Captain Campbell motioned him to sit down. She reached over to a brinewood panel, opened it to reveal a hidden control, and punched it hard. Almost instantly the ship's sprinkler system switched on, spraying everyone and everything in the salon with a high-pressure mist of extremely cold water. Very quickly the screams of anger turned into screams of shock and outrage, and then laughter.

Captain Campbell counted to ten, then reached over and switched the sprinklers off. "Does anyone else have anything to say?" she asked loudly. "The Justice has not adjourned the hearing. We will have order here—either the nice way or the not-so-nice way. You choose."

Harry reseated himself behind the table that served as his desk. Shariba-Jen handed him a new gavel—Harry looked at the robot in surprise, but Jen remained expressionless. He waited until everyone else had also quieted down and reseated themselves; most of them squelched when they moved, an effect that Harry found amusing, considering the circumstances.

"Your Honor—? May I speak to this issue please?" Finn Markham asked, rising weakly to his feet.

Harry looked at Finn, surprised the man could even stand. He nodded.

Finn Markham looked a hundred years old. He had to support himself by leaning on his brother's shoulder. Sawyer placed his hand on top of Finn's, but otherwise let him stand alone. Finn painfully levered himself around so he could address everyone in the room.

"I know that this situation came about because of something my brother and I did. We didn't realize the consequences of that action then. We've learned a lot better since, and we've done our best to repair the damage that we've caused. Nevertheless, nobody in this room owes either of us anything. We don't expect anything. We have no right even to ask for anything. . . ." Finn's voice failed him for a moment, but he waved away Sawyer's support. He turned back to the table, reached for a glass of water, and took a long, careful drink. He nearly dropped the glass replacing it on the table, but he retained his composure and faced the room again.

"We have come late to the Alliance of Life, but if we can learn what it means, then perhaps anyone can. Everyone can. We have learned the true meaning of brotherhood from all of you in this room. I would hope that you have seen us return that gift." Finn glanced down at Sawyer. "My brother even told me how he experienced a sense of brotherhood with Lee-1169, a man who has lost over two thousand brothers. I feel such pride in that knowledge.

"My brother has already donated three pints of blood to feed Zillabar," Finn said, surprising everyone. "M'bele will not take any more of his blood; it would endanger his life too. I have only one chance to continue the treatment I need. If everyone aboard this ship could donate a bit of his or her or its blood, then we could continue to feed Zillabar, and I could continue to benefit from the cleansing effects of her liver." Finn wavered where he stood, but he grabbed tightly onto Sawyer's shoulder and spoke with desperate sincerity. "I will not blame you if you refuse. I would not give one drop of my blood to feed Zillabar—and she has already taken more of it than I care to think about. But if Sawyer's survival depended on my willingness to give, I would give everything I have left. And if the survival of any other person in this room depended on my willingness to give, I still wouldn't stint. Thank you—for listening to what I had to say." He sank gratefully back down into his seat.

Harry Mertz looked around the room. The silence had become embarrassing and uncomfortable. This one stared at the ceiling, that one stared at the floor, the other one coughed into her hand, the last one pretended to have important business on a clipboard. Zillabar looked smug. Harry felt annoyed—but the source of his annoyance remained unsure. "I hate it," he said softly, as much to himself as anyone else, "when my enlightenment gets tested."

"I don't know—" said Lee-1169. "Maybe Sawyer experienced it as brotherhood; I experienced it as one long argument and a lot of uncomfortable bumpy rides and small dark places. It didn't seem like fun to me, let alone brotherhood." He shrugged, made a face, looked around, and let the words tumble blindly out of his mouth. "I mean—look, why should we, any of us, members of the Alliance of Life, lift even a single finger to save the life of a man who set out to track us down and betray us, who turned our Timebinder over to the Zillabitch? I think . . . I mean, I feel for you guys, yeah. You got caught in a bad situation, but why should the rest of us have to rescue you, when you really haven't done anything to benefit any of us? I vote no."

Beside him William Three-Dollar frowned. Something about Lee's words bothered him. Nyota also looked uncomfortable. But elsewhere in the room, Arl-N nodded his agreement, as did Gito. M'bele wore a dark expression, Azra looked unhappy. Ota scowled with some inner torment. Robin turned away to the wall. Kask rumbled annoyingly. Shariba-Jen remained expressionless.

"Excuse me—?" A tiny voice broke the silence. Ibaka stood up in Kask's lap and shouted for attention. "Please—? May I speak?" He didn't wait for permission. He leapt up onto the table in front of Zillabar. He allowed himself a tiny growl, then turned around to face the rest of the room. "I don't know about the Alliance of Life or what it means or anything like that, but I do know that these men"—he pointed to Sawyer and Finn—"these men saved my life and they . . . they tried to help my brothers. Even if no one else here owes them anything, I do. They can have as much of my blood as they want."

Harry Mertz found himself grinning with admiration. "Out of the mouths of puppies," he said.

The Dragon at the back of the room stood up then and grunted. Everyone turned to look at Kask. He said, "I will stand with my friend, Ibaka. If he gives blood, then so will I."

Ota resolved its inner torment then and turned around to face the others. "I too will volunteer my blood. Sawyer and Finn Markham helped rescue me from the Vampires, even though I had resigned myself to the inevitability of their appetites. I will donate blood."

Sawyer looked to M'bele hopefully. The dark man shook his head. "We'll need more than that."

Nyota tugged at his sleeve. "Father, you must donate too—"

"After what they did to you—?"

"Father, they gave me a life! They made it possible for me to speak to you and tell you how much you mean to me, how much gratitude I have for everything you've done for me. I would donate if you'd let me, but because I can't, you must donate for me. Please, I beg you—"

M'bele started to object, but he couldn't resist his daughter's pleading look. His expression crumpled, and he dropped to his knees in front of her. "I grieve for the daughter I think I've lost even as I celebrate the wisdom that comes out of your mouth now. I'll do what you ask."

Three-Dollar stepped forward. "As will I. I feel shame that I did not step forward first. The dog-child truly understands the Alliance of Life better than any of the rest of us aboard this ship."

"Oh, hell—" said Gito. "Me too."

Arl-N raised an arm grimly. Azra, the quiet woman, lifted her head. "If my Timebinder will allow me, then I will serve this cause too."

Robin spoke up. "I don't know if android blood will help, but if it will, I'll donate mine."

Harry shrugged and added, "Well, count me in—" He glanced over to Captain Campbell. "You have anything you want to say?"

Captain Campbell smiled wryly. "Some people have called me a bloodless bitch. I guess I should prove that I have some blood after all."

And then only Lee-1169 remained standing alone, arms folded, looking resolute and unmovable.

"Y'know," said M'bele, "I seem to remember something about the Alliance of Life guaranteeing Sawyer and Finn's lives in return for their services. And correct me if I misspeak this, but Sawyer renewed that contract on Burihatin-14; so this effort to save Finn Markham by keeping the Lady Zillabar alive does serve the Alliance—"

"I hear you," Lee snapped.

"When we commit ourselves to the Alliance, Lee," Three-Dollar said softly, "we commit ourselves to the sacredness of life everywhere—"

"I know, I know—"

Harry rapped softly with the gavel. "Lee, I cannot require any member of the Alliance to honor this obligation with his or her blood. Only the specificity of Madam Zillabar's obligation to the Markhams allowed me to rule in favor of Finn's treatment, but I cannot extend that ruling to include anyone else without setting a dangerous precedent. The process remains voluntary. But let me give you a gift—a thought to consider.

"At its most basic level, a crime—any crime, all crime—exists as an offense against your body and what you can do with it, what you can put into it, where you can take it; it always comes back to the body. Conversely, all laws exist as restrictions on what you may do to other people's bodies. Therefore, a just law cannot fairly compel anyone to donate their blood or their organs or anything else unless they have already promised to do so. So whatever else happens here, it no longer happens as an issue of law, but as a demonstration of our commitment to our belief in the sacredness of life. Everywhere.

"Look around, Lee. All of us here—all of us but you—have taken a stand to share our blood for Finn's recovery. Perhaps Finn Markham will not need your blood, and you will not have to take this on as a personal dilemma. On the other hand, you still might want to consider where you stand in relation to the most essential tenet of the Alliance."

Lee met Harry's gaze unashamedly. "You speak well, old man in a white robe. But I have my angers, and I have my memories, and I don't choose to let go of either of them yet."

Pfinglemas

□□□□□□□□□□□□□□□□□□□□□□□□□□□□□□

The Golden Fury drifted. A derelict. Empty. Dead.

The Black Destructor approached it warily.

Kernel Sleestak d'Vashti stood on the command bridge of his vessel, studying the slowly rotating image in the display. To all outward appearances *The Golden Fury* seemed undamaged. But repeated high-level scans detected no activity of any kind aboard the vessel. Even the ship's autonomous systems had shut down.

d'Vashti kept his outer face blank. He seated himself in his command chair and pretended to boredom. Inwardly, he seethed. The Dragon Lord had abruptly taken *The Golden Fury* off on some wild chase after an errant freebooter—and then just as abruptly all communication had ceased. The idea that the freefooter might have taken some successful action against *The Golden Fury* had so little merit to it that d'Vashti could only assume that the silence of the Imperial Starship represented some kind of dangerous ploy.

He wondered if he'd miscalculated by embarrassing the Dragon Lord so badly in front of the command officers of *The Golden Fury*. He'd known for years that the Dragon Lord intended his own rebellion against the Vampires. He'd admired the warrior-lizard's skill at seeming to track down relentlessly the leaders of the human rebellion, while in reality allowing it to grow and become ever more solid. The Dragon Lord clearly intended to use the human threat as a justification for seizing power over the Phaestor. d'Vashti wondered about that. Had he misjudged the Dragon Lord's timing? He'd hoped to consummate the relationship with Zillabar before dealing with the human rebellion and then the Dragons.

Idly, he gestured to the captain of *The Black Destructor.* "Dreegel, send a boarding party over. No Phaestor. Only lizards. And give us a full remote video feed."

"Yes, sir." Captain Dreegel turned away and began issuing orders.

Shortly, an armed shuttle eased itself across the intervening space and locked onto one of *The Golden Fury*'s exterior ports. A few moments later the view from the lizards' helmet cameras filled the display on the bridge of *The Black Destructor.*

The image moved warily through the air lock, into an antechamber, into a corridor. Nothing looked amiss. Captain Dreegel stepped up beside him, also studying the massive wall-sized image. The view swam through several more corridors, poked into storage rooms and chambers, finding nothing.

Then, suddenly—

Dreegel retched and turned away from the display. Cries of shock and outrage swept across the command bridge. d'Vashti kept his face stony and implacable, but the horrific image before him had a compelling power all its own.

Everywhere lay the remains of slaughtered Dragons and Phaestor, the bodies shredded and seeping, barely recognizable. The walls of *The Golden Fury* dripped with gore.

And everywhere they looked, they saw fresh green pfingle eggs. Industrial grade. Carnivorous. Pfingles had swarmed here, eaten everything they could, laid their eggs, and died. Here and there dying pfingles still moved feebly. Others lay torpid, too swollen to move, eggs slowly oozing from their bodies, one after the other. As the camera view panned, more and more active pfingles came into view, crawling directly toward the camera wearer. The image began backing away hurriedly.

Abruptly, terrible screams came from the remote channel. Lizard screams. For barely an instant something horrible flailed across the display. The image careened, rocked violently for several long, intolerable moments—betraying flashes of the boarding party covered with still-ravenous pfingles—and then suddenly the image toppled over sideways and became still. In the distance the sounds of thrashing faded away, replaced by the more terrifying noises of insectlike crunching. It filled the channel. A single pfingle crawled curiously across the display, leaving a trail of eggs behind it.

d'Vashti's face had gone pale. He had heard of such things. He had never believed them possible—certainly not on an Imperial Starship. But he knew instantly what had happened. He said softly, "That goddamned lizard and his goddamned appetite. I knew he'd eat himself to death one day."

And then he allowed himself an inner smile. Now he had one less problem to deal with. His salivary glands began pumping furiously. He could almost taste the triumph awaiting him at the Gathering.

"Dreegel," he said, "destroy *The Golden Fury*. Hit it with maximum force. Use full-strength disruptors to kill everything aboard, then nuke the carcass. When you've done that, take us into *otherspace*. To the Gathering."

Blood Brothers

Finn Markham lowered himself gently onto the operating table of the starship's sick bay. He still felt weak, and experienced spells of dizziness every time he exerted himself too much. He took a deep breath and allowed his fatigue to sink in again. The blood-cleansing process would leave him nauseous and upset, but ultimately it would cure him—he hoped. He stared resignedly at the paneled ceiling while M'bele plugged him into the cross-dialysis treatment.

On the table next to his, Zillabar rested impassively.

Finn tried to ignore her, but after M'bele stepped out of the room, it became impossible. He glanced toward her several times. Each time he noticed that she too stared silently at the ceiling as she waited for the process to reach completion. Every time he looked to her, she glanced back at him for a moment as if waiting for him to speak, then returned her gaze to the scanning panels above.

At last she spoke first. "The irony of it does not escape me either," she said. "Every situation has come back to me turned inside out. Now I suffer as victim and you humans torment me."

"Karma," said Finn in explanation. "The karmic chicken always comes home to roost."

"The Phaestor don't believe in karma," Zillabar said, effectively ending that line of discussion. "And you might want to notice something. After all the discussion has ended, I still get to drink the blood of all of you. That should tell you something."

"Yes, it does. It speaks volumes about the generosity of humans—even to those who have made themselves our enemies."

Zillabar didn't answer that. Finn assumed from her silence that she had decided to end the discussion. But a moment later she spoke again. This time her voice had a quality he'd never heard before. Honest curiosity. "Tell me something—?" she began tentatively.

"What?"

"Why did your companions willingly donate their blood to save your life?"

"You don't understand it, do you?"

"A Phaestor would not act this way, not unless he saw an advantage for himself in the situation. . . ."

"Yes, I know," Finn said with more compassion than coldness. "That particular quality of Phaestor thinking has brought us to this situation."

"You didn't answer my question. About the sharing."

"We call it *cooperation*," Finn said. "I can see why you would have so much trouble comprehending it."

"Explain that," she said, as if giving an order to a servant.

Finn dismissed the apparent rudeness of her tone, recognizing it as ignorance more than intent. He took a breath while he gathered his thoughts and said, "It comes from the way we breed—and from the way you breed too. We bear our young in our own bodies. We nurture our young; you hatch from eggs. You do not bond as we do, you depend on pheromones and lust for loyalty. You don't have the same feelings we do—and we don't have the kinds of feelings you do."

Zillabar considered that. "So you believe that the Phaestor lack the ability to care."

"I believe you lack the ability to care as we do. Perhaps I believe mistakenly, but if my belief has any accuracy at all, then I can't even hate you for what you've done. You have no choice in the matter but to act the only way you can."

Zillabar's voice betrayed her startlement. "You *pity* me?" On her inner face astonishment fought with rage.

Finn didn't answer immediately. He considered the import of her question—not simply the question itself, but what it meant to both of them. He'd never really thought about Vampires this way before, and it left him uneasy. He might have to give up his hatred too.

At last he said, "Yes, I do. Because whoever designed your species cheated you out of a whole range of emotions that make life worth living. They didn't give you the capacity for love. And I don't know that what they gave you instead serves as any kind of useful substitute. From my point of view, I don't think so. I've always doubted the myth of Phaestor superiority. Now I know why."

"But—" said Zillabar, allowing just a trace of her old self to smile through. "You should notice that even as we lie here sparring, my blood serves your body, and not the other way around. You have succeeded in reducing me from master to servant; so perhaps you have demonstrated the superiority of your race after all—and maybe even this bizarre hormonal phenomenon you call *love*."

"You wouldn't say that if you still held power over us." Finn chuckled back. "But I do appreciate your attempts at diplomacy. At least, while we remain tied together like this, we don't have to torture each other."

"And I appreciate your kindness. Thank you."

For a moment neither said anything more.

"Tell me something else," Zillabar said abruptly. "Do you think a *Vampire* can learn this thing—?" She said the word with audible discomfort: "Can a Phaestor learn how to *care* the way you people do?"

Finn thought about it. "I don't know," he admitted. "I don't even know if I'd want to try to find out. I don't think I'd ever feel complete trust in any Phaestor. I don't know that many others would either. The history of the Phaestor doesn't encourage enthusiasm for the prospect."

"Think about this, then," said Lady Zillabar. "If the Phaestor do have the capability to *care* and we choose not to, then you humans will have to hate us after all. And if we do not have the capability to care, you will always see us as your enemies. In either case your revolution cannot succeed, because the existence of an enemy—*any* enemy—represents a fatal flaw in the essential philosophy. If you cannot ever bring yourself to hold my kind of life sacred, then you will have established the precedent of separating out those kinds of life you find disagreeable. In such a situation the dissolution of mutual trust becomes inevitable. You will always have to wonder and worry, who will the Alliance declare unworthy next?"

Even in his weakened condition, Finn recognized that Zillabar had spoken the very same thing that had troubled him since he had first heard the distinctions of the Alliance of Life. How can we hold *all* life sacred when some forms of life hold nothing sacred, not even themselves? We make ourselves weak with such a philosophy, not strong.

He didn't know how to answer the Lady's argument. It made sense. He could have spoken it himself. He already had, several times.

"I don't know," he finally admitted. "Better minds than I have considered this question and have come to mutually contradictory answers. For my part I dream of a place beyond hate. Even before my brother and I came to Thoska-Roole, I had already grown tired of the violence. Now . . . after all we have come through, I feel it even more intensely. I have grown sick and tired of feeling sick and tired. I want something else. I think we all do. Perhaps we'll never achieve a world that works for everyone, with no one and nothing left out—but we still want to try."

Zillabar made a sound in response, maybe a snort, maybe something else, Finn couldn't identify the emotion behind it. He glanced over to her.

"I think you have resolved my question about caring," she said. Her expression revealed that she did not think *caring* had any value for her.

"Yes, I see that," Finn replied. "Your refusal to recognize what lies beyond your own beliefs may yet prove a fatal weakness, not just for yourself, but for your whole species as well."

"I'll surprise you," she said. "I'll grant you the possibility of that. Certainly, if I had accurately understood everything I dealt with on Thoska-Roole, I would not have ended up strapped to a table like this with my veins linked to yours and my liver cleansing your blood. Never mind, Finn Markham. At least one of us has a false set of beliefs—possibly even both of us. Does that surprise you to hear a Vampire speaking like that? It shouldn't. However you interpret the actions of the Phaestor, don't for a minute assume that we have no cunning behind our actions. If we have nothing else, we still have our intelligence, and you have six thousand years of history to see how well that has worked out."

"Yes," agreed Finn. "We have six thousand years of history to see how well that has worked out. Not very well indeed."

"Well said," acknowledged Zillabar. "And very shortly we'll both see the resolution of this question, perhaps even once and for all."

The Black Hole Gang

❐❐❐❐❐❐❐❐❐❐❐❐❐❐❐❐❐❐❐❐❐❐❐❐❐❐❐

Meanwhile, in another part of the starship ...

The crew of *The Lady MacBeth* had gathered in the engine room to consider their own options. Because of Harry's demonstrated skill as a judicial tap dancer, they had invited him to sit in on their meeting and advise them. Harry agreed, but only after the usual heated discussion concerning his rates for legal advice.

Robin spoke first, laying out the position for all of them. "Now that Captain Campbell has turned in her Guild Insignia, we think we should have our contracts renegotiated. Captain Campbell says no; freebooters don't show as big a profit as Guild spacers, so she says that if we renegotiate, we should take a cut in wages. We disagree; we think that as freebooters, we should become partners in the whole enterprise. We won't ask for equal shares, but certainly some kind of pro-rata formula should apply here, shouldn't it? I mean, Shariba-Jen certainly doesn't need as much as oh, say, Gito or myself. Robots don't have many needs. I wouldn't presume to speak for Ota, of course, but it seems to me that we should offset the cost of Ota's rescue against its share. And, personally—"

Harry listened politely for at least fifteen minutes. Finally he allowed himself a dyspeptic groan.

"Do you feel all right?" Ota asked solicitously.

Harry nodded. "Yes, I feel fine." He massaged his temples. "But you've just reminded me why I quit politics—and why someday I may even quit the law."

Something went *fwoop*.

Harry glanced up nervously.

Gito sat on the catwalk above the spherical cage

259

containing the starship's pinpoint black hole. He had a large orange fruit in his hand, which he peeled slowly and methodically. Periodically, he tossed pieces of the peel into the cage, where they first tumbled, then spiraled in toward the minuscule flare of blue-white radiation at the center of the sphere. They swirled around in ever-decreasing circles until finally they winked out with a flash and a *fwoop*.

Robin flinched too. So did Ota. Nobody appreciated this reminder of the dreadful power of a singularity. They knew that Gito did it deliberately—as a way of attracting attention.

"I think we should call a strike," said Gito in his gravelly voice. "Shut the ship down until Captain Campbell meets our demands to negotiate. We've come as far as we can. She won't move. Let's stop it all right here. She'll come around fast enough then."

Ota looked up at the little man, blinking thoughtfully. "Gito, we have nothing to negotiate. We lost the farm. The Dragon Lord took our eggs. We have no insurance. We have nothing. The Shakespeare Corporation will go into foreclosure in eighty-two days."

"We have the award that we won in the hearing—"

"And how will we collect it? Do you want to try? I'd like to see you serve a warrant on the Regency treasury."

"Then why did Harry give us the award if he knew we couldn't collect?" Gito called down to Mertz. "Hey! Justice-man! What good does the law do if no one can enforce it?"

Harry agreed grimly. "You've just stated the entire problem. I can rule, but I can't enforce. You'll have to wait for the Gathering for a resolution."

Gito tossed the rest of his fruit contemptuously into the singularity, swung himself around, and began climbing down from the cage. "Then we have nothing to discuss, do we? The hell with all of you. The hell with this spaceship. The hell with the Regency. And the hell with the Gathering. All this talk fills nobody's pockets. To hell with heroes."

He stumped out of his own engine room, swearing quietly in his native tongue.

The rest of the crew traded disheartened glances. Robin sighed sadly. "I guess we'll have to start looking for new postings. Maybe someone at the Gathering will want to hire us—"

Ota disagreed. "I don't think Captain Campbell will give up *The Lady MacBeth* that easily."

"She may not have a choice anymore. I don't know. You know her better than I do, but I saw the look on her face when we left Burihatin-14. I think the fight has gone out of her."

"I hope not," said Harry, but by then the others had already filed out.

Realspace

□□□□□□□□□□□□□□□□□□□□□□□□□□□□□

Otherspace ended.

Realspace began.

Time, distance, and form all returned to the space outside the starship.

Methodically, they took their bearings, they made their calculations, and determined that their transit through *otherspace* had brought them halfway across the Palethetic Cluster and into the dark open rift beyond. Captain Campbell looked at the time/distance display and grumbled a reluctant acknowledgement of Robin's skill at astrogation.

"I've set up a standard deceleration approach to the Forum," Robin said. "I'll bring us in to a hundred thousand kilometers before requesting final-approach instructions."

Captain Campbell nodded perfunctorily. After a moment she got up and left the bridge, leaving Robin and Ota staring after her sadly. The two exchanged unhappy glances. They'd never seen the Captain so worried before. She wouldn't show it to any of the passengers, of course, but the fact that she even allowed her crew to see her like this bespoke her terrible state of mind.

"I wish we could do something," said Robin.

"We need to find a way to serve that warrant," said Ota grimly.

As Captain Campbell passed through the main salon of the ship, Sawyer stopped her and asked for a moment of her time.

She frowned, but she looked at him expectantly. "Yes? What do you want?"

"I wanted to say thank you."

"For what?"

"For what you did for me and Finn. Everything. For the arbitration. For the blood donation—your crew and you showed me the real meaning of the Alliance."

Campbell looked at him blankly. "I didn't do it for you. None of us did. We did it for Ota. You saved her on Thoska-Roole. We had to repay that debt. We always pay our debts. When the ship lifts, so does the ledger. Or something like that."

"Nevertheless," said Sawyer, "Finn and I still have much to thank you for. If we can provide any service to you—"

"No," said Campbell. "I don't want your services. I don't want any more obligations. This time it cost us our blood. Who knows what it will cost us next time?"

"You don't understand—"

"No, *you* don't. Thanks for your gratitude. Please don't give anymore."

"All right." Sawyer gave in. He looked at her, oddly fascinated by a woman he couldn't charm.

On the other side of that look, Captain Campbell found herself annoyed at a man who didn't take even his own life seriously.

"Tell me one thing, Captain," Sawyer said. "This Alliance business, this political stuff—I honestly don't understand it. I don't understand why Ota suddenly has such a commitment to it. Or anyone else, for that matter. Do you?"

"Do I understand it? Yes. Do I agree with it? No."

"Explain it to me, then. Why would Ota take such a stand?"

Captain Campbell studied Sawyer. She replied blandly, "Because Ota doesn't think like a fish."

"I beg your pardon?"

"I said, 'Because Ota doesn't think like a fish.'" Captain Campbell pointed to one of several aquariums in the salon. "See that? A fish doesn't get to vote on the water it swims in. You do. Only *you* don't. You just accept it. Ota stopped accepting it. Maybe someday you will too."

"Hm," said Sawyer. "And what about you?"

"Me? I swim in a different tank. Now, if you'll excuse me—" She stepped past Sawyer and continued aft toward the ship's cargo bay, leaving Sawyer to exchange a glance with an amused Harry Mertz, who had come into the salon in time to catch almost the whole conversation.

"A different tank?" Sawyer asked.

Harry grinned. "Don't look at me. She made up the metaphor. I didn't."

"She meant paradigms, didn't she?" Sawyer asked, scratching his head. "No, that doesn't make sense. . . ." Shaking his head, he wandered off in search of his brother. Maybe Finn could explain it.

The Forum

This particular trick requires a couple thousand pinpoint flecks of neutronium. At least. You can do it with less, if you wish, but to construct a smooth gravitational gradient, you'll need many small individual gravity wells, equidistantly spaced.

First, build a disk-shaped lattice of passive-field

gravitational prisms, with each prism set to deflect all
horizontal gravitational fields 180 degrees. This will allow
you to put one piece of neutronium in the center of each
triangular cell with the certainty that it will stay there. If
any fleck starts to drift to one side or another, the increased deflection of the gravitational prisms will push it
back into place. Fill the lattice with your motes of
neutronium and wait a hundred years or so to verify its
stability. Then pave it over.

You will now have a flat disk, five kilometers in
diameter, with a planetary mass and a two-sided gravitational field.

This configuration will produce some unusual gravitational artifacts. If you've built it to specification, with
a thinner density of neutronium flecks around the edges,
the disk will have almost no gravity around its circumference. This will give you easy access to free space. You
can jump right off the edge, with minimal escape velocity
needed as long as you stay in the equatorial plane. This
property represents an asset rather than a liability, because it offers unique docking circumstances for star-
traveling vessels.

A perpendicular field of gravity will occur across the
entire flat surface of the disk, both sides; but due to the
sharp gravitational gradients of each of the individual
flecks of neutronium, the pull of gravity will diminish
rapidly as you rise away from the surface of the disk.
Nevertheless, the combined gravitational pull of all those
bits of condensed matter will still have sufficient strength
to hold and keep an atmosphere of Earth-normal pressure across both faces of the disk, and a much thinner
envelope at the equator. Balancing all of this will require
some tricky math, of course, but any good quantum me-
chanic can easily juggle the necessary equations.

Both sides of the disk will have equal functionality,
of course, but for convenience' sake, you might want to
use one side for the necessities of civilization, and the
other side for maintenance of the disk's very small
ecosystem. Use the top half for gardens, fountains,
meeting spaces. Use the bottom half for wilderness,

crops, and ocean. If you work it right, you can create some extraordinary weather effects in a very small space.

Install it at the Trojan point of a binary star system. Pick two fairly benevolent suns that allow some distance. Don't plan on sleeping at night. This structure doesn't allow for a convenient cycle of days and nights.

But . . . if you insist on having a day-night cycle, you can always install a shadow field in a slow elliptical polar orbit, which will give you a useful approximation of a diurnal/nocturnal cycle.

Install spokes around the circumference of the disk, extending straight out almost to the limits of the usable atmosphere so that visiting starships can dock safely and their passengers can walk or ride an elevator down to the main body of the disk.

Put the whole thing well away from the Palethetic Cluster—for no reason at all, except maybe to make it convenient to get to.

Call it the Forum.

A place to stand. A place to speak. Most important of all, a place to listen.

Here you will find—on one side, anyway—beautiful parks, luscious gardens, towering trees, crisp cold air, fresh blue streams, sparkling fountains, graceful bridges and pathways, a score of small gathering places, three fair-sized open-air bowls, and one great amphitheater at the center surrounded by thirteen columns, one for each TimeBinder. Here the air glows with its own light, the trees radiate luminescence, the ground itself sparkles, and the pathways glimmer.

The Lady MacBeth approached the Forum carefully, entering its atmosphere in a precise equatorial orbit. Approached this way, the Forum had only the slightest gravitational pull, but the small size of its intense axial gravity field also gave it a ferocious tidal effect. An unwary pilot could find himself with his ship ripped in half.

Shariba-Jen backed the shuttle gently up to the end of a docking spoke and secured the boat with tractonic clamps. Routinely, he checked the outside atmosphere before popping the seals. As he expected, the Forum provided a near-perfect atmosphere for oxygen-using life forms. He never used it himself, of course, but he had learned the hard way that Captain Campbell considered it one of the highest priorities for herself and her crew.

Star-Captain Neena Linn-Campbell stepped out of the rear access lock first. She looked off into the distance at the edge of the tiny world and experienced the faintest thrill of panic. The air had a hard, crisp feeling. The Forum had less atmosphere than a full-sized planet: it didn't have as much surface area; it didn't need as much volume of gas to maintain the same amount of atmospheric pressure. Consequently, it also lacked a soft blue sky. You could stare directly out at the bright, unwinking stars.

One at a time the others followed Captain Campbell out onto the thick spoke. It looked as wide as a blacktree limb, though it had a much more pleasant color. The designers of the forum hadn't tried to extend the disk's natural gravity field outward. Although they knew several ways to accomplish the feat, none of them would have stayed stable over a long period of time. Instead they covered the spokes with a natural stick-to-me surface, so although the gravity of the Forum diminished rapidly as one moved away from the outer edges, one could still walk along the spokes without the danger of falling off and into an unpleasant orbit around the edge of the Forum.

"Wow," said Sawyer, pausing to look around. Finn came out of the airlock after him and echoed his sentiment. Finn looked much better, almost his normal self again.

Harry followed them out, straightening his white robe. He glanced around and nodded his approval. "The place hasn't changed a bit."

"You've come here before?" Finn asked curiously.

Harry coughed in sudden embarrassment, then nodded. "Uh, yeah. A long time ago."

The others followed them, pausing to stare in wonder and amazement. Robin and Ota stood and gaped. Kask lashed his tail in apparent discomfort, but would not admit his fear of this place. Ibaka saw the distant trees and began whimpering in eagerness. "Let me down," he begged excitedly, and the Dragon did so.

Lee-1169 stepped out of the lock and grinned broadly. William Three-Dollar followed him out with a beatific smile. Equally at peace, Nyota came next, walking between Azra and her father. She held their hands and led them out into the light of the upper sun.

Gito and Arl-N had volunteered to stay behind on *The Lady MacBeth* to stand guard over Zillabar. The rest of the travelers moved slowly down the spoke toward the edge of the disk. They made a strangely drawn-out group. They chose their steps with care; they pointed and gaped like tourists.

"Why did they put it way out here?" asked Sawyer.

Harry stopped and pointed behind them. To the galactic east lay the great wheel of the Milky Way galaxy—the Eye of God. Its gaudy splendor hung in a brilliant ellipse across half the visible sky. For the first time anywhere, they could see it all at once. *The Lady MacBeth* appeared dwarfed before it. "We came from there," he said. "Our past." He turned and pointed. To the galactic west lay a single bright cluster of light—compact, almost solid. The Palethetic Cluster. "And that—that represented our future."

Harry stamped his foot to indicate the Forum itself. "Here—once a planet sat in this orbit. A predator killed it—one of the first to leap across the rift. We used the body of the planet to build the Forum. Here we created the Regency of Terra. We recreated ourselves as warriors to stand against the horror that tracked us through the darkness. Here we defied the predators and took our first stand."

Harry realized that he had struck an heroic posture and an equally pretentious manner of speaking; he shook it off in sudden embarrassment, grinned, and asked, "Any other questions?"

"No thanks," said Sawyer. "I don't think we could stand another answer." He grinned back, enjoying Harry's flush of discomfiture. Consequently, he didn't see what Harry saw. Instead he saw Harry Mertz freeze in horror and dismay.

Sawyer whirled around. His face hardened as he

recognized the figure who waited at the end of the spoke—

Standing alone at the edge of the platform, Kernel Sleestak d'Vashti waited patiently for them. He wore a look of triumph.

Confrontation

"Oh, shit," said Sawyer.

In reply d'Vashti smiled.

For a moment no one moved; then the travelers began edging closer, clustering together to face the black-clad Vampire in an angry and defiant group. They stood ten meters from him; their voices carried loudly in the cold air.

d'Vashti surveyed them without apparent emotion. After a moment he remarked. "I must say, it seems very rude to me to hold a Gathering about the future of the Regency without inviting a representative of the Phaestoric aristocracy."

Justice Harry Mertz stepped forward, his gleaming white robe dazzling in the broad sunlight. "Your point may have some validity, your excellency; but neither can you deny that your actions and the actions of other Phaestor have caused the calling of this Gathering."

"Perhaps. Perhaps not. Forget cause and effect. I have little interest in the past. That way lies only blame and despair. I care for the future. So do you, Arbiter. At least you acknowledge the validity of my claim. Good. Let's play politics. I have the Regency Starfleet on my side. What do you have?"

"You have one starship, d'Vashti. Your fleet lies scattered across a thousand suns, her captains and admirals squabbling like children—unless you can consummate a mating. We both know that, so let's not play games with words."

"Nevertheless, I have that one starship, *The Black Destructor*. With the power of that particular method, I have the ability to dispose of any object here. Including the entire Forum itself. What weapon do you have?"

"We have truth," said Harry. "It will have to serve."

d'Vashti laughed. Harry allowed himself a smile of his own. They had drawn the battle lines and declared their positions.

"I don't think," Harry said, "that you'll dare risk triggering a civil war in the Cluster. Assaulting a Gathering will demonstrate to everyone that the Regency has lost its soul."

"Not the Regency. Only me," d'Vashti retorted.

"It makes no difference anymore," replied Harry calmly. "You have wrapped yourself in the authority of your offices. You have become the Regency in the eyes of the Cluster. If you act badly, so does the Regency. If you fall here, so does the Regency. If we fall here—by your hand—so does the Regency. Either way you lose."

d'Vashti waved Harry's words away as if they had no relevance at all to him. "You'll die believing that, old man."

At these words Sawyer and Lee both stepped up beside Harry. Both drew their weapons. Harry stopped them. "No. Not here. Anywhere else, perhaps—but not here. I won't allow anyone to stain the Forum with violence."

"You can't mean that!" cried Lee. "After everything that son of a stinkbug has put us through—" He fired anyway.

The beam bounced harmlessly off d'Vashti. It splattered in all directions, but the bulk of it flashed back to Lee, knocking him down and stunning him. The splash of it left Harry and Sawyer stinging. Sawyer bent to help Lee back to his feet. "That son of a stinkbug has a reflector shield. Consider yourself lucky that you didn't hit him with a more powerful beam."

d'Vashti laughed wickedly at the others' discomfort. Abruptly, however, he cut off his laughing, and his expression hardened. "Now, hear *my* anger. You"—he pointed to Sawyer and Lee—"you kidnapped the Lady Zillabar. Even now you continue to hold her hostage. I order the release of the Lady Zillabar immediately."

"We can't do it," whispered Sawyer to Harry. "Not yet—not until we complete Finn's treatment. As long as the phage survives in his blood, he can still die."

Harry spoke up in reply. "The Lady Zillabar has had a judgment levied against her. Until the completion of that judgment, we cannot comply with your request."

"Not a request, old man," d'Vashti said. "An order."

"Nevertheless—" Harry spread his hands wide in an apologetic gesture of legal helplessness. "The judgement stands."

"You made this judgment yourself?" d'Vashti asked.

"I did."

d'Vashti dismissed Harry with a wave. "It has no merit. Produce the Lady."

"I apologize, your excellency. I cannot retract my previous ruling." He smiled broadly. "You would have to have me overruled by a higher body of law. If you can find one."

d'Vashti's eyes narrowed. "If I can find one? Look around, old man. We have a thousand Arbiters at our disposal here. I couldn't throw a rock without hitting a Senior Arbiter. I can appeal your stupid ruling here at the Gathering without taking ten steps. You'll see soon enough what authority you have to make your futile judgments."

"Go ahead," said Harry. "The law grants you broad rights to appeal. As a matter of fact, you probably have very good grounds for an appeal in that a licensed arbiter did not make the original ruling—"

"What the hell!" said Sawyer. Lee and the others also turned to look at Harry, surprised and alarmed.

Harry ignored them. "—and the second ruling in the matter did not occur in a venue in which the Lady Zillabar had full access to appropriate representation."

"You son of a bitch—" said Sawyer. "I'll kill you myself!" Lee and Finn had to hold him back.

But Harry kept right on talking. "However, the Lady

Zillabar *did* accept the rulings made in both those hearings, and legal precedents say that her acceptance validates those rulings. Oh, I should also point out that you'll have to stand as a codefendant in the matter of an unfulfilled contract with Sawyer and Finn Markham."

d'Vashti dismissed Harry's words as an idle threat. "I have no concerns with those two trackers. The dead can't sue anyone."

Sawyer replied to that. "Take another look, batbreath. My brother and I stand before you, both very much alive."

"Well, yes," admitted d'Vashti. "But that can change too." To Harry he said, "We'll play it your way for now. I'll see you in court." Then he turned and strode away.

Sawyer and Lee both turned to Harry, both already speaking, but Harry held up his hands to silence them. "Please—" he said. "We have to do this by the rules of the Gathering. If we don't respect the rule of law, we have no right to demand it of anyone else."

"I hate politics," said Sawyer.

"I think I agree with you," said Lee.

"So do I," said Harry. "And I know more of politics than either of you. Now, listen to me, both of you—and listen well, because if you can't get this through your thick skulls now, then we might as well all turn around and march straight back to *The Lady MacBeth* and head for whatever little ratholes we want to call home." Harry raised his voice to include all the rest of his listeners as well. "You can't work for justice if you only want justice for yourself. You have to work for justice for your enemy as well—otherwise you won't have any justice at all, only a tool for revenge that both sides will bludgeon each other with for centuries to come."

Lee looked at the Arbiter, astonished. "I thought you stood on our side."

"I don't take sides, you idiot. I took an oath of impartiality the first time I put on a white robe. Forget about sides now. You've reached the point where most revolutions fail. You have to create justice for all, or you won't have justice for anybody."

Sawyer and Finn exchanged unhappy glances. Sawyer muttered something.

"Say again?" demanded Harry.

"You heard what d'Vashti said. He won't give us one nth the same consideration. How can we have justice with a snake, with a Vampire? Sorry, old man, but I don't believe in justice anymore. Not your kind, anyway."

"I see," said Harry. "You believe in justice only when you win."

Sawyer didn't answer. He and Finn turned away curtly; they strode angrily back toward *The Lady Mac-Beth*, not with any specific purpose in mind, only to get away from Harry.

Harry shook his head sadly. Lee turned away, so did Captain Campbell, and after a moment all of the others as well. Glumly, they headed back to the starship to activate the vessel's security defenses. Only Three-Dollar remained behind. He smiled gently at the Arbiter. "I think I know where I remember you from," he said. "I think you have some explaining to do."

"No," said Harry curtly. "I don't." And he turned away from the others and headed out onto the main platform of the Forum.

More Justice

□□□□□□□□□□□□□□□□□□□□□□□□□□□□□

Sawyer felt despondent. To come this far only to have their success snatched away by a set of unfair rules—it didn't make sense. He didn't feel good about anyone or anything. Even Finn's spirits had apparently begun to wilt. He looked unhappy and retired to the cabin that he shared with Sawyer.

Around them the argument raged like a firestorm;

they sat unmoved at the heart of it, too exhausted to fight anymore.

Captain Campbell couldn't believe Harry's betrayal and after several hours of fruitless arguing, she gave up in disgust. "I thought we could trust you."

"You can trust me to uphold the law," Harry said calmly. "Or my word as an arbiter will have no value at all."

Campbell ignored that. "And meanwhile you plan on giving away the tracker's life? What'll you give d'Vashti next? My starship?"

Three-Dollar understood Harry's reasoning, but when he tried to explain it, no one wanted to listen. For the first time he and Lee engaged in a full-out shouting match. Nyota and her father exchanged angry words, with Azra in tears between them. Gito didn't say anything; he just methodically broke out every weapon in the starship, inspected each one, tested it to see that it still functioned up to spec—not the manufacturer's specs, but the specs of his special modifications—and then returned them carefully to stores. Arl-N and Robin assisted him. Ota withdrew into itself and stopped speaking. Ibaka curled up in a ball and whimpered while Kask went stomping up and down the docking spoke, looking for something to kill. Shariba-Jen moved politely through the starship performing routine maintenance tasks and carefully steering potential combatants away from each other.

Finally Harry—and both of the TimeBinders—left *The Lady MacBeth* altogether, moving instead into guest pavilions on the Forum disk. Azra went with Nyota; M'bele did not. He stormed up and down the corridors of the starship, fuming with undirected frustration and anger. He didn't know who to hate anymore.

By the time of the hearing, the ship resembled an armed camp, with half the travelers not speaking to the other half; allegiances shifted as easily as opinions; but when they finally all filed out again to head toward one of the lesser amphitheaters, they had achieved—if nothing else—the *appearance* of cooperation lent by mutual silence.

This time they made their way to the Forum without incident. The walkways on the disk took them easily to their destination, a small bowl-shaped theater, already half-filled with curious onlookers and representatives of other worlds.

Sawyer looked around as they entered, and shuddered. He noticed too many Vampires, too many Dragons, not enough humans to suit his tastes. But . . . he also saw members of species he'd never seen before at all, only heard about. Two huge women—they looked like relatives of Murdock—sat on the top level of the bowl. Nearby sat several humanlike creatures who had a second set of arms instead of legs; free-fallers probably—or humanoid monkeys, Sawyer wasn't sure. Below them three tall, spindly men waited calmly; they looked even taller than Arl-N. Sawyer hadn't realized humans could grow so long. On the other side of the bowl he saw several shaven-headed individuals in featureless robes; he couldn't identify them as either male, female, or neuters; he assumed the latter. Most of the humans wore clothing from their own worlds, a dizzying variety of kilts, skirts, pantaloons, vests, robes, caps, hoods, and ornamentation. Most of them displayed a variety of skin colors far beyond those which Sawyer had assumed possible; he saw red skins, white, yellow, blue, brown, green, deep purple, ebony, albino, pink, and even milk-chocolate like his own and Finn's.

Sawyer saw several Knaxx sitting patiently in the bowl; it didn't surprise him. Informants went everywhere. Anyplace where something interesting might occur, the Knaxx would have members in attendance. It did surprise him, though, to see so many robots scattered throughout the crowd—and so many bioforms and androids too. Why should they have any interest in this hearing, or even in the Gathering, for that matter? The Gathering only concerned natural life forms, like humans—and maybe tailored reconstructs as well—but certainly not artificial or constructed beings. They had no claims to representation here. Or did they? He scratched his head curiously. Perhaps he didn't understand all of this as well as he thought he did. Maybe he didn't understand it at all.

But . . . he did understand one thing. Zillabar owed Finn his life. Period. He would not accept less than that. He patted his weapon thoughtfully as he took his seat. Finn took a seat wearily beside him. Finn Markham looked terrible. His recovery seemed halted, and he had begun to look deathly again, as if suffering a relapse of the blood-burn. Streaks of gray had appeared at his temples, and his skin had taken on an ashen color.

The rest of the travelers from *The Lady MacBeth* arrayed themselves around the trackers in a phalanx of moral support. At one point Captain Campbell even reached down and patted Sawyer gently on the shoulder. He reached up and patted her hand in gratitude—then realized what Neena Linn-Campbell had done and turned around to smile at her, but her gaze had already shifted elsewhere across the bowl of the amphitheater.

d'Vashti and his aides—all clad in dull-black armor and capes—entered the bowl, looking arrogant and already triumphant. They ignored the humans and took their assigned seats 120 degrees away. A moment later three Senior Arbiters in shimmering white robes entered the bowl. As Sawyer and the others watched, the two women and one man crossed to their positions, equidistant from both parties in the case. Sawyer looked around and spotted Harry at the top rear of the bowl; observer or participant, he couldn't tell.

"This dispute," began the most-senior of the Senior Arbiters, "has attracted a great deal of attention here at the Gathering, so much so, that we have chosen to resolve it before proceeding to the much larger business at hand. Indeed, the resolution of this matter may well have serious import for everything else we will consider later. In any case, we will now hear arguments in the matter of Kernel Sleestak d'Vashti and the Lady Zillabar versus the brothers Markham, Sawyer and Finn."

Kernel d'Vashti stood up then, bowing with extravagant politeness. He presented an imposing figure, surrounded by his Dragons and Vampire aides. "Your Honors, I apologize for speaking out of turn, but we cannot begin. Not until the Lady Zillabar joins us. Those *people*"—he spat the words with contempt—"those people still hold her in involuntary servitude. I demand—" He caught himself, stopped, bowed again—this time only slightly—and rephrased his speech. "I *request* that this court see fit to compel these lawbreakers to produce Lady Zillabar immediately so that she may participate in this proceeding, which certainly affects her, and that we may see that her captors have not abused her and that she still enjoys good health." d'Vashti concluded with another bow, this one quite florid, and waited expectantly.

"If it please the court—" Harry's voice came from the back of the amphitheater. Everyone swiveled in their seats to look at him. Harry came striding down to the open circle at the center of the amphitheater. "As the Arbiter who judged the ruling contested here, may I ask a question of some pertinence of Kernel d'Vashti? I believe it will help clarify matters." Without waiting for the Senior Arbiters to confer, Harry turned to d'Vashti. "Do you accept the authority of these arbiters, this body of law, and this proceeding?"

d'Vashti hesitated. After a moment he said suspiciously, "Of course I do. Why do you even raise the issue?"

Harry nodded, satisfied. "With the court's permission, I'll explain. If you don't accept the authority of this body to rule on this matter, then we cannot act in good faith here. Additionally, the brothers Markham would have the right to request a dismissal of the case, and according to precedent the Senior Arbiters would have no option but to grant it. I raise the issue because you have previously indicated your unwillingness to accept the authority of this Gathering. Do you now state for the record that you accept the authority of this Gathering and all that proceeds from it?"

d'Vashti shook his head. "You just changed the question. I don't accept this Gathering as legal, but I do accept the authority of this hearing—"

"No," said Harry. "You can't have it both ways. These Arbiters derive their authority directly from this Gathering. If you do not accept the Gathering, then you don't accept their authority, and neither can you ask for an arbitration. Would you clarify your stand, please, so that we may proceed appropriately?" Harry allowed himself the slightest of smiles. He turned and looked directly at Sawyer and Finn and the others, as if to ask, "Do you understand now?"

d'Vashti nodded. He looked as if he'd just bit into something unpleasant. He looked as if he wanted to turn away from the entire proceeding. He looked dangerous. "You son of a bitch," he said softly. "You clever son of a bitch."

"Thank you," said Harry. "I appreciate the acknowledgment—all the more so because it comes from you, your excellency. Now, then, do you accept the authority of this court, and of the Gathering it represents?"

d'Vashti nodded slowly. "I do," he said.

"Thank you," said Harry. He turned to the Senior Arbiters. "Thank you for allowing me to help clarify this issue. As you know, I have placed myself at the service of this court, and of this Gathering, specifically to help expedite matters such as this. I do appreciate the court's forbearance here."

He bowed and returned to his seat.

Zillabar Redux

It didn't take long for the Senior Arbiters to make their ruling. And shortly after that Star-Captain Neena Linn-Campbell arranged for Shariba-Jen, Gito, and Arl-N to escort the Lady Zillabar—in shackles—to the site of the hearing.

Zillabar looked weak, but her spirit appeared undimmed. Despite the bindings she strode into the amphi-

theater as haughty and as arrogant and as nasty as she
could manage.

d'Vashti stood waiting to greet her, but she swept
coldly past him, deliberately snubbing him. She walked
to the open circle at the center of the amphitheater and
looked up at the Senior Arbiters. "Your Honors," she
said, "I request relief. The Captain of the starship *The
Lady MacBeth*, and her crew, and her associated
passengers—in specific, Sawyer and Finn Markham,
Lee-1169, Dr. M'bele, and the two TimeBinders, William
Three-Dollar and Nyota M'bele, and others—have kidnapped me and held me against my will. I request relief."

"May it please the court—" Harry Mertz came trundling down to the center of the amphitheater again. "A
judgment exists against the Lady, compelling her to fulfill
her part of a contract made with Sawyer and Finn
Markham. The restriction of her movements became necessary in order to satisfy the terms of the judgment. Previous to my ruling the Lady Zillabar had demonstrated
bad faith on this contract; Sawyer and Finn Markham requested relief, the Lady accepted the results of a subsequent arbitration."

"I had no choice," she said.

"Shall we retell the whole history of this affair,
then?" Harry asked. "Including the events that transpired
aboard your starship, as well as at your private nesting
camp?"

d'Vashti stepped quickly forward then. "That history
has no relevance here."

"Perhaps it does," said Harry. "We should let the
Senior Arbiters decide."

d'Vashti replied, "The Lady Zillabar represents one
of the most important families in the Regency—"

"All the more reason why we should not allow any
hint of dishonor to stain her name," agreed Harry. "Let's
bring the full story out into the light so that Phaestor everywhere may know how the Lady sets the standard of
behavior for the entire Regency."

Zillabar looked to Harry, her eyes filled with hatred.
"I have no need of your defense, you sniveling old

fool. I will keep my private affairs to myself. I have that right. I stand here now with only one request of the Senior Arbiters. Please release me from the custody of the Captain of *The Lady MacBeth.*"

"Point taken," said Harry, stepping back out of the way.

d'Vashti spoke up then. "Your honors. I would like to state for the record that my species, the Phaestor, does not produce many fertile females. One female will lay many eggs in her lifetime and will produce a significant number of offspring for the next generation. The Lady Zillabar serves not only as the ruler of her own family, she also represents the future of the Phaestor aristocracy. I believe that the deliberate imprisonment of this woman constitutes an act of racial war. Under the Charter of the Regency—a document we all hold sacred, and which remains in effect, despite the alleged purposes of this Gathering, and indeed even until this Gathering ratifies any new form of government—under the sacred Charter, which must remain inviolate, preserving the right of species survival remains the single most important commandment, one which takes precedence over all other claims of any kind. Therefore, you have no other option but to reject the claims of these terrorists and criminals." d'Vashti concluded with a triumphant flourish.

Sawyer and Finn exchanged worried glances. Sawyer started to whisper something, but Finn put a hand on his shoulder to stop him.

The Senior Arbiter had frowned at d'Vashti's last words. Now she said, "Please do not use offensive language, Kernel d'Vashti. The court will make its own judgments about the criminality of any individuals here."

"Your honor, I said criminals and I meant criminals. *Convicted* criminals. *Escaped* criminals. Sawyer and Finn Markham, Lee-1169, Kask, Harry Mertz, and Arl-N all escaped from detainment on Thoska-Roole. Sawyer and Finn Markham, Lee-1169, and William Three-Dollar also escaped from the Lady's Imperial Starship as well. Therefore, in addition to granting Lady Zillabar's petition, I request that this court authorize me to take these criminals back into custody and return them to the detainments from which they escaped."

"Your honors—" said Harry, bustling back down to the center of the amphitheater. "It seems to me that mitigating circumstances exist in the matter of these convictions. Indeed," he said, waggling a finger, "I agree that the mandates of the Regency Charter bear strongly on this case, and I welcome Kernel d'Vashti's raising of these issues. I think we need to hear the whole story of these criminal convictions and the circumstances of the subsequent escapes—"

"No," said the Lady Zillabar. "d'Vashti does not speak for me. I have no wish to continue prosecution against any of those the Kernel named. In my official capacity as the senior representative of the ruling authority on Thoska-Roole, I intend to recommend that the Department of Criminal Prosecution investigate this case locally. Without my testimony I expect that the Department will have to dismiss all charges and expunge the records; in which case this court should not trouble itself with this matter. I'll stipulate to that if the court will."

The Senior Arbiter conferred briefly with her two colleagues. They whispered feverishly among themselves. At last, shrugging, they turned back to the Lady. "As you wish. This court will respect your privacy. Although Justice Mertz obviously wishes to expand the scope of this hearing, at this point we see no reason to do so.

"Additionally, we find Kernel d'Vashti's argument about respecting the genetic heritage of the Phaestor aristocracy so compelling that we have no choice but to grant your petition for release from the custody of *The Lady MacBeth*. That claim takes precedence over any contractual obligation you may have to the brothers Markham."

"Thank you," said the Lady Zillabar, inclining her head in a noble bow. When she straightened, she turned around to face her antagonists and gave them a look of sheer venom. "Thanks for your blood. I'll return later for the rest of it."

The Rule of Law

□□□□□□□□□□□□□□□□□□□□□□□□□□□□□

They kept their faces carefully blank until they returned to *The Lady MacBeth* and had sealed and dogged all the hatches. They held their silence until Shariba-Jen reported that the latest sweep of the ship showed that no security breaches had occurred.

Then they started shouting, laughing, and slapping each other on the backs until Harry Mertz began coughing uncontrollably and Ota had to lead him to a chair.

"I can't believe it," said M'bele. "It worked. It *actually* worked."

"It had to work," said Finn. "We didn't have a lot of other alternatives."

Catching his breath, holding up a hand, Harry nodded and agreed. "It worked because they believed it. And they believed it because we did."

Finn had already begun removing the death-mask makeup that Robin and M'bele had so carefully applied. As he pulled off the gray hair and peeled the ashen skin from his face, he finally began to look like the Finn Markham of old—ruddy, dark, and wearing a good-natured ear-to-ear grin.

"All right," said Lee-1169. "Can we have some explanations around here, finally? I have no idea what we just did. Did we win a victory or not?"

"Oh, we won a victory, all right," said Three-Dollar. "We just don't know how big a victory yet."

M'bele spoke up then. "Finn Markham responded so well to the treatments that he shook off the worst effects of the blood burn before we arrived. I kept this information secret from everyone—even from Sawyer at first—because I didn't understand what had happened.

281

Then, in looking over the entire history of the treatment, I realized exactly why this occurred. Finn's dramatic improvement began only after Lady Zillabar began feeding on all the different flavors of blood that we made available to her. The Phaestor body produces all kinds of protections against various blood diseases. When the Lady fed, all of her responses kicked in simultaneously, and Finn Markham benefited from that protection. The Lady transferred multiple immune factors to him. So Finn Markham's dramatic recovery occurred as a direct result of the generosity of every person here.

"But more than that," said M'bele, looking extraordinarily pleased with himself, "I can now tell you that as a result of the extended course of treatments, Finn Markham has achieved a profound immunity to the blood-burn, one which I feel will not only prove permanent, but could equally well prove transferable—not only to other humans, but also to every other species whose blood helped feed Zillabar. If so, we have not only a cure, but a vaccine—and for that we can thank each and every one of us here."

"I didn't donate," said Lee, both bitter and regretful. To M'bele he said, "I let my anger overwhelm my compassion. Forgive me."

Sawyer turned to Lee. "You don't have to apologize. We all understood. Nobody condemns you. I don't. I don't know that I would have acted any differently if I had stood in your place."

Lee shook it off. "But—now I feel as if I have betrayed this Alliance." He looked around in confusion. "Sometimes what feels right turns out wrong. Sometimes what feels wrong turns out right. How can anyone know what to do?"

Three-Dollar went to him and touched him compassionately. "You have to stop looking to the past as a guide. Instead design the future that you want and then choose to step committedly into it. Always look to the future you want to step into for guidance. That will tell you what you have to do."

Lee accepted this information with a puzzled frown.

He would have to think about this for a long while. He sat down thoughtfully.

Now, Robin spoke up. "But—?" she asked. "Why the pretense that Finn still needed further treatments? Why did we have to make him look so deathly ill for this hearing? That part I don't understand."

Three-Dollar nodded deferentially to Harry. Harry shrugged modestly. "Well," he said, "I take the blame for that. I did not tell any of you what I intended because I feared that your foreknowledge might keep you from acting appropriately. We needed you to become angry and rebellious, so that d'Vashti would believe that we had lost our unity—so that d'Vashti would see what he wanted to see, our vulnerability. We needed to have him underestimate us."

"So . . . you knew that the court would overturn your ruling?"

"I expected it," Harry said. "Indeed, I hoped for it. We had no further need of Zillabar here. Keeping her in custody made us look like villains. We had to get rid of her. She'd served her purpose. Finn had his health. We couldn't just release her, could we? No, we needed to have her serve us once again. By letting d'Vashti have the appearance of victory, we've also guaranteed his ultimate failure. The moment he accepted the authority of the court, he also accepted the authority of the Gathering.

"The TimeBinders have to concern themselves only with the upcoming Unification and Speaking. But the Arbiters have had a much more compelling worry. Whatever the TimeBinders create, how will we enforce it on the Regency? By getting d'Vashti to accept the legality of the processes here, he has established the precedent that the Regency will also accept the Speaking of the 'Binders. Whatever else happened at that hearing, we always had as our real goal having d'Vashti speak his acknowledgment for the record. We achieved that by not letting d'Vashti realize what he had stepped into. I thank you all for your part in this marvelous subterfuge."

Sawyer stood up then, frowning slightly. "But what about all that stuff you said about justice—justice for the enemy as well as for yourself?"

"What about it?" Harry eyed him blandly.

"Those high-sounding words; did you mean them or not?"

"I meant them," said Harry. "Every single word. I believe that d'Vashti must have access to justice too. And Zillabar. You and Lee and others have correctly asked the question, How can we have justice if the Phaestor don't also subscribe to it? The question troubles others as well. This hearing that we just concluded represents part of the answer. First, you have to have the agreement of the Phaestor that they will subscribe to the same code. They have. Now we can truly talk about justice. As an Arbiter, I remain committed to justice. When I wear this robe, I will speak as fairly as I can. When I doff the robe, however, I retain a healthy awareness of my pitiful shortcomings as a human. I confess to some loyalty to my friends. But I promise you, I have never let my love of my friends overwhelm my love of justice. It pleases me no end that in this situation justice also serves those I have learned to love."

Harry noticed the look on Sawyer's face and said, "That troubles you, doesn't it?"

Sawyer nodded. "I don't have to list all the different ways that d'Vashti and Zillabar have broken their word, broken their oaths to the Regency, broken the law, broken the boundaries of common decency—and you know as well as I how they have repeatedly violated the Charter of the Regency. Why didn't you bring that up? Why didn't you force the discussion of that issue? We could have had them disgraced—"

"We could have risked triggering a civil war. d'Vashti and Zillabar would not walk willingly into their own destruction. Nor could the Phaestor allow the Gathering to take that kind of action against two of their highest leaders. No. First we erode their authority by getting them to accept the authority of the Gathering as a higher body. This way, my friend, we have the force of the law on our side."

"But it doesn't matter what you get them to agree to. They'll ignore it at their convenience. They always do.

You can't possibly expect them to keep their word about accepting the authority of the Gathering?"

"Actually, I don't expect anything from either of them. Remember, I have personal experience of their treachery too. But listen to me, Sawyer Markham. We will abide by the rule of law, even if they do not—for once we begin to play by their rules, then no matter what else happens, we have already lost."

The Lady and the Tiger

□□□□□□□□□□□□□□□□□□□□□□□□□□□□

Within moments after the Imperial shuttle docked with *The Black Destructor*, the Lady Zillabar had stormed off, with d'Vashti following stiffly in her wake. Neither had spoken to the other—not in the hearing of multiple aides, attendants, and guards, Dragons and Vampires alike.

As soon as they had both reached the private quarters d'Vashti had set aside for her, Zillabar turned to the waiting attendants and maids and dismissed them instantly. "I will speak to the Kernel alone." When the door dilated shut behind the last of them, she let the first signs of her anger appear on her outer face.

"They insulted me. They abused me. They vilified me. They violated my person. They tried to rape my spirit, but I retreated to my inner space and they did not touch the real me. Hear this, d'Vashti—I will have my revenge. They will not crush me."

d'Vashti bowed low in deference to her rage. He spoke softly, "I guarantee that you will have your revenge, my Lady. I have no intention of letting this Gathering proceed."

"You?" she asked. "Of all the fools who tormented me, you have demonstrated yourself the most dangerous.

You just acknowledged that this proceeding has authority over the Regency Charter. You gave them the right to dismantle the Regency, if they deem it necessary."

"They won't—"

"You think not? Why do you think they called this Gathering in the first place? A Gathering represents the only authority left to them to undo the reins of our control."

d'Vashti shook his head. "They need all thirteen TimeBinders. The TimeBand of Willowar disappeared. They can't manage either a Unification or a Speaking without it—"

"They have critical mass with twelve TimeBinders. Maybe they'll vote to replace the missing TimeBand. Maybe they'll operate without it. I sat in a cell in that damned little can, and I never heard a hint of what the TimeBinders planned. I'll find out soon enough, now that I've regained access to my network. But I can tell you this, d'Vashti; now that they've gathered, they won't allow a missing TimeBand to stop them from accomplishing their goals. They'll find a way to proceed."

"It won't happen," repeated d'Vashti.

"You idiot. Haven't you heard a thing I've said? The Regency has no authority over a Gathering. It never did—and now that you've acknowledged that the Gathering has authority over the Regency—"

"I don't need authority." d'Vashti kept his voice carefully blank. "I have other means."

Zillabar stared at him. "I don't believe you said that. You have no idea how precarious our position has suddenly become. If you think you can use this—this Armageddon-class insanity of yours to suppress this process, you'll set off a rebellion that will make the last hundred years of uprisings look like a weekend on Fontana's Folly."

"I have a plan," he said.

She couldn't read him. She thought she knew d'Vashti's thinking, but suddenly she realized that large areas of him remained blank to her. Obviously, he had some mechanism in place that she remained totally unaware of. She lowered her rage. "I've seen enough of your plans. I've seen how they turn out." She waited for him to expand his statement.

He didn't. He simply remarked, "This one will not fail. Trust me."

Annoyed at his arrogance, she let her anger rise again. "I've already suffered enough from your plans—and the Dragon Lord's plans. She spat in disgust. "And you ask me to trust you?"

"You need me, Lady Zillabar. You and I both know it. Who else has the family rank necessary to stand as your mate?"

Zillabar's face flushed with rage. "If I could prove that you had a hand in Lord Drydel's death, you wouldn't dare the presumption to ask such a question."

d'Vashti said, "Nevertheless, the fact remains. And when the day finally comes that I mount you, I expect to hear you cry out with such pleasure and delight that the mirrors on the walls will shatter. We will have such a mating, it will resound as a legend for all future generations—your sons and mine will own the Palethetic Cluster."

Zillabar remained speechless in the face of his words. She couldn't believe his audacity. She turned away, unwilling to dignify d'Vashti's remarks with an answer.

d'Vashti rang for the attendants. "You'll wish to bathe, to feed, to relax in dreamtime. I will see that no one disturbs you." To the attendants he said, "See that the Lady has everything she needs. And see that no one visits her without my permission."

He bowed again to the Lady as graciously as he could and then strode out, sweeping his cape around him imperiously.

Zillabar fumed as the servant-wasps swarmed around her. She knew what had happened. She had traded one prison for another. And from this one, she knew, she would not find as easy an escape.

The Trouble with Harry

□□□□□□□□□□□□□□□□□□□□□□□□□□□□□□

Later.

Night never came to the Forum. But periods of darkness did occur, and most diurnal individuals used that darkness as the equivalent of night. Most slept, but many of those who enjoyed keeping nocturnal hours would often go out and sit under the stars. Oftentimes they indulged in long, thoughtful discussions. Others enjoyed more personal and intimate pursuits.

And some just wanted a little peace and quiet.

Far away from the more-traveled parts of the disk—at least as far as remained possible on this tiny diskworld—Harry Mertz sat alone on a stone bench in a secluded clearing. To a casual observer Harry appeared so still that he seemed either dead or asleep.

He remained that way for quite some time.

After a while Harry opened his eyes and looked at William Three-Dollar sitting on the bench opposite.

"Hello," Harry said. He waited for Three-Dollar's quiet response.

"I sat down here a half hour ago," said Three-Dollar.

Harry nodded. "I heard you sit down. If you needed to talk to me sooner, you'd have spoken."

"You know too much about medicine, too much about law, too much about the history of the Regency—and now I discover that you also practice the disciplines of the Zyne masters. You wear the robe of an Arbiter, but I know that you have played many more roles than that in your life."

Harry smiled. "You've lived more lives than me. Or rather, your TimeBand has."

"On the contrary, old man. I recognize you. You can

stop pretending. You and I—we don't need to do this charade." Three-Dollar tapped his TimeBand. "I know you. I recognize you, Harry Mertz. The name has changed, but not the face, not the voice, not the cunning. I know you."

Harry nodded. "Yes, I guess you do. All the TimeBinders do." He smiled gently, sadly. "I wondered if it would happen, if any of you would recognize me. I guess I should have expected it. I thought I could stay away, I knew I couldn't. I hoped I could come here only to observe, but I knew I wouldn't. Do any of the others know?"

"We *all* know. We selected me to come and speak to you. We want to know where you've gone all these years."

Harry shrugged. "I've wandered the Cluster. Where else would I have gone?"

"But—" Three-Dollar looked puzzled.

Harry explained. "I've traveled from world to world, paying my way with the labor of my hands, my heart, my back, my mind, whatever the market will buy. I've stood under a thousand different skies, met the most amazing people, sung the most wonderful songs, and cried the most terrible fears and sorrows.

"I've dug ditches, I've waited tables, I've strung wires, I've driven wagons, I've piloted boats, I've cast my nets in the cold waters of the north, I've panned for gold in the hot south, I've peddled news, I've strung words together for tuppence and ha'pennies, I've slung hash—both dirtside and in the galley of a tramp freighter—what more do you wish to know?

"I've peddled my wares door to door, and I've worked behind the golden counters of the most elegant establishments. I've counseled the poor on how to earn more money and the rich on how to spend it foolishly, I've built automobiles, I've destroyed them, I've taken them apart and put them back together again, I've worked as a tube-man on the interplanetary runs, I've climbed the monkey cages with the best of them, I've labored as a member of the black hole gang on more ships than I can remember, I've established six Guilds, helped run over a dozen, and I've busted three, I've made speeches, led parades, roused the rabble, and raised the dead. I've healed the sick, comforted the dying, helped the bereaved. I've delivered babies, taught schools, raised children, trained parents, and coached both the successful and the failures of a hundred different worlds.

"I've done all that and less. But you know more than me, because you carry the memories in your TimeBand, and I carry nothing but stories. Yes, I've studied law and medicine and physics and humanity. Of them all humanity remains the most interesting. All right, yes. I acknowledge all of that. What do you want from me?"

"Why haven't you made yourself known to us, Father?"

"Don't call me that." Harry looked annoyed. And then he answered the question anyway. "I have no value to you. And you have no need of me."

"No. We have *every* need of you. We have memories from fifty generations back, of a man who looks like you, speaks like you, thinks like you—a man who gave us wisdom and then vanished. The long-liner, the leaper through the years—the wandering Jew, the man who doesn't die, the immortal. Harry, we created the TimeBinders so we could have the benefits of that kind of perspective available to the rest of humanity. But we needed you for the control. And you abandoned us."

"No, I didn't abandon you. I gave you freedom. Had I stayed around, making a nuisance of myself, you would have deferred to me for a thousand years, and then you would have all started hating me for not having the good grace to die and get out of the way. By disappearing I gave you the opportunity to invent yourselves as something altogether new. And you did."

"But you helped create the TimeBinders. You saw the Regency born, you saw how it spread—you helped spread the word. You witnessed the beginnings of the Phaestor, and all the other adapted and augmented humans—and all the constructed species too. Harry, your immortality may seem a curse to you, but to the rest of us you represent the gift of connection to our own ancient past."

"No," said Harry, a little too quickly. "You see and hear only what you want to see and hear. You've turned me into a legend. You've made me a thing apart—a myth. Listen to me. Even TimeBinders can fall prey to their own emotions. You've given me the burden of a reputation of wisdom and grace much too great for any person ever to live up to."

William Three-Dollar ignored Harry's plea. "Harry, I know you as a holy man. We all know it. You can't deny it." He dropped to his knees before the white-robed old man and bowed his head. "Father, forgive us our sins. Give us your blessings. Speak to this Gathering."

Harry grabbed Three-Dollar by the shoulders and yanked him to his feet. "Listen to me, you stupid son of a bitch. If you ever say that again in front of another person, I'll punch your heart out. I'll rip your lungs out through your nose. I'll tear your fucking head off! Don't you dare turn me or anything I say into a religion! You screw things up that way. Every time! You start wars that way. Every time! I won't let you worship me. I'll catch the first ship out of here rather than let you add one more dollop of misery to the human condition. Don't you ever again call me holy-man!"

"Your holiness shines through, Father. You can't deny it."

"Goddammit! Don't confuse holiness with age. I have no more holiness than anyone else!"

But William Three-Dollar remained unconvinced. "You may believe that all you want, Harry, but you can't escape the truth. Both you and I know it. And both you and I know what you have to do to have this Gathering succeed."

Harry stared at Three-Dollar, almost horrified. "Go to hell," he said. He turned and walked away into the darkness, shaking with fear as much as anger.

Arrivals and Greetings

By the time of the first session, over a thousand vessels had arrived at the Forum, carrying representatives from over ten thousand worlds. The disk swarmed with a multiplicity of languages, cultures, species, breeds, and political positions. Walking through the gathering crowds, Sawyer and Finn gaped in wonder at all the varieties. They identified several species of bioforms they'd never seen before, some new forms of animaloid cyborgs, and a delegation of reconstructed humanides. They also saw large numbers of robots, lektroids, demonics, androgynes, Zetabeds, Meta-Lunans, Andalorians, Informants, Kasimirs, Rashids, and Loyers. More than once they stopped to stare at forms of alien and created life that they could not identify at all.

Likewise many of those same individuals also stopped to stare in wonder at Sawyer and Finn, some even so bold as to approach them and ask, "Unreconstructed humans, yes? May I touch you? Photograph please?"

Elsewhere on the disk Ibaka had found a delegation of his own species; a pack of adult canines, accompanied by several children like himself. He barked in joy when he saw them and went careening madly across the lawns, yipping in wild enthusiasm. Kask rumbled slowly after, suspicious and wary.

The dog-people stared upward at Kask in alarm, their hackles rising all along their spines—they knew their history too well—but Ibaka scampered back to Kask and jumped proudly up into his arms and announced to his new friends, "Kask saved me from Vampires. Kask saved me. Kask, look—I've found people like me!"

The dogs gathered around the Dragon warily; but the children overcame their hesitation first. If Ibaka could climb safely into the Dragon's hands, then surely they could approach close enough to touch his huge green tail. The parents barked and growled at their children, but listened with interest when Ibaka began to explain. When Kask told of his part in the massacre at the Dragon camp, the dogs began to look up at him with new respect and even wonder.

At one point, however, one of the other dog-children looked up in alarm and wailed. On a nearby rise three Phaestor boys stood and studied them thoughtfully, perhaps even . . . hungrily. Two of the larger dogs stood up, growling; but Kask lumbered to his feet and turned toward the Vampires with a distinctly angry expression on his face. The boys hesitated, then turned and ambled away—not for a moment revealing their inner faces.

Elsewhere on the disk Shariba-Jen sat on a workbench in a daisy chain of repairs. Before him he had the back of another robot open and exposed to his probing tools. Behind him a third machine had opened his back to likewise tinker with Jen's innards. "Yes," it said. "I think I can trim this. You'll notice an immediate improvement in your flexor rods."

"Jen, I have a question for you," said the machine in front. "I've heard that you'll have to seek a new posting soon. We might have room on *The Mangled Logic*. If you wish, I could arrange a meeting with captain Jhimmie."

Jen did not reply. The machine behind him spoke up instead. "Everyone has heard the rumors about *The Lady MacBeth*'s troubles, Jen. I've heard that Regency marshals intend to serve a warrant of foreclosure on Captain Campbell before the Gathering concludes. If you'll allow me to advise you, you'd do well to find yourself another ship. You should do it soon. If the court sees your indenture as part of the assets of the corporation, you could end up in foreclosure too. I wouldn't like to see that happen to you."

"Thank you for your concern," said Shariba-Jen. "I will consider your suggestions at length."

"Please do."

Elsewhere on the disk Harry Mertz walked with two TimeBinders—one, a thin, frail-looking man; the other, a heavy-gravity woman with the musculature of a bull.

"Thank you for coming with me," he said to them.

"We do it to honor you, Father."

"Don't honor me. I've had enough honors for a hundred lifetimes. Now I have more important things to do than to listen to any more acknowledgment. If I had had the good grace to drop dead a thousand years ago, you would have long ago put your memories of me into the proper perspective. Now, please just give me a little simple courtesy, and that will suffice to please a cranky old man. Now, come with me. I want to show you something." He led them to the largest meeting place on the Forum, the central amphitheater, a place of cylindrical speaking pedestals that rose up from the floor to make the speaker visible all over the bowl-shaped arena.

"Imagine a place that looks like this," said Harry. "Imagine a place constructed to honor this Forum—now imagine that a corrupt government has turned such a place into a detainment, filled the arena with water, filled the water with carnivorous beasts, and marooned their most feared political prisoners on the pedestals. Periodically, for the amusement of the guards, they cause one pedestal or another to sink slowly into the water, putting the prisoners at the mercy of the beasts. Imagine that they do this as a deliberate mockery of the Gathering."

The two TimeBinders listened to Harry's words with pained expressions. "Surely you exaggerate. We've heard the rumors too, but—"

"I have brought with me six witnesses. Kask, a Dragon; Ota, a bioform; Lee-1169, a clone-brother; Sawyer and Finn Markham, trackers; Arl-N, a poet. And I have seen it myself. The Kernel of the Phaestor aristocracy, d'Vashti himself—and the Lady Zillabar—imprisoned me in the Old City detainment of Thoska-Roole, a place that exists exactly as I have described. Listen to me, and listen well. The Phaestor have desecrated their own Forums on a hundred separate worlds. They will desecrate this one, if they have the chance."

"And what do you want from us, Father?" the heavy-muscled woman said. "What do you want us to do?"

"First, I want you to stop calling me 'Father,' " Harry said. "Second, I want you to listen to what the delegates have come here to say. I want you to listen and listen and listen, for as long as it takes to hear all the grievances—every single one. And then, and only then, I want you to do the job you came here to do. If the system has broken, then either fix it or give us one that works."

"Will you participate in this process?" asked the woman. "We need you."

Harry shook his head. "My presence will only pull the process off purpose."

The frail man blocked Harry's path. "No. On the contrary, your august presence will only validate the proceedings. Already the rumors have begun circulating that the immortal has come to the disk. If you don't participate, the Phaestor will say that you don't support the process. They will argue that the Speaking lacks credential. Already d'Vashti has challenged the Unification, because the Willower TimeBand has disappeared." The frail man took Harry's hands in his own. "Please join with us. We need you more than you realize."

"No! You must do this without me," Harry insisted.

The heavy-muscled woman looked at the old man defiantly. "Will you reconsider that decision?"

"No, I won't."

"Then hear this, Harry Mertz. Last night the TimeBinders spoke together—not as a Unification, only as individuals. We took a vote. If you won't participate in this Gathering, then neither will we. We will announce that we cannot proceed without you, and we will return to our homes."

Harry's eyes went wide in shock, horror, and finally anger. "You idiots! Don't you understand that you dismantle your own authority that way?"

"Nevertheless, we will stand by our vote. Will you participate, or do we go home?"

Harry hung his head in shame and stared at his feet. He looked up at the sky. He looked around the empty Forum facility. He sighed. He took a breath. He scratched his cheek. He said a word that no one had spoken for five millennia. He wiped his nose. "You drive a hard bargain," he said.

"So you will participate, then?"

Reluctantly, Harry nodded. "I will make myself available to you."

"Thank you. We want you to do the Speaking at the Unification—"

This time Harry said a whole bunch of words that no one had spoken for five millennia. The two TimeBinders understood the language of the words, but not the entire cultural context. Later they would spend some time remembering; the frail man would blush, the heavy-muscled woman would laugh uproariously.

Elsewhere on the disk Ota confronted an officer of The Great Palethetic Import and Export Distribution Consortium. The bioform politely said, "Captain Campbell wants to know what recompense we can expect from you."

The man tried to brush it aside. "We had a fair contract—"

"You didn't honor it. You sold us overage pfingle eggs."

"We sold you four-month green pfingle eggs."

"You sold us three-month eggs. We expect a full refund on our cargo deposit."

"You may have to wait until Hell freezes over."

"If necessary we'll push that particular planet out of its orbit to guarantee that fact. Nevertheless, we will demand a settlement on this issue. Perhaps you've heard of Captain Campbell's brinewood salon? You might want to consider what that particular artifact might mean to you and your colleagues."

The man grinned at Ota. "You can't scare me. I've heard from a reliable source that a Regency marshal has an arrest warrant for your Captain and her entire crew of malcontents, criminals, and terrorists. My company will probably offer the highest bid on your starship, just so we can see the expression on Captain Campbell's face."

Elsewhere on the disk Star-Captain Neena Linn-Campbell addressed a gathering of officials of the Spacers' Guild. Despite her reputation for reckless words and angry actions, she lowered her voice and spoke with tact and diplomacy. She spoke with candor. But she also said many things that the Guild officials did not want to hear. Their faces froze as she discussed the need to restructure the Guild. The Guild had caved in to the Phaestor tyranny, leaving itself blind and toothless. As a result the Vampires controlled the commerce of the Cluster, no one else.

Captain Campbell spoke all of this patiently and then acknowledged, "I know that you do not want to hear bad news. And what I have said here will not give you cause to cheer me. But you need to know this—I have had my ship's intelligence engine exchanging data with the intelligence engines of every other ship that has come here to the Forum. We have compiled some very interesting statistics.

"Four hundred years ago the construction rate for independent new vessels in the Palethetic Cluster began to level off. One hundred years ago it began to actually decline. This contradicts all of the long-term growth predictions that we should have seen realized by now. Looking underneath these statistics, we have discovered that starship construction actually increased during the past half-millennium; but the Phaestor aristocracy has taken control of an increasing majority of those new vessels.

"It seems to me—and to many others—that the Phaestor intend to take over all interstellar shipping and commerce. In those markets that they already control, we've seen prohibitive user-fees and tariffs. I don't have to list them for you; Guild ships no longer choose to serve those markets, because of what we euphemistically call 'local restrictions.' Freebooters serve some of those markets. I suggest you pay some attention to what the freebooters have discovered about the Vampire idea of free trade.

"I will make this information available to anyone who wants it. I think you should take it as a warning. They intend to put us all out of business and feed on our bones."

The head of the committee nodded sympathetically.

"We've heard about your problems, Captain Campbell. We sympathize with your situation, but we don't believe that your conclusions reflect an accurate understanding of the—"

At this point Neena Linn-Campbell finally lost her composure. "Take your sympathy, fold it into a sharp-cornered object, and stuff it where the sun doesn't shine," she said. "If this Guild had done its job properly, you wouldn't have to offer me much sympathy; you could offer me congratulations instead. How much more sympathy will you need to offer to the other Captains here when the Vampires come for them next?"

Elsewhere on the disk Lee-1169 came silently to a small clearing. He stood alone, with his hands clasped before him. He bowed his head and allowed himself a small prayer of memory for the two thousand genetically identical individuals that the Dragons and Vampires had hunted down and murdered. He stood there for a long time, letting tears roll softly down his cheeks.

"Lee—" a distant voice called, a childish voice. "Hi, Lee—?"

Lee-1169 turned around to see two men and a pre-pubescent boy approaching. Surprise registered on his face like an impact. His mouth fell open. "Lee?" he called back. "Hi, Lee—?"

The boy broke into a run and came trotting eagerly up to him, yelling in delight. Lee-1169 recognized his own features at a younger age. He felt a hot flush of emotion rising through him.

"1714," said the boy, introducing himself happily. He held out both his hands in a long-familiar ritual of greeting.

"1169," Lee replied. He took the boy's hands gratefully, and the two just looked at each other, beaming in mutual recognition and pride. "You fill me with joy," 1169 said. "I had not known that any of us had survived."

"Not many," said Lee-1714, "but enough." He pulled himself into his older brother's arms, and the two of them hugged intensely. By the time they released each other, the two other men—also both Lees—had come up along side them.

"1066," said one, holding out his hands to 1169.

"984," said the other, taking 1169's hands in turn.

One by one they hugged each other. And now fresh tears rolled down all of their cheeks. "We've survived the worst," said 984. "We'll rebuild—and we'll grow stronger than ever."

At that 1169 smiled, but his expression had a bitter-sweet edge. "Just us four?"

"No," said 1066. "We have twenty-two other brothers scattered safely around the Cluster. Perhaps more, but we have definitely located those. Don't worry; they have all found safe places to hide. When the time comes that we can reunite ourselves, we will. For the moment we bide our time and—" He stopped, his face hardening as he caught sight of something approaching from another direction.

1169 turned around to see Kask the Dragon approaching. The Dragon saw them at the same time.

Lee-1169 looked sideways. He moved fast and caught Lee-1066's arm before the gun left the holster. "No," he said. "Not that one."

"You defend a Dragon? One of the killers of your brothers?"

"Not that Dragon. Trust me. Please." Lee-1169 stepped in front of Lee-1066 and stared deeply into his eyes. "I know that Dragon. He saved my life. If we ever want peace between Dragons and ourselves, it has to start here—with us. Please, let me handle this." Lee-1169 turned around to face Kask.

The Dragon's face had become a mask of conflicting emotions. His old convictions fought with his new ones. He believed in honor—but he didn't know what actions really represented honorable behavior anymore. He shifted his feet nervously; his tail lashed back and forth.

"Kask—" Lee-1169 approached him cautiously. "I want you to meet my brothers."

The Dragon grumbled something unintelligible.

Lee-1169 held out his hands to him, the same greeting he had just offered his brothers. "You and I have shared much together. I think we know each other better

than any Lee and any Dragon have ever known each
other before."

Kask grunted.

"Listen to me, then. You have lost your brother
Keeda, and now that I know you this well, I know something of what you felt then and what you must feel now.
I cannot share all of your sorrow, but I claim a piece of
it, because I care about you. I cannot bring your brother
back, but please let me share my brothers with you. If I
can share your sorrow, Kask, then you can share my joy
at discovering that some of my brothers still live."

Kask shook his huge head. "I cannot."

"Yes, you can."

"No," the Dragon rumbled. "I have taken an oath to
kill Lees wherever I find them. I have already broken
that oath once. If I meet your brothers, I will have to
break it three more times. Or I will have to keep it four
times. Please do not do this to me, Lee-1169."

Lee nodded. "I understand. Kask—?"

The Dragon turned back to him. "What?"

"May I ask you one other favor, then?"

"If I can."

"Please, let me know what it would take to release
you from that oath. My brothers have an oath too that I
would like them to forswear. Perhaps you and I can find
a way to create peace among our families?"

The Dragon hesitated. "I will consider it," he said
after a moment. And then he lumbered away.

Lee-1169 turned back to his brothers. They stared at
him as if he had become something alien and monstrous.
"Hear me out," he said. "I'll tell you my history. And
then maybe you'll understand. And then, if you still believe we can never have peace, I'll accept the decision of
the family." He began speaking quietly. He began by telling them of the events in the Old City detainment on
Thoska-Roole, of two trackers named Sawyer and Finn
Markham, a dog-boy named Ibaka, an Arbiter named
Harry Mertz, a Star-Captain called Neena Linn-Campbell, a bioform named Ota, a TimeBinder, a doctor, a
Vampire, a child—and even a Dragon named Kask....

More Greetings,
More Arrivals

Elsewhere on the disk of the Forum, three TimeBinders walked together. The smallest of them, a young dark girl, spoke knowledgeably to the other two—a frail-looking man and a heavily muscled woman. She went on at some length about her experiences, and the other two nodded in understanding as they listened. Following at a distance, the TimeBinder's father and her servant both watched with a strange sense of pride.

Elsewhere on the disk three Loyers argued over the philosophies necessary for a Cluster-wide standard of justice. One of them, the eldest, clicked its mandibles thoughtfully and wondered aloud about the wisdom of including humans in any new government. "This one has never believed that humans have the rationality for self-government."

"Yes, I agree entirely," the second one replied as it chewed on the carcass of a mutated rat. "But of all the species represented here, which one do you think will behave so foolishly as to accept the responsibilities involved?"

"True," acknowledged the third, rubbing its foreclaws over its carapace in a ritual cleaning. "For that reason alone the rest of us *need* them. If only they didn't *smell* so bad. . . ."

Elsewhere on the disk Robin had found a gathering of androids and joined them cautiously. Although technically human, most androids felt profound feelings of alienation from "natural humans." Few of them had ever admitted it around their human friends, but among themselves it often came up as a topic of conversation—the feelings of rage, attraction, shame, despair, and hurt.

Much of this had to do with the fact that contractors often created androids without full sexuality. Adult androids usually felt cheated, betrayed, disabled, and resentful. Most had learned not to express these feelings; even worse, most had learned not even to admit these feelings to themselves, let alone each other. They pretended happiness or competence or even mechanical professionalism—anything but their own true selves. Androids often committed suicide. Few humans ever understood why, and assumed both correctly and erroneously at the same time that the flaw lay in the original blueprint for construction.

But . . . among their own kind, androids became *something else*, something not quite understandable to any other race or species or construct. Unlike every other form in the Cluster, the androids had in humans a model for their own behavior that they could never quite attain. Knowing that they could not achieve humanity, they became *inhuman* in the most amazing ways. They abandoned the pretenses to gender, reason, emotion, logic, and dignity. Instead they achieved *something else*, something without a name—but something that every android knew and understood, almost as if by instinct.

Robin sat alone and watched the others as they chatted and exchanged information. Most of them had stripped off their human clothes, reveling in the opportunity simply to stand naked in a group of their own. Here the full extent of the designers' crimes against their children stood revealed for all to see—individuals with the shapes of men but without nipples, without genitals, even without hair on their bodies; others in the shapes of women, again without nipples, without genitals, only empty curves to give them the appearance of something desirable. All neutered. And emotionally, all without gender or orientation. Without sexuality, gender remained irrelevant.

Under the erotic spell of a mysterious dark music, filled with suggestive rhythms and sad, seductive harmonies, the androids *danced*. They moved among each other, touching freely, exploring, wishing, pretending. They looked into each other's eyes with hope and longing. They pretended affection and intensity. They moved into each other's arms, pseudo male to pseudo female, pseudo female to pseudo female, pseudo male to pseudo male. None of it mattered.

An android male-form sat down next to Robin. He too remained clothed. "You don't play?" he asked.

She shook her head. Then she glanced over to see who had spoken. Her glance lengthened, became a studied look. The male-form had an infectious grin, a friendly expression. Robin couldn't help herself, she smiled back. He had a strong and handsome demeanor.

Again he indicated the dance floor. "You don't dance?"

"Not naked," Robin admitted. "I would appear as a freak, even among my own."

The male-form nodded knowledgeably. "I too," he admitted.

Robin looked at him with surprise. "You have . . .?"

"Yes," he said quickly. "I have full functionality." He said it as if embarrassed.

"So do I," said Robin. "They built me for . . ."

"I know," he said. "Me too."

"I've never admitted it before," said Robin. "I don't know how I can say it even now."

"I know," he said.

"I learned the ways of the human body—they wanted me to learn it so I could provide greater pleasures. But I learned it so I could kill. I killed the customer who kept hurting me," she said. "Then I killed my owners. Then I burnt their brothel. I forged my release." She looked sideways at the male-form. "You may hate me for this, but I worked as an assassin-for-hire for three years. I killed only men. Only men who hurt women or children or androids." She added, "I became very adept at it. I enjoyed it."

"Why did you stop?" he asked.

"Because I enjoyed it so much. Because one day I looked in the mirror and saw the face of the customer who kept hurting me. He enjoyed it too. I nearly killed myself that day, but I didn't."

Neither of them spoke then.

After a while she asked, "And what about you?"

"I . . . envy your courage."

"You hated your master?"

"No. I fell in love with him. And, in his own way, I think he loved me too. But he used me until he didn't want to use me anymore. And so he . . . sold me. I felt betrayed. I thought he cared."

"Humans never *care*."

"I don't know," the male said. "I think they care. I just don't think they know how to care about *us*. They don't know how to feel about us, because they don't understand what they've made us into."

"You have more compassion than I."

"You work with humans, though. I can see by your uniform. I would think—"

"The woman I work for—well, we have an agreement. She doesn't care about me, and I don't have to care about her. We do our jobs without letting our feelings get in the way. It works—"

"But you care about her anyway."

"Yes," Robin admitted, her voice starting to crack. "I do. They built me to care, and I can't *not* care."

"Me too," he admitted. "If only they would leave out the caring—"

Shyly, he laid his hand on top of hers. "Would you like to walk with me for a while? We wouldn't have to talk, if you don't want to; but I'd appreciate the company."

Robin wiped her eyes. "Yes, thank you," she said. She took his hand, and they left the place of music and bodies together.

Elsewhere on the disk a group of children—all kinds, all species—played happily together with a ball of lambent energy; they batted it about with great paddles, laughing excitedly at the sparks and the noise they made. From a distance Nyota watched them wistfully.

After a moment Ibaka came running up to her,

laughing and giggling. "Play with us?" he asked. Nyota shook her head.

From a distance M'bele observed this with a sad expression. His daughter had gained six thousand years of memory. She had lost her innocence and laughter. Once again he wanted to weep.

Elsewhere on the disk the Dragon Kask had met a distant branch of his family. He stood among the other Dragons, once again allowing himself to feel *accepted* by his own kind.

The Dragons compared their ornaments and trophies, their medallions and their armor. They admired each other's war-paint and weapons and helmets. They posed and postured proudly for each other, demonstrating the ferocity of their war-cries. Kask laughed harmoniously with them—until one of his brothers remarked, while sharpening his knife, that he looked forward to the chance of killing Lees. "I've heard that several of them have come to the Forum. I can hardly wait to taste their blood."

Kask did not share the laughter. It troubled him, and he couldn't explain why—not even to himself. He remembered Lee-1169's question. He wondered anew about loyalty and honor. Did it lie in following rules? Or did each person have to invent honor for himself as if no one else had ever invented honor before? He'd never had to consider these questions. It made his head hurt.

Shortly after that he wandered away from the other Dragons. Kask decided that he didn't like their jokes about killing Lees . . . or anyone else. He went off and sat alone for a very long time.

He thought he wanted the companionship of his brothers again. But no—he didn't want them. He didn't even like them anymore. What he wanted remained unattainable. He wanted his simplicity again. He didn't want to have to think about things like this anymore. He wanted . . . he didn't know what he wanted.

Elsewhere on the disk Gito wandered alone, feeling very much left out of the gatherings and celebrations of all the others. Because of his height—or rather, the extreme lack of it—he often felt as if he belonged to a

whole other human species; a species not yet represented here at the Forum. If any other high-gravity
dwarves had come to the Gathering, he had not yet met
them. He would have given anything to speak with another person from Tharn.

And then—it happened. He heard a soft, gravelly
voice behind him. He turned and saw her. And his emotions plummeted. She had a certain crushed-rock quality
about her that he found attractive, she moved with stolid-
ity and assurance; but she also wore a dark-red Regency
uniform. Despite himself Gito drifted closer. Her name-
tag identified her as Juda-Linda; she smiled at him tooth-
ily, and he couldn't help himself, he smiled back; but the
insignia on her uniform revealed that she served on
d'Vashti's starship. She held the rank of fluction supervi-
sor on *The Black Destructor*.

Simultaneously intrigued and repelled, Gito didn't
know whether to approach, to flee, or merely to stand in
one place, as if struck dumb by lightning. He shifted his
feet uneasily.

She came to him, glancing at him curiously, and
then as she saw the insignia of *The Lady MacBeth* on his
chest, she frowned; but then her frown eased as if Gito's
ship didn't matter at all to her, and she approached the
rest of the way. "Hey, fella—" she said.

Gito flushed with embarrassment. "Hey, yourself."

"Do you have any news from Tharn?" she asked.

Gito shook his head. "I haven't seen Tharn in . . . too
many years. Yourself?"

She laughed. "I've served on *The Black Destructor*
so long, I can't remember the last time I walked on a
planet."

"Do they treat you well?"

"As well as one could hope for. The Phaestor give orders. We follow them. If everything works the way they
want, nobody cares about anything else."

"Hm," said Gito.

"Why do you ask?"

"I may have to find a new posting soon. I thought
that I might start asking around at the Forum. So many
ships, so many opportunities—"

At that moment Ibaka and another shaggy dog-boy came running past, yipping and barking in excitement. Seeing Gito, Ibaka stopped to say hello, wagging his tail happily.

Juda-Linda stiffened rudely. "Get away from us, you little son of a bitch!" She raised her arm as if to strike the boy.

Ibaka yelped and ran away. His friend followed. Gito felt ashamed. He should have stopped her. He should have said something. Now he would have to apologize to the dog-child. He looked at Juda-Linda again. Somehow some of her attraction had vanished.

Elsewhere on the disk Star-Captain Campbell sat and chatted over an evening meal with Sawyer, Finn, Harry, M'bele, Nyota, Three-Dollar, and several other of the TimeBinders and their attendants who had come to the Gathering. Despite all their individual concerns, they discussed little of importance. For a brief while, at least, they had put aside their troubles in favor of a moment of relaxation. They sat around and swapped bawdy tales and obscene stories. The TimeBinders each had six thousand years of dirty jokes. The evening quickly became uproarious.

Sawyer's eyes met Neena Linn-Campbell's for just the briefest of instants, and then they both looked away quickly, equally embarrassed—

Suddenly—

Somewhere Ibaka yelped. A Dragon growled. The light of the day winked out. Darkness swept across the Forum.

Sawyer leapt to his feet; so did Neena Linn-Campbell. Then all the others. They looked up into the sky, aghast. As their eyes adjusted to the sudden night, they saw an edge of darkness sweeping silently across the stars.

"What the hell—?"

And then—an ominous and terrifying red light swept over the entire disk of the Forum. It came from a thousand different sources, spaced across a wall of something gigantic—

Sawyer recognized it first. "Oh, my God—"

And then Captain Campbell did too. And Finn. And then all the others.

Kernel Sleestak d'Vashti's enormous Armageddon-class warship had moved in position directly *above* the disk of the Forum. A flying mountain of metal and guns. Even though it remained above the ceiling of air, beyond the limits of the atmosphere of the disk—even at that great distance it filled the entire sky. It blotted out the stars, the suns, and even the Eye of God.

Across the disk, every eye—human, bioform, robot, construct, android, alien, Vampire, Dragon, whatever— turned upward. They stared in awe and wonder and horror at the size of the kilometers-long vessel. It drifted silently across the roof of the world, both a challenge and question. What did d'Vashti intend? Had he done this as a bluff? Or would he actually fire on the delegates to the Gathering?

"Goddammit," said Harry softly.

Finn said it for all of them. "He's outmaneuvered us. How can we hold a Gathering under the guns of the Regency?"

War Councils

□□□□□□□□□□□□□□□□□□□□□□□□□□□□□

They retreated to *The Lady MacBeth* to escape the fearsome eyes of *The Black Destructor*.

The TimeBinders expressed the greatest concern. Seven of them sat in the starship's salon, anxiously discussing their alternatives. Harry, Ota, Lee, Sawyer, M'bele, and Captain Campbell sat in on the discussion too.

One of the TimeBinders, a boyish-looking fellow named Grolder, put it into words. "How can we proceed? Even if the Gathering declares the Regency dissolved, how can we enforce it? If we take a stand here, he has the power to scourge our worlds."

Nyota stood up then to reply. "I don't argue with your logic. But I want you to look at something else for a moment. Look at how we have all reacted to the sight of a single starship in the sky. We knew that d'Vashti had the power. We just hadn't had our noses rubbed in it. Suddenly he flies overhead and turns on his red lights, and we all go into a panic. We let our fear and our anger speak for us. We fall into the trap of our own emotions. We have reacted exactly as d'Vashti wanted us to. Now we have to ask ourselves—do we proceed as d'Vashti wishes, or do we take control of our own destinies and act as *we* wish?"

"But, Nyota—d'Vashti can't allow this Gathering to begin at all. He needs to break it up before it starts. If he has to create an incident, he will."

Nyota nodded in understanding. But she simply looked across at Grolder and asked, "Do you want to go home empty-handed? Do you want to go back to your people and say, 'd'Vashti had a starship, and we grew so afraid that we decided not to proceed with the Unification'—do you really want to do that?"

Grolder shook his head no. "I admit my fear. d'Vashti terrifies me. But . . . let me tell you something else. I had heard the stories of Phaestor atrocities—from you, from William Three-Dollar, from Harry Mertz—but I didn't believe them because I didn't want to believe them. Until now. d'Vashti has demonstrated his contempt for this process. He gives us no choice. We must proceed with the Gathering."

"I have a thought," Finn said. "I know that I don't have the same perspective of any of you, but if I might—" He glanced around expectantly, but no one objected. The TimeBinders looked to him politely. Finn nodded and continued. "I don't think that d'Vashti acted rashly or foolishly or impetuously. I think he acted with deliberate forethought. I believe that d'Vashti wants the Gathering to proceed. He moved his ship into position not to frighten us into quitting in panic, but because he wants to challenge us to continue on in anger. For some reason—I have no idea what or why—he *needs* for us to have the Gathering. He did this to strengthen our resolve, not weaken it. And look around—it's working.

"We thought we tricked him into recognizing the authority of this body; what if we miscalculated? What if he's tricked us into having exactly the kind of Gathering he wants?"

The TimeBinders scratched their heads thoughtfully as they considered the import of Finn Markham's suggestion. "But what does he want? What does he gain?"

"He wants power. He wants Zillabar. He wants the Gathering to provide the mechanism by which he will attain both."

Three-Dollar spoke then. "On Thoska-Roole we knew for many years that the Dragon Lord had no intention of breaking the back of the rebellion while we remained useful to him. We never believed that this idea came entirely from the Dragon Lord. We always suspected that d'Vashti had reasons of his own for wanting the rebellion to grow powerful. Perhaps he wanted this Gathering all along."

"If so," said Harry Mertz, "then we have to ask ourselves why. We may have a much bigger problem here than we ever expected."

In the engine room of *The Lady MacBeth*, Robin and Gito engaged in a similar conversation while Ota and Shariba-Jen looked on.

"I don't care about politics," said Gito. "Tall people do politics. Short people work. And we have to work twice as hard just to get half the recognition. I just want a fair share. You want to know the truth? I don't care who wins, I'll go with the winner. Yeah. Don't look so surprised. The Chief Fluction engineer of *The Black Destructor* has asked for a copy of my rating. Maybe she'll offer me a job."

"She doesn't want your brain, you idiot!" Robin said. "She wants your dick."

"Big head, little head. I don't care. I want to work on a bigger ship. Maybe they'll serve better food. Maybe they'll appreciate me more than I see here."

"What about your loyalty to Captain Campbell?" Robin asked, shocked at Gito's audacity.

"What about her loyalty to us?" Gito rasped back. "Whatever happened to that renegotiation of our contracts?"

"Do you think you'll get a better deal from the Vampires?"

"The Phaestor will pay me on time. I can't work for a bankrupt corporation—neither can you!"

Robin stopped, speechless. She started to reply, then stopped herself in frustration. At last she said, "For the first time in years, I regret that I took a vow of nonviolence. You make me wish I had a weapon in my hands, you nasty little pig-fucker."

"Wait," said Gito nastily. "I'll get you a needle-beam. You can lower yourself to my level."

"I have never seen such a display of disloyalty, dishonor, and terminal stupidity in anyone! Stupid me. I expected better from you! I thought that this crew stood together as friends—as a family! I accepted you without question. We all did—even though we knew your history, your family, your personal disgrace. And we thought you stood with us the same way. Now we know the truth. Anyone with enough money can buy your loyalty."

Gito took a step back, startled. "Wait a minute—" he said, flustered. "Captain Campbell says it, and you say it, and Ota says it—everybody says it—that the corporation has gone bust. We've all started looking for new postings. Don't deny it. You've asked around. Ota has. So has Jen. So why should I take the brunt of your anger? I have to take care of myself too—"

"But . . . not with the very people who've brought down Captain Campbell. Don't you understand *anything*, you cretin?" Robin stormed out of the engine room, followed by Ota and Jen, leaving Gito behind, shaking his head and muttering curses about women, androids, and bioforms who didn't know their aft orifices from a black hole.

Robin stamped through the keel of the ship, coming up onto the Operations Deck of the bridge, where she stopped in surprise. Sawyer and Finn sat over the tactical display, huddled in private conference.

"Who gave you access to the bridge of the vessel?" she demanded.

"Captain Campbell. We need to confer with EDNA."

"About what?" Robin looked at them sspiciously. She still felt angry at Gito; she had no intention of letting anyone else win a confrontation.

"About ways to fight back."

"You?" queried Robin.

"Sawyer and Finn Markham, experts in mayhem," Sawyer explained.

"It says so on our business cards," Finn added.

"At your service," Sawyer bowed.

"Well . . . ?" Robin said grudgingly.

"Help us," Sawyer said. He gestured upward. "Why can't we do something about *that*?" He indicated the unseen vessel that still dominated the sky over the Forum.

"Sure," said Robin. "If you could get aboard her, you could do any number of things to take her apart. Hell, a virus program to reverse her passive levitators just before transit would turn the damn thing inside out—"

"Too obvious," remarked EDNA, *The Lady Mac-Beth's* intelligence engine. She put up a display showing the Armageddon-class warship. "If I had the responsibility of taking that ship into *otherspace*, I would run tell-me-three-times checks of all gravitational generators and prisms, every thirty milliseconds."

"But if we could do it—?" Finn asked.

EDNA caused the image of *The Black Destructor* to shred itself. "Unfortunately, you'd have to wait until the vessel left the Forum. It won't help you any in the present situation."

"Hm," said Sawyer. "I wonder if we could get her to self-destruct somehow. EDNA, has an intelligence engine ever gone suicidal?"

"Sorry. Intelligence engines hardly ever demonstrate unstable behavior."

"Hardly ever?" asked Finn.

"It depends on the ancillary motivations. I would assume the I.E. on *The Black Destructor* does not have many ancillary features. The Phaestor don't really like intelligence engines with too much independence."

"Hm," said Sawyer. "Maybe we could give it some."

"Not a good idea," suggested EDNA. "The more independence an engine has, the less likely it will commit suicide."

"If we could get an antimatter kernel aboard—or even nearby. Hell, if we could just launch one in its general direction . . ."

EDNA caused the display to show the results of such an event. *The Black Destructor* disappeared in a flash of light—but so did the Forum, *The Lady MacBeth*, and several hundred other vessels.

Sawyer sank back in his chair. "All right, I've run out of ideas," he announced.

Finn looked at him, surprised. "Really?"

Sawyer said, "Well . . . no. But this frustrates me. We can't get aboard the ship, we can't get near it, and anything we could do to it will hurt us as much as them. We need something elegant."

"Sorry," said Captain Campbell stepping onto the command bridge of her vessel. "But we don't have any more pfingle eggs."

"It doesn't matter," said Finn. "Vampires don't like pfingle eggs enough—at least not enough to get stupid about them."

Neena Linn-Campbell glanced curiously at Sawyer. "May I ask you something?"

"Sure."

"I thought you two didn't get involved in politics. Why now?"

Sawyer shrugged. He scratched his ear. He frowned. "Politics?" He shook his head. "Nah. We decided to take this one personally."

Neena Linn-Campbell smiled. "Why don't I believe you?"

Finn smiled gently and admitted it. "All right, maybe we do care a little. Maybe all this politicking stinks just like all the other politicking in the Cluster. But maybe also this time it might actually make a difference for the better. If we really do believe in justice, and if we have even half a chance here, we have to try, don't we?"

"Besides," said Sawyer. "We don't think like fish."

"Right," said Captain Campbell skeptically. "And maybe you heard that Dragons don't care what they eat, fish or foul-smelling."

Sawyer grinned. "I guess that might have something to do with it too." He turned back to the display. "EDNA, by any chance do you have a schematic of the keel of *The Black Destructor*? I have another idea."

"It won't work—" said EDNA. But she put up the display anyway.

The Edge

□□□□□□□□□□□□□□□□□□□□□□□□□□□

Nevertheless, not all of the TimeBinders felt as strongly as Three-Dollar and Nyota. Not all of them reacted as Grolder. Several still expressed concern about the wisdom of continuing with the Gathering in the face of the Regency's obvious disapproval. These included Fariah of B'rik'yno, Lord K'aenar of Ascuto, and Calvin of Canby.

Even as the first hour of the Gathering approached, the informal politicking continued. Many of the attendees came from worlds where the Phaestor aristocracy had not yet exercised their authority as dramatically as they had on Thoska-Roole and Burihatin. Some of the TimeBinders remained skeptical of the stories and rumors they had heard of atrocities and violations of the Regency Charter. Nevertheless, across the disk of the Forum, various groups still came together to consider their next actions. With the full weight of d'Vashti's Armageddon-class warship hanging over them all, many of the arguments against the Phaestor had taken on a new credential.

At a gathering place at the outer edge of the Forum, Lee-1169 spoke patiently with Fariah, Lord K'aenar, and Calvin, three of the most conservative TimeBinders. Fariah had glowing red skin and long black hair that reached to her waist; she wore an elegant gown of pale silk. Lord K'aenar had olive skin and shadowed eyes; he wore an ornate ceremonial kimono, so intricate that it defied easy description. Calvin wore only a simple harness for his weaponry; he had orange hair that covered his entire body; and Lee remained uncertain of his genetic heritage. The three TimeBinders listened patiently as Lee presented his case to them. They stood at the top of a rise of wide marble steps near the edge of the disk. Here, where the atmosphere thinned considerably, they had a remarkable view of the stars.

Around them the other surviving members of the Lee clone-family stood, occasionally interjecting their own thoughts and comments, but mostly allowing their more world-wise brother to say it for all of them.

"I can't speak for the rest of the Cluster," said Lee, "but I can tell you what I've seen in my lifetime. Ask me about the Kilpatrick Massacre,[11] and I'll tell you of one of

---

[11]Seventeen years earlier an "unfortunate incident" occurred at the small mining settlement of Kilpatrick's Folly on the backwater world of Morpaline. A troop of Regency Dragons sought revenge for an inadvertent insult to one of their number. (The original insult was not even caused by an inhabitant of the settlement, but by a visiting traveler, known only as Mr. Costello, "professional hero.") The Dragons' revenge got out of hand; they slipped into a killing rage and ran amok through a mountain settlement, killing 117 of the 183 inhabitants.

The Regency Prefect (a member of the Lee clone-family) on Morpaline summarily ordered the entire troop of Dragons dishonorably executed. This incident triggered a three-year civil war between the Lee clone-family and the Moktar Dragons. This war never officially ended; the Dragons simply ran out of Lee clones to kill. They exterminated almost the entire Lee family. Nevertheless, the vendetta remained in effect.

Of some peripheral interest, a number of children survived the massacre, including two boys; Finn Markham, age fifteen, and his younger brother, Sawyer, age eight. Already hardened by the tough conditions on Morpaline, Finn made a personal vow to accomplish two things in his life: First, he would see that Sawyer was raised and educated to be worthy of their family name. Second, he would track down and kill Mr. Costello, the traveler who insulted the Dragon Guard in their village.

The Regency Prefect transferred Finn and Sawyer (and most of the other orphans) to the custody of a human-services placement agency—a kind of high-class slave trader. Later the Regency agreed to pay "compensation fees" to each of the sur-

316 David Gerrold

the great turning points in the history of the Regency. The Dragon Guards have taken it as a sacred oath to kill judges and councilors and clone-families ever since. The Regency has become a partner in the commission of these illegal acts."

As he detailed the events of the Kilpatrick Massacre, a small crowd began to gather around, their faces rapt with attention. His passion and his fury made Lee a compelling speaker. The force of his personality infused his whole presentation, and the crowd reacted with gasps and anger as he spoke of the Dragons' rage, their killing frenzies—the way they slashed fathers to death in front of their sons, the way they tormented and looted and laughed at the pain of others. Lee spoke calmly at times, furiously at others, but overall he evoked an emotional response from his listeners that no mere dry recanting of facts could ever produce.

At the back of the crowd, two small humans watched with sour expressions, Gito and Juda-Linda. Neither had any great concern for the problems of other species; partly this grew out of their own sense of alienation from the taller elements of their species, partly it came from their own personal resentment at the patronizing way that others had often treated them, and partly it came from the built-in bias of their culture. The people of Tharn didn't complain—and certainly never in public—they got even. Gito frowned uncomfortably. Robin's words still haunted him. He knew that he had failed to understand something. It bothered him. Now

---

vivors of the massacre. Unfortunately, the Dragon Guard challenged this attempt at compensation in court as an insult to their honor. The case dragged on for many years, and by the time that all parties finally came to agreement, little remained of the award to the remaining survivors; the legal corporations representing them claimed the bulk of the money. Sawyer and Finn collected almost nothing for their parents' death. As a result of these events, Sawyer and Finn developed a lifelong distrust of both lawyers and governments.

Sawyer and Finn finally contracted for adoption by a military colony, where both learned significant survival skills. Unfortunately, their personal agendas kept them from being fully assimilated. They used their small share of the Kilpatrick settlement to pay off their indentures to the colony and left by the first ship they could book passage on to become trackers.

They still haven't found Mr. Costello, the man responsible for triggering the Kilpatrick massacre, but neither have they stopped looking.

Lee's words disturbed him even more. Lee *understood* it. But listening to him, Gito still couldn't hear what he *really* meant. It just sounded like more weeping and wailing at the unfairness of the universe.

Something rumbled behind them. Automatically, Gito stepped out of the way, pulling Juda-Linda with him. Several Dragons had appeared around the edges of the gathering. Some of them grumbled uncomfortably—deep sounds of warning and danger. The listeners in the crowd began turning their heads to stare at the Dragons. Standing to one side, the other Lees began to show their concern as well. They whispered among themselves, wondering if they should withdraw or stand by their brother.

Finally even Lee-1169 acknowledged the presence of the warrior-lizards. "Ho," he said. "Here I stand. A Lee that you missed."

One of the Dragons, the biggest, spoke in a voice like doom. He wore black armor, trimmed with silver. "Anywhere else in the Cluster, we would punish your treason with instant death. Here we have to let you speak with impugnity."

Around them the crowd had grown enormously. Word of this confrontation had spread across the disk, and people of all races and species moved quickly toward the scene—like bystanders rushing toward the scene of an accident, hoping to see the bloodshed.

Lee remained unfazed. "I know that you want to kill me. And hear this. In my heart still burns a desire for revenge as well. I want to hurt those who hurt me. As do you. As do we all.

"I came here to tell the TimeBinders that the corruption that caused the Kilpatrick Massacre has spread throughout the Cluster—that we can't trust the Phaestor nor the Moktar Dragons. But in the journey to get here, I discovered something else. I discovered that I had to give up part of my hatred."

Now Sawyer and Finn came charging up to the crowd, began trying to force their way through the thickest part of it. Sawyer pointed out the Dragons to Finn.

Finn replied, "I don't like the looks of this. They

came to create an incident." The brothers pushed through to stand beside an unhappy-looking Kask. "Will they attack?" Finn asked.

Kask rumbled. "I would—if I still believed in Dragons' honor."

Lee-1066 whispered up to Lee-1169, "This looks dangerous, Lee—please come down."

1169 waved his brother away. "We have to take a stand. We have to take the chance." To the scowling Moktar lizards he said, "Yes, I thought I wanted to kill Dragons; but I have learned that Lees and Dragons do not have to kill. Not each other, not anymore. I have shared bread with a Dragon. He and I served together in the battle against a larger foe than either of us alone could defeat. And from that we learned a larger truth. We can both stand for the same possibility—that all of us together can serve the Alliance of Life. We don't have to fight. We can build.

"So now I ask you the same question that I asked him. What will it take to end the enmity between your family and mine?"

Two of the Dragons grunted. "We'll show you what it'll take—the silence of the Lees." They started for Lee-1169; the crowd scattered, scrambling to get out of their way. The Lees tried to get to their brother, but the surge of the crowd pushed them sideways and away.

"Here they go," shouted Finn.

"And here *we* go," said Sawyer.

Gito started forward too, not knowing what he intended to do, but Juda-Linda grabbed his arm and held him back. "No. This argument belongs to the tall ones, not you and me."

The brothers Markham jumped up onto the raised steps to stand beside Lee, so did Robin—and Kask and Ibaka. He pushed them all away, angrily. "No. This argument belongs to me."

"It belongs to all of us," said Sawyer.

"No, it does not," said Lee. "I have to stand alone here. I let you stand alone when your brother needed my blood. Let me reclaim my honor my own way." Standing on the side, the other Lees watched in horror, not knowing whether to run—or to leap up to stand beside their brother.

Abruptly Kask put himself between Lee-1169 and the two advancing Dragons. He growled warningly. "No, you cannot kill him. I won't allow it."

"*You* won't allow it?" The Dragons laughed. "By what authority?" Several other Dragons pushed through the crowd now. Sawyer and Finn exchanged worried glances.

"Don't you listen?" said Kask to his brothers. "This vendetta has brought dishonor to the Dragons. Further killing will only increase the size of the stain. It has to stop somewhere. Let it stop here."

One of the Dragons grunted disdainfully. "The expert on dishonor speaks. You've stained yourself a hundred times over."

"I know the meaning of honor," said Kask. "The death of this man will not honor the Moktar. You'll have to kill me before I'll let you kill him."

"No," said the biggest of the Dragons. "We don't waste our time on the stained and the nameless."

Abruptly, three of the Dragons tackled Kask—the four struggling Dragons careened sideways, tails lashing, biting and snapping and roaring ferociously. The biggest Dragon, the one in the black-and-silver armor, charged Lee-1169, grabbed him in his claws, held him high over his head, screaming triumphantly, and then flung the hapless clone-brother as hard as he could *out and away*—right off the edge of the disk of the Forum!

The others released Kask, and the Black Dragon snorted at him. "You see? We don't have to kill when we can just throw the trash away."

"Let's get the others—" another Dragon started to say, and lowered his head preparatory to charging the other Lee clones; but Kask broke free and came barreling headlong into the Black Dragon, knocking him tail over windpipe, snarling and slashing at his throat. The two lizards tumbled and writhed for a moment, snapping and biting at each other, grunting and roaring. For a moment it looked as if Kask had no advantage, but the bigger Dragon couldn't maneuver as easily—and suddenly,

Kask ducked under the Black Dragon, lifted, and toppled the bigger beast onto its back. The Black Dragon came crashing down with a ground-shaking thud. Kask had his mouth around the other's throat so fast, that for a moment none of the onlookers realized that the fight had ended.

"Kill me swiftly," said the Black Dragon.

"No," said Kask. "Killing solves nothing. I will let you live with the disgrace that even a dishonored Dragon can beat you. Or you can learn the lesson that something other than killing defines true honor."

"I'd rather die!" the Black Dragon rasped.

"You don't have that choice," Kask growled. "By my victory I order you and your team to leave the disk of the Forum never to return—until you can return as a force for peace." He released the other's throat. "Now, go! Before I inflict a bigger disgrace."

The Black Dragon levered himself ruefully to his feet. Without a word he stamped away. The other Dragons stared after him in confusion, then followed unhappily.

Much of the crowd had already rushed to the edge of the disk, where Lee still struggled in the air. Even as they watched, he tumbled away toward the edge of the atmosphere. The Lee brothers screamed in rage and horror.

"We've gotta do something," Sawyer shouted.

"What—?" Finn asked. "Throw him a rope? What rope? Go after him? How?"

Lee-1714 swore and cried and shrieked until both of the Markham brothers had to grab him to keep him from jumping after Lee-1169. Robin grabbed the boy from behind in a hug and pulled him close to her, holding him tightly, and turning him away from the edge so he couldn't see what happened next.

Lee had already stopped struggling. He had fallen into the thin outer reaches of the envelope of air and passed into unconsciousness. Moments later, even as he shrank away into the distance, they could see his blood boiling out of his mouth and ears and eyes—

"Hmpf. He deserved it," observed Juda-Linda. "For preaching treason."

Gito looked at her, shocked at her disregard of life. He found himself wondering—*Do I look like that?* He turned away, troubled.

Critical Mass

◻◻◻◻◻◻◻◻◻◻◻◻◻◻◻◻◻◻◻◻◻◻◻◻◻◻◻

The three TimeBinders looked stricken. The crowd swirled around them. Angry voices called for action, demanding that the TimeBinders respond.

Abruptly, Calvin of Canby spoke to the throng. He removed a ceremonial rod from his harness and held it out before him. "I have seen enough. I have heard enough. I stand ready for the Gathering now." He started toward the center of the Forum, then stopped and look back to the other two 'Binders. "Do you intend to stand there waiting for a silver invitation? We've seen a crime committed on this Forum. Do you need any more evidence that the Gathering must proceed?"

Fariah nodded solemnly and joined Calvin. Lord K'aenar bristled; he put his hand on his sword, then nodded curtly. He stamped proudly over to stand with Calvin and Fariah. As they marched toward the center of the disk, the crowd swarmed around them, surrounding them, shouting defiance at the warship above and screaming for justice.

They flooded into the central amphitheater in a torrent of bodies. Calvin strode directly to the slender central pedestal and laid his ceremonial rod of authority on top of it. "I, Calvin of Canby, stand ready for Unification." Then he stepped back out of the way. A great bell-like tone sounded across the entire disk of the Forum. The first TimeBinder had laid down his authority. All over the disk, people looked up from their conversations, startled, delighted, worried, thrilled, alarmed, excited—

The slender red woman laid her ceremonial rod next to his and announced, "I, Fariah of B'rik'yno, stand ready also." The solemn note rang again. Deep and resonant, it rolled out across the tiny world.

And finally Lord K'aenar produced his glowing rod of authority and laid it with theirs. "Let the Gathering begin." He waited until the last echo of the third chime faded away into silence. He grunted once in satisfaction, then stepped into position. The three of them stood there waiting. They had issued the call. They knew it would not take long for the word to spread.

"We've got a problem—" said Finn.

"We can't stop them," Sawyer said.

"If we intend to act, we'll have to do it now—"

The two brothers started to turn away, nearly tripping over Gito. The dwarf grabbed Sawyer by the leg and pulled him down to the ground with a sudden strong jerk, then pulled him halfway back up again to growl in his face. "You don't need a warhead, you idiot. Use a singularity in a vacuum bottle. They'll never detect it."

It took a moment for Sawyer to realize what Gito meant. "Do you know how long it would take to shove a warship that size into a pinhole?"

"Put it at the bottom of a gravitic lens. If it takes longer than fifteen minutes to go down, I'll eat my own underwear."

Robin looked at the dwarf oddly. "Gito, you don't wear underwear."

Gito shrugged and let go of Sawyer's shirt. Sawyer climbed back to his feet.

"Y'know," said Finn. "I think he might have something there—"

Gito snarled. "Shut your feeding hole and listen. Plant it in the keel of the ship, expand the event-horizon with a hyperspace injector-valve—three meters oughta do it, but you can make it as big as you need—then get out of the way. *Fwooop*! The singularity will eat the hyperspace valve for dessert, and the whole thing will collapse back to a pinhole."

Robin, Sawyer, Finn, looked at each other and grinned. "Y'know. It just might work."

"Of course it'll work," snarled Gito. "Clean. Fast. Nasty. If you have luck on your side, you'll have maybe ten minutes to get out. If you have no luck, well, at least death will come quickly and painlessly."

"Let's do it," said Sawyer.

"Wait a minute," said Robin. "Where do you plan on getting the singularity from—?"

Sawyer and Finn exchanged a glance, then looked back to Robin expectantly.

"Oh, no, you don't. You can't! That would leave *The Lady MacBeth* without a heart for its engines."

"Uh-huh. And the last I heard, Regency marshals had other plans for *The Lady MacBeth*. Let's ask Captain Campbell how she wants to decommission her command."

Gito said, "Hey, if you do it right, you can retrieve the singularity afterward and reinstall it. Hell, with the extra mass it'll probably gain between three and five percent efficiency."

"Let's do it," said Robin, ready to move.

"We still have the problem of getting the damn thing aboard *The Black Destructor*," said Sawyer.

"I'll do that," said Gito. "I'll accept the posting Juda-Linda offered me."

Robin looked at him, surprised. "You would do that—?"

Gito shrugged. "I like her, but not enough to work for her. She has a nasty mean streak."

"Too mean for you—?"

"Let's go," said Sawyer. "We'll talk about Gito's love life later." The four of them headed out toward the edge of the disk and the docking spoke of *The Lady MacBeth* at a run.

As Sawyer and Finn, Robin and Gito, hurried off in one direction, Harry Mertz and William Three-Dollar arrived at the central amphitheater from the opposite side.

"Oh, shit," said Harry, looking at the waiting TimeBinders—five of them stood there now; their rods of authority lay on the central pedestal. "I feared that something like this would happen."

"d'Vashti got tired of waiting. He triggered an incident."

"It works that way sometimes when you try to plan a revolution. The plot comes to a boil before you want it to."

Three-Dollar put his hand on Harry's shoulder. "We need you more than ever now. You know that."

Harry shook off Three-Dollar's hand. "I've heard that before. I don't believe it. You know why? Because when I do help, I never see that I make a difference. When I don't help, everybody still survives. They solve their problems without me and keep on going."

"Harry—" Three-Dollar grabbed him by the shoulders and looked him directly in the eye. "We need you to stand as the Nexus. You will give us the credential, because you have the moral authority of history ingrained in every fiber of your soul."

Harry glanced away, uncomfortable. "Please, not me. Find someone else."

"Listen to me, you cranky old son of a bitch," Three-Dollar said. "You have to do this. If you don't, then every TimeBinder in the Cluster will know you for a hypocrite. Starting with me."

"Do you know what happens to the person who stands as Nexus?" Harry asked uncomfortably.

"Yes. It changes you. It leaves you with a head full of memories and a vision big enough for the Cluster. I would think that a man like you would deeply desire such an opportunity."

"Not a *second* time!" said Harry to Three-Dollar's astonished stare. "Yes, it changes you. But not always for the better. Do you know how much pain comes with it? All the pain in the Cluster. Everything that every TimeBinder knows. Please don't ask me to do this *again.*"

Three-Dollar gaped at Harry, amazed. "No wonder I remember you so vividly! No wonder that we all do. You stood as the Nexus when the first TimeBinders created the Regency."

"Yes," Harry admitted. "I did."

Three-Dollar sagged in resignation. "Forgive me. I had no right to make any more demands of you. You have already served us. We have no right to ask for anything more."

"Damn straight," said Harry, satisfied.

"But will you do it anyway?" said Three-Dollar, still meeting his eyes.

"You never give up, do you?"

"No. Neither do you. We stand on the same side, only you don't realize it yet. As soon as you do, you'll know what you have to do—"

Harry snorted. "I've known what I had to do since before we arrived. I just don't want to do it." He pushed past Three-Dollar, muttering something nasty.

"But you'll do it?"

"But I'll do it," he conceded.

A Romantic Interlude

On the bridge of *The Black Destructor*, Kernel d'Vashti and the Lady Zillabar studied the aerial view of the Forum. The crowd around the amphitheater swelled as they watched. From above they could see the entire disk; the word had obviously spread quickly. People moved down the spokes from their various vessels; they threaded their way across the paths and the lawns and the gardens. They rode the moving walks and filled the layered rows of the great arena.

As she watched, Zillabar's expression turned as brittle as ice. She didn't bother to hide her feelings anymore. She said coldly, "I assume that this little demonstration below represents the successful workings of your great secret plan . . . ?"

d'Vashti returned her gaze with equanimity. "I expected the Gathering to proceed. That it now appears as if it will begin earlier than either of us expected neither helps nor hurts the actions I intend."

"I can't believe how you've mismanaged everything. The Regency will crumble because of your stupidity. I should have you flayed alive."

"Shut up, you stupid sow," d'Vashti said. "I control you now."

She stared at him aghast.

He stepped in close to her and lowered his voice. "You have no ship, you have no Dragon Guards, you have no authority on this vessel—or anywhere else for that matter. You have no power at all except that which I choose to let you have."

Zillabar's face flushed with rage. "How dare you speak to me that way!"

"I'll speak to you any damn way I want, you arrogant bitch. You belong to me now. If you want courtesy, respect, even the simplest privileges of your rank, you'll have to purchase them. Do I need to tell you what price I expect?"

"Never. I'd sooner feed my eggs to scavenger dogs than let you father the next generation of my family line."

"That anger will only make the mating sweeter. When I finally subdue, you, my Lady—when I finally turn the passion of your anger into the even hotter passion of lust, your screams of ecstasy will blister the air."

Zillabar spat at d'Vashti's feet. He just grinned, a very un-Phaestor-like expression. "The more you revile me, the more aroused I get. I think I'll have to get a larger size of underwear."

Zillabar couldn't stand it anymore. d'Vashti had even taken away her ability to rage. She turned away, shaking, quivering, already beginning to feel the first stirrings of . . . of the weakness and hunger that she knew . . . would lead inevitably to . . . d'Vashti's chambers . . . and her eventual enslavement to the needs of her body.

No! She had to resist the hormonal storm. She had to! She wanted to wail aloud. She could feel herself poised on the precipice of—*dreamtime*! Yes. She needed dreamtime. A lot of it. That would help her retain her focus. She began freezing herself solid again—"

d'Vashti snapped his fingers at the attendants. "Return the Lady to her quarters. Keep her there. Oh, and don't let her go into dreamtime. I'll need to consult with her later." He didn't even bother to bid the Lady a good day; he strode to the opposite end of his command bridge and began snapping out orders to his Captains.

"Ready my shuttle for immediate departure. I have a Gathering to attend."

Another Romantic Interlude

Using the massive singularity injector suspended from the overhead crane, Gito began the delicate process of extracting the pinpoint black hole from the spherical singularity cage of the The Lady MacBeth's main engine. While he performed this delicate operation, Finn and Sawyer argued between themselves.

"Sawyer," he said. "I just want you to consider something. Okay, maybe I still have too much Vampire blood in me. Maybe it's affected my thinking. But just consider this for a moment. If we truly believe in the sacredness of life everywhere, then we don't have the right to destroy d'Vashti's ship and its crew like a band of terrorists."

"Absolutely," Sawyer agreed. "But if we don't destroy that vessel, then no one will have a life anywhere to hold sacred."

"Yes, but—remember what Harry said. We have to play by *our* rules, not theirs! Else we've already lost."

"I have to tell you, big brother. This discussion does not make me happy. I don't like hearing you argue for the enemy."

"I want to suggest something . . . an alternate plan. What if we connect the trigger to the weapons monitor?"

Sawyer snorted. "And you think that'll stop him?"

"It'll stop him damn quick if he breaks his word to respect the sanctity of the Forum. If he fires his weapons, the trap goes off," Finn said.

Sawyer thought about it. A series of expressions passed across his face so fast, Finn couldn't follow them. Abruptly, Sawyer said, "All right."

"Huh? You gave in too easy. Why?"

Sawyer shrugged. "d'Vashti represents a danger to us only if he keeps his word. When has he ever kept his word?" He grinned. "I like the idea of him squeezing the trigger on himself."

"All right—" said Gito. "Here we go." He pressed a button. The singularity injector moved like a piston. It extruded a shining cylindrical part of itself directly into the center of the spherical cage. Gito watched his displays carefully. "I have it," he announced calmly. He encapsulated the singularity, sealing it within the enclosed magnetic bottle, and then slowly withdrew the injector from the cage. His fingers danced across his keyboard. The machinery made some sounds, lights flashed, chimes sounded, and then the injector swung around and released the magnetic bottle into Shariba-Jen's waiting arms.

The robot took the bottle carefully, readjusting his stance to allow for its weight. The singularity itself, suspended in both a magnetic and gravitational bottle expressed almost no weight at all; but the bottle itself had considerable mass. Gito approached now and slid a small ring over the end of the bottle, the gravitational lens. He locked it into place, attached the Limited Intelligence Engine, armed it, withdrew the key, and handed it to Finn. "All right. Let's go."

"Wait—one second." Captain Campbell stepped into the engine room. "Sawyer?" she said. "May I speak to you?"

Sawyer looked at Gito and Finn apologetically. "Excuse me, guys." He jumped up onto the deck circling the engine room and crossed to where Captain Campbell stood. She looked into his eyes meaningfully.

"I want to tell you something . . . *important.*"

"Sawyer," she said slowly. She stopped, swallowed, lowered her lashes shyly, then brought her eyes back up to his. "Please . . . don't fuck this up."

"Uh—" He nodded quickly to cover his disappointment. He had hoped for something a little more personal. He started to turn away, then figured—what the hell, go for it! He turned back to Captain Campbell, grabbed her hard into his arms, and drew her face to his. He kissed her long and deep—and when he finally let go of her, she looked red with embarrassment and anger. Her chest rose and fell with quick, ragged breaths.

"You—" she said. "And I—" she added. "—will have to have a serious conversation about this—" She took another breath" "—Just as soon as you get back."

"Yes, ma'am," Sawyer agreed solemnly. He grinned all the way back to Gito and Finn.

The Nexus

□□□□□□□□□□□□□□□□□□□□□□□□□□□□□□

The last of the TimeBinders arrived. Nyota laid her rod of authority on the pedestal with all the others. The twelfth great note rang out across the disk of the Forum, summoning all to the central amphitheater. Nyota smiled, almost with childish delight, then joined the eleven other men and women waiting to one side. They looked solemn and proud and grim, all of them.

Around them the crowd rustled and waited. They gossiped among themselves. They worried, they speculated, they tried not to look upward at the great red starship still hanging over them like a threat.

Abruptly, Harry strode down into the center of the

Forum amphitheater. He wore a new white robe that gleamed like starlight. He turned around slowly, as if meeting the gaze of every set of eyes in the stadium. "I stand before you, Godfrey Daniels Harry Mertz, ready to assume the responsibility of the Nexus. I have done this before. You know me as the immortal, the long-liner, the leaper of years, the wanderer, and the man from Earth. You know me as a legend, but I stand here as flesh and blood.

"Six thousand years ago I stood here as the Nexus, and now, today, the twelve wearers of the TimeBands have asked me to perform this task again. Does anyone here object?"

A rustle of awe swept through the crowd. Several people screamed. A few fainted. Many of those in the closest rows dropped to their knees in worshipful posture. But Harry went to the nearest individuals and began pulling them back to their feet. "No, you mustn't. Don't do that. Please—"

Around the amphitheater, one by one, people began standing. Slowly, they began applauding. The sound of it grew louder and louder, a steady, rhythmic wave of acceptance and acknowledgment and honor.

Harry bowed his head, sadly. Tears filled his eyes. "You leave me no choice. I accept."

Harry went to the central pedestal. A headband lay there, next to twelve rods of authority. He lifted the headband and placed it on his own temples. He waited a moment as the fields shifted and solidified, focusing on the patterns of his brain. He had to grasp the edges of the pedestal to steady himself, but after a moment the dizziness passed and he straightened again.

Now each of the twelve TimeBinders came forward, one at a time. Each one lifted his or her baton off the pedestal and handed it to Harry. Calvin of Canby, Fariah of B'rik'yno, Lord K'aenar, and then William Three-Dollar—he looked at Harry worshipfully; they all did.

Harry accepted the batons one at a time, gathering them into a single bundle. As he took each new baton, Harry met the eyes of the presenting TimeBinder in mutual understanding. As he added each new staff, it linked itself with the rest. The rods became united—and they began to give off light. They gleamed stronger and brighter with the addition of each new length. At the same time Harry seemed to grow taller and brighter himself. Harry kept his emotions solemn until little Nyota M'bele placed the last baton in his hand. He *winked* at her. And she *winked* back.

Now Harry held his newly assembled caduceus aloft and proclaimed, "By the authority of the TimeBinders, I stand here as the Nexus of the Unification. Let the word go forth. The Gathering has begun!"

Harry had become the Nexus.

When the Nexus spoke, it no longer spoke in Harry's words or with Harry's voice. The Nexus had become the living presence of all twelve TimeBinders speaking in unison, embodied in a single mind.

The Nexus stepped to the center of the arena. A circular area lifted up slowly, becoming a rising dais, a pedestal, a place to stand. Everyone in the amphitheater could see him. An expectant hush fell across the waiting crowd.

In the Mountain

☐☐☐☐☐☐☐☐☐☐☐☐☐☐☐☐☐☐☐☐☐☐☐☐☐☐☐☐

As one shuttleboat dropped away from *The Black Destructor*, another one approached. Nearly a hundred docking ports lined the bottom of the great vessel, and almost that number dotted her upper hull. The tiny shuttleboat slid into one of the lesser ports near the tail of the mountain-sized vessel.

The air-lock doors slid open, and Gito, Sawyer, Finn, and Shariba-Jen debarked. Each of them carried a duffel over his shoulder—their personal belongings. Gito greeted the waiting Juda-Linda. She eyed them all suspiciously.

"As I told you I would, I brought my assistants," Gito explained.

Juda-Linda's gaze slid up Sawyer's slim frame and down Finn's thicker one. Sawyer offered a genial, but unconvincing, smile to the dwarf-sized woman. She barely glanced at Jen.

"Too big. Too ugly," she decided. "But what the hell, you can keep them for now. Later, though, we'll have to reassign them. The Phaestor don't like humans—at least not where they have to look at them. Come this way."

Sawyer and Finn exchanged glances. "The little woman has even less charm than Gito," Sawyer whispered.

"Good," Finn whispered back. "It just makes the job easier."

"I've got the perfect quarters for you," Juda-Linda said. "Below the keel."

Again Sawyer and Finn looked at each other. Having your quarters below the keel signaled extreme disrespect—almost disgrace. "Perfect," said Sawyer. "Below the keel? I wanted the keel. I like the keel. The keel appeals to me." He turned around and waggled his eyebrows suggestively at Jen, whose duffel contained a magnetic bottle wrapped in shield-cloth and rags.

Trying to suppress his own laughter, Finn poked him hard in the ribs. "Shut up."

Still grinning, they followed Juda-Linda deep into the bowels of *The Black Destructor*.

Elsewhere in the mountain other events began unfolding.

Through corridors much more elegant than the ones traversed by Juda-Linda, Gito, and the others, four of d'Vashti's insect-guards escorted a quiescent Lady Zillabar toward her quarters. d'Vashti had assigned her a spacious guest chamber low in the aft of the vessel—the location represented a deliberate insult, though not one as severe as if he had placed her below the keel. Had he placed her there, the Lady Zillabar would have had no choice but to commit suicide to rid herself of the stain.

As they came down along the wide corridor, a pale Phaestor youth and several Dragons came up the passage from the opposite direction. Neither party acknowledged the existence of the other, but as the Dragons came alongside d'Vashti's guards, they all turned in unison and quickly dispatched them, killing them easily and efficiently. One had his back broken, another had his head bitten off, a third collapsed under the blows of a Dragon's hammering fist, and the fourth—well, the Dragon just reached into his chest and ripped his beating heart out with his bare hand. And ate it.

The Phaestor youth ran to the Lady, dropping to one knee and offering his service. "We have brought your salvation, holy mother," he offered.

Zillabar reacted with anger. "It took you flaming long enough, you stupid bazoons!"

The boy hung his head with shame. "I apologize, my Lady. We have had some difficulty keeping up with you."

"Oh, the hell with it. I don't have time for bitchery anymore. Let's go."

"We have a shuttleboat waiting, ma'am, and we have a long-range cruiser waiting for you, deep in the rift. This way, please—"

They headed up the corridor at a brisk pace. The Dragons carried the bodies of d'Vashti's insect-guards, not willing to leave either evidence or a potential snack behind.

The Word

"When last we met—we TimeBinders—when last we put our minds and our hearts and our memories together, we gave birth to a Regency, a body with the authority to muster the resources to fight the Predators that threatened the worlds of the Palethetic Cluster.

"We redesigned ourselves. We re-created our children. We turned them into the most vicious possible fighting force. We gave them a language of their own, and we turned them loose to patrol the rift between ourselves and the Eye of God. They succeeded in stopping the Predators. They succeeded—and we succeeded in our original goal of security and safety throughout the Palethetic Cluster.

"But we also made a mistake. At that time we did not look far enough ahead. We did not ask ourselves, What will we do when the Predators no longer represent a threat? What will become of our children then? Well, now we have the answer to that question, and it dissatisfies us.

"Let me tell you what has happened. Six thousand years ago we designed a language for our Phaestor children that would channel their thinking into action and results. We gave them a language that not only denied passivity—you could not even express the concept of it. The Phaestor language has no words for surrender or weakness or failure.

"The language *worked*. It helped to make our Phaestor children invincible, because they could not conceive any possibility other than victory. The language obliterated the alternative. But—" said the Nexus. "That same Phaestor language has come home to torment the parents. When the Phaestor ran out of Predators to destroy, they needed a new challenge. They reinvented themselves as an aristocracy, and they gave themselves a goal—the Regency would expand its authority over the Cluster worlds, to include not just their defense, but their governance as well.

"We do not deny that the Phaestor won a great victory over the deadly planet-killing Predators. We will always owe them our gratitude for that—but the excellence they demonstrated at making war does not also imply equal excellence at making peace. We have found instead that the mind-set needed for winning a war interferes with the processes of peace, over and over and over again.

"The Phaestor have mostly succeeded in extending their authority. They have mostly succeeded in assuming the governance of the Cluster. And they have mostly succeeded at transforming the way the rest of us think and feel and speak, because they have made their language—*the language that we invented for them*—the language for all of us.

"I speak to you now, as the Nexus, as the voice of all the TimeBinders. I give you the first decision. *We must return to the Old Tongue.* We cannot continue to use the language of the Phaestor. It channels our thinking away from the methods of respect and cooperation. As long as we use the Phaestor tongue, *we speak in a crippled language!*

"I will demonstrate. The Old Tongue contains a verb not found in our present speaking. The verb *is* . . . *the verb of existence.* It allows one to assign a static quality to a moving object. It allows one to discuss occurrence, to describe, identify, or amplify. It allows one to indicate status, it allows one to discuss the past, as well as the future, as identities—

"But the same word does not exist in the Phaestor language. And because we now use the Phaestor language, it does not exist for us either. Because we do not have it, because we do not use it, we cannot say many of the things we most need to say. I now give you back the word. The verb *to be!*"

The Nexus took a deep breath. His voice rolled out across the entire arena. "I *was* the first Nexus. I *am* the Nexus again. I *am* the immortal man. I *was* born in the Eye of God. I slept for a thousand years in a vessel that plunged across the rift. I *am* the oldest human *being* alive.

"I *am* connected to the minds of twelve TimeBinders. I *am* the sum total of all of their lives and all of their past lives. I have *been* male and female, child and parent. I have been dreamer and peasant, poet and soldier, servant and served, teacher and student, savior

and saved, idiot and savant—I have *been* all of this and
more. I *am* humanity.

"And speaking for a thousand thousand thousand
separate voices, I have this to say about the state of the
Cluster today: *This shall not stand!*"

The Keel

ᗕᗕᗕᗕᗕᗕᗕᗕᗕᗕᗕᗕᗕᗕᗕᗕᗕᗕᗕᗕᗕᗕᗕᗕᗕᗕ

Long tubes of light lined the keel of the mountain—the
spinal cord of the machine's communication network.
The thoughts of its intelligence engine passed back and
forth through the optical cables. The corridor glimmered
off into the distance, fading out into an indistinct blur.
Thick stanchions framed the passage; polymer decking
felt like slabs of stone underfoot.

As Juda-Linda led them down toward the access-bay
to the underquarters, Gito fumbled around in his duffel.
"I brought you a gift," he said.

"Don't need no gifts," Juda-Linda grumbled. "Tall
people give gifts. Gifts patronize."

"No," said Gito. "This gift doesn't patronize." He
swung around abruptly and hit her with a hypo-spray injector. Juda-Linda's eyes rolled up into her head, and she
toppled over like a small brick dumpling. "Urgh," said
Gito. "She might not forgive me for this." He shrugged.
"No loss, I guess." He dragged her over to the wall and
propped her up, trying to make her comfortable.

"All right, let's go to work," said Finn, pulling a gun
out of his duffel. Shariba-Jen had already identified an
access panel and had popped it open. He plugged himself into the network and went silent for a moment.

"Hey," said Sawyer, pulling out his own gun. "I forgot to ask. Can we get out of here again?"

Gito glanced up and down the keel as he assembled

his weapon. They didn't expect anyone to interrupt them, but they had come prepared anyway. "Probably not," he said, answering Sawyer's question.

"I didn't think so," Sawyer said.

Abruptly, Jen began cursing in fluent binary. To the others he said, "Some son of a lizard has changed the protocols. All of the intelligence engine's internal messages travel through this network. Multiple monitors exist throughout the vessel. The redundancy guarantees no data loss—only someone has implemented a very nonstandard data coding. Stand by while I search for the translation protocols. They have to have them somewhere—"

"What does all that mean?" Sawyer asked.

Finn scowled. "It means we can't connect the bomb-trigger to the starship's weapons."

"You mean we can't resolve our previous dilemma about the sanctity of Phaestor life?"

"Sure we can," said Gito. He opened Shariba-Jen's duffel and began attaching a new control chip to the magnetic bottle containing the singularity. "We'll just put the damn thing on a time fuse."

"No," said Sawyer. "We made an agreement—with ourselves. About the sacredness of life. We have to keep our word. Innocent people will die."

Gito blinked at him, astonished. "No one aboard this vessel can claim innocence. They share responsibility by their presence. You know that. So do I."

Sawyer shook his head. "I wish I could believe you—but you almost signed on board. And you know that Juda-Linda doesn't share the Phaestor hunger. Don't you think that others here might deserve the same compassion?"

"You've spent too much time with Harry Mertz. You've caught his madness. You've turned into a weakling." Still, Gito hesitated. He stopped himself from arming the new control chip. He turned around and looked at the optical cables running along the walls. He studied the access panel, frowning, worrying, scowling, and muttering to himself.

Abruptly, Gito said, "Gotcha!" He pointed. "See that

regulator-channel? That controls the arming of the weapon systems. I can set a channel detector right next to it. If an abnormal increase in message-traffic occurs, the detector will notice it and can use that stimulus to trigger the singularity expansion. That'll accomplish the same thing without the need to tap into the ship's computer network. Good!" He turned to Sawyer. "Will that make you happy? Will that let you sleep well at night?"

"It will make me *ecstatic*. I'll sleep like a baby."

Gito reached into his duffel and pulled out a third command chip. He clipped it into place on the magnetic bottle, armed it, and locked it. "Done!" he said. "If they target their weapons, it arms itself. If they arm their weapons, it goes into time-bomb mode. If they fire, it triggers. The first thing that'll happen, it'll break this cable, interrupting their ability to fire. By the time they re-route, the lens will have begun eating the ship like a Dragon in a garbage dump." With Jen's help they slid the bottle into position, securing if firmly to the wall so it looked as if it belonged there.

"What if someone spots it and tries to remove it?" Finn asked.

"It'll go off. Even I couldn't remove it now. If anyone even thinks a dirty thought near it, it'll go off. Now, let's get out of here before somebody thinks a dirty thought."

They gathered up their equipment. At Gito's urging Shariba-Jen stuffed Juda-Linda into his empty duffel and slung her over his shoulder. They headed back the way they had come as fast as they could.

To Be

☐☐☐☐☐☐☐☐☐☐☐☐☐☐☐☐☐☐☐☐☐☐☐☐☐☐☐

"We stand here, all of us, as a question. A question asked with a thousand different voices. We *are* this question: What does it mean to *be* a human *being*? Who *are* we? Who *are* the rightful members of this body?"

The Nexus looked out over the crowd thoughtfully.

"We could spend the rest of our days asking this question, seeking to define ourselves—and in the end we will accomplish nothing of value. We will end up only with another collection of reasons, explanations, rationalizations and justifications—excuses for turning one against another."

He paused, as if gathering his strength for the leap of faith to follow.

"Let me *be* dangerous. Let me suggest that the question has no answer—no answer that *is* worthy of any further expenditure of our valuable time and energy. I say this, I assert that the definition of sapience—of sentient life itself—*is* irrelevant to the real issue.

"The real issue *is* not who is worthy, but who *is* willing to *be* accountable. Who *is* willing to take a stand here?

"I say that any of us who step forward and say, 'I *am* sapient,' *are* demanding not a privilege, nor invoking a right, nor even an authority. I say that any of us who dare to make that statement *are* simply claiming our fair share of the responsibility."

The Nexus paused, letting his words sink in across the Forum. Some of his listeners frowned unhappily. Others nodded. Many looked puzzled. What did all of this mean?

"And if that *is* true—then it follows that this *is* true

as well: that none of us here, nor any of us hereafter, may claim the right or the authority to deny any other sapient being its fair share of the common responsibility.

"Or let me put it another way. I ask each and every one of you. What *are* you willing to die for? What *are* you willing to live for? That *is* the place where justice lives."

Or Not To Be

CCCCCCCCCCCCCCCCCCCCCCCCCCCC

Suddenly—

The sound of clapping came ringing down from the top rank of the amphitheater. A single pair of hands clapped slowly and methodically. The Nexus turned to see who stood there. The audience swiveled in their seats, craning their necks as well.

Kernel Sleestak d'Vashti stood poised at the rim of the arena, flanked by a regiment of ferocious-looking Dragons. As he stood there, the rest of the Dragon Guards stepped into position around the stadium. They had surrounded the Gathering. Gasps of surprise and horror came from the crowd. Many leapt to their feet. Shouts of anger and fury arose.

d'Vashti ignored them all. He came striding down the steps, his great dark cape flowing out behind him like a black flame. He walked down almost to the center of the Forum and took a position opposite the Nexus. They stood at eye level.

"You speak bold words, old man. But your Gathering has no validity."

The Nexus shook its head. "This *is* the place where the law *is* made. Here, we *are* all its servants and none of us may *be* above it. You yourself have already acknowledged that."

d'Vashti laughed, amused. "If you insist, I'll play your charade: I *am* sapient. I accept the authority. I have to. No one else has the power to enforce it."

The Nexus responded in the voice of the Twelve. "Responsibility *is* not authority. You may claim only your share—and no more than that."

d'Vashti pointed to the mountain in the sky. "That *is* my authority. Where *is* yours? You don't have thirteen TimeBinders here, do you? Where *is* Willowar?"

The Nexus didn't answer that. He frowned.

"Tell me it doesn't matter. Tell me that you have critical mass," d'Vashti said. "I say it does matter. I demand that the TimeBinder of Willowar step forward and add his authority to this Gathering. Where *is* Willowar?"

And abruptly, the Nexus knew what d'Vashti wanted. He said, "If the TimeBinder of Willowar *is* present, let him step forward and join us. He will *be* welcome."

d'Vashti smiled. He reached into his robe and pulled out a shimmering headband. "Thank you," he said. "I will." He lifted it to his head and lowered it carefully to his temples. Gasps of horror rippled across the arena.

The Kernel of the Phaestor authority staggered for a moment, but he held himself erect, letting the headband establish itself. Then, abruptly, he became another person. His face relaxed, became peaceful—and at the same time, shaded with emotion. He stared across the intervening space at the Nexus.

"Do you feel me now? Do you feel my strength? My power? Do you feel the authority of the Phaestor in your head? Go ahead, old man—create something for me. Create a new Regency. One even more powerful than before!"

The Nexus staggered as if two great armies fought a war within his head. He collapsed to the floor of the pedestal, struggled for a moment, clutching his temples, clutching the constricting headband, as if trying to pull it off, then he uttered a great gasp of horror and shook as if possessed by a fit.

Around him, the TimeBinders also staggered. Nyota began wailing in pain. Three-Dollar sank to his knees.

The others collapsed where they stood or clutched painfully at their skulls.

Only d'Vashti remained unaffected. "None of you can match the power available to a single well-trained Phaestor. You gave us *dreamtime*. We used it to master ourselves—and now I will use it to master all of you!"

Harry Mertz pulled himself laboriously to his feet. The connection to the TimeBinders had been broken. He spoke only for himself now. It would have to be enough. Somehow, he managed to get the words out. "Your authority exists only because we gave it to you. Now we revoke it. The stand we take here will outlive us. Already the word goes forth. The Regency *is* dissolved."

"On the contrary," said d'Vashti. "I *am* the new Nexus. The Regency will continue, stronger than ever—with myself as its ultimate leader. I now order this Gathering dissolved." He flung his arms wide, as if in victory. Harry Mertz staggered as if struck. He sank to his knees. Several of the TimeBinders fell to the ground, gasping and clutching their heads or their chests.

"You see?" said d'Vashti. "You never had a chance. I've had you under my guns since the moment you started. Now—" He started to gesture.

Somehow Harry managed to get the words out, laboring to make himself heard. "You fool. You don't understand the power of the linkage—"

d'Vashti laughed. He completed the gesture.

Nothing happened.

And then . . . everyone in the arena looked up. A soft puff of light had flashed against the hull of *The Black Destructor*.

"What *was* that?" asked d'Vashti.

Escape

□□□□□□□□□□□□□□□□□□□□□□□□□□□□□□

"Oh, shit —" said Gito.

"Uh — ?" asked Sawyer.

"Somebody had a dirty thought."

"Huh?" Finn didn't want to believe it either.

"Didn't you hear it? Something went *fwoop!*"

They looked back down the seemingly endless corridor. Something dark grew there. The channels of lights blinked and pulsated alarmingly.

"Goddammit," said Finn. "I knew we couldn't trust the little bastard, but I didn't think he'd go off that quickly!"

The walls of the starship nearest the singularity began to wrinkle. The event-horizon of the pinpoint black hole now stood as a three meter sphere. It flickered like an uneasy ghost. Around it, the panels began pulling off the walls. They flung themselves through the air and tried to wrap themselves around the event horizon— then they just *vanished* into it. The bigger pieces folded themselves into crumpled balls and pulled themselves into the black hole with a dreadful crackling and crunching sound—flickers of radiation and static electricity began flashing across the surface of the sphere, and every object coming near it. St. Elmo's fire danced up and down the corridor.

The devastation expanded. The radiation increased, growing brighter every second. A great wind began sucking into the flickering sphere. The ship's atmosphere poured into the artificially widened singularity, pulling pieces of debris and scraps of material along with it. A stanchion crumpled and broke with a great creak and clang of poly-ceramic. A section of corridor collapsed.

At the far end of the passage, Shariba-Jen said calmly, "We have less than ten minutes." He pointed. "The docking ports lie that way."

The mountain shook then. The great ship shuddered with an impact that knocked Sawyer sideways into Finn and both of them to the floor. Gito grabbed a stanchion. Still carrying Juda-Linda, Jen compensated and held his balance. Alarms began going off. Loud clanging noises, raspy saw-toothed buzzers, klaxons, bells, chimes, and crisp metallic voices announcing, "We have a breach of integrity in the lower keel."

All the air-tight doors on *The Black Destructor* began slamming shut, one after the other. They knew it wouldn't help. The pinpoint hole had become a sucking maw with an incredibly intense gravitational pull. It would pull the entire starship into it, inexorably. The monster ate. The vessel crunched and crashed and continued collapsing loudly into it.

Sawyer and Finn came up against a sealed door. Sawyer kicked it and slammed it with his hand, instantly regretting his anger.

Jen said, "Up there—we'll have to use the manual accesses." He pointed toward a metal ladder. Finn went up it first, popping the hatch into the main escape corridor. Immediately, he turned around and pulled Sawyer up after him. Jen handed up Juda-Linda, and Gito followed.

Panicked crewmembers came running from all directions, racing toward their emergency stations. Sawyer wanted to warn them that they should abandon ship, but he knew he didn't dare. They ran past him, ignoring the strangers in the passage. The corridors had begun to shake now, as if the ship had caught itself in a state of perpetual earthquake.

Jen scooped up Juda-Linda and began leading the way again, straight toward the aft docking bays. But as they charged around the last corner, they came colliding up against—Lady Zillabar and her guardians, just coming in from the opposite side!

For a moment, all of them stared at each other in a horrified tableau.

"You?!" Zillabar said to Sawyer and Finn Markham. "You?!" They said in reply.

And then—without even thinking, they fired. Gito shot the first Dragon Guard right between the eyes, Jen tossed the still-unconscious Juda-Linda to the rear and used the reaction from that gesture to plunge his arm right into the chest of the closest Dragon. He activated his industrial laser-finger and burnt out the creature's heart. Finn shot the third Dragon in the balls, then sliced his beam upward to stab out the creature's eyes. Sawyer hit the fourth one with a stun-grenade, then kicked sideways to disable the Vampire youth who led the party. They had the advantage of surprise and readiness. The Dragons toppled like dominoes.

Finn turned to check behind—and saw Zillabar going for one of the Dragon's guns. He leapt after her, grabbing her arm and pulling her back. He let her have it with a roundhouse punch.

Coming up quickly to cover him, Sawyer said, "That ain't no way to treat a lady."

Finn grimaced. "She ain't no lady. Come on, let's go." Finn bent down and scooped up Zillabar, tossing the woman over his shoulder. He headed for the nearest shuttle. Shariba-Jen had already grabbed Juda-Linda again, and Gito had popped the door.

"Huh?" Sawyer stared. "Why—?"

For some reason, Finn felt he had to answer in the Old Tongue. "Because," he said. *"Life is sacred. Everywhere."*

Around them, the great structure of the Armageddon-class warship continued to creak alarmingly. It sounded like a slow-motion avalanche, a death-rattle, a metallic cry of despair. The scream of the poly-ceramic frame went on and on and on, as it bent and cracked and poured itself into a three-meter hole. Sparks and explosions echoed somewhere in the distance. They heard screams and panic.

As Finn climbed down the tunnel, Zillabar pounded on his shoulders. "Put me down, you stinking son of a human!"

"Nope. I insist on rescuing you!"

"To make me a slave again! An act of ridicule? Never!"

"No. I just want to prove you *wrong*."

"I'd rather *die*!"

Finn stopped, very annoyed. "All right," he said. "Have it your own way." He dumped her disgustedly to her feet, left her there, jumped through the shuttleboat door and slammed the hatch in her face.

"What about the Lady?" Sawyer asked.

"She changed her mind."

"Just as well. She never did get along with the rest of us."

Shariba-Jen sat at the controls of the shuttleboat, swearing furiously. "The damn thing won't start. The pod bay doors won't open. And the ion-drive modules keep going pocketa-pocketa instead of rrrrm-rrrrm."

"Kick it!" Gito hollered. "That always works for me."

The Final Collapse

□□□□□□□□□□□□□□□□□□□□□□□□□□□□□□□□

Now the outer hull of the great vessel began to crumple. Sparks and explosions flickered along its hull.

Far below, on the disk of the Forum, the crowd watched in horror as the silent tableau unfolded. Shuttleboats dropped away from the vessel, one after the other; bright sparks of light rushing toward safe harbor.

Even d'Vashti stared — stunned into speechlessness.

The great vessel slowly imploded, collapsing inward around the singularity at its heart. The last few escape pods fell away from it. The great ship sucked inward in a sudden final rush — and finally vanished in a blaze of brilliant blue light.

And then ... a great cheer went up all across the flat disk of the Forum. Whoops and shrieks of joy. Whistles and catcalls of hysteria. Delirium and delight. A celebration of emotional release. Cries of victory resonated and echoed. People grabbed each other, tears streaming from their eyes; they pounded each other on the back. They hugged. They kissed. They held each other close, turning around and around. They opened their arms and their hands and united their hearts.

The Dragons shifted among themselves, uncertain and wary. They looked as if they thought they should take action, but they held themselves back. They had no experience with this kind of situation.

And then ... the Nexus stood up again in the center of the arena and looked across the intervening space at Kernel Sleestak d'Vashti. "You are fighting the TimeBand, d'Vashti. It works only when you submerge your identity in the sea of memory. You cannot impress your will on six thousand years of history, hoping to reshape it with a single hunger. It doesn't work that way. You must relax and let us in. Swim in the sea of community. Relax. Surrender to the community of minds and become one with the rest of us. Let your mind be part of ours—that's the way. Now, you can see the larger vision and realize that this small tiny hunger of yours, this dreadful lust for power and authority serves no one, not even you. We welcome your strength in the new vision. You have much to give us. But you must surrender to the inevitable now so that we can all end the dreadful killing together. The choice *is* yours, Kernel Sleestak d'Vashti. How say you?"

d'Vashti recoiled. He staggered backward. "No!" he screamed. "No! I will not *be* beaten." He gestured and the Dragons instantly unslung their weapons and pointed them all at the Nexus. "Do you think you are stronger than this?"

"Listen to the TimeBand, d'Vashti. Listen—! This is your last chance."

d'Vashti nodded mockingly. "Yes, I thought so. You have brave words and no weapons. Now, I'll teach you the dead man's victory."

"Ahh," the Nexus smiled. "So be it." He bowed in a

curiously inviting gesture. "If that is your choice, then go for it. This will *be* an interesting death." The Nexus held up the caduceus he carried so all could see it. He held it aloft like a shield of virtue.

For just the barest instant, a flicker of doubt flashed across d'Vashti's face. Then he shook it away and lashed out in anger. "You get to have an interesting death. I get to *be* right." He gestured to the Dragons above, giving the order to fire.

The needle beams struck then. They bounced off the Nexus like water splashing off a wall. The beams splattered outward in all directions. They leapt out across the arena, directly back to the Dragon Guards, striking one after the other, igniting them instantly ablaze. The Dragons' screams cut off sharply as each one flared brightly and exploded into nothingness. One after the other, they disintegrated, shriveling into shadows of ash that whipped away quickly in the breeze.

d'Vashti stared in horror. His gaze circled the upper rim of the arena and then came slowly back to the center where the Nexus still held the caduceus high. It gleamed and dazzled. Intelligent energy crackled off of it, sparking and fizzing.

"See what you have created!" The Nexus roared at him. "Your own hatred comes back to you amplified by the TimeBands, aimed by our memories, enlarged by our wisdom, expanded by our vision of what *is* possible. Your own mind focuses the energy, because you are wearing a TimeBand too!"

"No!" said d'Vashti. "I am the authority of the Regency here! I speak for the Cluster—" He put his hands to his temples and appeared to concentrate. He tried to focus his thoughts. He screamed for dreamtime. He turned around and around, staring at each of the TimeBinders in turn, focusing the fury of his thoughts on them, one after the other.

The Timebinders flinched. Several of them staggered. Two of them sank to their knees. And then, little Nyota M'bele wailed in pain. "Daddy!" she cried. "He's *hurting* me!"

M'bele, the dark man, came charging down the

steps, a one-man avalanche of anger. But before he could leap—

Nyota screamed again, but this time her voice was amplified out of a dozen throats—all of the TimeBinders in unison, and the Nexus too. "No! No! No! You *nasty little bug*! I'll squash you back!"

d'Vashti staggered. He clutched at his head, as if trying to pull the TimeBand off. He clutched at his chest, his heart—he whirled around, as if something had grabbed him and seized him. He screamed. He began to crumple and collapse, as if that same invisible force were now squeezing him, compressing him into a smaller and smaller space. His cries of pain choked off abruptly. The power of the TimeBinding wrapped him like lightning. He shrank away into nothingness.

Only the TimeBand remained. It clattered to the ground, empty.

And then there was silence.

The Nexus lowered the caduceus. He looked tired, but victorious. He smiled. He grinned. He laughed. "I said it would *be* an interesting death."

And then the whole arena roared and cheered.

The Nexus held up his hands and waited for silence to return. He had to wait a long time, but when at last the crowd was ready again, he resumed his speaking for the twelve remaining TimeBinders.

"The Regency *is* dissolved.

"Now, let us renew ourselves. Let us recreate ourselves. Let us redesign the future.

"The Regency *is* history. In its place, we give this Covenant to you—" The voice of the Nexus rang out as clearly as a bell. He could be heard not only across the disk of the Forum, but across the entire Palethetic Cluster.

"We hold that life *is* a gift. We hold that intelligence carries with it the responsibility to use the gift wisely and in the service of life. We hold that life should *be* a marvel and a delight.

"Therefore, we take this stand—that life *is* sacred everywhere. We make this commitment—that we will build a future that works for everyone, with no one and nothing left out. We *are* the promise — that justice *is* forever possible."

The Nexus looked around the arena, appearing to meet the eyes of every person there. "Let us begin," he said. "I *am* sapient. I accept the responsibility."

And then—the Nexus stopped. The moment ended. Silence fell.

Only Harry Mertz remained in the center of the stadium. He had stopped *being* the Nexus. The Gathering was over. Harry looked around himself, a little confused. At last, he nodded a perfunctory thank you and let the pedestal sink back into the ground, thinking he had failed.

The silence stretched out.

And then, high in the upper tiers of the seats, a small voice was heard. Little Ibaka stood up and yipped for attention. "I *am* sapient," he said, almost stumbling over the word. "I accept the responsibility too."

The silence deepened. Ibaka looked embarrassed. But he took a deep breath to renew his courage and took another step forward.

But then—a huge green warrior lizard stepped forward to join him. Kask rumbled loud enough for everyone on the disk to hear. "I too *am* sapient. I too accept the responsibility."

Ota stood. And other bioforms too.

Robin rose to her feet. Beside her, a male android stood up.

Captain Campbell frowned unhappily, not quite understanding, but at the same time understanding all too well. Slowly, she rose to her feet. Her features relaxed, her expression eased into one of peacefulness. All over the amphitheater, all kinds of *beings* were rising to their feet now; informants, constructs, the remaining members of the Lee family, servant-insects, robots—everyone. And now, Shariba-Jen, Gito, Sawyer and Finn entered the group from the back. Juda-Linda followed grumpily and uncertainly as they pushed their way forward to stand near Captain Campbell, Ota and Robin. Shariba-Jen said, "I *am* sapient." Gito hollered, "So *am* I!" Beside him, Juda-Linda silently wept. Gito turned to her to comfort her, but she pushed him away. Gito stared after her, tears filling his eyes, but he didn't know what else to do.

Sawyer and Finn looked around themselves, looked around at this massive celebration of selfhood. It was beyond their understanding; and yet, at the same time, they understood exactly what it was.

Finn stepped forward and shouted joyously, "I accept the responsibility."

Sawyer joined him, "I *am* sapient!"

Finn poked his brother. "Well, thank god for that. You had me fooled for the longest time."

Harry Mertz looked over at them and they exchanged happy grins. Harry did not look the same—but then again, no one did.

Sawyer stepped forward, far enough for everyone in the arena to see him. He began to applaud Harry Mertz. Then Finn also began applauding. And then the people around them picked it up as well. All around the Forum, sapient beings stood up, clapping and cheering and celebrating their mutual declarations.

The applause grew and grew, it gathered throughout the Forum. It swelled into a roar of thunderous approval as they all acknowledged their mutual acceptance of The Alliance of Life and what it had brought forth, A Covenant of Justice.

The Beginning

Later.

As they walked away from the amphitheater, only Harry was solemn. The others bounced like balloons in the wind. Finally, Sawyer looked to him curiously, and asked, "What's the matter, old man? You should be happy."

"Perhaps I'm tired," Harry admitted. "I seem to remember being very depressed the last time I did this."

"Why?"

"Because the easy part is done. Now, the real job begins. There's a lot of work to be done out there. We may have dissolved the authority of the Regency, but there are a lot of little d'Vashti's scattered across the million worlds who are going to be slow to get the message. All of us—" Harry indicated the thinning crowds. "We're all going to have to build a new agreement for cooperation in the Palethetic Cluster." He pointed them toward *The Lady MacBeth*. "Are you going to be a part of it?"

Sawyer and Finn looked at each other. "Oh, no—we don't work for governments."

"This isn't government work," Harry said.

"It's close enough. No, we got you here. You had your Gathering. It was fine. We wouldn't have missed it for the world, but we'd like to get back to our real business, if you don't mind."

Harry glanced at them curiously. "I thought you said you accepted the responsibility of sapience."

"Hey, we only said we accepted the responsibility. We didn't say we were giving up the right to complain about it."

Harry took them both by the elbows. "Come on," he said. "I've got a job for the two of you. And I won't take no for an answer."

Elsewhere on the disk, Star-Captain Neena Linn-Campbell stood brooding by herself. She was staring out off the edge at her beautiful, battered, rugged, old starship. *The Lady MacBeth* hung useless off its docking spoke.

As they approached, she turned and waited for them. "Congratulations," she said to Harry. "You won. I've been . . . thinking. About what it cost me. I guess the price was worth it. I didn't think I'd come through this unscathed—" She shrugged. "I'd like to think I still have the strength to start over, but . . . I don't know. Anyway, I'm happy for you."

"Are you done?" Harry asked. "I'm here to offer you a contract. The Alliance has asked me to travel the Circuit and spread the word of the new Covenant to the other worlds. It'll be my job to enroll them in the idea of universal sapience. But I'll need a ship."

Star-Captain Neena Linn-Campbell shook her head sadly. "I wish I could accept that contract, Harry. But I don't have a ship."

"You're wrong," said Finn.

"What? Do you know something I don't?"

Finn nodded and waved to someone approaching from the other direction. Shariba-Jen and Gito came down the docking spoke from *The Lady MacBeth* and approached Captain Campbell. He had drawn a big grin on his otherwise blank robotic features. The effect was both bizarre and affectionate. "I've got our singularity locked in a tractor beam. EDNA's pulling it in slowly. It's gained a considerable bit of mass, so we should be gaining some efficiency there. Gito says he can have it reinstalled in a few hours."

"See?" said Finn. "I told you that you still had a ship."

"That's nice," said Captain Campbell sadly. "But the corporation is still bankrupt."

"Um, no—it isn't," said Sawyer. And now Ota, Robin, Arl-N, Kask, and Ibaka approached.

Ota spoke for the crew. "We'd like to purchase shares in the Shakespeare Corporation. We've pooled our resources and we have enough to help you forestall foreclosure. We've already decided that you should accept the Alliance contract to ferry Harry around the Cluster."

"For one thing," said Gito, "it'll be a lot safer."

"No," said Neena Linn-Campbell. "I don't pay you enough for you to have enough money to make a difference."

"Oh, we know that," said Robin. "But you will. We've worked it all out. The pension fund, the insurance trusts, some bounty money, that's a start—plus we've arranged to float a little paper here, a little paper there. That, with the deals you know how to arrange, should give us enough to keep going for a while. If we can't make it work after that, we don't deserve *The Lady MacBeth*."

Captain Campbell frowned. She looked to Ota and Robin. "Was this your idea?"

They both shook their heads.

"I wish it were my idea," Robin admitted. "But it's Gito's."

"Gito's?" Campbell looked to the high-gravity dwarf with incredulity etched upon her face.

Gito scowled and tried to shrug it off. "Well, Sawyer sort of suggested it. But I did the arm-twisting. I figure this is the only way that we can guarantee that we'll get a fair share of the profits. We'll have the bookkeeper working for us, for a change."

"It'll be the *same* bookkeeper, Gito," Captain Campbell explained.

"Yep, but Ota will have an equal stake in it too. I ain't worried."

Robin looked to Gito, surprised. "Y'know—for a moment there, I almost thought that you cared about us and *The Lady MacBeth*, but no. I must have been mistaken."

"Right," growled Gito. "You were mistaken."

Star-Captain Neena Linn-Campbell scratched her head thoughtfully. "I dunno," she said. "I'm skeptical, dubious, doubtful, and even cynical about the whole idea. But what the hell! If the crew wants to go down with the ship too, why should I deny them that pleasure? All right! We're still in business!" She turned to Harry Mertz. "You've got yourself a ship, old man."

ABOUT THE AUTHOR

DAVID GERROLD made his television writing debut with the now classic "The Trouble with Tribbles" episode of the original *Star Trek®* series. Since 1967 he has story-edited three TV series, edited five anthologies, and written two non-fiction books about television production (both of which have been used as textbooks) and over a dozen novels, three of which have been nominated for the prestigious Hugo awards.

His television credits include multiple episodes of *Star Trek*, *Tales From the Darkside*, *Twilight Zone*, *The Real Ghostbusters*, *Logan's Run*, and *Land of the Lost*.

His novels include *When H.A.R.L.I.E. Was One Release 2.0*, *The Man Who Folded Himself*, *Voyage of the Star Wolf*, as well as his popular *War Against the Chtorr* books—*A Matter for Men*, *A Day for Damnation*, *A Rage for Revenge*, and *A Season for Slaughter*. His short stories have appeared in most of the major science fiction magazines, including *Galaxy*, *If*, *Amazing*, *Twilight Zone*, and *The Magazine of Fantasy & Science Fiction*.

Gerrold has also published columns and articles in *Starlog*, *Profiles*, *Infoworld*, *Creative Computing*, *Galileo*, *A-Plus*, and other science fiction and computing periodicals. He averages over two dozen lecture appearances a year and also teaches screenwriting at Pepperdine University.

David Gerrold is currently working on the new Chtorr book and a sequel to *Voyage of the Star Wolf*.